Hollywood Husbands

Jackie Collins burst on to the publishing scene in 1969 with the first of a string of provocative and controversial bestsellers, *The World is Full of Married Men*. Since then she has written eleven novels, including the phenomenally successful *Hollywood Wives*, which rocketed to the top of the international bestseller lists throughout the world, and has now been made into a highly successful mini-series.

Jackie Collins lives in Los Angeles with her husband and three children and is currently working on a new novel.

Also by Jackie Collins
in **Pan Books**

The World is Full of Married Men
The Stud
The Bitch
Sinners
Lovehead
The World is Full of Divorced Women
Lovers and Gamblers
Chances
Hollywood Wives
Lucky

Jackie Collins

Hollywood Husbands

Pan Books
in association with
Heinemann

To the wives who told me plenty . . .
And the husbands who told me more than
I ever wanted to know . . .
And special thanks to special friends
who tried to tell me nothing at all, but did
not succeed!

Extract from 'The Thrill is Gone' by
Henderson and Brown © Chappell Music
Co. Inc. 1931.
Used by permission of Redwood Music Ltd.

First published in Great Britain 1986 by William Heinemann Ltd
This edition published 1987 by Pan Books Ltd,
Cavaye Place, London SW10 9PG
in association with William Heinemann Ltd
9 8 7 6 5 4 3 2
© Jackie Collins 1986
ISBN 0 330 29722 8
Printed and bound in Great Britain by
Richard Clay Ltd, Bungay, Suffolk

Somewhere in the Midwest . . .
Sometime in the seventies . . .

The nightmare began for the child when she was fourteen years old and alone in the house with her father. Her brothers and sisters were long gone. As soon as they were old enough to earn a living they left — quickly — and never came back to visit. Her mother was in the hospital, "women's problems", a neighbour had sighed. The child did not know what that meant, only that she missed her mother desperately, even though she had only been gone two days.

The little girl was an accident. Her mother often told her that. "You're a late accident," she would say, "an' too much work for me. I should be restin' now, not raisin' another kid." Whenever she spoke the words she would smile, hug her daughter, and add warmly, "I wouldn't do without you, my little one. Couldn't. You understand me, darlin'?"

Yes. She understood that she was loved by the frail woman in the carefully patched clothes who took in other people's washing and treated her husband like a king.

They lived in a run-down house on the outskirts of town. It was freezing in the winter and too hot in the summer. There were hungry roaches in the kitchen and giant rats that ran across the roof at night. The child grew up with fear in her heart, not because of the vermin, but because of the many times her father beat her mother, and the terrified screams that continued throughout the night. The screams were always followed by long, ominous silences, broken only by his grunting and groaning, and her mother's stifled sobs.

Her father was big, mean and shiftless, and she hated him. One day — like her brothers and sisters before her — she would leave, just sneak off in the early dawn as they had done. Only she had more exciting plans. She was going to go out in the world and make a success of her life, and when she had enough money she was going to send for her mother and look after her properly.

I

Her father yelled for his dinner. She fixed him a steaming plate of tripe and onions just as her mother had taught her. It wasn't satisfactory. "Slop!" he shouted, after he'd eaten most of it, belching loudly as she hurriedly removed the plate and replaced it with his fifth can of beer.

He looked her over, his eyes rheumy, his face slack. Then he slapped her backside and guffawed to himself. She scurried into the kitchen. All her life she had lived with him, and yet he frightened her more than any stranger. He was brutal and cruel. Many a time she had felt the sharp sting of his heavy hand across her face or shoulders or legs. He enjoyed inflicting what he considered his superior strength.

She washed the solitary dish in a bowl of water, and wondered how long her mother would be in the hospital. Not long, she hoped fervently. Maybe only another day or so.

Wiping her hands, she made her way through the cramped parlour where her father snored in front of a flickering black and white television. The buckle of his belt was undone, and his stomach bulged obscenely over a grimy tee-shirt, an empty beer can balanced on his chest.

She crept outside to the toilet. There was no indoor plumbing; a cracked basin filled with luke-warm water was the only means of washing. Sometimes she cleaned herself in the kitchen, but she wouldn't dare to do that with her father home. Lately he had taken to spying on her —creeping up when she was dressing and sneering at her newly developed curves.

Wearily she pulled off her blouse, stepped out of her shorts, and proceeded to splash water under her arms, across her chest, and between her legs.

She wished there was a mirror so that she could see what her new figure looked like. At school three of her friends and she had crowded together in a toilet and examined each other's developing buds. It wasn't the same as seeing her own body — she had no interest in looking at other girls' breasts.

Carefully she traced the swell of her small nipples, and sucked in her breath because it gave her such a funny feeling to touch herself.

So intent was she on examining her new body, that she failed to hear the clump of her father's footsteps as he approached the out-house. Without knocking he flung open the creaking door before she had time to cover herself. The buttons on his fly were open. "Gotta take a piss," he slurred. And then, as if working on a slow fuse, he added, "What you doin', girl, standin' around naked?"

"Just washin', pa," she replied, blushing beet-red as she frantically

2

reached for the towel she had brought in with her.

He was too quick for her. With a drunken lurch he stepped on the flimsy towel, and blocked the door with his bulk. "You bin seein' any boys?" he demanded. "You bin sleepin' around?"

"No." Desperately she pulled at the towel, trying to dislodge it from under his foot.

He staggered towards her, all beer breath and bloodshot eyes. "Are you sure, missy?"

"Yes, pa, I'm sure," she whispered, wanting to run and hide in her bed and die of embarrassment.

He watched her for a long moment. Then he touched himself and grunted loudly.

Her heart was pounding – signalling DANGER DANGER. She held her breath. Instinct told her she was caught in a trap.

He fiddled with his thing until it was completely visible, sticking through his trousers like an angry red weapon. "Ya see this?" he growled.

She stayed absolutely still and silent.

"Ya see this?" he repeated, his face as red as his weapon. "This is what ya gotta look out for." He stroked his erection. "This is what every boy ya ever meet is gonna want to stick ya with."

As he reached for her she began to scream. "No! No! No!" Her voice was shrill and unreal as if it belonged to someone else.

But there was no one to hear her. No one to care.

And then the nightmare really began.

PROLOGUE

Hollywood, California
February 1986

There were two major events taking place in Hollywood on a cool weekend in February 1986.

The first was a funeral.

The second, a wedding.

Some people felt obliged to attend both. Although, of course, they changed outfits for each occasion.

BOOK ONE

Hollywood, California
April 1985

Chapter 1

Jack Python walked through the lobby of the Beverly Hills Hotel with every eye upon him. He had money, charisma, a certain kind of power, razor-sharp wit and fame. It all showed.

He was six feet tall with virile good looks. Thick black hair worn just a tad too long, penetrating green eyes, a two-day stubble on a deep suntan, and a hard body. He was thirty-nine years old and he had the world by the balls.

Jack Python was one of the most famous talk show hosts in America.

"Hello, Jack," cooed a voluptuous woman sprayed into a mini tennis dress.

He smiled his killer smile – he had great teeth – and looked her over appreciatively, knowing eyes sweeping every curve. Standard greeting – "How's it going?"

She would have been happy to tell him, only he didn't break stride, just kept walking towards the Polo Lounge.

Several more people greeted him along the way. Two tourists paused to stare, and a very thin girl in a red tank top waved. Jack did not stop until he reached his destination. Table number one, a cosy leather booth directly facing the entrance of the Polo Lounge.

A man was already seated there. A man with a slightly manic look, clad in white sweats, black Porsche shades, and a Dodgers baseball cap. Jack slid in beside him. "Hiya, Howard," he said.

"Hiya, Jack," Howard Soloman replied with a wink. There was something about the perpetual motion of his features which gave him the crazed look. He was always mugging, crossing his eyes, sucking in his cheeks. In repose he was quite nice-looking – the face of a Jewish doctor who had strayed into the wrong business. However, his constant mugging gave the impression

9

that he didn't want anyone to find out. "What was the action last night?" he asked, restlessly rimming the top of his glass with a nervous index finger.

"You've been to one screening at the Goosebergers' house – you've been to 'em all," Jack replied easily.

"Good movie?"

"Lousy movie."

"I coulda told you that," Howard said smugly.

"Why didn't you then?"

Howard took a gulp of hot coffee. "Adventure is finding out for yourself."

Jack laughed. "According to you *no* movie is any good unless it comes from your studio."

Howard licked his lips and rolled his eyes. "You'd better believe it."

"So invite me to one of your screenings."

"I always invite you," Howard replied indignantly. "Is it *my* fault you never show? Poppy's quite insulted."

"That's because Clarissa has very particular taste," Jack explained patiently. "Unless it's a film she's been offered and turned down, or unless she's actually *in* it, she has no desire to see it."

"Actresses!" spat Howard.

"Tell me about 'em," agreed Jack, ordering Perrier and two eggs over easy.

Saturday morning breakfast at the Polo Lounge had once been a ritual for Jack and Howard and Mannon Cable, the movie star, who had yet to appear. Now they were all too busy, and it was a rare occasion when they were able to sit down to breakfast together.

Howard headed Orpheus Studios, a recent appointment and one he relished. Heading a studio had always been his big ambition, and now he was there, King of the whole fucking heap – while it lasted. For Howard, like everyone else in Hollywood, realized that being a studio head was an extremely tenuous occupation, and the position of great and mighty power could be snatched away at any given moment by faceless corporate executives who ran the film industry like a bank. Being a studio head was the treacherous no man's land between high-powered agent and independent producer. The saving speech of every deposed studio head was: "I need more creativity. My talent is stifled here. Too much to do and too little time. We're parting amicably. I'm going into indie prod." In the industry, "indie prod" (independent production to the uninitiated) equals out on your ass. Canned. Can't cut it. Tough shit. Don't call us, we'll call you. And so . . . most indie prods faded into oblivion after one failed movie.

Howard Soloman knew this only too well, and it scared him. He had struggled too long and too hard to allow it to happen to him. The one consolation he could think of was that at least when you failed in Hollywood you failed up. Out at one studio – in at another. The old pals act reigned supreme. Also, he was lucky. Zachary K. Klinger – the multi-powerful magnate – owned Orpheus. And Zachary had hired him personally.

Tapping the tabletop with bitten-to-the-quick nails, Howard said, "Since Clarissa wasn't in the goddamn movie, I guess it was one she vetoed. Right?"

"Her decision made her very happy last night," Jack replied gravely. "*Terms of Endearment* it wasn't." He extracted a pair of heavy horn-rimmed glasses from his top pocket and put them on. He didn't need them to see, but as far as he was concerned they took the curse off his good looks. So did the two-day growth of stubble he carefully cultivated.

Jack did not realize that the glasses and the incipient beard made him all the more attractive to women. Ah . . . women . . . The story of his life. Who would have thought in seventh grade that shy, studious Jack Python would have developed into one of the great lovers of the century? He couldn't help the effect he had on women. One penetrating glance and they were his. No rock star had a better track record.

Not that Jack went out chasing. It had never been necessary. From the onset of puberty and his first conquest at fifteen, women had fallen across his path with monotonous regularity. Most of his life he had indulged shamelessly. One, two, three a week. Who counted? A brief marriage at twenty-five barely stopped him in his tracks. Only luck and a certain sixth sense had prevented him from catching various sexual diseases. Of course now, in the eighties, it was only prudent to be extra careful. Plus he felt a more serious image was in order, and for a year he had been desperately trying to live down his lover boy reputation. Hence his relationship with Clarissa Browning. Clarissa was a serious actress with a capital S. She had won an Oscar, and been nominated twice. No bimbette movie star she.

"I'd like to get Clarissa to do a film for Orpheus," Howard said, chewing on a bread roll.

"Have you anything in mind?"

"Whatever she wants. She's the star." Reaching for the butter he added, "Why don't you tell her to call me direct. If I operate through her schmuck agent nothing'll get done." He nodded, pleased with his own idea. "Clarissa can whisper in my ear what she wants to do, and *then* I'll do the dance of a thousand agents."

"Why don't *you* phone *her*?" Jack suggested.

Howard hadn't thought of anything as simple as that. "Would she mind?"

"I don't think for her. Give it a shot."

"That's not a bad idea . . ." His attention wandered. "Christ!" he exclaimed. "Willya look at that ass!"

Jack cast an appraising glance at a very impressive rear-end clad in tight white pants exiting the Polo Lounge. Recognizing the sway, he smiled to himself. Chica Hernandez — Queen of the Mexican Soaps. He would know that sway anywhere, although he didn't let on to Howard. Kiss and tell had never been his style. Let the tabloids guess their smutty little hearts out. Jack never spoke about his many conquests — even though it drove Howard and the other guys crazy. They wanted names and details, and all they got was a smile and a discreet silence.

Since the start of his year-long affair with Clarissa there wasn't much to tell. A couple of production assistants, an enthusiastic bit-part actress, a Eurasian model. All one-night stands. As far as he was concerned he had been scrupulously faithful. Well, with a woman like Clarissa Browning in your life you couldn't be too careful. Their romance was headlines, he had to watch his every move.

Jack Python was smart, charming, a concerned citizen interested in maybe pursuing a political career one day. (Hey — remember Reagan?) And although he understood women very well — or thought he did — he still believed (subliminally, of course) in the old double standard. It was okay for him to indulge in the occasional indiscretion — after all, a quick lay meant nothing to a man. But God forbid Clarissa ever did it.

Not that she would. Jack knew that for sure.

*

"Faster!" gasped Clarissa Browning fervently. "Come *on*. Faster!"

The young actor on top of her obliged. Although in shock,

12

he was managing to perform nevertheless. Well, he was twenty-three years old, and at twenty-three a hard-on is only a hand-shake away.

Clarissa Browning had done more than shake his hand. Shortly after their first meeting on the set of the film they were appearing in together, she had requested his presence in her dressing room. He went willingly. Clarissa was a star, and this was only his second movie.

She offered him a glass of white wine and a pep talk about his role. Even though it was only ten o'clock in the morning he accepted both gratefully. Then, in clipped tones, pushing strands of fine hair away from her delicate but interesting features, she said, "You do know, that on film reality is the core of everything."

He nodded respectfully.

"You play my lover," she said. Clarissa was twenty-nine years old with a long face, limpid eyes, a nose just saved from being too long, and a thin line of a mouth. In life she received no awards for beauty. However, she had proven more than once that her ordinary looks created incandescent magic in front of a camera.

"I'm looking forward to it," the young actor said enthusiastically.

"So am I," she replied evenly. "Realize, though, that anticipation is not enough. When we interact on screen it has to be real. We have to generate *excitement* and *passion* and *longing*." She paused. He coughed. "So," she continued matter-of-factly, "I believe in working our roles through *before* we get in front of the camera. That way we are never caught with our pants down – metaphorically speaking, of course."

He tried for a laugh and wondered why he was beginning to perspire.

"Let's make love and get it out of the way," she said, her intense brown eyes challenging his.

Who was he to argue? He forgot about his California blonde perfect girlfriend with thirty-six-inch boobs and the longest legs in town.

Clarissa reached over, unzipped his Levis, and they went to work. Even though he was somewhat shell-shocked that he was sticking it to Clarissa Browning. *The Clarissa Browning! Who would believe it?!*

When they were finished she said briskly, "Now we'll both be able to concentrate and make an excellent film. Just know your lines backwards. Listen to our admirable director, and *become* the character you're playing. *Live* the role. I'll see you on the set."

Just like that, he was dismissed.

As the young actor left her dressing room, Clarissa reached for a thermos of vegetable juice and poured herself a small glass of the nourishing liquid. She sipped it thoughtfully. Interaction with her fellow actors, that's what real theatre was all about. Making love to the young man had put him at ease, given him the confidence he would need for the difficult role. He would no longer be in awe of her – Clarissa Browning – Oscar-winning actress. He would see her as a passionate woman – flesh and blood – and react accordingly. This was very important, although some people would think she was mad if she confided that she always made love to her on-screen lovers. It worked – and she had an Oscar to prove it.

Jack Python would throw a fit if he ever found out. Macho chauvinist. All-male stud. Did he honestly believe she didn't know about his little dalliances?

She laughed quietly to herself. Jack Python – the man with the wandering cock . . .

Ah well . . . as long as it didn't wander *too* far. Right now it suited her to have Jack as her permanent lover. Who knew what the future held. . . .

*

"I got a friggin' heart palpitation yesterday," Howard Soloman announced with a grim expression.

"What?" Jack wasn't quite sure he'd heard correctly.

"My friggin' heart," Howard continued in outraged tones, "started bouncin' around like a ping-pong ball."

Jack had long ago decided Howard was a hypochondriac. He changed the subject. "Where's Mannon?" he asked. "Is he coming?"

"Mannon would come very day of his life if he could," Howard said slyly.

"We all know that," Jack agreed.

Mannon Cable – movie star, director, producer, hot property (in Hollywood when you're hot you're hot, when you're not you may as well be dead) – made his entrance. As with Jack before him, every pair of eyes swivelled to get a better look. In fact Mannon actually stopped conversation. He was handsome. If you threw Clint Eastwood, Burt Reynolds and Paul Newman into a blender, you would come up with Mannon Cable. His eyes were cobalt blue; his skin sunkissed to a sexy leather brown; his hair a dark, dirty blond; his body powerful. Six feet four inches tall – "Every inch a winner," he would mock when he made frequent guest appearances on the Carson show.

He was forty-two years old – fit, fast, and right up there box-office-wise with Stallone and Eastwood. Mannon Cable was hitting a peak.

"Hey – I'm one hungry sonofabitch," he said, sliding into the booth. He grinned. He had the *I am a big movie star* grin down pat. He also had a great set of caps (lost the shine on his originals when he laboured as a stunt man for a couple of years) which enabled him to grin from here to eternity without any trouble at all. "What are y'all eating?"

"Eggs," replied Jack, stating the obvious.

"Looks like a couple of fried tits to me," laughed Mannon.

"Everything looks like tits to you," Jack replied. "You should see a shrink, you've got big problems."

Mannon roared. "The only big problem I've got is my dick. *You* should have such problems." He signalled to the waiter and proceeded to order an enormous breakfast.

Jack stared at Mannon and Howard. Sometimes he wondered why the three of them remained friends. They were all so different now. And yet, whenever he got to thinking about it, he knew why. The truth was that they were brothers under the skin, sharing their pasts. They had made it to the top together, and nobody could split them up – although many a wife and girlfriend had tried.

Howard had gone through three wives, and was currently on his fourth, the curvaceous Poppy. He had children everywhere. Mannon was still carrying a torch for his first wife, Whitney, and the new one, Melanie-Shanna, had not yet killed the flame. Jack had Clarissa, although deep down he knew she wasn't the right woman for him – a knowledge he refused to admit.

"I've got a great idea," Mannon said suddenly. "Why don't we fly down to Vegas next month? Just the three of us. We never get to see each other anymore. We could play the tables, raise hell, cause some trouble, just like old times. Whaddya say?"

"Without the wives?" Howard asked hopefully.

"You bet your *cojones* without the wives," Mannon said quickly. "We'll drop 'em off at Neiman's – they'll never even notice we're gone."

Mugging excitedly, Howard said, "I like the idea," forgetting that Poppy would singe his balls if he tried to go away without her. This one was a clinger, as opposed to the other three before her, who were strictly takers.

"How about it, Jack?" Mannon looked at his friend expectantly.

Jack had promised Clarissa a week in New York. Long walks through the Village. Off-Broadway theatre. Never-ending dinners with her strange, broke friends. Guess who would pick up the bill?

He hated walking, only liked movies, and her so-called friends were a pain in the ass.

"Yes," he said. "Set it up. Work permitting, you can definitely include me in."

Chapter 2

Jade Johnson was totally addicted to Bruce Springsteen. She had no desire to meet him, just lust from afar like a mildly randy fourteen-year-old. She put *Born in the U.S.A.* on her stereo and danced around her new apartment.

Jade Johnson was twenty-nine years old. She had shoulder-length shaggy copper hair, gold-flecked widely spaced brown eyes, a full and luscious mouth, and a strong square jaw which saved her from being merely beautiful, and made her face challenging and alert.

She was five feet ten inches tall, one hundred and thirty pounds, with very long legs, a lithe, supple body, broad shoulders, and an incredible swan-like neck.

Apart from being kind-hearted and a good friend when the need arose, she had an acerbic wit and a wild sense of humour. She was also smart, independent, and one of the highest-paid photographic and commercial models in the world.

The doorbell rang and she rushed to answer it, clad in blue jeans and an oversized sweatshirt.

It was the foreman of the delivery crew who had just stacked fifteen large packing cases in her hallway. "That's it, lady," he said, handing her a slip to sign. "All present an' correct. I hope you're satisfied."

Signing, she slipped him a fifty–dollar bill. "Buy a beer for you and the guys."

Pocketing the money appreciatively, the man thought about what a knockout broad this one was. Not only good-looking in her skin-tight jeans and sweatshirt, but generous too.

"Thanks," he said, and added with a smirk, "that commercial you got runnin' on TV sure is blistering!"

She grinned, displaying very white, even teeth, and a warm, sexy smile. "Glad you like it," she said, subtly edging him to–wards the door. Once they started on about her famous coffee commercial she knew the time was ripe to move them out, having learned, very early on in her career, to be friendly yet unreachable to her many unknown admirers. Once, at eighteen, she had been attacked and nearly raped by a crazed fan who had fallen in obsession with a swimsuit poster she had posed for. Only the intervention of a concerned neighbour had saved her.

The delivery man paused at the door. "Maybe ya gotta photo y'can sign for me," he said hopefully.

Out she projected silently. She was looking forward to being alone and beginning the great unpack. "I'll send you one," she said pleasantly.

"Scrawl, I love ya Big Ben," he leered. "That'll give the boys somethin' t' think about."

Big Ben! Was he kidding?

She waited patiently while he laboriously printed his address on a slip of paper. "Thanks again, Ben," she said, finally closing the front door on him.

Alone at last! In L.A. Who would have thought she would ever make the long trek west again? New York was her kind of town, always had been. California never beckoned. Well, once, when she was twenty and naively accepted the offer of a screen test. *Stupido.* She was no actress, and held no ambitions in that direction. But she was young and curious, and what the hell – a trip was a trip.

She had arrived to be met by a block-long limo with a youngish agent lounging on the back seat. He wore *multo* gold chains with his open-to-the-limit silk shirt and carefully pressed designer jeans. He had a suntan, a mini-mogul cigar, a receding hairline, and an attitude. He offered her grass in the car and an invitation to dinner.

She turned down both, which caused frown lines to appear in his perfect suntan.

A suite at The Beverly Hills Hotel was reserved for her. Flowers and fruit abounded. She stayed five days, tested with a broody actor who tried to kill her close-ups, turned down several more invitations from the bronzed agent, returned to New York, and never heard another thing.

Several years later when she was really hot, Hollywood beckoned again. "Forget it," she told her New York modelling agent. "I'm going to be the best model in the business, *and* the highest paid. Who needs to travel the starlet route? Not this girl, baby."

And she was right. Jade Johnson *was* the best. And she was – due to the deal she had recently signed – the highest paid.

The deal was the reason she was once more in Los Angeles. Cloud Cosmetics made her an offer she couldn't refuse, and part of it was spending a year on the West Coast to make a series of million-dollar TV commercials. Normally she would never have considered leaving her beloved New York. However, she had just come out of a six-year relationship with a married man, and getting away seemed like an appealing prospect.

She wandered around the apartment kicking off her tennis shoes and unzipping her jeans as Springsteen belted out *Born in the U.S.A.* The sound of his raspy voice filled the room, and she was content. This was going to be a new beginning, the start of a whole different life. No more Jade Johnson – mistress. Oh no, sirree. That trip was over, *finito*. What a fool she had been. What a gullible idiot, falling for every cornball line he threw her way. She was hardly naive, and yet for six long years he had kept her captive with his tongue – in more ways than one.

She thought of him briefly. Mark Rand. An English Lord. An English asshole. A wild-life photographer of world-wide repute. They had met on assignment in Africa. She was doing leopard swimwear for *Vogue*, and he was shooting the photographs. He had curly hair, amused blue eyes, and fascinating conversation. It wasn't until a week of passion had passed that his fascinating conversation included mention of a wife, Lady Fiona Rand.

Jade remembered her fury. She had fallen for the oldest lines in the world . . . *My wife and I live together in name only . . . when the children are older . . .*

And Jade Johnson — smart, worldly, hardly a babe in the woods — listened to his corny bullshit and actually believed him! For six years she believed him. And she would have gone on doing so if Lady Fiona hadn't given birth to yet another little Rand heir, and Jade found out about it by accident while leafing through an English magazine.

The end had been acrimonious, her move to California swift.

Gazing around her new apartment she decided it was a great find. Situated on Wilshire near Westwood, she had leased it furnished, although there was no way she could think about getting through a year without her things around her. Books, records, her collection of china dogs, tapes of favourite movies, clothes, family pictures, and other personal possessions. Hence the delivery from New York a timely day after her own arrival, courtesy of TWA.

Contemplating the many cartons piled high in the hallway, she wondered if she could summon the energy to start on them now. With a sigh she realized she'd better. Grabbing a 7-Up from the kitchen she set to work.

Chapter 3

It was Silver Anderson's forty-seventh birthday, and she awoke with the thought that she was one year older foremost in her mind. She lay in bed for a full ten minutes ruminating on this fact, and then reluctantly she arose, first buzzing her houseman and ordering bran muffins, fresh orange juice, and lemon tea to be on her table in exactly fifty minutes. That was how long it took Silver to be ready to face the world. Rather quick considering the transformation that took place.

The woman who left the luxurious king-size bed was quite ordinary looking.

The woman who left the bedroom fifty minutes later was a television superstar.

Silver Anderson was ready for a *Vogue* photo session – the cover, of course, Silver only did cover stories. She was fully made up. Heavy base, dramatic eyes (she still wore false lashes, giving her a commanding but rather old-fashioned look). Her lips glistened with scarlet gloss, and her cheeks were sunken with shading. She wore heavy gold earrings, a white silk turban, and a pale beige leather outfit liberally studded with diamanté. It was only ten a.m. but Silver knew she owed it to her fans to always look like a star. She was five feet three inches tall, and had maintained her girlish figure. It took diet and exercise, and although it was a bitch keeping to the routine, the results made it worthwhile. From behind, with her tight ass and sassy strut, she could easily be mistaken for a twenty-year-old.

Sweeping downstairs, she ignored her Russian houseman, Vladimir, who was gay and couldn't care less *how* she treated him as long as she kept him in her employ. He dined out on his personal intimate Silver Anderson stories twice a week. To his friends *he* was the star, living vicariously through his mistress's exploits. Silver was *always* making headlines. She segued from men problems (two ex-husbands, dozens of boyfriends) to drink problems (thank you, Betty Ford, for making it legitimate) to feuds with directors, writers, producers – whoever was around to vent her anger on. Silver was very proud of saying, "I am a professional. And I *will not* be screwed around by unknowledgeable amateurs trying to step in my limelight. Let them remember just exactly who they are dealing with."

*

Silver Anderson first became a star at twelve. She was discovered singing and dancing in a school play by the talent agent father of one of her friends, who recommended her to the casting director of an important musical film. She auditioned, got the role, and went from there to ministardom singing like a bird in a series of hits. She certainly had a wonderful voice, full of power and extraordinary clarity. And so she should – her mother, Blanche (a failed singer herself), had made sure that her daughter had singing lessons from the age of five. Blanche often used to say to her, "I never made it. But you, my dear, will take the talent you inherited from me, and become the biggest star in the world."

Blanche had also insisted on dancing lessons and acting classes. As a result, when she was growing up, Silver never knew childhood, just vigorous training for the stardom her mother was convinced would one day be hers. When she was sixteen, the bottom fell out of musical comedy movies in Hollywood, and her agent suggested New York and the theatre.

"You're not going to New York," objected her father, George, a college professor and sometimes inventor of what her mother referred to as "useless devices". They lived in a large, rambling house in the Valley, bought with Silver's earnings, and he had no intention of uprooting.

"Daddy, I must!" Silver protested tearfully, as her mother had told her she should. "My career is at stake!" She overdramatized everything, even at sixteen.

Blanche agreed with her daughter. "We can't ruin her life, George. We must encourage her to soar!"

George stared mournfully at his domineering wife with the carrot-coloured hair and unfulfilled dreams. He knew there was no stopping her, so it was arranged that she would accompany Silver to New York for six months while he stayed at home with their son, Jack — at nine, seven years younger than his famous sister.

Both Silver and Blanche adored New York, and the feeling was mutual. Silver opened in a new show called Baby Gorgeous, *which ran for a phenomenal five years. During this time she married her first husband (tall, dark and weak), divorced him (he asked her for alimony), helped her mother to divorce George, and attended Blanche's remarriage to a twenty-six-year-old stage hand (her mother was thirty-eight at the time) and neither of them ever had any desire to go back to Los Angeles and the Valley. New York suited them just fine.*

"George and Jack are better off without us," Blanche reasoned. "You were born to be a star. And I was born to live in New York and enjoy myself."

That, she certainly did, what with her successful daughter and new younger husband.

After Baby Gorgeous *there was another smash show, a huge-selling record album, and sold-out cabaret appearances wherever Silver cared to appear.*

It took her ten years to go home. And then she didn't go home as such, she took a bungalow at The Beverly Hills Hotel with her current lover, a Scandinavian stud. And in between giving head and interviews she finally called her father. "Drive into Beverly Hills and I'll treat you and Jack to lunch tomorrow," she announced grandly, not letting on that Newsweek *were doing a cover story on her and needed to get some family pictures.*

George demurred; he had given up on Silver long ago. Just because she

21

*was his daughter did not change the fact that she was selfish and
egotistical, thinking only of herself. He held her responsible for breaking
up his marriage, and he would never forgive her for that.*

*Jack was home from college. At nineteen he was handsome, smart,
and curious to meet the sister he could hardly remember. "I'll go,
dad," he said eagerly.*

*George agreed under protest. He wouldn't put it past Silver to try
and lure Jack away from him too, a risk he would just have to take.*

*Jack went off to meet his famous sister in high spirits. He returned
two hours later, a frown on his face and criticism on his lips. "She's
fucking unreal!" he exclaimed. "She acts like the Queen of England."*

*George did not show his relief. "Don't swear," he admonished
sternly. "Is this how they teach you to talk in college?"*

"Dad! I'm nineteen, for crissake."

*"Then I should think you know by now that swearing does not
make you any more of a man."*

*"Okay. Okay. Sorry," Jack said quickly, and thought that next
time he came home from college in Colorado, he would take his friend
Howard Soloman up on his idea that they rent an apartment together
in Hollywood. "It'll be an ace move," Howard enthused. Jack had
said no. Next time he would say yes.*

*Silver thought her baby brother was a handsome dolt. He certainly
had the family looks, although all the talent had obviously gone in
her direction. One meeting was enough. She did not bother to call
again, and it was another four years before they came face to face at
the funeral in New York of Blanche, who had died of an untimely
cancer.*

*Jack often wondered why he went. When his mother divorced his
father she had divorced him too. He would never forget George's grim
face when he sat him down one day and gave him the bad news.
"Your mother won't be coming home," he'd said. "It's best this way."*

*As a kid, Jack could remember crying himself to sleep for many
months, trying to figure out what bad thing he had done to make his
mother desert him so brutally. In his teens he had considered contacting
her, making her tell him. But he always put the dreaded visit off, and
when she died it was too late, and he knew he must at least attend her
funeral.*

*Silver was playing drama queen to the hilt. She was dressed in
black fox furs and a pillbox hat with a veil. She clung to Blanche's
husband, sympathy brimming from over-made-up eyes, while photographers bobbed and weaved around the graveside.*

Silver failed to recognize her only brother. He tapped her on the arm to jog her memory. "Thank you for your good wishes," *she murmured, and moved on to the next fan.*

He could smell the liquor on her breath, and tried to understand. Three months later she married her former stepfather in Las Vegas vowing that this one was "forever". Ten months later there was an acrimonious divorce which caused nasty headlines.

It seemed that Silver always rode the wave of bad publicity and rose from the ashes smiling. The next year she bore a daughter, refused to name the father, and went off to live in Brazil with a very rich man (some said a plasticized Nazi war criminal) for two years. Then she returned to Broadway at the age of thirty-four and starred in two hit shows one after the other for a total of five years.

Meanwhile Jack was getting his life together. After college he shared an apartment in Hollywood with his friend Howard Soloman. Howard wanted to be an agent, mainly because he felt it opened the gateway to "unlimited pussy". He got himself a job at a big talent agency working in the mail room.

Jack wasn't sure what he wanted to do. Everyone said that with his looks he should be an actor — he shuddered at the thought. Writing interested him. Newspapers interested him. The journalistic world beckoned. He started to review movies and records for a small magazine, and to make his half of the rent he became a tour guide at a television studio. Within six months he was promoted to a researcher on a local talk show.

"You've got a way with people," said the head researcher, a woman who recognized raw talent when she saw it.

"Thank you," he replied, deftly avoiding her offer of a night of ecstasy in her Westwood condo.

He then proceeded to sleep his way through all the good-looking female guests on the show, while learning everything there was to know about television.

One day a young movie actor — one of the guests — grabbed Jack backstage. "Hey, man — you're fucking my girlfriend," the actor protested.

"I am?"

"You can bet your ass on it."

Jack couldn't figure out which one might be the actor's girlfriend so without naming any names he gave a blanket sorry.

"So you goddamn well should be," huffed the actor. "She won't let me get beyond first base. What's she like in the sack?"

Conversation led to the nearest bar, and Mannon Cable — newly discovered and busted out — became the third roommate to Jack and Howard. They called themselves the Three Comers — a reference to their

career goals rather than their colourful sex-lives. Howard was a walk-
ing hard-on. Mannon had looks and humour to lure them between the
sheets. Jack had everything.

One thing Jack never advertised was his famous sister. Howard
knew, but kept it to himself. Mannon found out, and thought it was a
hoot. "Why the secret?" he asked.

Jack shrugged. "I hardly know her. Who needs the connection?"

Fortunately, Silver, at the start of her career, had chosen to use her
mother's maiden name, which was Anderson. Jack preferred the more
dramatic family surname — Python.

And so the Three Comers' careers rose.

Howard by the age of twenty-six became a fully fledged agent, and
at twenty-eight he was hot. Along the way he got married, took out a
mortgage on a too-expensive house in Laurel Canyon, purchased his
first Mercedes, and gave great meeting.

Mannon hit the road to big stardom via a centrefold in a popular
woman's magazine. He out-Reynolded Burt Reynolds, starred in
several sure-fire hits, bought the requisite beach house and cream Rolls-
Royce, and supported a constant stream of beautiful ditsy girlfriends.

Jack went off to Arizona and worked on a local television news
station. After two years he was hosting everything they had to offer.
He got an anchor position in Chicago, then Houston. He tried his
hand at everything from serious news to fluff pieces, covering politics,
film festivals, murders, movies, child molestation. You name it — he
knew something about it. In Houston they gave him his own show,
The Python Beat. He out-rated everyone and everything in the vicinity.
His fan mail was legion. By the time he hit New York to host a nightly
network show, Silver was on her way to Hollywood to star in a movie
version of one of her Broadway hits. He often wondered if she would make
contact to congratulate him. After all, like it or not, they were brother
and sister, and maybe they could forget the past and start again.

He never heard a word from her.

The movie Silver starred in bombed. It wasn't just an ordinary
bomb, it was a mega-explosion, a nuclear disaster, wiping out all
connected with it. Silver fled to Europe, humiliated. Everyone seemed
to blame her. As far as she was concerned she was the best thing in it.

She went through what she now delicately referred to as her "nervous
breakdown" period. Actually it was a serious flirtation with booze and
drugs which very nearly ended her life — let alone her plummeting
career.

That's when Jack heard from her. Well, not from her exactly, he got
a call from London, and a ten-year-old girl named Heaven. "Are you

my uncle?" she demanded. "Can I come and stay with you? Mama's sick. They've taken her away."

Jack cancelled a week's interviews and took the Concorde to London. He found Heaven living with a transvestite in Chelsea. Silver was locked up in a mental institution.

"She tried to take her own life, poor dear," the transvestite whispered. "Can you imagine what it must be like when the looks go, and the talent. I did what I thought was best. Oh, and by the way, she owes me two thousand pounds. I'd like cash, please."

Jack took care of everything. He paid the bills, arranged for Silver's transfer to a private nursing home, hired twenty-four-hour nurses and the best psychiatrists.

When he visited his sister she stared at him blankly. Without makeup she looked like a pale white shadow, but her eyes burned with heat. "How's George?" she asked. Forty years old and she was finally asking after her father — the father she had abandoned at sixteen.

"He's doing okay," Jack replied. "I'm taking Heaven to stay with him. If that's all right with you."

"Yes," she replied listlessly, her tapered fingers plucking at a loose strand of hair. "I'm finished, you know," she continued matter-of-factly. "All washed up. In Hollywood they can't see real talent for shit. All they want is twenty-year-olds with big boobs. I'll never come back."

Jack felt uncomfortable with this pale, wan woman who spoke with such bitterness. This was not the Silver Anderson he had watched throughout the years. In a way it was a relief to know he was out from under her shadow — although the shadow had only existed in his eyes.

"Hey —" he tried to give her confidence. "You're still a beautiful woman. And you'll always be a big star."

"Thanks!" Her tone was full of sarcasm. "Words of encouragement from baby Jack. God! When you were still in diapers I was a star. I don't need you to tell me."

She made no comment on his career. Jack Python. Man of the hour. His own network show.

Settling everything, financial and otherwise, he flew back to California with Heaven. "You'll camp out at your grandpa's house," he told the child. "He's quite a character. And when your mother is better she'll send for you."

"No she won't," replied Heaven, wise beyond her years. She was small, with pinched features and enormous amber eyes.

"Yes she will," he countered.

"Bet?" questioned Heaven.

"Sure. You're on, kid."

Heaven won her bet. In London, Silver recovered and never did send for her daughter.

Jack was disgusted. He talked to the head honchos at his network and asked for his show to be moved to Los Angeles. They agreed, and he was delighted. At least Heaven would have someone around – apart from her grandfather – who genuinely cared for her.

Silver resurfaced on the English stage in a new production of Pal Joey, *which brought her excellent reviews and a resurgence of fame. English fame. She loved being back in the spotlight and basked in the light. But it was only English light, and that wasn't enough. England was a small pond and she wanted America. With that thought in mind she acquired a new agent in Hollywood, Quinne Lattimore, and badgered him to do something about it.*

Quinne did not think they were going to create any fires. Silver Anderson was hardly hot news – she had been around too long and stepped on too many toes to set the town alight. He suggested her name for a few projects and heard everything from "She's too old" to "The broad's a lush." And then along came the unexpected offer of a role in Palm Springs, a daytime soap. Normally Quinne would have rejected the project immediately. Silver wanted to come back, but hardly on daytime television playing an ageing torch singer. However, when City Television came in with an offer that was too tempting to ignore, he called her in London and said, "I think this might be the showcase to get you here, so that the people who matter can see you."

"I'm not doing a soap," she steamed.

"It's a six-week guest spot," Quinne interrupted. "Top dollar, unlimited budget for wardrobe, and you get to keep the clothes, approve the script, and anything else we want to throw at them. They're anxious."

"So they should be," she sniffed. "A soap indeed!"

"Sleep on it," he suggested.

"Why should I?" she argued.

"Because it's the only ballgame in the park."

Silver did Palm Springs. She was fabulous. The show's ratings rocketed. The producers made her an offer she couldn't refuse, to stay on. And Silver Anderson became the hottest actress on daytime television.

For three years now she had reigned supreme. She was bigger than she'd ever been, and revelled in every minute of her success.

*

A black stretch limo waited outside the front door of Silver's mansion high up in Bel Air. Inside the limo sat her publicist,

Nora Carvell, a fifty-nine-year-old lesbian with knowing eyes and a gravelly voice (who else could possibly put up with Silver?), and her personal assistant — a tall, jumpy young man who had held the job for two weeks and was about to get fired.

"Good morning, everyone," Silver beamed.

There was an imperceptible sigh of relief. Silver was in a good mood — thank God for that!

Chapter 4

When Mannon Cable got up to go to the john, Howard Soloman leaned anxiously towards Jack Python and said, "You're never gonna believe this, but I ran into Whitney at a party last night, and I swear she's got the hots for me."

Jack started to laugh. Whitney Valentine Cable was Mannon's ex-wife, a stunning-looking actress for whom Mannon still carried a torch. "Whitney," Jack said slowly, "has the hots? For *you*?" He continued laughing.

"For crissakes," Howard said irritably. "What's so funny about *that*?"

"Because you and Whitney hated each other when you were Mannon's agent. Christ! If I had a nickel for all the times you bitched about her, and likewise she about you."

"A hard dick an' a soft pussy creep up on people in a variety of ways," Howard said wisely.

Jack almost choked. "I love it when you wax poetic."

"Fuck you."

"When I'm at a loose end I'll think of you first."

Howard belched, not so discreetly. "I'm tellin' you, *she* came on to *me*. The next move is mine an' I'm gonna make it."

"You'll make it when Mannon's six feet under," Jack warned. "You move on Whitney and he'll have your balls for breakfast."

"What's the big friggin' deal?" Howard waved his arms

27

excitedly in the air. "They've been divorced for nearly two years. Mannon's married to Melanie what's-her-name. And Whitney hasn't exactly acted like a virgin since they split."

"You're talking like a dumb asshole," Jack said, bored with the conversation. "Has it ever occurred to you that Whitney suddenly getting the hots for your body coincides very nicely with your primo position at Orpheus?"

"Are you saying –" Howard began indignantly. He stopped abruptly as Mannon slid back into the booth.

"I've been thinking," Mannon said expansively. "Somebody should do a movie about middle-aged broads who follow movie stars into the can. I just got trailed by a real prize. She bird-dogged me into the goddamn john and asked for my autograph while I'm in the middle of taking a leak! Can you believe it?"

Jack could easily believe it. The same thing had happened to him a week before at a fashionable restaurant. Fame. It was the one part of his life he did not enjoy. Sister Silver revelled in it. You couldn't pick up a magazine without seeing her face staring at you. Her come-back was phenomenal, and yet fortunately it hadn't affected him. In the public's mind they had two very separate identities. Like Warren Beatty and Shirley MacLaine, the fact that they were brother and sister rarely came up.

Today was Silver's birthday. He hadn't spoken to her in months. The only conversations they did have concerned Heaven, who was now sixteen years old. When Silver first came back to America, the expectation was that the child would leave her grandfather's house and return to live with her mother. However, one week in Silver's company put paid to *that* plan, and Heaven returned to her grandfather, who had continued to bring her up ever since. It pissed Jack off. George was getting older and needed a little peace and quiet in his life. Heaven was turning into a wild child and Silver was the last one to care. She wouldn't even reveal who Heaven's father was.

"What d'you think, Howard?" Mannon demanded. "How about doing a movie called *Old Groupies* or *How I Learned to Take a Piss in Public*? Is the idea grabbing you?"

"I think you *should* do a film for Orpheus," Howard said seriously. "Name the deal and it's yours."

"C'mon. *You* know better than anyone that I don't even have a minute to scratch my ass."

Swooping on another roll, Howard said, "Let's get something

28

in the works. When you're free we want you. Remember, Orpheus is first in line."

"What is this, calling-in-favour time?"

Howard nodded vigorously. "Yeah."

"In that case," Jack joined in, "when are you going to do my show? You've promised for God knows how long. What is this unswerving loyalty to Carson?"

Throwing up his hands, Mannon grinned. "I'm in demand! I love it!"

He had been in demand for over fifteen years now, and he was still enjoying every minute, not to mention the public's adoration and the millions of dollars he made.

Mannon had everything he wanted. Except Whitney. She had left him just when he needed her most, and he was taking his time getting over her. His new wife, Melanie-Shanna, had not solved any problems. She was a recent Miss Texas Sunshine, pretty and sweet, but Whitney she wasn't, and marrying her had been a grave mistake. If it wasn't for alimony and community property, he would have dumped her a week after the wedding. Like a jerk he hadn't gotten her to sign a pre-nuptial agreement limiting her demands. However, his lawyers were working on it, and as soon as he got the all-clear he was going for a divorce. Naturally, Melanie-Shanna knew nothing of his plans. It wouldn't do to forewarn her. Let her think everything was perfect until D-Day – and then bye-bye, pretty little beauty queen.

He must have been insane marrying her. It was a revenge strike aimed at Whitney, who had moved in with his ex-friend, a Malibu stud named Chuck Nielson. The guy couldn't even act, and only appeared in the movies Mannon turned down. Fortunately their affair was shaky, and now Mannon (as soon as he could arrange a divorce) planned to win her back.

"I can't do your show," he said gravely. "You're too serious."

"Serious!" Jack shook his head. "I guess you missed me and Ms. Midler last week."

"Great tits!" interjected Howard.

"Great talent," scolded Jack.

"*And* great tits," added Mannon.

Jack couldn't help laughing. "You two!" he said. "Tits 'n' ass. The story of your lives."

"And you never think about it, right?" Howard and Mannon said as one.

"Only when I'm horny," Jack replied, and the three friends laughed.

*

Whitney Valentine Cable had a spectacular body and a striking face. Her eyes were a dreamy aquamarine, her nose straight and freckled, her mouth drooped at the corners until she smiled, and when she did, Whitney Valentine Cable had the biggest, the best and the whitest smile in Hollywood.

Her hair was blonde and long and fluffy. Grown men fantasized about her hair. And grown women copied whatever style she chose to wear her luxuriant tresses in.

She was a personality and a star, but sad to report, Whitney Valentine Cable could not act.

This did not seem to matter very much, for in the five years she had pursued an acting career she had ridden the crest of mild popularity. Countless magazine covers helped. And a year-long television sit-com, followed by a string of exploitation movies featuring her in various scanty outfits. Whitney had worn everything from three strategically placed fig leaves, to a mink peek-a-boo ball gown. She had *never* shown EVERYTHING. Oh no. Gorgeous as she was, Whitney knew the good sense in keeping *something* hidden. So the great unwashed public had never spied upon her luscious nipples or her silken furry bush. Even though *Playboy* and similar magazines had begged, pleaded, even cried for her to reveal all – offering vast sums of money for the privilege.

It was never enough. If Whitney was going to show off the goods it would be for a million dollars or not at all. And that offer hadn't materialized yet.

*

Whitney Valentine made the trek to Hollywood the easy way. Working as a hairdresser in a small town outside of Fort Worth, she was as eager as the rest of the town to watch the location shoot of a genuine Hollywood film taking place. She visited the outdoor set with her girlfriend on a Saturday afternoon, and immediately caught the eye of Mannon Cable, the macho star of the movie.

It was not exactly love at first sight for Mannon. More If it moves – nail it. And delectable Whitney was the most nailable girl he'd seen all week. She was eighteen and innocent, or so she said when he tried to initiate her into the joys of going to bed with a movie star.

30

Whitney was not happy living in a small town. She wanted out, and Mannon Cable seemed the perfect exit visa. Holding back, instinct told her, was the only way to get him. And she was right. He called her everything from a dumb broad to a prick-tease, but six weeks later he married her, and when the movie finished shooting he brought her to Beverly Hills as his bride.

For five years Whitney played the model wife. Cooking, shopping, taking care of their Malibu ranch house, posing for photo layouts with her famous husband, and generally behaving like the woman every man wished was his.

And then, one hot Malibu Sunday, with the jacuzzi going full force, and the waft of barbecue in the air, Mannon's friend and agent, Howard Soloman, whispered in her ear that there was a role in a television pilot for which she would be perfect if only she were an actress.

Excitement lit up her face. "Put me up for it, Howard," she begged. "Oh, please! You must!"

"Mannon'll kill me," he groaned.

"And so will I if you don't," she hissed.

Secretly she tested for the role.

Secretly she got the job.

When all was revealed to Mannon he was furious. "You stupid asshole," he yelled at Howard. "The last thing I need is a starlet for a wife."

"It's what she wants," Howard argued lamely.

"Well, you're no longer my agent, I can tell you that," Mannon screamed, then turned his wrath on Whitney.

"I want to work," she told him calmly. "I'm bored."

"Bored!" He was outraged. "You're married to me, for crissake. How can you possibly be bored?"

"You're always working," she complained. "I have nothing to do all day. I'm lonely."

"So how about starting a family? We've talked about it enough times. You know it's what I want."

"And I want to do something with my life before I settle down and have babies. Please, Mannon, you've got to understand that this is what I need."

Reluctantly he agreed that she could take a shot at it. Whitney was the only woman he wanted to spend his life with, and if she required a few months messing around in show biz, let her do it. She'd soon find out what a crap-shoot it all was.

The first thing she did was dye her light brown hair blonde. And then she decided to call herself Whitney Valentine — adding the Cable to please Mannon (it also pleased the press department of her television show, but that's another story).

And so began her climb to stardom. It wasn't difficult. The sit-com was a hit, she had all the right requirements in abundance, plus a very famous husband, and the publicity mill took it from there.

Five years and five hundred magazine covers later she was a star — just as she'd wanted. And she and Mannon were history. She hadn't planned to divorce him, but he was jealous of her success, and there was nothing she could do about that. They had been divorced for eighteen months. The moment the decree was final Mannon had married some Texas beauty queen. Whitney could not help feeling hurt, for it was she who had instigated the divorce, not Mannon, who had declared undying love right up until the moment he married again. For a while she was tempted to do the same with the guy she was living with — Chuck Nielson, an ex-friend of Mannon's. But Chuck was great when he was straight, and insane when drugged out. Besides, she was enjoying her new-found freedom.

*

As she sipped a glass of iced tea beside her kidney-shaped swimming pool in the garden of her house on Loma Vista, Whitney thought about Howard Soloman. Who would ever have imagined that one day he would be running Orpheus Studios? When he was Mannon's agent she couldn't stand him. And when he launched *her* career she tolerated him, until he left agenting to form his own production company. A few powerful jobs later he was head of the studio. She was impressed.

Extending a delicate foot, she admired the pearly glow of the polish on her pedicured toenails. Howard Soloman. One of Mannon's best friends. Funny, vulgar, street-smart Howard.

She shivered uncomfortably. Even thinking about going to bed with Howard was crazy; she had known him for too many years — *and* all three of his wives, including Poppy, the present one. And yet, last night at the Fields' party, Howard and she got to talking — quietly, in a corner, with no one else around — and something had happened. He understood her. He understood her career needs. And sometimes that could be the most important part of any relationship.

Chapter 5

Springsteen belted, and Jade felt good. She had unpacked three boxes and already the apartment seemed more like home. The doorbell buzzed and she peered through the spy-hole – an old New York habit. "Who is it?" she called out.

"Pizza."

"I didn't order any."

"You've *always* got an order of pizza on the way."

"Corey!" She flung open the door. "What a sneak! You told me you couldn't get here until next week."

"For you, sis, I worked magic."

He placed the box of pizza on the floor and hugged his sister. There was no family resemblance. Corey was shorter than Jade, and several years younger. He was pleasant looking, with uniform features and none of his sister's mesmerizing charisma.

"This is *so* great!" she exclaimed.

"Me or the pizza?"

"The pizza, what else? Let's eat. I'm starving! It's double mushroom, I hope?"

"And cheese and bologna and meatballs and peppers. Does that suit you?"

"Oh, Corey, baby – *you* suit me. It's fantastic to see your silly smiling face."

He grinned. "Likewise, pretty sis. It's been too long."

"I know."

He picked up the box of pizza. "Am I coming in?" he asked jokingly. "Or are we eating out in the hall?"

"Sorry! C'mon. In. Now. Food. And all the news. Right?"

"You got it." He followed her into the ultra-modern kitchen and placed the box on a counter top.

Jade reached for plates and a knife. "How's Marita and the Johnson heir?"

Corey looked around. "This is a really nice place," he said admiringly.

"Better than my rabbit hole in New York, huh?" she teased.

"Bigger."

"What do you want to drink? Shall we live dangerously and open a bottle of wine?"

He consulted his watch. "It's only twelve-thirty."

"Y'know, sometimes I think you never moved to the big city."

He glanced out of the window. "Sometimes I wish I hadn't." Turning towards her he added, "Have you spoken to mom and dad lately?"

She handed him a bottle of white wine and an opener. "I'm going to call tomorrow. I always call on Sunday. If I change the routine they get panic-stricken and think God knows what. Why?" her tone became anxious. "There's nothing wrong, is there?"

He wrestled with the wine. "They're fine. I spoke to mom yesterday."

"Good." She busied herself with dividing the pizza into two huge pieces.

Uncomfortably he said, "It's just that I figured if you'd spoken to them you would've heard."

She fixed him with a sharp look. He had something to say and she wasn't sure she wanted to hear it. "What's on your mind?"

"Marita and I split up."

"Oh, shit!"

Shrugging defensively he said, "It's no big deal."

"Yes it is," she replied grimly. "You have a child. That makes it a *very* big deal."

He glared. "No lectures. Not unless you want me to talk about *your* situation."

"I'm *out* of my situation," she said pointedly, a determined set to her jaw.

Sensing a weakness he pounced. "You've wasted six years of your life with a married guy, so if you're planning to give *me* advice I'm not interested."

Anger filtered across her face. "Don't get uptight with me," she snapped. "What *you* do and what *I* do are two different things."

34

As soon as she'd said it she wished she hadn't. All his life Corey had played second to her. She was the successful one in the family. He'd never made it. She was at the top of her profession. He had a mediocre job with a public relations firm in San Francisco. He hadn't even left home until he met and married Marita – who was Hawaiian – and moved with her to California four years ago.

"I'm sorry," she said quietly. "I guess I'm upset. Marita and you seemed so terrific together. What happened?"

He made a gesture of defeat. "I don't know."

Jade found she had lost her appetite. Her brother's happiness was important to her and his news was a bombshell. She couldn't wait to get on the phone to her mother and discuss it.

"I wanted to tell you myself," he said, getting up and restlessly pacing the kitchen. "Mom and dad know, but that's about it."

"Is it irrevocable?"

"'Fraid so. I'm moving to L.A. I've got a transfer from the San Francisco office."

"At last some good news. You can move in with me."

Shaking his head he said, "I've got a place. I'm sharing a house with a friend."

The scene became clear. Corey was involved with another woman. Hopefully, when his hard-on wore off he would hurry back to Marita and the baby.

"Can I give you some advice?" she ventured.

"No, thank you. Look, sis, I've got to run. There's a lot of stuff I have to organize."

"You only just got here," she protested.

Kissing her forehead he said, "We'll be living in the same town. We haven't done that since we were kids. It'll be just like old times, won't it?"

The shine was off her day, but she nodded anyway.

"I'll call you," he said, "as soon as I'm settled."

The moment he left she phoned her mother, who knew no more than she did, and was very upset about the situation.

"Has anyone spoken to Marita?" she asked.

"Corey says she's gone back to Hawaii with the baby to stay with her family," her mother said.

"Not permanently, I hope?"

"I don't know."

As soon as she hung up, she felt an urge to talk to Mark.

They had been apart for five weeks and she still had withdrawal symptoms. For six years they had shared each other's lives. Except he had led a separate life of his own in England, one she was supposed to know nothing about.

Bastard.

That didn't mean she couldn't miss him if she wanted to.

Without thinking she wolfed down the rest of the pizza, an act she immediately regretted. Mark would have laughed at her. Sometimes, when she went on eating binges, he called her the Fat American. Hardly a title suited to her slim curves. When they had fights – and it had not been a peaceful six years – she called him the Uptight Englishman. They used to joke about writing a sit-com with the two nicknames combined. "It'd be a smash!" Jade would laugh.

"Only with you in it," he'd reply.

They always used to go on trips together. She enjoyed his world as much as he was fascinated by hers. Twice a year she had accompanied him to Africa on his photographic safaris, and she would certainly miss the breathtaking beauty of waking up in the wilderness with the most incredible dawn skies and the sounds of nature all around.

Mark Rand.

He was part of her past.

She had to stop thinking about him.

Chapter 6

Wes Money shared a birthday with Silver Anderson, only he didn't know it, and even if he had he wouldn't have cared. He was thirty-three years old and getting nowhere fast. The trouble with Wes was that he had no direction in life. Having tried a little bit of everything, he had failed to succeed at anything.

*

Wes Money was born in a slum area of London to a sometime hooker and her part-time pimp. Childhood was not exactly made in Disney-land; growing up was a tough game, and Wes learned early on in life to play it fast and dirty. When he was twelve, his mother found herself a rich American (or at least she thought he was at the time), married him, and moved to New York. Wes thought he had died and gone to heaven. He was getting laid at thirteen (all the little high school girls just loved his cockney accent), getting arrested at fifteen (shoplifting — nothing lethal), and getting out at sixteen. He did not say goodbye to his mother — she probably never even noticed he was gone. By the time he split, she had divorced her husband and returned to her old ways. Hooking suited her better than cooking.

Wes moved in with a buxom stripper who thought he was twenty. He did a little pimping of his own, but his heart wasn't in it, and a small amount of drug dealing led him to the fringes of the rock business, and what he thought at the time was his true love — music. He dis-covered he could sing, unearthing a low throaty growl which lent itself to the heavy-metal sounds popular in the seventies. After toiling as a roadie for a year with a group called In the Lewd, *his chance came when the lead singer came down with an acute case of the clap. Without hesitation Wes stepped into his shoes if not his pants.*

Ecstasy followed. He was twenty-two and singing with a group. Fourteen-year-old virgins threw themselves at him. He met Mick Jagger and Etta James. He was going to be famous!

In the Lewd *disbanded after ten months. They hadn't even gotten a record deal. Wes was pissed off, although he quite expected other groups to be lining up to sign him.*

Nothing happened. Absolutely nothing. So he moved to Miami in search of the sun, and took a job as a bartender in a night club where he met a Swedish divorcee of forty-two, with money, steel thighs, and no sense of humour. She kept him for three years, which was all right with him, especially as he was making it with her maid, a well-stacked Puerto Rican girl.

Both relationships ended when the Swedish woman decided to get married again, and the bridegroom-to-be was not him.

Reluctantly he went back to tending bar at one of the big hotels. A suitable job for someone who couldn't make up his mind what to do next.

Vicki entered his life when the last thing he was looking for was a woman with no money. Vicki was twenty and perfect. There was no way they couldn't team up. Love was a new experience for him, and it made him uneasy. Vicki was a dancer in one of the lavish hotel shows, and unfortunately she made even less money than he did. They lived together in a tiny ocean-front apartment, and before long Vicki was making ominous mumblings about marriage.

A picket fence, unpaid bills, and babies was not the future he saw for himself, so he cheated on Vicki with her best friend, and made sure she found out. Then he left town and returned to New York, where he soon realized it was too cold for him —but not before doing a small part in a porno video for a fast thousand bucks cash.

The money brought him a one-way ticket to Los Angeles, where he rented a two-room run-down house in Venice —on the boardwalk — and worked as an extra in a few movies. After a while he got bored hanging around film sets, and drifted back to tending bar at a variety of Hollywood hang-outs.

One day he woke up and he was thirty-three.

*

Luckily Wes was not in his own bed, as he would have been so depressed he might have killed himself. He groped for a cigarette and looked around, while a thousand needles jabbed relentlessly at his temples. He had no idea where he was.

A half-full glass of scotch stood on the bedside table next to a pink telephone and a frilled Kleenex holder. There was also a cheap plastic alarm clock, and an ashtray shaped like an owl, overflowing with old cigarette butts.

Well, he obviously hadn't hit pay dirt. For years he had been looking for another Swede. Being kept by a woman was the kind of cushy lifestyle that appealed to him.

Yawning loudly he sat up. A stuffed ginger cat stared down at him from a shelf. "Good morning," he said amiably.

Was it his imagination, or did the cat wink?

Shit! Too many late nights and hard women.

The bedroom was small and hot. No air conditioning. He had definitely lucked out.

"Anyone home?" he called, and his hostess made her entrance. She was a plump blonde with teased hair, caked makeup, and silicone breasts displayed through a polyester negligee.

"I thought ja'd never wake up," she said. "Y'can put it away quicker than my old man, an' *that's* goin' some."

He could swear that he'd never set eyes on her in his life. And he must have been very drunk to have honoured her with the pleasure of his cock. "Do I know you?" he asked.

She eyed him appreciatively. "At least y'can get it up, which

38

is more'n *he* could when he ran out on me. You'd be amazed at the number of fagolas around today."

"Really?" He dragged on his cigarette and pretended to be surprised.

"I ain't kiddin' you, hon." She fluffed out her hair and gave him a long, lingering look. "I gotta be at work in half an hour . . . What the heck, I've time if you have."

He would sooner have walked on hot coals all the way back to New York. This drinking of his had to stop.

She began to divest herself of the negligee. Underneath she wore a red garter belt, red patterned stockings and nothing else. Her bush – wiry and black – grew all the way to China. He was surprised she didn't back-comb and style it.

"Nothing I'd like better," he said, lifting the sheet and peering down at his penis – rigid, but only with the need to take a piss.

"Looks good t' me," she leered.

"Just checking," he said.

"What for?"

"I've got this ongoing case of herpes. The doc says it's only catching when it flares up. However, in the interest of not passing anything on, I like to keep an eye on it."

She froze. "You *low*-life!" Quickly she struggled back into her negligee, rolls of fat shaking indignantly. "Get out of my bed and take a powder."

"It's not communicable now," he protested.

"Just get lost, scumbag."

She turned her back while he pulled on his pants and shirt. He left her house without another word being exchanged, and was surprised to find himself in the Valley. *How* had he made it to the Valley in the condition he must have been in?

Fortunately his car was parked outside. An old Lincoln won in a poker game. He did have his moments.

Stopping at a coffee shop on Ventura Boulevard, he went straight to the men's room. In the mirror above a cracked basin he wished himself a happy birthday. On the wall somebody had scrawled MY MOTHER MADE ME A HOMOSEXUAL and underneath someone else had written IF I GIVE HER THE WOOL WILL SHE MAKE ME ONE TOO?

Leaning closer to the mirror he saw the marks of time and too much booze. Right now, unshaven, with a hangover and bleary eyes, he didn't look too good. But he washed up nicely, and when he had lived with the Swede he had been positively good-looking. Of course, manicures and facials and massages and new expensive clothes helped anyone look good. Life with the Swede was quite a few years ago though. He missed her steely thighs, *and* her money.

Anyway, he could still get most women if he put his mind to it. He had longish brown hair and regular features marred only by a broken nose (acquired in a bar-room brawl), and a small inch-long scar beneath his left eyebrow (the result of an argument with Vicki when they split). His eyes were the colour of fresh seaweed, and while he didn't exercise or any of that crap, his five feet eleven inches was in pretty good shape – give or take a few extra pounds.

He knew how to please the ladies too. Sober or drunk he could still make 'em sing Streisand.

After coffee and a couple of sugar-packed doughnuts he set off home, almost stopping for a teenage hitchhiker in red shorts – only changing his mind when he realized he was playing Russian roulette with his sex life. There were all sorts of things to consider nowadays: herpes, which he didn't have – not to mention AIDS, which did not mean a shot of pencillin and goodbye Charlie. AIDS meant death. Slow and lingering.

Shuddering, he decided he definitely had to clean up his act. No more lost-weekend nights. In future he had to *know* who he was sleeping with.

Outside his house lurked a local prostitute. Once, when he was really busted, he had let her use his bedroom for a week. She entertained forty-two men and the place had smelled like a doss house toilet. Never again.

"Hiya, Wes," she trilled. "I brought you a present."

He was touched. The local hooker had remembered his birthday.

No such luck. It was a packet of cocaine he had ordered for an acquaintance.

"How much?" he asked.

Money was exchanged for goods, and he realized funds were alarmingly low. Even though he could sell the coke at twice the price, it was time to find another job.

Inside his house nothing had changed. Dirty clothes, dirty ashtrays, dirty sheets – the usual mess. Idly he wondered if he could hire the hooker for maid service. Probably not. She would think it was beneath her.

Punching on his phone answering machine he waited for the

message that would tell him he was wanted for another group. Singing was his life – only he hadn't done any in years.

"Listen, pal," said the voice of his friend Rocky. "You gotta do me a big favour. Tonight there's this party up in Bel Air at some TV star's place. Silver Anderson. Me and Stuart were supposed to take care of the bar, only the stupid sonofabitch broke his arm jumpin' out of a movin' car. Don't ask me why. Sixty bucks for a coupla hours. You can't let me down. Okay, pal?"

It was his birthday. He had nothing else to do.

Chapter 7

Jack Python drove a dark racing-green Ferrari. He did not like anyone else behind the wheel, and as most of the parking valets in town were aware of his idiosyncrasy they were quite happy for him to park it himself.

Leaving The Beverly Hills Hotel, he walked briskly to his car, trailed by a couple of tourists from Minnesota who, camera in hand, hoped to get his picture. Before they could summon the courage to ask, he roared off into the hazy afternoon sunshine.

He was supposed to play tennis, but breakfast with Howard and Mannon had sapped his energy and he didn't feel like it, so he cancelled the appointment on his car telephone, making it for the next morning. Then he tried Clarissa at the studio, only to be informed that she was on the set and unavailable.

"I know who you are!" a girl in a white convertible at a stoplight yelled.

His smile of acknowledgment was uncomfortable. He honestly did not enjoy public recognition – unlike Mannon, who revelled in it, or Howard, who craved it. When Howard was first made the head of Orpheus, his finest moment was getting the front round table at Morton's restaurant, wiping out two movie stars and a very important producer.

The Three Comers. Well, they sure had come a long way. Three guys with big ambitions sharing one small apartment. And they'd all made it to the top. He was proud of their achievements.

He drove slowly to his penthouse in the Beverly Wilshire Hotel, preferring the looseness of hotel life to the responsibility of his own apartment or house. It gave him a nice sense of freedom.

Clarissa rented a home on Benedict Canyon, and he spent a lot of time there. Lately he had been thinking of leasing a place at the beach for the summer. Not in the Malibu Colony, that was too full of recognizable faces. More like Point Dume or Trancas. The idea really appealed to him. Maybe he'd just take the summer off and become a beach bum. He also thought it would be good for Heaven, who might like to come and stay with him for the summer.

Clarissa wasn't thrilled at the prospect. She was a city person, more comfortable with dust and smells and bustle. She was always complaining about Los Angeles as opposed to New York. And she hated the beach.

They had met in New York at a fund-raising party for a Democratic Senator, who he later found out she was sleeping with. Their meeting was no big deal, apart from the fact that she dumped the Senator and ended up in *his* bed. After that they saw each other intermittently for a couple of months, always pursued by frantic paparazzi.

When Clarissa appeared on his show it was considered a big deal, a first, because she didn't do television talk shows. Struggling through an hour with her he understood why. She was a difficult guest, and he was sorry he'd asked. *Face to Face with Python* depended on a lively exchange of interesting conversation between Jack and his guest of the hour. He wanted people to feel that after they'd watched his show they walked away from their television set with a new knowledge and understanding of the person in the hot seat. With Clarissa they found out nothing She was a brilliant actress, and a lousy interview.

Face to Face with Python had been running with consistently excellent ratings for six years. The show aired once a week on Thursday nights, which left him plenty of time to pursue other activities. He had formed his own television production company five years before, and oversaw the making of docu-dramas with something important to say.

Jack had an image problem. He was too good-looking to be

taken as seriously as he would like. And his womanizing reputation was hard to live down. But he was trying.

*

Howard Soloman drove a gold Mercedes 500 SEC. He stood, or rather fidgeted, beneath the portico of The Beverly Hills Hotel and waited for the valet to bring it round.

To his eternal disgust Howard was on the short side for a man. He barely made five feet six inches, although when he wore his specially made European shoes with the hidden lifts he could sometimes add another four inches, making him a respectable five feet ten inches. In his weekend uniform of sweat pants and Adidas jogging shoes, lifts were not possible. Yet. Howard had asked his shoemaker in London to work on it.

Howard was also – at only thirty-nine – losing his hair. It had started to thin alarmingly years before, and prudently he had added a custom-designed hairpiece before people began to notice. The hairpiece was good, the only drawback being that it made him sweat. Once, on a weekend in Las Vegas, he had taken a girl to his hotel room. He had removed his clothes, shoes, and then his hairpiece, because it was so damned hot and she looked like a certain maniac who would pull crazily at his hair in moments of passion.

She had stared at him in amazement. "*Shee . . . it!*" she exclaimed. "I came up here with a nice lookin' guy, an' I end up with a bald midget!"

Which, of course, had swiftly ended *that* night of sexual high jinks.

The only time Howard removed his hairpiece now was in the privacy of his own home with only his wife and visiting children to mock him.

There had been four wives – one of them current, three of them ex. And there were five children. Nobody could ever say that Howard Soloman didn't have what it took. He was a walking hormone!

Wife number one was a black activist who moonlighted as an "artistic dancer". In spite of Jack begging him not to, he married her when he was nineteen and she was forty. It was not a lasting marriage. They both decided it was a mistake, and after forty-eight hours of fucking their brains out they got an annulment.

Wife number two was somebody else's wife when he met her. She was pretty and sweet – nothing to get into a lather over.

43

Howard railroaded her into divorcing her husband. Then he married her, fathered three children by her, and divorced her – all in the space of five years. She was exhausted by the time it was over, and now lived in Pacific Palisades with the kids and a new husband.

Wife number three was an incredibly tall, sophisticated, Brazilian ball-breaker. She generously gave him a child and two years of her life, and then hit him for so much alimony he thought he might never recover from the shock.

Wife number four was Poppy, his former secretary. They had been married for three years and had a daughter named Roselight. Their daughter was the reason they married in the first place. Poppy did not believe in abortion, so when she became pregnant she put the screws to him and he married her. Well, what else could a nice Jewish boy do?

Poppy made the Brazilian ball-breaker look like the good fairy.

"Howard!" A hand clapped him on the shoulder. "You old son of a gun! I haven't seen you in too long."

Howard recognized Orville Gooseberger, the producer. He wished he had on his lifts: Orville was tall enough to make him feel uncomfortable. The only tall people he wasn't uncomfortable with were women. That feeling of dominance was a turn-on. Once, he had made a very tall woman stand open-legged on a table while he went up on her. He got quite horny just thinking about it. It was definitely a scene to be repeated, only not with Poppy, who was short. And besides, there was no way he'd suggest an act like that to her – she thought he was perverted as it was.

"You know, Howard," Orville boomed, "we have to do a project together. It's about time."

Why hadn't it been time *before* Howard was head of Orpheus?

"Why?" said Howard.

"What?" said Orville.

Ah, the hell with it. Orville was an ace producer, *and* he brought his pictures in on time *and* within budget, which is more than you could say for most of the assholes running around calling themselves producers.

"We'll take a meeting," Howard said expansively, using Hollywoodese.

"Lunch?" Orville suggested. "Perhaps here. On Monday or Tuesday?"

"I gotta check my book," Howard said. "Call the office on

Monday. My girl knows every move I make better than I do."

He realized he could see right up Orville's nose and the view was not pleasant.

The parking valet zoomed up with his Mercedes. Howard slipped him a ten, impressed with his own generosity, and slid behind the wheel, inhaling the smell of the rich leather which never failed to please him. There was nothing like having money. No thrill in the world. Even naked ladies standing on table tops with their legs spread.

*

Mannon Cable drove a blue Rolls-Royce. The Roller, he called it.

He did not leave the hotel at the same time as Jack and Howard, because he had to pick up Melanie-Shanna in the hotel beauty shop.

She was not ready when he arrived, which infuriated him. Major movie stars were not supposed to cool their heels while ex-beauty queen wives primped and fussed.

Whitney had never spent hours in the beauty shop. She was naturally beautiful, and how could he have ever let her go?

The final split, when it came, was clean-cut. They had been fighting for months, mostly over her career, which had taken off with alarming speed – thanks to Howard Soloman, who Mannon barely spoke to for a while, until he got out of agenting and left Whitney alone. She had become an enormous television star and the demands on her time were insatiable. Mannon had just finished a difficult movie and needed to get away. "Let's go to the south of France," he'd suggested.

"I can't," Whitney replied. "I've got fittings, interviews. Oh, and I promised to do the Bob Hope special. *And* the photo spread for *Life* magazine is being scheduled now."

"I can remember when *I* came first," he'd said angrily.

She had turned on him, all hair and teeth and pent-up frustration. "And *I* can remember when I wanted you to."

"Jesus! I took you out of hick town to be my wife, not some trumped-up starlet. I've giving you a choice, Whitney. It's me or your career."

He never weighed his words before saying them. In retrospect he wished he had, for they were both too stubborn to retreat.

"You want me to choose?" she'd said, very slowly.

"Goddammit. *Yes*."

"Then I'll take my career, thank you very much." Her eyes, filled with hurt and anger, challenged him to back down.

He didn't. He packed a suitcase and left the house.

A week later she started divorce proceedings.

One thing about Whitney, she was scrupulously fair. No Hollywood Wife she. There were no demands. She didn't want alimony or a settlement. She kept half the money from their house when it was sold, and that was it.

"I don't believe your luck!" Howard had exclaimed.

"I'd still be married if it wasn't for you," Mannon growled. He had never stopped wanting her back.

Chapter 8

The photo session was going well. Lionel Richie tapes flooded the studio, and Silver, watched by a large entourage, put the photographer through his paces.

He was a famous Italian photographer, a star in his own right. Only Silver remembered when he'd photographed her *before* superstardom, and had treated her like shit. He'd also made her look like shit, which wasn't surprising considering he'd only shot one roll of film, and any idiot knew you never got anything worthwhile until the third roll at least. He'd also forced her to use his own makeup and hair people. A bad mistake.

Now *she* was in charge, and enjoying every minute.

"Antonio, dear," she said, stopping the click of his shutter. "Do you know that today is my birthday?"

Antonio threw up his hands as if she had just declared World War III. '*Bellissima!* You don't have the birthday. You have the celebration!"

"Exactly." She smiled sweetly. "So where's the caviar and champagne?"

Antonio looked concerned. "You want some, *cara*?"

"I'd love some, Antonio, dear. And if you are *very* good, I'll invite you to my party later."

He beckoned one of his assistants. "Champagne and caviar for Signorina Anderson. *Pronto. Pronto.*"

The assistant, a girl dressed like a boy, held out her hand. "I'll need money," she said, wondering how much he would come up with. His stinginess was notorious.

A scowl flitted across Antonio's small but perfectly formed fifty-five-year-old features. He reached into the back pocket of his impeccably cut trousers and reluctantly pulled out a hundred-dollar bill.

Silver laughed loudly. "My God, Antonio, you're as tight as your own ass! The poor girl will need more than that. Let me see –" she played to her entourage – "there must be at least ten of us. We'll want three bottles of Cristal, and a nice big jar of fish eggs. Give her your credit card."

Give her yours, bitch! Antonio wanted to snarl. Only he didn't. He knew she was getting her own back for the last session, and in a way he didn't blame her. One had to admire Silver Anderson's success. A few years ago she was washed up, completely finished. And now she was sizzling, at what – forty-three? Four? Nobody knew her exact age. She was up there somewhere and that's all that mattered. In a town comprised mostly of big-bosomed twenty-two-year-olds, her achievement was certainly something.

He produced his MasterCard with a flourish. Let Silver see that the great Antonio accepted defeat with style.

She stretched languorously. "How about a break?" she suggested in a low, husky voice, standing up before finishing the sentence, uninterested in whether Antonio cared to break or not.

"My idea too, *bellissima*," he said quickly.

Strolling behind the camera she playfully peeked through the viewfinder. "Hmmm," she said. "Let me see the Polaroids again."

Dutifully her hairdresser Fernando, her makeup artist Yves, *and* the stylist for the shoot sprang forward – each waving an instant photo for her inspection.

She gazed at the pictures of herself like an uninvolved critic.

"Your hair looks *mah*vellous," raved Fernando, who wore his own spiky locks in a currently fashionable purple Mohawk.

She touched her long wavy wig. "I'm not sure it's dramatic enough."

"Ah, but it is! It is!" he protested. "Very *you*."

"I like the short wig better."

"We can change it."

Shaking her head she said, "I don't know . . . I'm not sure. What do *you* think, Nora? Isn't this style a little too young for me?"

Nora Carvell, a cigarette butt attached to her lower lip, squinted from her seat on the sidelines. "Cut the crap, Silver. You know you're the youngest lookin' broad over forty in this town. Y'can wear anything an' get away with it."

Nora had worked with Silver as her publicist for three years. One of the reasons they continued to get along was that Nora always spoke her mind and never kissed ass. Surrounded by sycophants, Silver respected and enjoyed Nora's honesty. It was good to have someone around who wasn't afraid of opening up her mouth.

Silver giggled. It was true. She looked early thirties, not a day over. All the husbands and lovers, fights and booze had left nary a mark. She was sensational for her age. Any age, in fact.

"You're right," she agreed, holding the Polaroid at a distance and squinting slightly. She needed glasses, but vanity would not permit it.

The rest of the shoot progressed without incident. Above all else Silver was a professional. So professional, in fact, that when the champagne and caviar arrived she touched neither, opting instead for a plain glass of Evian water.

Antonio was furious as he observed her entourage scoff the lot.

"I've changed my mind," she said sweetly, when offered a glass of Cristal and a tasty cracker with a mound of imported caviar on it. "Mustn't smudge my makeup. Besides, I don't want to feel hungover for my party tonight."

*

"You think it's easy?" the young girl with the multi-coloured punk hair demanded of the eighteen-year-old boy lounging against the side of an old Ford Mustang smoking a joint. "I am in like a very negative position," the girl continued, snatching the roach away from him and taking a healthy drag. "Like first of all I'm *me*. An' then people find out all the garbage, an' then I'm Silver Anderson's daughter, or Jack Python's niece. Sometimes I'm even George fucking Python's grand-daughter – ever since he invented that stupid pool-cleaner." She looked outraged. "Get this action, Eddie. I'm over at a girlfriend's house the other day totally sitting around bullshitting, and her father comes in the room – her *father*. So she says, 'Daddy, I want you to meet Heaven.' And *he* says, 'Aren't you George Python's grand-daughter? He's saved my weekends with his machine.' I mean, I ask you. With a name like Heaven there's no escape."

"Y'could change your name," Eddie mumbled, retrieving the joint from her multi-coloured fingernails.

Heaven widened startlingly amber eyes. "Why should I?" she demanded. "It's *my* name. My identity. It's like the only *positive* thing in my life."

"Y'got me," Eddie said.

"*And* my music," she added.

"Our music," he corrected.

"*I* write the songs," she pointed out. "And I sing 'em."

"Yeah, an' who would you be singin' 'em *with* if me an' the guys didn't back you?"

She wasn't going to hurt his feelings, only she knew that the group meant nothing. *She* was the star when they appeared at local events, not Eddie and his group.

She yawned loudly and executed a little dance in the front yard of Eddie's house.

He watched her through slitted eyes. She was a difficult girl to figure, most of the time she kept him confused. He liked her a lot, even if she *was* totally screwed up because of all her famous relatives. "Wanna go for a drive?" he asked. "Get a hamburger?"

"No, thank you," she replied, picking at the material of her jagged denim micro skirt.

"What *do* you wanna do, then?"

"I thought you said your parents were away this weekend."

"They are."

"So why can't we go in your house an' fix something? I won't eat you."

"I wish you would," he leered, shifting his weight from the side of the car.

"Eddie," she sighed, tipping her head to one side. "I thought you'd *never* ask."

He wondered if she was teasing him as he felt the start of something big build up in his pants. Heaven had been flirting with him from the day they met three months ago, only every time he made a move she shoved him off. "C'mon," he said quickly. "In the house. I'll show you who's asking."

She followed him inside. His sisters were out and the small neat house was very cool and quiet.

"I wanna see your room," she said.

Hastily he thought about whether there was anything around to embarrass him. He decided it was all clear. She would just have to understand about the life-size poster of Daryl Hannah on his wall.

His room was overloaded with stuff and very untidy.

"Slob!" she exclaimed. "Like I mean you totally get off on disgusting mess."

Grabbing her from behind he rubbed his hands across her small breasts – bra-less beneath a baggy tee-shirt.

She didn't push him away as usual; instead she stood very still allowing him the feel he had been waiting months for.

His hard-on chafed for escape as he slid his hands underneath the flimsy tee-shirt and reached bare tit.

Still she didn't object.

He fingered the tips of her nipples and groaned, waiting for her to stop him.

She turned around and faced him. "Do you wanna do it?" she asked, her eyes unusually bright.

Did he *want* to? There was *smoke* coming out of his ears as he tried to appear casual. On the surface he was Mister Cool, but in reality he was nervous as hell.

"Do you?" she persisted, amber eyes staring into his.

"Yeah," he managed.

"So do I," she said, slowly pulling her tee-shirt over her head.

*

"You invited Heaven tonight, didn't you?" Nora asked in the limo on the way back to the house.

Silver gazed out of the tinted side window. "As a matter of fact, no," she replied coolly.

Nora grunted her disapproval, which caused Silver to come up with a list of reasons why she had not invited her only child to her birthday party. They ranged from "There'll be nobody else her age there" – which was a lie, because two of the actors from *Palm Springs* were under twenty, and they would certainly be there – to "She hates parties." Which was something Silver could not possibly guess, as she knew nothing of her daughter's

50

likes and dislikes. In fact, since being back in America, she had managed to see Heaven as little as possible. "It wouldn't be wise for me to disrupt her life," she told anyone who asked. And then she would add with a conspiratorial laugh and a knowing wink, "Besides, I'm hardly a mother figure, am I?"

The truth was that having a teenage daughter did not suit Silver one bit. It made her feel her age, and anything that made her feel that was banished from her life.

Nora projected silent disapproval.

"Why?" Silver asked at last. "Do you think I *should* have?"

"Given that you've invited a hundred and fifty of your closest friends, and more than a smattering of the press, I don't think it's such a terrible idea. After all, she'll be reading about it in every gossip column in town, so maybe you should give *her* the choice of attending or not. There's still time to ask her."

"God!" Silver sighed dramatically. "As if I don't have enough problems!"

Chapter 9

Unpacking boxes had lost its thrill. Corey's visit had upset Jade and she found that she could no longer concentrate. In frustration she sat down and consulted the L.A. pages of her phone book. Several of the friends listed belonged to Mark, so she left them alone, and tried a fellow model and ex-roommate, black and exotic Beverly D'Amo. Beverly had moved to Los Angeles two years ago to pursue an acting career, and was now, according to her answering service, in Peru, and not expected back for a while. Disappointed, Jade called another model friend from New York. The girl kept her on the phone for thirty-five minutes complaining about an errant husband. Next, she spoke to a married girlfriend; this one was in the throes of a messy divorce. Man trouble was obviously catching.

A more fun group seemed to be the way to go, so she telephoned Antonio – the photographer, an amusing friend once you got over his *I am a star photographer* trip. They had worked together often and enjoyed many a great night out in New York when he visited.

"I'm here," she announced. "And the good news is that I'm a free agent, so let's get together. Preferably tonight."

"Bellissima!" he crooned. 'My *bella* Jade. What *dee*-lightful pleasure to hear your voice."

"You too, baby. How's Dix?"

"Dead!" was the dramatic retort.

"Another one hits the dust, huh?" She was not surprised. Antonio had a new boyfriend every month, and according to him they all let him down.

"He was *Eeenglish*," Antonio snorted, as if that explained everything.

"Well . . ." she said. "That makes two of us with dead boyfriends. I gave Mark back to his wife."

"Bene. He was *Eeenglish.* Tonight I take you to the birthday part of the true beetch."

"Anyone I know?"

"Seelver Anderson. The woman *kill* when she see you. Dress up, *bella*."

Hanging up the phone she decided a big Hollywood party in the company of the waspish Antonio was just what she needed. Usually the word *party* produced an instant excuse. Mark shied away from them – probably because he did not wish to risk being photographed with her.

What *had* he told his wife? They had often been caught by stray paparazzi leaving Elaine's restaurant in New York, or attending the opening of a new art gallery. Knowing Mark, he no doubt passed her off as a casual acquaintance, and aristocratic Lady Fiona must have believed every lying word. Mark and his clever lies. God!

Pouring a glass of wine, she allowed herself the pleasure of reliving the denouement.

*

Lord Mark Rand returned from a photographic trip, his thin features flushed with enjoyment, his brown wavy hair untidy –like a little boy's. He was almost fifty, but looked no more than thirty-five. The plan was that he spend six days in New York with her, and then return to London. Usually he divided his time between England and America, with numerous foreign assignments in between.

Dropping various camera cases, he put both arms around her. "Hello, lovely lady. Are you ready to give home and comfort to an extremely tired Englishman?"

Six years was just about to be part of her past. She didn't want to rush it. "You smell like a camel," she remarked, wrinkling her nose.

Laughing, he said, "Bathe me. Cover me with sweet oils. Massage my tired body and I shall be yours forever."

What a corny English asshole. Why had it never bothered her before?

He walked into the crowded living room of her Village apartment. Quite a few times he had suggested she move uptown to a more expensive place. "You can afford it," he would complain. "Why stay here?" Never once had he offered to share the rent. Not that she needed his money, she did very nicely on her own. Still . . . the offer would have shown commitment.

It never bothered her until they split.

"How was the trip?" she asked.

"God, it was unbelievable!" he said enthusiastically. "Sunsets the like of which even I have never seen before."

"And the girls?" She referred to the three models he had been photographing for an upmarket nude calendar layout.

"Young. Boring. And stupid."

"Did you sleep with them?"

Raising an eyebrow he looked at her quizzically. "What a strange question."

"Do you sleep with your wife?"

Frowning, he said, "What is the matter with you? You know I don't. We've discussed it many times."

She stared at him. "I want you to tell me again."

Shaking his head he chanted, "I did not sleep with my three dopey little model girls. And I do not sleep with my wife." He paused. "Does that satisfy you?"

"How long is it since you have slept with her?"

"Jade —" an edge crept into his voice — "I'm tired and I'm very hungry. It's been an arduous journey and I would like to relax."

"How long, Mark?"

She was giving him one last chance to be truthful and tell her everything.

"Fiona and I have not slept together since I met you," he snapped. "You know that perfectly well, and I resent being questioned in this way."

Her eyes glittered dangerously. "Not even once?"

He returned her gaze unblinkingly. "Not even twice." Removing his jacket he added, "Now, please may I have a scotch and soda. A hot bath. And the unadulterated pleasure of your beautiful body. In that order."

It was over, but why not prolong it? Make him suffer, as he had done to her.

"Certainly, sir," she said lightly. "One large scotch with a dash of soda coming up. And I'll get your bath ready."

He relaxed. "What a girl!"

What an English asshole!

In the bathroom she turned on the water to fill the tub — only the hot. Then she went into the kitchen and poured Kentucky bourbon into a plastic glass — Mark hated plastic glasses almost as much as he hated bourbon — and added two cubes of ice — which he couldn't stand.

Whistling, and looking ridiculous in baggy boxer shorts, Mark strolled into the bathroom. She followed him with his drink.

Stripping off his shorts he stepped into the steaming tub. "Jesus Christ!" he screamed, hopping out immediately. "It's scalding hot!"

"Sorry," she murmured, handing him his drink.

He took a healthy sip and almost gagged. "This is bourbon," he said accusingly. "You know I hate bourbon."

"Oh, dear." She stared at him without feeling. He was not the most attractive sight in the world standing in her bathroom, naked. His legs were too skinny, and bright red feet and calves from the boiling hot bath water did not help matters. He had a limp penis, a slight paunch, and a chest matted with gingery hair flecked with grey.

This was exactly how she wanted to remember him.

"There appears to be something on your mind," he said at last. Apparently he was not completely insensitive to her feelings.

Reaching into her pocket she pulled out the crumpled clipping of Lady Fiona cradling the latest little Lord or whatever it was.

Keeping his cool, he glanced at it. "Oh," he said calmly. "That's a printing error. Damned silly mistake. This is a picture of Fiona with my brother's child."

He must think she was an idiot. And why not, indeed? She had behaved like one for six years.

"I checked," she said coldly. "This is your son."

He stretched for a towel and tied it around his waist, his eyes refusing to meet hers. "How did you do that?" he asked, a tad nervously.

"It's all right," she said flatly. "I didn't call Fiona and ask her. You're perfectly safe to go home."

"Now, listen," he said, pulling himself together. "This whole baby thing was an accident, pure and simple." Warming to his theme he added, "I didn't tell you about it because I didn't want to upset you."

Staring at him scornfully she said, "An accident, Mark?"

"Let us go and sit down and I'll explain it to you over a drink."

He attempted to pass her. She blocked the bathroom door.

"Explain it to me now," she said icily. "I can't wait to hear."

He cleared his throat and gathered his thoughts. "It's quite true that since being with you I have not slept with Fiona," he began.

"What does that make the baby — an immaculate conception?" she interrupted sarcastically.

He continued, seemingly unperturbed, not to be stopped from telling his story. "A while ago I returned from a trip. Fiona was depressed. Her favourite uncle had died, and she had been thrown from her horse on a hunting trip, which bruised her self-esteem more than anything else."

Watching him make up the story as he spoke was pure theatre. He was the best instant liar she had ever seen.

"Yes?" She wanted more.

He tightened the towel around his waist. "It was her birthday. She drank too much champagne. When we went to bed that night she was crying, and came to me for comfort. I didn't have the heart to reject her. It was only once in six years, and the result was Archibald."

"Archibald!"

"It was her uncle's name," he said sheepishly. "She wanted to remember him."

Jade began to laugh uncontrollably.

"I'm sorry, darling," he said, believing all was forgiven.

She managed to control herself enough to say, "Take off the towel."

"What?"

Touching her fingertips to his nipples, she brushed them lightly. "I said, take off the towel. Or do you want me to do it for you?"

"Do it for me," he replied, feeling the swell of relief followed by a generous erection.

She pulled the knot on the towel and it fell away from his body. "My, my," she said admiringly. "Look what you brought me back."

Relaxing, he leaned against the tiled sink.

With practised moves she stroked his chest, then his belly, and as she reached lower she sank to her knees and teased his excitement with her tongue.

He leaned back even further and surrendered to the sensual caress of her luscious mouth, his enjoyment mounting as she increased her rhythm.

Just as his pleasure was reaching lift-off, she bit down roughly with scissor-sharp teeth.

He yelled in agony.

Calmly she released him, and stood up. Catching him off balance and unprepared, she pushed him into the scalding water of the bath-tub.

"You bloody maniac!" he screamed.

"You goddamn liar!" she replied. "Her birthday, indeed! That line is older than George Burns!"

Marching to the bathroom door she turned for one final look. He was struggling from the burning tub like a hyper fish. With satisfaction she noticed the faint trace of teeth marks on his rapidly shrinking penis. "Goodbye, Mark," she said. "I'm going to dinner. When I come back I want you and all your worldly shit out of my life forever."

He was gone when she returned three hours later.

Once she split from him she found out he had been cheating on her all over town. Why hadn't anyone told her? The general excuse was that it didn't seem proper while they were together.

She felt duped. Getting out of town was the best tonic she could think of.

*

Sipping her wine, Jade went to the closet and chose a suitable outfit for the night's activities.

A party with Antonio. It might be fun, it might not.

Whatever. It was better than sitting home.

Chapter 10

"Lighten up," Wes Money said. He was speaking to his landlady, Reba Winogratsky, who had arrived unexpectedly to collect two months' overdue rent. "I'll have it for you next month."

"Wesley, Wesley!" she sighed despairingly. "One of these days I'm gonna have to throw you out."

With an appealing look he said, "You wouldn't do that to me, Reba, would you?"

She ran her tongue slowly across her top teeth. "I might."

He tried to ascertain whether she was in line for a screwing, decided that if she ever turned up alone she would be. Today she had what appeared to be her son with her – a fat boy of about ten with a sulky expression. They had arrived in a new Mercedes which she quickly explained belonged to a friend. He didn't believe her. The car was hers and she didn't want anyone to know lest they struggled even more about paying her exorbitant rent demands. She wore a tight halter top, shorts, and stiletto heels. Her legs were waxed and so was her moustache. She was no beauty. From her left shoulder hung a huge leather purse. She was obviously out on a rent-collecting binge.

"Can I offer you a cup of coffee?" he asked politely. If the kid wasn't with her he would have offered her more than that. Last time she turned up it had been with a Mexican maid who cleaned the kitchen floor while they argued over a rent increase.

"Come up with some cash soon or you're just gonna have to go," Reba decided.

"I will."

"I hope you mean it, Wesley. You owe me two months, an' next Saturday I'm sendin' the collector."

"Who's the collector?" he asked, alarmed.

"Better you should never find out," she replied, absent-mindedly scratching her crotch.

I could cure that itch for you, he wanted to say, but curbed the impulse.

She ran a finger across a table top, leaving a fresh and shiny trail through the dust. Then she peered into the cramped kitchen, which was stacked with filthy dishes and half-eaten food. "The way you keep this place is an open invitation to rats," she remarked, without too much concern.

"Can we go?" whined the fat kid.

"Clean up your act, Wesley, an' get me my money."

He followed her to the door. "Yes, *ma'am*."

She gave him an appraising stare. "Y'know, you're not bad lookin' if you took better care of yourself. You've got a kinda Nick Nolte quality."

Nick who? "Thanks," he said. "I'm working on it."

"Get a job," she scolded.

He decided to impress her. "Tonight I'll be at Silver Anderson's house helping her out. She's havin' a party."

"*The* Silver Anderson?"

"No. Silver Anderson who works as a checker at Von's Market," he said sarcastically.

"Huh?"

"Of course *the* Silver Anderson."

"Really?" She didn't quite believe him, but she gave it a shot anyway. "Get Timmy here" – she patted the fat boy on the head – "an autographed picture, an' I'll knock ten bucks off the money you owe."

"If I can."

"Good." She took the boy's hand and clicked her way across the wooden porch out onto the boardwalk.

Hazy sunshine caught Wes's attention as he watched her go. A pretty Chinese girl skate-boarded by. He thought he might grab a few rays and liven up his complexion. Somehow, in his busy schedule of screwing, boozing and partying he never found time for the sun.

His nextdoor neighbour emerged from her house at the same time. She had moved in six weeks ago, shortly after the previous tenant overdosed on heroin and was carried off in a body bag. He'd never seen her before, but sometimes he'd had to hammer on the dividing wall in the middle of the night (when he was home) for her to turn down the godawful classical music she liked to play. It figured. She looked like a school teacher: brown hair in a bun, baggy clothes, and John Lennon glasses. She appeared to be surprisingly young, probably only early twenties.

"Hello, neighbour." He waved a friendly greeting.

She pretended not to notice, and set off along the boardwalk.

Snob. She was no doubt pissed off he'd banged on the wall. He followed her because he had nothing better to do.

She turned up a side street and climbed into an ancient Volks-wagen. Bored, he headed in the other direction, across the sand, down to the sea. It was a mild day and the ocean was calm. He liked it better when the surf was up, and the waves came belting in. He loved it when it rained. And a storm was a special treat.

He sat down on the sand, and the next thing he knew he must have nodded off for a couple of hours, because when he awoke, water was lapping his feet. Nearby, a lone dog sat on the sand staring at him.

Wes was not partial to animals. An old girlfriend had once kept a monkey. It pissed and crapped everywhere, and for a grand finale jerked off whenever they made love. No more pets after that.

He consulted his copy of a Cartier tank watch. Fifty bucks from a travelling Iranian. It lost five minutes a day and sometimes stopped altogether. He ascertained it was late afternoon and hauled himself up. Rocky would be getting panicky. Better put him out of his misery.

Chapter 11

Poppy Soloman was getting dressed, and when Poppy got ready for a party – watch out!

Howard repaired to his own bathroom, locked the door, and had his second snort of the day. Cocaine. A little habit he had been indulging in for a few months now.

Carefully he laid out the white powder on a special mirror-topped tray, coaxed it into two neat lines, and with the help of a straw, snorted it into his nostrils. One long, deep breath and the rush was incredible. Better than sex. Better than anything. Howard felt like he could own the world. He *did* own the world. He owned a fucking studio, for Christ's sake. Well, not exactly owned it, ran it. The same thing. It gave him the power he wanted, only to really enjoy the power he needed an occasional snort. Nothing habit-forming, mind you. Howard knew when enough was enough, and duly limited himself. Once in the morning to get off on the right foot. And once in the evening *only* if they were going out or entertaining at home. Since they went out or entertained every night, he regularly snorted twice a day. Not such a terrible thing. Some actors, producers and studio people couldn't get through a meeting without visiting the john three times.

Howard considered himself a very conservative user, one who could certainly never get hooked. Stopping was no problem. But why stop something that made you feel so goddamn good?

Howard had concerns. Once you reached the top, where else was there to go but down? And the pressure was on.

A huge conglomerate owned Orpheus Studios, headed by Zachary K. Klinger, a major powerhouse. Zachary K. liked Howard – in fact it was he who had chosen him for the top position. But that was now. What if Howard was unable to deliver? Zachary K. wanted box office giants in whammo grossing movies. He wanted Howard to turn the failing fortunes of Orpheus around, and he wanted him to do it fast. Maybe too fast.

Picking a movie that's going to soar is like singling out a puppy from a large litter. You could end up choosing the runt – whatever its pedigree.

Howard sweated every time he had to make a decision. But now, with the coke to fortify him, he decided that in the few months he had been at the helm he had done a marvellous job. His first move had been to pick up a couple of sleepers for distribution – which meant he took two small independently produced movies, and had Orpheus distribute them as they were short of product. The results were sensational. Both films went through the roof. Howard was a hero.

Now all he had to do was oversee some hits of his own. Just make absolutely sure that every new picture he gave the green light to was a potential smash.

The following month Zachary K. was coming to town to check up on progress. Not that he didn't get a daily report from one of his spies. Howard knew for a fact that there were at least two stationed in key jobs.

He wasn't going to let it bother him. Nothing bothered him. Look what he had done with his life. He was a genius, for crissakes.

*

Howard Soloman was born when he was sixteen, and his mother divorced his father, fled from Philadelphia to Colorado, and shortly after, married Temple Soloman. He couldn't wait to change his name from Jessie Howard Judah Lipski to the much more simple Howard Soloman. What an escape! His natural father was a rabbi, a cruel, hard man who treated both his wife and son as if they had been put on this earth solely to do his bidding, and he made sure that their lives were pure misery. When Howard — or Jessie as he was then — reached his teenage years he begged his mother to get out. "I'm going," he told her, "an' you'd better come with me."

She didn't take much persuading, and one dark night they fled to New York, and from there to Colorado, where an old school friend of his mother's put them up. It was like getting out of prison, and when his mother married Temple Soloman six months later, it was as if God had smiled on them for doing it. Temple was an easy-going mild-mannered man. He was the senior partner in a clothing manufacturing business, and while he wasn't exactly rolling in it, he had enough money to buy Howard a second-hand car and send him to college.

Howard felt like a Russian who finally saw America and all it had to offer. He was alive and free. And so was his mother. The early years were just a bad dream.

As a teenager Howard was plump and plagued with acne, until he discovered girls. Once that happened his weight soon dropped, and the acne vanished overnight. Temple sat him down one day and gave him a lecture. "Always use a johnny," he said, snapping a Durex in front of his stepson's face. "And give the girl a good time too." Big wink. "Only don't get anyone pregnant."

Howard thought about Temple's remarks. What did he mean by "give the girl a good time"? Wasn't she having a good time just by being in his company?

The next time he had a young lady in the back of his shined up old Buick he asked her casually as he humped away, "Hey — you havin' a good time?"

"You're heavy," she whined. "Why is your back so hairy — it's . . . ugh! My mother will kill me if she ever finds out I'm doing this."

So much for conversation. He almost lost his erection. God forbid!

It took Howard's first wife, the fierce black activist whom he married when he was nineteen, to teach him the joys of getting a woman off too. "Just go for the button an' liiiiift–off, babee!" she instructed while clasping him around the back of the neck with ebony legs he thought might strangle him.

Hitting the button on his third attempt, he realized there was a difference. Instead of the female being a reluctant participant in the act of sex, she turned into a stark raving maniac! Why hadn't Temple mentioned buttons to him! Look at all the time he had wasted!

One day Howard read a book about Howard Hughes. He liked it so much he reread it three times. Temple had told him — early on in their relationship —that he was the heir to the manufacturing business of which Temple was the senior partner. "When you graduate," his *stepfather had said, "I'll teach you everything I know. You're like my own son, and when the time comes I'll hand the business over to you."*

Howard was grateful, but not at all sure he wanted to stay in Colorado and make ladies' dresses. He had bigger plans. He wanted to be like Howard Hughes. He saw Hollywood in his future. "What's it like?" he asked his friend Jack Python, as they struggled through a business administration course together. "You're from L.A. Is Hollywood really something?"

Jack shrugged. "I live in the Valley. I don't go over the hill much."

"What hill?"

"The Valley is separated from Hollywood and Beverly Hills by several large canyons. You drive over Benedict Canyon or Coldwater or Laurel."

"And? What's it like when you get there?" Howard asked impatiently.

"Streets. Palm trees. Tourists. It's no big deal."

"Well, I'm going there. Summer vacation I'm getting a job and renting an apartment. Why don't we take a place together?"

Jack shook his head. A year later he changed his mind, and when they graduated they moved into a two-bedroom apartment just off Hollywood Boulevard. No luxury abode, but it was functional and convenient.

By that time Howard had already spent the previous summer in Los Angeles, and returning he felt like a veteran. He knew where to get the cheapest hamburger, the fastest dry cleaning, the best place to hang out for the price of one cup of coffee — and where to find the prettiest girls. He had already been married (though it was annulled), worked at one of the studios in the mail room, and had his first case of the clap (unfortunately not his last). Temple Soloman had been disappointed but understanding of his need to try his luck in Hollywood. "What do you want to do there?" he had asked.

"Be an agent," Howard blurted in reply. And the seed was sown. Why not be an agent? With his conversational skills he could be the greatest.

So he changed positions, and instead of going back to his old job at — yes — Orpheus Studios — he started in the mail room of S.M.I. Specialized Management Incorporated. And from there, history was made.

It had taken him seventeen years to get to the very top.

*

"Howard!"

He could hear Poppy calling. Clearing up his coke paraphernalia, he unlocked the bathroom door.

"Howard," she sighed, in the little-girl voice she had recently affected. "What do you think?"

She twirled for him.

Poppy was five feet two inches tall, rounded and perky looking. She had very long blonde curls, slightly protruding blue eyes, and a self-satisfied permanent smile which went nicely with her retroussé nose. She also had new tits – thanks to a man she referred to reverently as "plastic surgeon to the stars". She wore a turquoise frilled, strapless dress, and many real diamonds. Her new tits protruded nicely.

"You likee my dress?" she asked.

He wanted to say no. He wanted to say that she looked like a short, tiered Christmas cake. He wanted to say, cut your hair, lose fifteen pounds and put on a plain black dress. He wanted to say – *Bring back the old tits, I liked them better*.

"Dynamite!" he exclaimed, wondering if Whitney would be at the party.

She smiled happily. "I knew you'd like it."

When she was his secretary she had worn neat tailored suits and plain, well-cut dresses. She had kept her hair up and featured little jewellery. Now she looked like a walking advertisement for a fancy jewellery store.

She held up a bracelet-laden wrist. "You likee?"

He inspected multiple diamonds. "Very nice."

"Very nice!" she squealed, grabbing him in a hug. "You're the most generous man in the world!"

Wasn't he just! Even his accountant – a seasoned veteran of Hollywood marriages – was beginning to blanch at the constant stream of bills. "Can't you keep her home at least *one* day a week?" he'd complained. "The woman is a walking charge card!"

Howard saw no way of stopping her, short of breaking both her legs.

"Get dressed, Howie," Poppy said. "It's party time. We don't want to be late, do we?"

It was the first time she had been ready before him in five years of marriage. He was too busy thinking about Whitney to wonder why.

Chapter 12

"I invited her," Nora Carvell said.

Silver felt a small stab of annoyance. Who needed a teenage daughter to remind her of the creeping years? "Is she coming?" was her casual response as she stripped off her clothes in the privacy of her bedroom and pulled on a silk robe.

Nora lit a fresh cigarette from the smouldering butt attached firmly to her lower lip. "She said she'll try."

What Heaven had actually said was a sarcastic "Why doesn't she wait until it's all over to ask me? Don't count on me bein' there. As if she gives a shit." For her years Heaven was quite eloquent.

"Why don't you try to get along with your mother?" Nora had rasped. "You haven't even sent her a card."

Heaven's laughter rang out. "She's *never* sent one to me. In fact I'm lucky to get a cheque three weeks later when *you* remind her."

Nora couldn't deny the truth. "Try and make it tonight," she urged before hanging up.

There was nothing she would like better than to see mother and daughter get along. A lot of people – including Heaven – thought Silver was a bitch. Nora saw another side of her. She saw a successful woman alone in the world with no real friends. She saw an ambitious woman who had been hurt and used by men. She saw a woman who had alienated her family yet needed them desperately.

"God!" Silver exclaimed. "She'll try, indeed! You would think she would run barefoot over hot coals to attend my party."

Nora said, "I'm going home to change, I'll be back in an hour."

"Fine," Silver responded, as she tried to decide whether to refresh the heavy makeup she had worn for the Antonio photo session, or take it all off and start again.

She compromised. Left the dramatic eye makeup intact, and cleansed her skin with cotton pads soaked in witch-hazel.

The cold lotion on her face was delightfully soothing. She walked over to her luxurious king-size bed and pulled down the purple satin cover. Pratesi sheets awaited. A welcome lie-down for fifteen minutes was just what she needed.

Her bedroom was peaceful and cool. Pale lilac silk walls complemented the deep purple of the carpet. Mirrors abounded.

Lying back on the bed she tried to empty her mind, but tonight it was impossible. All she could think about was Heaven's father, and what a bastard he had been.

★

Silver Anderson met "The Businessman", as she always referred to him, when she was thirty-one and he was fifty-two. He was extremely rich, very powerful, and naturally — married. Silver was starring on Broadway at the time. She was also divorcing her ex-stepfather and rekindling an affair with her co-star.

"The Businessman" walked into her life at a party and took over. He was a big man in every way: tall, portly, with heavy features and hooded eyes. Some whispered that his early connections included organized crime. Some whispered that he had the ear of the President. Some whispered that the late Marilyn Monroe was once a girlfriend.

His wife was a social lioness. Small and petite, forever clad in designer clothes, groomed to within an inch of her life, she ruled their three homes with an elegant iron fist.

"We never fuck," was one of the first things he revealed. Silver had heard that before, from every married man who ever cheated on his wife.

"What do you do?" she asked sweetly.

"We socialize," he replied gruffly, and presented her with a hundred-thousand-dollar diamond necklace from Cartier.

"The Businessman" was a very demanding man when he found the time. His sexual appetite was voracious, and Silver, who was no slouch in the sexual stakes herself, found him hard to keep up with. He was rough and crude, but God he was exciting!

Silver fell in love with a married man twenty-one years her senior, and she fell hard. On the one hand he treated her like a whore. On the other he showered her with expensive gifts — the diamond necklace was just the beginning.

One day he arrived at the penthouse apartment they used as a meeting place, with two other women. A seductive-looking redhead, and a soigné black girl with the style of a fashion model. Instinctively Silver knew they were hookers. High-class ones, and very costly, but hookers all the same.

Angrily she cornered him in the kitchen after he had fixed them all drinks. "What's going on?"

"Nothing, if you don't want it to," he replied blandly.

She knew it was what he wanted and her stomach churned. Silver Anderson had been around, but never that much.

They returned to the living room and polite chat. The two girls were good, they knew their stuff. "Isn't it a little hot in here?" one of them murmured, taking off her light silk jacket.

"Very hot," the other agreed, stretching out her legs and removing her shoes and stockings.

Silver felt "The Businessman" tense beside her on the couch.

The black girl stood up and smiled seductively. "You don't mind, do you?" she asked, unwrapping her crossover dress. Underneath she wore a scarlet lace G-string and that was all. Her breasts were pointed and polished like the finest onyx.

The redhead stood too. "I love to take off my clothes," she said softly. "I need to feel nothing between me and nature." She stretched, allowing her full breasts to fall free of her blouse.

The penthouse apartment was hardly the great outdoors, but Silver got the drift.

Idly the two girls began to touch each other. Fingers caressing breasts and other, more secret places. Tongues warm and soft. The secret places exposed for all to see.

"The Businessman's" breathing was laboured. Beneath his trousers Silver saw the proof of his excitement. Without moving from the couch, and without taking his eyes off the two call-girls, he urged Silver to lift her skirt.

She had tried to remain unaffected by what was going on — an impossible task. And to her shame she knew she would do anything he asked. So while the womem writhed together on the floor, Silver Anderson lifted her skirt, removed her panties, spread her legs, and allowed "The Businessman" to mount her and take his ride of perverted passion.

When it was over she felt dirty and humiliated. She was Silver Anderson, not some cheap tramp to be taken and used in front of whores. She was furious with him, and angry at herself for succumbing so easily.

The next day he sent her a ruby as big as an egg and a note. We'll do it again soon. Like hell they would. She refused to see him in spite of his bombardments of gifts and flowers.

Six weeks later she realized she was pregnant.

The first thing she did was consult her gynaecologist. "I don't want this baby," she told him flatly.

He was a charming man with grey hair and a crinkly smile. "Why not, my dear? You're in excellent health."

"I know that," she said irritably, searching for a suitable reason. "I'm not married." That would shut him up.

He laughed. Charmingly. "Silver, Silver," he sighed, placing the tips of his fingers together and rocking back and forth behind his desk. "You're a very famous woman. What does it matter whether you're married or not? You'll have a beautiful baby with none of the in-conveniences of a husband in the house." He chuckled at his own wisdom. "You'll make single motherhood fashionable."

She liked the idea. Silver Anderson, a pioneer for women! Also the thought of an abortion terrified her. Eventually she decided to go ahead and have the baby.

By the time she gave birth, "The Businessman" was gone from her life. She had threatened him with exposure to his wife if he didn't leave her alone. He had no idea the baby was his.

The press went crazy in their quest to find out who the father was, but Silver remained silent. Three months after Heaven was born she moved to Rio with a Brazilian polo player. Heaven was left in New York with a nanny.

As Silver watched the child grow, she regretted giving birth. Every time she looked at Heaven, she was reminded of "The Businessman" and her unforgettable night of degradation.

Heaven had never asked who her father was. Jack did once, when he came to London to pick up the child. "He doesn't exist," she'd said coldly.

Unfortunately he did.

*

Silver sighed and stretched. Opening her eyes she stared at the silk draped ceiling above her bed. If Heaven appeared tonight she was not going to be pleased. *Damn* Nora for asking the girl, and bringing back all the bad memories.

The Baccarat clock on the bedside table told her it was time to start getting ready for her party. She wished she could sleep for ten hours. When was the last time she'd done that? Work . . . Work . . . Work . . . Parties . . . Parties . . . Parties . . .

Ah, well . . . for great fame you paid a price . . .

It was worth it.

Almost.

Chapter 13

Mannon Cable worked out in his private gym before getting ready for the party. He didn't really want to go, he was not fond of parties. This was a favour for Nora Carvell. She had phoned a week before and asked him to attend. Nora was an old friend, and one of the few people in Hollywood he would do anything for. Well, not quite anything – however, if she wanted a favour, she was on. At the beginning of his career she was the one person who was always there for him. The crusty old publicist was in his corner from day one. He recalled walking into her office on the lot the day he signed for his first important movie. Fifteen years ago to be exact.

*

Mannon Cable was twenty-seven years old and the best-looking hunk ever to cross Nora Carvell's path when he walked into her office. Not that she was interested. She preferred girls, always would. Only Mannon didn't know that, so when he first set eyes on the middle-aged woman with the cropped hair and the permanent cigarette dangling from her lips, he went into his number. Sexy walk. Macho scowl. Cobalt blue eyes scorching everything in sight.

"Take a seat," Nora snapped. "And tell me your life history. Then we'll make something up." She shuffled some papers around on her desk. "Have you been over to the stills department yet?"

"Nope." He shook his head.

She squinted at his sun-kissed good looks, trying to decide how to sell this new piece of beefcake. "Go ahead. Shoot."

He told her about being born in Montana, coming to Los Angeles at nineteen. Studying at various acting classes, working as a waiter, an extra, a gas pump attendant, a repossessor of cars, and a stunt man.

"Married?" she asked.

"Nope," he replied.

"Homosexual?" she persisted.

He shifted uncomfortably. "Are you kidding?"

Pencil poised, she checked him out for signs of lying. "I'm not gonna make it public knowledge, sonny. I just have to know these things so I can protect you."

"I am not a queer," he said stiffly.

She scribbled on a piece of paper and said, "Come back tomorrow. I'll have you all figured out."

He returned the next day to be handed a typed sheet of imaginative accomplishments. He was a football hero, an English honours major, who had been injured in a football game and told that he would never walk again. For two years he had lain in a hospital bed unable to move, until — miracle of miracles — blind faith pulled him through and he came to Hollywood and was discovered for this very movie he was about to make.

"This is all lies," he protested.

She shrugged. "So I bent the truth a little. Big deal."

"I don't like it."

Inhaling cigarette smoke she said, "You don't havta like it, sonny, just remember it."

He shook his head. "No way."

"It's studio policy. Bio info's gotta grab 'em. Whaddya think's gonna grab 'em about your background?" A cloud of smoke enveloped her and she began to cough. "Are you sure you're not a fag? Y'live with two other guys. What's the deal?"

"Get fucked," he steamed, and walked out.

After that they became good friends. It was Nora's idea that he do the Burt Reynolds spoof centrefold. He did it with a big, shit-eating grin and a large picture of a strutting cock (the barnyard variety) covering his strutting cock (the Mannon Cable variety). It caused quite a stir, and everyone knew who Mannon Cable was after that.

When Nora left the studio a few years later she came to work for him as his personal publicist. Eventually she went off to live in Italy with her companion of many years, and when her lover died she came back to America and took a job at City Television. Her first assignment was Silver Anderson. She had worked with her ever since.

*

Mannon finished a series of gruelling press-ups, and threw a towelling robe over his shorts. When he was married to Whitney, parties were a rare event. Whitney was content to stay at home on the ranch, just the two of them. She liked to ride their horses, walk on the beach, and join him in fixing a barbecue. Until she started her dumb career and fucked everything up. Now the Malibu ranch was sold, the horses too. Home was a formal mansion on Sunset Boulevard, and he wasn't happy.

Melanie-Shanna waited in the games room, which featured a pool table, full western bar, and his collection of guns on the walls.

When Mannon had showered and dressed he joined her.

"Hi, honey," she greeted him quietly. "Feeling good?"

"Yeah, great."

He didn't know what it was about Melanie-Shanna — it wasn't her fault, she just aggravated the hell out of him. Maybe it was because *she* was his wife and Whitney wasn't. They had met when he went to Houston to make a movie. While he was there, recovering from Whitney's walk-out and her subsequent affair with Chuck Nielson, he had judged a beauty contest. Melanie-Shanna, with her mane of auburn hair, her clean, long-limbed body, and her sweet smile, was the natural winner. He had taken her out to dinner a few times. Then he had taken her *in* to dinner. One thing led to another and he made love to her on the floor of his sumptuous suite. She was only twenty years old when they married a week later. Whitney was nearly thirty. Let her eat her heart out.

Basically Mannon married Melanie-Shanna to make Whitney jealous. It didn't work. And it left him in the crapper with a young wife and no pre-nuptial agreement. To make matters even worse, Melanie-Shanna adored him.

"Can I fix you a drink, honey?" she asked.

"Why do you always have to tag *honey* onto the end of every sentence?" he said aggressively.

"Sorry, hon — er, dear. I'm not aware that I do."

"Well, *be* aware," he warned. "It makes you sound like a cheap dance hostess."

She turned away so that he couldn't see her large eyes fill with tears. What was she doing wrong? For months he had hardly had a good word to say to her. When they first met he had been so loving and kind, truly the man of her dreams. He hadn't known that for years she'd had his picture tacked on her wall after seeing him in *Sweet Revenge*. Mannon Cable had always been her favourite movie star.

Now she was Mrs Mannon Cable, and it wasn't making either of them happy.

Quietly she poured scotch into a glass, added ice cubes and handed it to him.

He swallowed the drink in two gulps. "I suppose we'd better go," he said dourly, walking to the door. "And I'm warning you, I don't want to stay late."

"Neither do I," she said, following him out. Tonight she wanted to come home early. Because tonight she was going to tell him they were expecting a baby.

Chapter 14

"Wanna go party?" Heaven asked Eddie on the phone.

He laughed, low-down and dirty. "I thought we had our own party this afternoon."

"Some party," she giggled.

"A blast, right?"

"A *big* blast."

"You wanna repeat it?"

She paused. "I have another sort of party in mind."

"Aw . . ." Eddie said. "I hate those open parties. They're always full of kids, an' I hate not gettin' in the house, an' being treated like garbage, an' —"

"This is a *proper* party," she interrupted. "Like a *Beverly Hills* party, with movie stars and fancy food and probably some dumb band."

"Food?" Eddie questioned. "Real food?"

"I guess."

"Who invited us?" he asked suspiciously.

"Nobody invited *you*," she responded tartly. "Only *I* can take you," she taunted. "That's if I *want* to, an' if your car'll get us over the hill."

"Whose party is it?"

"My mother finally remembered I'm alive."

"Silver Anderson?"

"I'm not related to Linda Evans, you geek."

There was a short silence while Eddie digested this information. Finally he said, "What'ud I have to wear?"

"Anything you like," she replied blithely. She herself planned to cause a sensation in her red leather micro-dress, and the longshoreman's overcoat which she had just bought at Flip on Melrose with money from her singing gigs.

"Do y'*wanna* go?" Eddie inquired, remembering how she felt about her famous mother.

"I dunno," she replied, unsure for a moment. "I don't see why I *shouldn't*. I *am* her daughter."

"Uh . . . let's do it then," he said.

"Oh . . . I don't know." She changed her mind quickly.

"Aw, c'mon, H. Get on the track 'n' stick to it."

"Maybe I will. I'll call you back."

She hung up on him before he could argue. She enjoyed playing games with Eddie. Especially *now*. Anyway, she couldn't make up her mind whether she wanted to go to her mother's dumb party or not. On the one hand it might be a real blast to spy on the Hollywood set first-hand. On the other – who would Silver have there? Certainly not Rob Lowe and Sean Penn. More like a bunch of doddering old farts.

As if to make up her mind, her grandfather, George, appeared at the door of her room. He was a tall, thin man, with a shock of thick white hair and a preoccupied expression always in place on his deeply lined face. He didn't look like Silver, and no way resembled Uncle Jack. He had a sort of nutty professor air about him. Heaven liked him a lot. For a grandfather he was ace. And he left her alone. *Most* important.

"Are you home for dinner, dear?" he asked, fiddling with his glasses which hung from a blue cord around his neck.

"I think I'm going out, pops."

"Good, good," he said absent-mindedly. "Then I can let Mrs Gunter go."

Anything to let Mrs Gunter go. She was their housekeeper/cook/busybody, and she drove Heaven nuts.

"I'm not bothering with dinner myself," George added vaguely. "I shall be in my workroom all night." His eyes fixed on a half-naked poster of Sting tacked to her closet. "Where are you going?" he asked.

"Out with Eddie," she replied, deciding the hell with it – she *would* go to her mother's party. Why shouldn't she? "We're playing a gig."

"Twelve o'clock curfew," George reminded.

"Sure, pops," she agreed. She could walk in at four in the morning and he wouldn't know it. Once he was in his workroom nothing disturbed him. Usually he carried on through the night, losing all track of time.

She didn't mention Silver's party. It would only upset him, and he might try to dissuade her from going. George and his famous daughter did not speak. It had been that way for thirty years.

Oh well ... Heaven didn't blame him ... Maybe she shouldn't talk to her mother either. Silver treated her as if she hardly existed. Never called. Never asked anything about her life when they did get together. Usually it was a twice-yearly dinner at La Scala with Nora in attendance. The woman was a bitch.

Big fucking deal. Who cared?

She did.

Chapter 15

Clarissa Browning rented a secluded house on Benedict Canyon. She leased it from a young director who had gone to work in Europe for a year. The house was dark and old, surrounded by tall trees and untended grounds. Clarissa liked the coldness of the house, the bathrooms that were over fifty years old, the dark wood panelling everywhere, and the general gloom.

Even the swimming pool was not of the usual California variety. There was no jacuzzi. No floating pool furniture. It was always filled with leaves, as the filter rarely worked. And it was always ice cold, as the heater *never* worked. At night coyotes howled, and other small, wild animals scurried across the old tile roof. Sometimes snakes slithered into the pool and drowned.

Clarissa enjoyed lighting a log fire in the bedroom and reading from her extensive collection of classics. She liked to bundle up in a long flannel nightie with a hot mug of cocoa for company, and pretend she was back east.

Arriving home from the studio early Saturday evening she was pleased to see Jack Python's dark green Ferrari parked out front. He had his own key to come and go whenever he pleased. It suited her. Clarissa never brought her homework to the house.

He was in the bedroom watching television. Or was he watching? On closer inspection she discovered he was asleep.

Silently she observed him for a moment – so still . . . so quiet. Usually Jack was always on the move. The green eyes probing, finding out things. The hard body ready, poised. The sharp mind, clickety clickety click.

He excited her. He always excited her.

The first time they met she had thought – *Handsome son of a bitch with a hard cock and not much else*. She had changed her mind soon enough. He had a hard cock all right, but that wasn't all. Jack Python had energy and curiosity and a steel trap of a mind. He was a fast thinker with words to back up his thoughts. He was not just a pretty face.

They slept together immediately, in spite of friends warning her that Jack Python came and ran. Not with Clarissa Browning he didn't. She had no intention of becoming just another name on his long list.

Patiently she attempted to get to know him. It wasn't easy. Charming and warm and intelligent as he was, Jack never allowed anyone to get close. Clarissa understood. She was the same way herself.

She moved to California to do a movie, and when he eventually got around to calling, she played his game, and refused to see him. It soon became clear that Jack did not like rejection.

When they finally saw each other it was understood they were an item. They had been an item for over a year now. It suited both of them.

Clarissa scrubbed off her studio makeup, removed her clothes, and stood over the sleeping figure of her lover. She forgot about the young actor at the studio that morning. Merely business. Jack Python was pleasure. Such pure exquisite pleasure . . .

She shuddered in anticipation of what was to come. In bed he was a master. He had an uncanny knack of knowing her every need, combined with the most impressive staying power.

"Just a trick," he said one day, when she asked him how he did it.

"Tell me!" she persisted.

"Just call it mind over matter," he grinned.

Her presence was not waking him. She clicked off the hated television. (Hated by her, loved by him. "How can you not watch *Hill Street*?" he demanded every Thursday night at ten o'clock.) The sudden silence disturbed him, and he rolled over, still asleep and still dressed in his usual weekend clothes of Levis and a sweater.

She unzipped his jeans with her teeth.

He woke up and groped for her.

Pushing his hands away she rolled his Levis down. He wore no undershorts. He never did. She bent her head to his sudden interest.

"I surrender," he said, throwing his arms to the side.

"I knew you would," she murmured.

Later they shared a cigarette and discussed their plans for the evening. There were several possibilities. A screening of a new Mel Brooks film. "I'm too tired to laugh," Clarissa demurred. An industry dinner honouring an old actor. "Why?" Jack questioned. "He was a no-talent when he was young. What's the trick in growing old?" And dinner with Clarissa's agent at Spago. "He's a lunch," she decided.

"What do you feel like doing?" he asked, clicking on the television. "Want me to send out for Chinese?"

Clarissa flicked the television off. "What about going to your sister's party?"

"Huh?" He was surprised. "How do you know about Silver's party?"

"I was invited."

"You don't know her."

"Maybe I should."

"Why?"

"Because she's your sister, and I've never met any of your family. Not your father, or your niece. I think Silver Anderson is an interesting woman, and I'm intrigued to meet her."

"Shit!" Jack said, jumping from the bed and pacing around the darkened bedroom.

"Are we nervous of being in her company?" Clarissa chided. "Does she make you feel inferior?"

"You talk such crap sometimes."

"Yes? My psychiatrist says that to conquer fears you simply have to face them."

"You pay two hundred bucks an hour for advice you can get out of a Chinese fortune cookie?"

"He's helped me a lot."

"Hey — I'm not going to get into a fight over this. Silver doesn't make me nervous. She doesn't make me anything."

"Then we'll go?"

"If that's how you want to spend your Saturday night."

"It is."

He wasn't going to fight it. Clarissa was a stubborn woman, and if she wanted to do something they usually ended up doing it.

He did not believe in fighting. He believed in exiting. Quietly. If it ever got to be too much.

Chapter 16

Silver Anderson's party was being paid for by City Television. Silver was notoriously tight with a buck, and there was no way *she* was shelling out thirty or forty thousand dollars — even if it *was* for her, and she could certainly afford it.

City was planning a big celebration for the cast of *Palm Springs* before the summer hiatus, when Nora suggested it might be a better idea to make it a party to celebrate Silver's birthday. "Do I have something for you!" she told them. "Glamour. Style. Stars. A media event with sensational coverage." They fell in love with the idea immediately, and once she had them hooked all she had to do was convince Silver.

It wasn't difficult. Not when Silver discovered City Television was paying. "I'll have the party," she agreed. "And when it's all over and done with I want my entire house re-carpeted. A little gift. They can afford it." A dramatic pause.

"Oh, and by the way, Nora, forty-*five* is my official age this year. Not a moment older."

Nora didn't want to get into *that* one. She reckoned City Television would certainly pay for the carpeting of Silver's house. Where else could they get this kind of world-wide publicity for such a steal? And the coverage would be sensational. No problem. For Nora Carvell knew plenty about publicity. Television was taken care of, and then there were photographers from *U.S.A. Today*, *People*, *Newsweek*, and a personal photographer who would capture shots to be sent out world-wide on all the wire services. The paparazzi would be outside, flanking a red carpet and crash barriers to the house. Along with several of Beverly Hills finest, who would take care of the vigorous security.

Nora had personally supervised the guest list, inviting a hand-picked group of important industry people, and a mix of very famous actors, actresses, sports stars and assorted V.I.P.s from other fields.

Dressed in a plum velvet suit with clumsy pearl jewellery not complementing her short, untidy grey hair, she rushed back to Silver's house early. Swamped in Ma Griffe scent and cigarette smoke she parked in the back next to Wes Money, who was just alighting from his old Lincoln.

"Who're you?" she asked tartly, ever wary of uninvited spies from the *National Enquirer* or *True Life Scandal*.

"I'm bar. Who're *you*?"

"I'm publicity. Pass the word. Anyone calling the super-market rags with overheard gossip will not be working in this town again. Got it?"

Wes nodded. The old broad had just come up with a great idea for scoring extra bucks. She hurried off, and he took a leisurely stroll down a garden path to the back door, which led him into an overcrowded, very large kitchen.

"I'm bar," he said to an elderly Chinese women who stone-walled him with a glare. "Bar?" he said to a big-bosomed girl in a white uniform.

She gestured vaguely towards a door.

He walked through into the house proper. Some house. Marble floors. Overstuffed couches. A series of luxurious rooms all leading into other luxurious rooms. And finally a glass wall overlooking a black-bottomed swimming pool, at the end of which was a curved black marble bar.

A frantic Rocky waved to him. "Hey, man, thank Christ you're here," he said, busily unloading boxes of booze. "What took you so long?"

"I had to find it, didn't I?" Wes complained. "Fucking Bel Air is like one of those mazes in an amusement park. You told me Bellagio. It goes on for fucking ever in every direction. You're lucky I'm here at all."

"You really crack me up," said Rocky, who looked like a poor man's Sylvester Stallone — hence the name. "Only *you* could get your ass lost in Bel Air."

"And only *you* give out shit directions," Wes responded. "I wasted gas driving up and down."

"Do me a favour — get to work," Rocky said, shoving a heavy box of wine in his direction. "We've only got an hour before blast-off." He lowered his voice. "There's a mixed box I've put together, it's over there." He gestured. "Get it out to your car whenever seems like a good time. I'll come by tomorrow to split it."

"Why *my* car?" Wes asked peevishly.

"'Cos it's *me* they'll be watching."

Sure. If anyone was to be caught stealing booze it was good old Wes Money.

Screw Rocky. He must think he was some schmuck. But so what? He'd do it. Life was a risk, and in a kind of perverse way he enjoyed taking 'em.

*

Silver discarded five outfits before deciding on chiffon purple harem pants, a floating top embroidered with gold, and a long Cleopatra wig. She looked exotic, like an Egyptian queen. Especially when she added solid gold slave bracelets, giant hoop earrings, and several huge diamond rings.

She hadn't touched a drink in months, but she certainly wasn't an alcoholic, and she quite fancied a glass of ice cold Cristal to put her in the mood for the evening's activities. Decisively she picked up the intercom and buzzed the kitchen.

Her houseman, Vladimir, elbowed the Chinese woman out of the way to answer his mistress's call. The woman almost fell, and cursed in Chinese about rude American pigs. Vladimir, who spoke a little Chinese (thanks to a five-year live-in relationship with a Chinese waiter who unfortunately fell off Santa Monica pier and drowned) ignored her insults and cooed into the phone.

"Yes, madame?" His English was almost impeccable except for his mispronunciation of *w* as *v*. "Vat can I get for you?"

"Champagne, Vladimir. Very cold. Very soon."

"Yes, madame." He grabbed Wes, who was passing by on his way to the back door with the box of contraband carefully prepared by Rocky. "You!" he said sharply.

"Who, me?" replied Wes innocently, thinking – *Oh fuck, now I'm caught.*

"Champagne. For Madame. *Pronto.*" (The *pronto* came from an Italian waiter who shared his affections for two nights and screamed *pronto, pronto* every time he came, which was often.)

"Madame who?" asked Wes patiently, thinking the Russian queen probably meant Madame Wong who was glaring at both of them, and what had *she* done to deserve champagne?

"Madame Silver," said Vladimir, raising a scornful eyebrow at this cretin's ignorance. "Cristal. In a Baccarat glass. And make sure it's icy. Hurry, hurry!"

"I'll be right back," Wes said cheerfully, realizing the game was not yet up. He hurried out to his car with the box and loaded it into his trunk.

When he returned to the kitchen, Vladimir screamed, "Vere is it?"

"What?"

"The champagne for Madame."

"Oh. That. Just gettin' it."

"Now!" Vladimir leaped excitedly in the air. In his youth he had trained as a ballet dancer – long before he defected to the West and freedom.

Wes mock saluted. "Yes *sir, Kapitan*. One glass of bubbly comin' right up."

*

The 1965 Mustang spluttered to a full stop halfway up Coldwater Canyon.

"Like I don't believe this!" Heaven screeched.

"Jesus!" groaned Eddie.

"This can't be happening," she yelled, jumping from the car.

"Jesus!" repeated Eddie, following her. "It was runnin' fine when I picked you up."

"Like what are you gonna do?" she demanded, venom in her voice.

"What are *we* gonna do," he corrected.

"It's *your* fault," she pointed out. "It's *your* dumb car." She kicked the side of the old Mustang with a sharp booted toe.

"Don't do that!" he objected.

"I will if I want," she replied in a childish sing-song, and for good measure she gave the car another solid kick.

He was incensed. "Cut it out. What's the matter with you?"

"I'm pissed off," she said. "I'm *really* pissed off."

"You think *I'm* dancin'?"

They glared at each other. Heaven, with her spiky multi-coloured locks. Eddie, with his black hair greased back in true sixties style.

"This is like the bummer of all time," she announced flatly.

Eddie headed for the hood of the car. "Don't worry 'bout a thing. I'll fix it," he said, less hopeful than he sounded.

With an exasperated sigh she sank down on the grass verge muttering, "Yeah. You an' who else?"

*

Silver did not like being kept waiting. When she wanted something she wanted it *now*. Ten minutes had elapsed since her request for champagne, and her taste buds were on full alert. With a snort of annoyance she buzzed the kitchen a second time, and Vladimir, who was knee deep in Chinese caterers, grabbed the phone.

"Are you keeping me waiting, Vladimir?" she asked icily.

"*Never*, madame."

"Then *why* are you still in the kitchen?"

"The bartender is on his vay up to you at this very minute, madame," Vladimir lied.

"I should hope so." She replaced the receiver with a crash.

Vladimir muttered ominous words of Russian under his breath. Reverting to his mother language relieved him when he was about to undergo a stress attack. "Bar!" he screamed loudly.

Five minutes later Wes was found. Vladimir equipped him with a silver tray, a Baccarat glass brimming with chilled Cristal, and dispatched him upstairs to face Madame's wrath. Vladimir knew when to make himself scarce.

Whistling a Beatles' song as he negotiated the sweeping staircase, Wes reflected on the vagaries of life. That very morning he had woken up in a little house in the Valley with a cheap dyed blonde. Now he was heading – tray in hand –

towards the bedroom of one of the biggest television stars in America, who lived in a frigging mansion! Pity he wouldn't be sharing *her* bed. Although he would sooner it was Whitney Valentine Cable. Now *there* was a real stunner. Not that he watched television much – just sports and late movies if he was in the mood. In fact, he wasn't quite sure what Silver Anderson looked like. All he had was a vague memory of a big dark woman staring out at him from countless magazine covers.

Wes was in for a surprise. Silver Anderson was dark all right, with her long jet hair and almond-shaped heavily outlined eyes. But big she wasn't. She was small and slender, almost petite. And beautiful in a dramatic and compelling way. He eyeballed her as she flung open the door of her bedroom as soon as he finished knocking.

She gave him an icy stare, and said coldly, "Exactly *how* long does it take to pour *one* glass of champagne and bring it up *one* flight of stairs?"

Walking past her into the purple wonderland of a bedroom, he looked for a place to put the tray. "Search me," he said cheerily. "Next time I'll put a stopwatch on it."

"I beg your pardon?" she said, hardly believing his cheek.

He spotted a mirrored dressing table and figured that was as good a place as any to dump the tray. As he placed it down, their eyes met in the mirror, and for a split second they held each other's gaze.

Silver saw an unruly attractive man, with a certain restlessness about him and a don't-give-a-damn attitude.

Wes saw a good-looking, if slightly older woman – and with unusual sensitivity for him, he sensed a mixture of need and loneliness coming off her in waves. The combination, with her mature beauty, was quite appealing.

Sexual chemistry was strong in the air.

He knew there was a moment to be seized, only it wasn't *his* place to seize it. *She* had to be the one, and if she didn't make a move *he* certainly wasn't going to set himself up for rejection by some big-time television star. It was probably all his imagination anyway.

He gave her an opening shot, just to play the odds. "Can I get you anything else?" he asked, his words loaded with innuendo.

Silver was no fool. The last thing she needed was some deadbeat bartender hitting on her. She iced him off with her eyes and a cold "No."

The moment was over. Leaving the star's bedroom he returned downstairs.

Vladimir pounced on him. "Vas Madame happy?" he asked anxiously.

"Yeah," replied Wes easily. "Why?" The Russian queen had obviously expected him to get torn off a strip. Tough tit. He was unscathed.

Or was he?

Chapter 17

Rule One: Smile for the photographers.

Rule Two: Be charming for the television cameras.

Rule Three: Always leave a good impression among the staff. They are the people who made you famous in the first place, so never forget them.

Whitney Valentine Cable knew all the rules by heart. And so she should. They were *her* rules, and she abided by them religiously.

She alighted from Chuck Nielson's red Porsche, and allowed the paparazzi to capture the widest smile in America. Chuck, who was boyishly handsome although he would never see thirty-five again, joined her, and the two of them posed.

The paparazzi clicked desperately. This was a hot picture, and one the entire world would want to see. The previous year Whitney Valentine Cable and Chuck Nielson had been an item – an on/off affair of epic proportions, complete with public fights and equally public reconciliations. Then they split, and Chuck stole the French actress wife of an English director – which made wonderful copy; while Whitney dated a series of different men – which also made wonderful copy. Now it appeared they were back together. A paparazzi's dream! Second only to Whitney reuniting with Mannon Cable.

Slowly the two of them moved inside, and Jeanne Wolf for *Entertainment Tonight* greeted them effusively.

Meanwhile, Howard and Poppy Soloman drew up in a very long, very flashy limousine. Howard failed to see why he should drive himself at night when he could use a studio limo any time he pleased.

The paparazzi failed to spring to attention, which aggravated Howard and devastated Poppy.

A lone flash captured their consternation. And then all the photographers surged forward to focus on Michael Caine and his beautiful wife, Shakira.

Howard and Poppy entered the house, and the first person they saw was Whitney, sensational in a white strapless dress. Hollywood kisses were exchanged. Howard inhaled her scent and wondered if she wanted him as much as he wanted her.

"I've been thinking about a project you'd be just right for," he blurted, with a manic twitch.

Her gaze was direct and interested. "Have you, Howard?"

"Are we speaking of the Weissman script?" Poppy joined in.

He turned to her with a frown. What the fuck was she talking about? "What Weissman script?"

She clung to his arm. Poppy Soloman had decided that as the wife of a studio head she must make it her business not to get left out of anything. "The script on your desk, darling. I read it yesterday. Whitney would be *wonderful* as the girl. It's such *off* casting." She planted a wifely kiss on his cheek. "You're brilliant to think of her."

He was brilliant and he didn't know it! His comment to Whitney had just been a ploy to talk to her later. He had no project she was right for. Now he had the Weissman script. He'd better have someone read it for him fast and find out if there *was* anything for Whitney in it.

Howard did not read scripts. It was too time-consuming. He had three readers whose opinions he trusted, and they analysed every story and gave him a succinct two-page synopsis. Poppy was not one of them. He wouldn't trust Poppy's opinion of Army Archerd's column in *Variety*, let alone a script!

"Yeah, Whit," he said quickly. "I wanna have a word with you about it later."

Whitney smiled. She hadn't been wrong about Howard; he was interested in her as an actress *and* as a woman. Perfect.

Chuck Nielson appeared at her side with two glasses of orange juice; neither of them drank alcohol – one of the few things they had in common.

Howard was disturbed to see her back in his company. Chuck Nielson was a low-life and trouble. He specialized in stealing other men's wives, and he couldn't get himself arrested as far as starring in a movie was concerned. Nobody wanted to hire him. In the past he'd starred in a couple of hits. But that was five years ago, and in Hollywood memories are notoriously short.

The two men greeted each other affectionately – macho slaps on the back and mild insults. Poppy brightened considerably. She still thought Chuck was a star, which just showed how much *she* knew.

While she spoke animatedly to Chuck, Howard threw Whitney a low aside. "What are you doing back with *him*?"

She shrugged. She probably had the most beautiful shoulders in the world. "Desperation," she whispered. "I couldn't get a date for tonight and I didn't want to miss seeing you."

Howard's ego pumped. Whether the Weissman script was right or not he would make sure it was rewritten to accommodate the fabulous Miss Whitney Valentine Cable. And when she starred in the movie for Orpheus Studios he would also make sure she dropped the Cable. Who needed to be reminded of Mannon every time he heard her name?

*

Outside the gates of Silver Anderson's estate, Mannon and Melanie-Shanna were fighting as they sat – captive prisoners in his blue Rolls-Royce – trapped in a line of expensive cars waiting to gain entry to the party. They were at least eight cars away from the uniformed guard at the gate, and Mannon was steaming.

"If we'd left home on time," he said angrily, "we wouldn't be caught in this mob scene."

"*I* was ready," Melanie-Shanna protested, not prepared to take the blame for everything.

"Then why didn't you make sure that *I* was?" he shouted.

She shut up. She had learned with Mannon that sometimes silence was the only way to handle his frequent temper tantrums. To the outside world being married to a superstar seemed like a dream. But the reality was far different. Sure there were advantages. Money. Position. And sharing the bed of a man millions of females wanted to sleep with.

There were plenty of disadvantages too. No privacy. No

peace. The ever-present army of people to tend to his every need. The relentless come-on from every single woman he ever met. The bad moods only *she* witnessed. The insecurities – an affliction suffered by every actor, be he superstar or bit player.

Mannon was right at the peak of his career now. Melanie-Shanna shuddered to think what he would be like should his star ever dim. She hoped he would be thrilled when she told him about the baby.

She wasn't sure he would be.

*

And so they came.

A legendary movie star with a rugged profile, foreign wife, and dead career.

A younger movie star (but only by a decade or two) with a starlet girlfriend, and a nearly dead career.

A cheating producer and his socialite wife.

A cheating wife with her gay husband.

A young hot actor with an even hotter coke habit.

A pretty young actress who only liked other pretty young actresses.

Nora was pleased by the turn-out. Everything was proceeding without a hitch. The only slight hiccough was Silver's non-appearance. A late entrance wasn't a major tragedy, only Nora wished the star would get her act together. Several times she had popped upstairs to check that all was well. Silver, dressed and ready, sat by a large picture window in the bedroom gazing out at the magnificent view, smoking a cigarette. Los Angeles at night, as seen from high in the hills, was a fairyland of twinkling lights – Silver seemed mesmerized.

At nine o'clock – the party started at eight – Nora trekked upstairs again.

"Who's here?" Silver asked anxiously.

"Everyone," Nora replied. "You can come down now."

"In a minute. Don't rush me."

Nora decided it was time to put the pressure on. *"Now,"* she said pointedly. "Otherwise they'll start going home."

Silver sighed, and arose obediently. Moving over to a full-length mirror she inspected the image

"Perfect," flattered Nora.

Silver took a deep breath. "I should hope so. I work hard enough to create it."

One last, lingering glance and she walked towards the door.

Silver Anderson was having a birthday party. She didn't want to miss it.

Chapter 18

"Are you sure you want to do this?" Jack asked quizzically as his Ferrari negotiated the winding curves of Bel Air.

"Yes," Clarissa replied curtly. "Why wouldn't I?"

He felt he was being tested and he wasn't sure he liked it. "Because," he replied slowly, "parties have never been your favourite way to spend an evening. Especially not big glitzy bashes filled with press."

She smoothed down the skirt of her tailored brown gaberdine suit. "I didn't say this was my favourite way to spend an evening." She spoke in a measured tone. "I said I was interested in meeting your sister. I'm sure you must understand my curiosity."

No. He didn't understand at all.

"You've never really explained why you don't get along," she persisted.

And I have no intention of doing so now, he thought.

"We're different people," he said shortly.

"I know *that*."

"So if you know it, let's drop the subject."

"As you wish."

They drove the rest of the way in silence.

*

When Jade partied she threw herself into the spirit of the evening. She knew that a night spent in Antonio's company was not exactly a cultural event. It was more a blast, an experience, a let-it-all-hang-out-and-get-down! So she dressed accordingly in tight black satin pants tucked into matching boots. A long black shirt cinched at her twenty-two-inch waist with a wide belt. Fake jewellery galore from Butler & Wilson in London: gifts from Mark – he had a surprising knack for picking out just the right pieces. In retrospect she thought that maybe another woman had chosen them. Who knew? He no doubt had mistresses everywhere; she had just been his New York connection.

Piling her shaggy copper hair on top of her head, she secured it with a couple of pins, deftly arranging strands to fall artfully free. Then she applied tawny makeup, and emphasized her widely spaced gold-flecked eyes with brown shadow and thick kohl pencil. Plenty of lip gloss over a gold-toned lipstick, and she was ready when Antonio and three of his friends came piling into her apartment laden with flowers, record albums, bottles of wine and an assortment of gourmet Chinese tidbits picked up at Chinn Chinn on Sunset Boulevard.

"I thought we were going out," she said, as they proceeded to make themselves at home.

"We are, we are, precious," insisted Antonio, instructing his minions. One to the kitchen to warm the snacks in the microwave. One to the bar to open the wine. And a third to arrange the profusion of glorious flowers.

She began to laugh. "This is an invasion," she protested.

"A welcome." Antonio showed off his neat, precise little grin. "To Los Angeles, *bellissima*."

"Won't we be late for the party?"

He pursed his lips. "Who cares? Nothing happens until *Antonio* arrives!"

His companions all nodded their agreement as they fussed around.

Antonio kissed the tips of his fingers. "You look a dream, *cara*. A death in the family it suit you."

"You're *bad*, Antonio."

"But of course!"

"*Very* bad."

"Naturally!"

*

Nora greeted Mannon with a warm hug. "*You* are a prince," she whispered.

"No, I'm a putz," he responded. "Have you any idea how long I've been sitting in my goddamn car waiting to get in here?"

"I'm sorry."

"So am I."

She summoned a waiter. "What'll you have?"

"Scotch. You'd better make it a double."

Melanie-Shanna stood silently by his side. Nobody asked *her* what she would like to drink. Nobody cared, as long as Mister Superstar was taken care of.

"I'd like a glass of white wine," she told the waiter quietly.

Mannon was still complaining. Nora listened attentively, then teased him and flattered him, and gradually Melanie-Shanna felt him relax. Until Whitney, his ex-wife, appeared, and Melanie-Shanna felt herself go hot and cold, for they had never met.

"Christ!" Mannon muttered to Nora. "What's *she* doing here?"

"I didn't know you two weren't talking," Nora said.

"We're talking," he replied gruffly, although he wasn't sure if they were or not. The last time he'd seen her she had been distinctly cool. In fact, she had brushed him off completely. Well . . . understandable, really. He had just had a piece published in *People* where he called her a career-mad starlet, and Chuck Nielson a washed-up beach bum.

Thank Christ she was no longer with *him*. And as these thoughts crossed his mind, Chuck materialized beside her, and the very idea of *his* Whitney with Chuck Nielson *again* drove Mannon wild with fury.

"Fuck!" he mumbled under his breath.

"What?" asked Melanie-Shanna.

"Nothing," came the surly reply.

They were on a collision course. There was no way they could avoid coming face to face.

Mannon steeled himself for confrontation.

*

"I'm going," Heaven said impatiently, rising from the grass verge and brushing dead leaves and debris from her long overcoat.

"Whattya gonna do — fly?" demanded Eddie, as he fiddled with the engine of the Mustang, getting nowhere fast.

"I'll thumb a ride," she announced, now determined to get to her mother's party.

"You can't do that, it's not safe."

"Ohhh! Listen to daddy!" she mocked. "I *can* look after myself, y'know."

He straightened up. "Yeah — you get a ride from one of those mass murderer freaks an' you'll *really* be able t'look after your-self."

"Oh, *sure*. Every one of these cars goin' by is just *crammed* with serial killers waitin' to grab little ole me!"

"Cut the crap," he said angrily. "You're not takin' any rides on your own. I'll leave the Mustang here an' come with you."

"About time!" she huffed.

*

Working the party kept Wes busy. Whatever Rocky was paying him wasn't enough. He grabbed a couple of beers behind the scenes, but basically he was sober. Well, he had to be, didn't he? There was a lot of action going down.

First of all Rocky was operating a lucrative sideline selling coke to a number of studio hot shots. And once the word got around, business was brisk. Rocky brought him in on a com-mission basis, and between the two of them they scammed the party pretty good.

Behind the bar out by the swimming pool, Wes didn't get a lot of opportunity to observe Silver Anderson. But he saw her make a dramatic entrance at nine o'clock, and the assorted press went crazy.

"Is she married?" he asked.

"Naw," Rocky drawled. "The fag in the kitchen tells me she has a different boyfriend every week."

"Who's the one this week?"

Rocky belched. "What the fuck do y'think I am — a gossip hack?"

They both stopped talking to observe Whitney Valentine Cable as she undulated past.

"Now *there's* a broad." Rocky smacked his thick lips with relish. "I could stick it to that one any way, any day."

"Yeah," agreed Wes.

Later he sold a gram of coke to Chuck Nielson. He felt like asking him about his gorgeous girlfriend, only he didn't. Wes knew how far to go and with whom.

*

Nora couldn't believe her luck when Jack Python arrived with Clarissa Browning. All she had to do was get him with Silver for a picture, and the front pages of the world's press would be hers. The brother and sister had never been photographed together.

89

She greeted Jack effusively and tried to guide him in the right direction.

He shook her off with his customary charm. "Why don't you take Clarissa to meet Silver, she can't wait."

"What about you, Jack? Aren't you going to wish your sister a happy birthday?"

"Maybe later, Nora." He gave Clarissa a gentle push in the right direction. "Off you go. That's what you came here for, isn't it?"

Spotting Howard, he strolled over.

"You're the *last* person I expected to see here," Howard said in surprise.

"Me too," Jack agreed. "Hopefully I won't be staying."

*

"Hello, Mannon," Whitney said in her silky voice, her mouth downturned, no dazzling smile in sight.

"Whitney." He nodded curtly. "Chuck."

Once, the three of them had been close friends. They had lived in neighbouring beach houses and spent all their time together. In fact Mannon could remember going on location and asking Chuck to look after Whitney for him. Ha! What a laugh! Chuck had looked after her all right: he was probably trying to get her in his well-used bed even then.

"How're they hangin', pal?" asked Chuck.

The bum was stoned as usual. Whitney loathed drugs. Why was she with him again?

"Have you met my wife?" Mannon asked tightly, and introduced Melanie-Shanna, who realized immediately this was an uncomfortable reunion.

"Melanie," said Chuck, swaying slightly. "What an unexpected pleasure. You're lovely. But then my old buddy always did have great taste."

"Thank you."

Mannon gripped her by the arm. What was she thanking the creep for?

Whitney began to edge away. She looked stunning. She always did. Melanie-Shanna was pretty, but every woman paled in comparison to Whitney.

Chuck, sensing Whitney wanted to split, dutifully followed her. "Nice seein' ya, pal," he said to Mannon. "And I liked meeting *you*." He gave Melanie-Shanna a burning look. "Come and visit us at the beach sometime."

"Goddamn moron," muttered Mannon, watching them move off.

"He seems pleasant enough," Melanie-Shanna said, knowing, even as she spoke, that it was the wrong thing to say.

"Jesus!" Mannon rolled his eyes. "When will you learn!"

*

Silver enjoyed playing star hostess. She circulated and smiled and flirted. She posed with the cast from *Palm Springs*. She gave witty quotes to George Christy from the *Hollywood Reporter*. She chatted to friends and acquaintances. Eventually she instructed Nora to get rid of the press. Their constant questions and the bright lights of the television crews stationed by the door – they weren't allowed beyond that – were beginning to annoy her.

"I want them to get a picture of you and Jack," Nora fretted.

"Who?"

"Your brother."

"Oh God! What's *he* doing here?"

"He's with Clarissa Browning."

"Hmmm . . . Her taste must be slipping."

When it came to family Silver was not a warm and wonderful person. Once Nora had asked her about it. "We're not close," Silver had admitted. That could be the understatement of the year.

Nora had been observing Jack Python. He always made absolutely sure there was a roomful of people between him and his sister. Obviously he had no intention of getting anywhere near her.

*

"Can we have lunch?" Howard asked Whitney. His palms were slippery with sweat as he watched her contemplate her reply.

"Is this about the movie you want me to do?"

"The film and uh . . . other things."

"What other things, Howard?" she teased, and her down-turned mouth broke into a wide smile.

"Don't get me hot, baby. I think you and I have been heading in this direction for some time."

"I *can* have lunch," she decided sweetly. "I'll bring my agent."

"Your agent my ass."

"Does that mean his presence is not required?"

"When?" he asked urgently.

91

"Let me call you."

Howard glanced outside. Poppy had Chuck Nielson pinned against the bar. "What are you doing with that stoned Nielson schmuck again?" he asked, leaning closer to her smooth outdoor beauty.

"He's convenient."

"He's also crazy."

"I can handle him."

"I hope so."

Nora cut in. "Do you mind, Howard? Whitney dear, the press will kill for a photo of you with Silver. *Newsweek* wants it for their 'Newsmakers' page."

"Sure," Whitney said pleasantly, kissing Howard on the cheek. "Be patient," she whispered. "I'll call you on Monday."

*

Mannon said, "What were you talking to Whitney about?"

"Orpheus wants her," Howard replied. It wasn't a complete lie. According to Poppy there was a suitable script, and besides – *he* was Orpheus and *he* wanted her. To hell with his twenty-year friendship with Mannon.

*

Heaven and Eddie got a ride down the Canyon with a couple in a station wagon who were going into Hollywood to see their first porno movie. They were a young couple, and tried to persuade the teenagers to accompany them.

"Forget it," Heaven said when they hit Sunset, having encouraged them all the way.

Outside The Beverly Hills Hotel, by the bus stop, they hitched a lift with two girls heading for a party at the beach. They got off at the West Gate into Bel Air, and walked for twenty minutes before they flagged a security patrol car. The two guards listened to their story and took them up into the hills, letting them off right outside the gates to Silver's mansion.

"Some place!" exclaimed Eddie, as Heaven informed the sceptical guard who she was.

"Yeah," she agreed. "I guess it's okay."

"Why don't you live here?" Eddie asked as they traipsed up the driveway to the house – having got the go-ahead from the guard.

"I dunno," she said vaguely. "I like it where I am."

She didn't care to mention that her mother had never suggested she move in. Not that she wanted to.

"Jeez!" said Eddie. "I'd be here like a rocket!"

As they neared the house they could hear music playing and the clink of cutlery and glasses.

"I guess dinner is served," Heaven joked. "Silver is into all that formal crap."

"Are you sure we're dressed okay?" Eddie asked, anxiously tugging at his black leather studded jacket.

"Whadda we care?" Heaven said defiantly. "She's lucky I'm here."

They entered the house. Two photographers walked by them on their way out. They did a double-take, but Heaven was used to that. She wasn't exactly Sally Prom. With her spiky multi-coloured hair, heavily streaked makeup and outlandish outfit, she looked like a cross between Twisted Sister, Rod Stewart and Cher.

She was wearing her red micro-dress with a huge overcoat. The dress was cut out in strategic places, exposing much bare flesh. On her feet were lace-up black boots covering zebra-striped tights. Cheap plastic jewellery jangled from her person like baubles from a Christmas tree. One ear – pierced four times – held four different earrings.

"Holy shit!" Eddie exclaimed as they stopped and took stock of their surroundings. "This place is a freakin' palace!"

"Yeah," Heaven said confidently. "And I'm the visiting princess!"

Chapter 19

Jade, Antonio and friends demolished four bottles of red wine and all of the delicious Chinese tidbits before leaving for the party at ten. Antonio's companions were an animated group. One makeup artist with a pageboy bob and oriental eyes. One hair stylist with the thinnest body Jade had ever seen. And one U.S.C. film student, who was obviously Antonio's latest love.

The student, who had only consumed one glass of wine, drove Antonio's Cadillac Seville. They entered Bel Air by the West Gate, and immediately got lost. There were loud shrieks of "This way! That way!" Contradicted with "*Down* the hill, not up. We're going around in circles."

Jade had no idea where she was, it was all foreign territory to her.

Al Jarreau blared from the car stereo as they drove up and down the hills.

They found the house by accident an hour later.

The guard at the gate glared suspiciously into the car.

"Spray perfume, darling," Antonio stage-whispered. "Otherwise he get stoned just breathing our air!"

Jade obliged with a quick spritz of Opium. The Cadillac was alive with the fumes of the joint Antonio's friends had been enjoying.

"Thank you!" squealed the makeup artist.

The guard consulted his guest list, found Antonio's name, and waved them on.

★

When Heaven and Eddie swaggered into the party, Jack had just persuaded Clarissa to leave. Coming across his errant niece on her way in stopped him abruptly. "I don't believe this!" he said.

"Uncle Jack. What are *you* doing here?"

"God knows. More important, why are *you* here?"

"Beats me," she shrugged. "It seemed like a good idea at the time!" She giggled. "This is Eddie. Y'know, I told you about him. I sing with his group."

Jack shook hands formally with the dark-haired boy, and duly introduced Clarissa to them both.

Heaven was impressed. She had heard about Jack's affair with the famous actress, yet she had never met her.

Clarissa was amused by the girl. "So *you're* Heaven," she said, looking her over. "A most unusual name."

"Yup. That's me."

"I like your hair."

"Thanks."

"And your coat."

"Got it at this brilliant place on Melrose."

"You must take me there."

"God! *Me* take *you*!"

Clarissa nodded. "If you're free sometime, we'll go shopping and have lunch."

"Wow! If *I'm* free!"

"Does Silver know you're coming?" Jack interrupted.

"Like I guess so. Nora invited me."

Jack wondered why Nora would do that. He could hardly imagine Silver begging that her daughter be present. She had never taken any notice of Heaven before, why would she start now? Maybe, on her birthday, she'd had a change of heart. Wouldn't *that* be something?

"We're going," he said. "Try and have a good time – although somehow I don't think this is quite your scene."

Heaven pulled on the sleeve of his jacket. "Uncle Jack. Eddie's car broke down comin' over the canyon. How'll we get back to the Valley?"

She was exasperating, but he loved her anyway. "Is that my problem?"

She giggled. "It is now." One thing about Uncle Jack she knew for sure – he was always there for her, which is more than she could say for her mother.

He groped in his pocket and produced some bills. Peeling off a couple of fifties he said, "Have Nora call a cab when you're ready to leave." He peered at his watch. "And don't make it too long. Your curfew's still twelve, isn't it?"

"Yup."

"Don't break it."

"Nope."

"And if you do something normal with your hair we'll take you out to dinner one night."

"What's normal?" she asked innocently.

He touched her cheek affectionately. "*You're* certainly not. I love you anyway, kid." He nodded at Eddie, and said curtly, "Look after her, or you'll have *me* to reckon with."

"Yes sir!" replied Eddie, standing to attention.

"Isn't he the best?" Heaven said as she watched him go. "And you know something – she's nice too. Like not big-time or any of that film star crap. Don't you agree?"

Eddie wasn't listening. His eyes were popping. He was star-tripping and loving every minute.

*

"How do you like my niece?" Jack asked, putting his arm

protectively around Clarissa's shoulder as he guided her towards the front door.

"I think she's a lost little girl."

"She needs her mother," Jack said tightly. "Only she's never going to get her. Silver lives only for herself."

"Maybe she has to," Clarissa replied. "She's created the image – every day she must fuel the fire."

"What a wise lady," he said, "for an actress!"

He handed his parking ticket to an attentive valet who leaped forward. "Coming right up, Mr Python."

"And you are a rude man, Mr Python," Clarissa mocked.

He studied her long pale face and the intense eyes. "Let me take you home and show you just how rude I can be, *Miz* Browning."

She nodded and allowed the anticipation to begin.

The parking valets were not expecting any new arrivals. They were busy jockeying the cars for departing guests when Antonio and his group drove up.

"Is everyone leaving?" Antonio asked, jumping from the car and flapping his hands.

"No sir," replied a surfer type. "Just a few people."

"Dahlings!" Antonio spotted Jack and Clarissa.

They broke away from each other and greeted the famous photographer. He was – as usual – surrounded by a group of eccentric misfits who came piling out of his car. Among them was a great-looking girl Jack knew he had seen somewhere before. He did a classic double-take, and immediately wished he hadn't, for Clarissa missed nothing.

The girl was tall and slim, with direct, challenging eyes, a sensual body, and a tumble of copper hair piled on top of her head. Her eyes flicked right past his intent gaze as if he didn't exist. Jack was used to more attention than that.

"Your car, Mr Python," said the parking valet, holding open the door.

"*Divine* to see you both," sighed Antonio. "And such a *surprise!*"

Jack climbed into his Ferrari, revved the engine, and shot off a little too fast.

Clarissa rested her hand on his thigh. "Home," she said coolly. "And get that bimbo off your mind. You are no longer stud of the year. Remember?"

How well she knew him.

*

96

"Let's get out of here," Mannon said.

"Any time you want," Melanie-Shanna responded obediently, anxious to be alone with him so she could tell him their good news.

Mannon had endured more than enough of viewing his ex-wife across a crowded party. He wanted her back so badly he could taste it, and he was in no mood to watch her with the likes of Chuck Nielson.

He planned to call his lawyer first thing in the morning and hammer out a settlement to offer Melanie-Shanna. He wanted to be fair about it – she was a sweet kid, but not for him. Things had to be done at once, even if it did cost him. And then he would be free to concentrate on getting Whitney back.

*

Nora saw Heaven first. At least, she assumed it must be Heaven, for who else could possibly turn up looking like that? She hurried over, almost speechless, and for Nora that was something. "I hardly recognized you," she said.

Heaven grinned cheekily and turned in a circle, her long overcoat trailing behind her. "I'm an original!" she said proudly. "So's Eddie."

Eddie nodded, hungry eyes still scanning the room.

"I can see that," Nora remarked dryly. She hadn't seen Heaven in over a year. The child had certainly changed. Silver would be horrified.

"Eddie an' I, we've got our own group," Heaven confided. "He plays the guitar. I sing an' write all our stuff. We've got a couple of other guys involved – like a drummer an' a second guitar. If you'd given me the word we could've played here tonight."

"Not quite suitable," Nora said quickly. "Have you seen your . . . er . . . Silver?"

"Nope." Heaven ran her hands through her spiked hair, pulling at it to make sure it stood at attention.

"I'll take you over," Nora volunteered. She knew it had to be done, and she was the one to do it.

"Sure," Heaven said casually. "C'mon, Eddie."

The two of them followed Nora across the room, and outside to the tented patio where Silver held court at a table for ten. She was in the middle of telling a joke, and the other people at the table listened with rapt attention – waiting for the punch line. "I don't recognize Elvis," Silver concluded, barely controlling her own laughter. "But the one in the middle is Willie Nelson!"

The entire table broke up.

Nora took the opportunity to grab her attention. "Look who's here," she said.

Silver turned graciously, ready to greet yet another power broker or fellow star. When she saw Heaven she visibly blanched. "God God!" she said. "What have you *done* to yourself? You look *dreadful*!"

Only Nora observed the flash of pain which flitted quickly across the girl's face. And then a rebellious expression took over, the amber eyes hardened, and Heaven blurted, "Gee, mom, nothing changes. You're still as old-fashioned as ever."

Silver didn't like *that*. She stood up from the table to prevent her guests from hearing any more, and said in a low voice, "And you're as rude as ever, I see."

"I guess it runs in the family, mommy dearest," Heaven replied defiantly.

"Don't call me that," Silver hissed, and glared at Nora as if to say – *I told you so*.

Nora shrugged. "C'mon kids," she said, "I'll get you some food."

Eddie was not to be shifted so quickly. He stuck his hand in Silver's direction and said in an awe-struck voice, "Miss Anderson, I love your work, you are the very best."

This was news to Heaven, who shot him a filthy look. Eddie. *Her* Eddie. Her confidant and friend. And as of that very afternoon – her lover. He was behaving like a star-struck fan. And to her mother of all people! Outrage enveloped her.

Eddie stood there with a stupid sloppy grin on his face, while Silver bestowed the royal handshake, and even managed a charming smile.

"Garbage city," Heaven muttered to herself, and began to edge away.

"Aren't you going to wish your mother a happy birthday?" Nora said pointedly.

"Oh yeah – Happy birthday, mom." She raced for the bar, leaving Eddie behind – what a geek!

*

By chance, Howard had purchased a small glassine envelope of what he was assured was first-rate Peruvian cocaine. A young actor he knew assured him. And since Howard's connection at the studio (a rather flaky female production executive) was not altogether reliable – there were days when she never even bothered to turn up – he decided to accept the actor's offer of a "great deal". Little did Howard know he was paying twice the amount the actor had given to one of the barmen. He made the buy discreetly, underneath a palm tree out by the pool. "This isn't for me," he explained to the actor, who couldn't have cared less. "It's for a friend."

He felt secure with the coke stashed on his person. So secure, in fact, that he saw no reason why he shouldn't have a small snort on the premises – just to rev himself up.

Finding an empty toilet in the pool house, he laid out a suitable amount of the white powder. It wasn't that he needed it or anything like that, he just felt like testing out his new source – making sure it was primo.

*

"Give me a vodka martini," Heaven said to the barman. She had no idea what a vodka martini was, but it sounded like a sophisticated enough choice.

Rocky checked her out. She looked like she could be a customer. He was carrying Quaaludes and other assorted goodies apart from cocaine. As he fixed her drink he mumbled, "Y'can score anythin' else y'like if you've got the honey."

"What?"

"Honey – money."

She wanted to giggle. Silver, with all her fancy trappings, had ended up with a dealer behind her bar!

"I'm not in the mood for buying," she said haughtily. And then she remembered the money Uncle Jack had handed her, and thought – *Why not?* It certainly wouldn't cost a hundred dollars to get a cab back to the Valley.

"I'll change my mind. Do you have any joints?"

"How many?"

Shrugging vaguely she said, "Three or four."

"Ya look like a rock star, an' ya buy like a kid."

Heaven propped her arms on the bar. "Do you *really* think I look like a rock star?" she asked eagerly.

Rocky, adopting the Stallone stance, said, "Yo, pretty lady."

She gave him a second look. He was of medium height and muscular, with drooping eyes, a funny crooked nose, and a shock of longish black hair. He was an older man, he must be at least thirty, but so what? Eddie was behaving like a jerk-off. He had joined the court of Silver, and a quick glance across the

99

room confirmed that he was *still* hanging onto her mother's every stupid word. "Thanks," she said. "I *am* a singer, only I can never get anyone to listen to my tapes."

"Poor pretty lady," Rocky crooned sympathetically. Lately he liked them younger and younger. This one looked positively illegal. If he wasn't so stoned he would go for her now. "I have a friend in the record biz," he added, thinking he could save her for another time.

"You do?" she asked hopefully.

"Oh yeah yeah yeah, I sure do. He's a good buddy. Maybe I can fix it for him to er . . . hear your tapes."

Her amber eyes sparkled. "Really?"

"If I can do – I will do." He winked suggestively.

"Two brandies," demanded a fat man in a too-tight cummerbund and rented tux.

"Comin' up," said Rocky agreeably. He scribbled his number on a paper napkin and slipped it to her. "Give me a call. Maybe I'll be your manager. I'm the kinda guy can make things happen."

She took the napkin and stuffed it in her pocket. He was probably full of crap. Most people, she had discovered early on in life, were full of crap.

*

Antonio and his group fussed around Jade, keeping her a part of their own private circle. "You're a new face in town," Antonio warned. "So, *cara*, we protect you."

"Come *on*," she laughed. "I'm the *last* person who needs protecting. I'm from New York – remember?"

"This is a place filled with beautiful women, but you, *bellissima*, are special."

Jade couldn't help smiling. Antonio the flatterer. He got some of his best pictures that way.

"Okay, okay. I guess I'm surrounded," she sighed grudgingly. "Only I want a running commentary on everyone and everything. For a start – who's that?" She pointed out Heaven, lounging defiantly against the bar hanging onto her vodka martini.

"Who indeed?" echoed Antonio, peering over. "*Another* new face, and one that's not been lifted either."

"She looks completely out of place," Jade remarked. She had already observed that the party was filled with impeccably groomed and well-coiffed women in expensive designer clothes.

"True," agreed Antonio. "And so young. José!" He snapped his fingers at the makeup artist with the careful pageboy bob and oriental eyes. "Bring the young lady over. She has the peculiar style. Maybe I photograph her."

José sprang to his feet.

Jade smiled. "Still collecting strays," she mused.

"It makes the life exciting," agreed Antonio.

Jade looked around the tented patio filled with tables. Dinner was over, and now the party guests table-hopped and danced to the strident disco music. Antonio had commandeered his own table, and he proceeded to point people out as they boogied past. He had a line of gossip on everyone. "*She* take the heroin." "*He* a bigamist." "*She* in the porno films." "*He* only like two women."

"Stop!" Jade held up her hand sternly. "I don't want to know any of this."

"Why?" inquired Antonio, quite hurt by her lack of interest. "Is true."

"I don't care."

"You *should* know these things now you live here, *cara*," he said huffily.

"Why?"

"Why . . . she ask me why . . .?" He trailed off as José brought Heaven to their table.

The girl was indeed an original. Very pretty. And young. Glowingly, vibrantly *young*.

*

Silver wanted the evening to end. Fortunately people were beginning to depart. She couldn't be more pleased. She had a strong desire to strangle Nora. Did the stupid woman honestly expect her to be thrilled and delighted by Jack's presence? Not to mention Heaven, who arrived late looking like a reject from a rock concert.

She had struggled long and hard to regain the title Silver Anderson — Superstar. And tonight was to have been her crowning triumph. Now everything was ruined by her daughter and her brother. Just the very sight of them put her in a bad mood, and what the hell did Nora think she was gaining by inviting them?

Poppy Soloman tapped her on the shoulder to say goodbye. "We *must* have lunch," Poppy gushed.

"I'm far too busy for lunch," Silver dismissed her crisply. Then, remembering that Poppy was married to Howard Soloman, and Howard *was* the head of Orpheus, she added, "Perhaps dinner." There was no reason, now she was a major television star again, that she couldn't return triumphantly to the big screen.

"I'll *give* a dinner for you," Poppy promised.

"What a nice idea." Silver warmed to the plump blonde with the pink and white complexion. They had hardly spoken before, although both realized the advantages of a dinner party in Silver Anderson's honour.

"I'll have *my* secretary call *your* secretary," Poppy said, well versed in Hollywood protocol.

"Do that," replied Silver graciously, and moved on to the next departing guest.

Chapter 20

Wes had back-ache. He surveyed the stragglers at the party and wished they would all go the fuck home. He was tired and fed-up, not even slightly bombed, while Rocky was stoned out of his head.

Rocky was a dangerous friend to have. He was heading for big trouble, and Wes had no intention of being dragged along for the ride. Selling a small amount of cocaine on the side was one thing, but as soon as Rocky realized he had more customers than he could handle, he made a call and dispatched Wes to the front gate to accept a fresh delivery. Some black dude in a white stretch limo arrived all set to join the party.

"No *way*," Wes told him. "It's a private event."

"C'mon, man, you look like y'can get me inside," the occupant of the limo coaxed. "There'll be somethin' sweet 'n' extra for you. I just *looove* that Silver Lady. She's got *reeeeeal* style."

"Sorry," Wes said firmly, accepting delivery and hurrying back up the drive before the guard at the gate became suspicious.

Rocky was way gone even then, and while he developed his lucrative sideline, Wes got to fix everything from a Marguerita to a frozen strawberry daiquiri. And he was pissed off. Rocky was making all the money while *he* was doing all the work. Fuck it! Rocky was treating him like a paid lackey, not a loyal friend who was kindly helping out.

Wes did not like fixing drinks for rich jerk-offs in dinner jackets and their ladies – if that was the right description. Most of the women had tight mouths, and anyone who knew a thing or two about the female sex knew if their mouths were tight their pussies were too. Waiting to get laid. The guys were so busy with their big deals and their drug habits, they didn't have time to service their old ladies. And usually the broad wasn't old *or* a lady.

Wes knew these things. He had worked enough bars around town and listened to enough stories.

Working a bar in a club was a whole different ball game. There, he was his own boss. He had attitude and authority – even a little bit of power. Working bar at a party it seemed he was just hired help. A servant. At everyone's beck and call.

Wes decided no more favours. He was nobody's errand boy.

*

"And so," Heaven continued, "like Eddie formed this group, an' I sing an' write the songs. And we're really, *really*, totally brilliant!"

"What do you call yourselves?" asked Jade.

"The Rats," Eddie joined in. Boy, was he having a good time! Not only had he got to meet Silver Anderson, now he was sitting talking to this fantastic model whom he'd seen on television in the sexiest freakin' commercial ever! What did it matter that Heaven was ignoring him – he was on a roll!

"The Rats!" Jade repeated with distaste.

"No *bene*, dahling," interrupted Antonio – ignoring Eddie and concentrating on Heaven. "You must have a name – people they love – they remember."

"Heaven and the Boys," Jade suggested.

"No! No! No! I have it!" exclaimed Antonio. "*Heavenly Bodies!* What a name! *Heavenly Bodies*. It must be. Antonio, he say so."

"I don't know . . ." Heaven cocked her head on one side, enjoying all the attention.

"What about *me*?" interjected Eddie. "I can't be in a group called Heavenly Bodies. It sounds like we're all freakin' dead! We're called the Rats. And we're not changin' our name. Nobody's complained before."

Antonio dismissed him with a wave of his elegantly manicured hand. "Tonight things they change," he stated. "I, Antonio, have decided to help this young lady to succeed." He smiled benevolently at Heaven. "The same as her mama, she too will be the big star."

"Wow, and you haven't even heard me sing," Heaven protested, thrilled by this unexpected turn of events, yet also frightened lest she didn't live up to this funny little man's expectations.

"Ah, but I don't need to," Antonio said with a Cheshire Cat smile. "When Antonio decide to photograph someone, that someone become the star. Antonio *smell* talent!"

★

Vladimir's kitchen was almost clear. The Chinese caterers had departed, and only a few waiters and the two barmen remained, servicing the last guests who seemed reluctant to leave, even though Madame Silver had retired upstairs at least half an hour ago.

Vladimir had his eye on the waiters *and* the barmen. The end of any party was a dangerous time. That was when bottles of liquor, bar implements, and cartons of cigarettes always seemed to mysteriously vanish. Vladimir checked everyone at the back door as they prepared to leave. He double-checked a waiter who vaguely resembled Rob Lowe. He sent out signals, and the young man responded.

"Vould you care for a night hat in my apartment?" Vladimir tempted.

"Sure," the waiter responded.

"Good, good." Vladimir was excited. He had been eyeing the boy all night. "Valk across the courtyard to the garage. Vait for me." He gave a winning smile, and shooed him on his way.

Silver Anderson's instructions were explicit: "No entertaining on my premises." Surely she did not consider *his* apartment above the garage her premises?

"Hey, chief." Wes smiled his way through the kitchen. "I'm taking off."

Vladimir eagle-eyed him. He seemed contraband-less.

Wes eased himself out the back door. Most of the fags who

ran these rich houses didn't know their ass from a hole in the ground. This Russian dude was checking him over because it was the end of the evening, and yet at the beginning of the evening he had calmly walked past him with a full box of booze and not a question asked. Stupid.

Rocky was stupid too. Somewhere along the way Wes had made a couple of scores of his own with the new supply of cocaine, and Rocky hadn't even noticed. When he woke up in the morning maybe he'd realize – maybe not. That's what happened when you snorted your own business.

Getting into his car Wes took a long deep breath. He was tired. Exhausted. Tomorrow was another day. A Sunday. He planned to sleep it through.

Chapter 21

The morning after the party . . .

Silver Anderson stirred at noon, adjusted her royal-blue sleep mask, and returned to a wonderful dream about herself.

Jack Python was up at seven. Swam twenty lengths in Clarissa's pool, then drove to his hotel and worked on ideas for his upcoming series of shows.

Clarissa Browning waited until she heard his car leave, and then arose and spent a solitary day absorbing her latest role. She enjoyed being alone.

Howard Soloman surfaced. Felt lousy. Snorted coke. And played three sets of punishing tennis with a movie star, another studio head, and a female executive they all wanted to fuck.

Poppy Soloman covered her face in rejuvenating creams, submitted to a thorough massage from a sadistic woman with a genteel voice and cruel hands, and spent the remainder of the day gossiping on the phone.

Jade Johnson, got up at ten. Dressed in sweats. Went to a

coffee shop, had breakfast (prune juice and a danish), bought the papers and a selection of magazines, and spent the day by herself.

Mannon Cable left his bed at eight. Called his lawyer at eight-fifteen and had a lengthy discussion about how to get rid of Melanie-Shanna.

Melanie-Shanna Cable left her bed at nine, marched into the kitchen where Mannon was on the phone, and announced that she was pregnant.

The rest of their day was spent in long discussions.

Whitney Valentine Cable woke up on Chuck Nielson's water bed in his Malibu beach house. They made love – which he was very good at. Afterwards they managed to consume a large breakfast, then they swam in the ocean and lazily sunbathed.

Wes Money was disturbed by the phone at eleven o'clock. "Get lost, whoever you are," he mumbled into the receiver. It was a woman. Naturally. Why did they find him so goddamn irresistible?

He was forced to say she could come over. Which she did. And he was sorry, because he was too tired to get it up, and she was determined to have at least three orgasms.

They parted company on bad terms, and he went straight back to sleep.

Heaven floated through the day planning what totally brilliant outfit she could wow the great Antonio with when she turned up for the photo session he had promised her.

Vladimir got rid of the young waiter early in the morning, and spent the rest of the day agonizing over his latest conquest. How could he continue to be so indiscriminate when dreaded disease roamed the streets?

Later, dressed in red, he cruised Santa Monica, and took home a sixteen-year-old runaway who did unspeakable things with his queen-size tongue.

Silver Anderson would have a fit if she knew what went on above her garage.

Fortunately she didn't.

Another lazy Sunday drifted by.

Somewhere in the Midwest . . .
Sometime in the seventies . . .

The girl put up with the unwelcome attentions of her father for almost two years. After his initial attack she learned to stay out of his way as much as possible, and with her mother home from the hospital it was not so easy for him to get to her.

But he managed. In spite of her fear and pain. He grabbed her whenever he could, and forced himself on her.

She was too ashamed to tell anyone, for she blamed herself for tempting him, and withdrew into a shell, unwilling to make friends or mix with the other children at the local school she attended. Whenever she could she avoided school altogether. There was a place in the woods she could hide, a large oak tree with a hollow in its trunk she could squeeze into. For hours she would stay there, curled in a ball, her arms wrapped around her knees, her thoughts tumbling around in her head.

She loved her mother. She didn't want to hurt her.

She hated her father. She would gladly kill him.

When she was almost fifteen she got her first period. The blood confused and shocked her. It was just like the first night when he'd mounted and thrust into her. Now the blood was back again. Bad blood. A sign she was unclean.

When her father found out he mumbled drunkenly, "We gotta be careful. Can't getcha in the family way. Can't do that."

But he wasn't careful, and it was only when her stomach began to swell that she realized with horror that a baby was beginning to grow inside her.

She didn't know who to turn to or what to do. Her mother was sick again, and back in the hospital. Her father found himself a lady friend and brought her to the house. The woman was big, with huge, floppy breasts and a raucous laugh.

The girl cowered in her bed and listened to their animal sounds.

When her mother died, the woman moved in permanently. That same night, at three in the morning, they came for her, the two of them. They were drunk and mean-spirited, out to have some fun.

. The woman watched while the man stripped the cover from his daughter's bed, and the thin nightdress from her young body.

The girl began to scream, but the sound of her anguished cries was cut off when he covered her mouth with the palm of his hand. With a grunt he fell on top of her and roughly began to thrust with brutal strength, while the woman crowed her encouragement and urged him on.

The girl felt waves of nausea. She pushed his heavy body away and begged him to stop. His weight was crushing her so she could hardly breathe. He was hurting her.

When the pains started she knew with an ominous feeling of dread that something was wrong. In vain she continued to struggle. It did her no good.

When he was through the woman took her turn, using anything that amused her to torment the girl.

And at last it was over. The two of them staggered off, too drunk to care.

Silently, in unbelievable pain, the girl staggered to the outhouse. Her body was racked with contractions, as thick trails of blood trickled down her thighs.

Squatting on the floor, all alone, she witnessed the birth of her baby. Only it wasn't a baby, it was a four-month-old foetus, and when the girl felt strong enough to walk, she wrapped it in a towel, took it to her favourite tree, and buried it in the earth.

After that there was only one thing left to do.

She was calm as she collected a can of gasoline from beneath the kitchen sink, and poured it around the perimeter of the small wooden house.

Lighting the first match was easy. . . .

BOOK TWO

Hollywood, California
June 1985

Chapter 22

"What do you want out of life, Miss Anderson?" the English journalist asked. She was a middle-aged woman with brittle looks and dyed yellow hair. She was a failed actress, a failed singer, and a failed writer of novels. Finally she had made her mark with a weekly page in a London daily newspaper, and was now known for her vitriolic dislike of successful actresses, singers, and novelists. She attacked them in print whenever she could.

Silver summoned up a meaningful look. "Happiness," she said wistfully. "After thirty years in this business I think I deserve it, don't you?"

The journalist, who went by the unfortunate name of Cyndi Lou Planter, and looked like a man in drag, leaned closer to the famous star to see if she could spot any signs of a face lift or an eye job. Alas, nothing, except a mask of smooth, expertly applied makeup. Later, when she wrote her piece she would say:

> Silver Anderson exists beneath a two-inch layer of Max
> Factor. While relentlessly pursuing a thirty-year career she
> searches for happiness. Maybe if she scraped off some of
> her makeup she'd have a better chance of finding it.

"You certainly *do* deserve it," Cyndi Lou Planter gushed. The poison oozed from her pen, not her lips. She was too much of a coward to insult anyone to their face.

"Thank you." Silver smiled graciously. "That's very kind of you."

Where the hell is Nora? she thought. This Planter woman with her phoney smile and dull, unoriginal questions was getting on her nerves. Apart from anything else she had body odour, and the room was beginning to stink.

Nora! Silently she summoned her publicist.

Magically Nora appeared. Cyndi Lou Planter's hour was up, and Nora knew how to get rid of them better than anyone.

Silver rose and offered the journalist a friendly handshake. She was aware that the woman was a bitch, in print and out. So what? Someone had once said *As long as they spell your name right.* Yes. And possibly Ms. Planter could just about manage that.

Silver retired to her bedroom while Nora got rid of the journalist. She was the last in a day of interviews for England. *Palm Springs* was to be shown on television there, and they wanted immediate impact. The English company that had bought the series had asked Silver to fly to London for a week. She wasn't sure if she wanted to. England conjured up mixed memories. It was the scene of her lowest point in life, and although she had made a miraculous comeback, she was not sure if she ever wanted to return. Hence the parade of journalists through her house.

Nora bustled into the room. "Done!" she announced triumphantly.

"Thank God!" replied Silver, stretching with relief. "Nobody can ever say I don't work hard for my money."

Nora had to agree. Silver never stopped. Her energy level was quite incredible. Mere twenty-year-olds would kill for her dynamic vigour.

"Tonight's the opening of that new restaurant you promised Fernando you'd attend," Nora reminded. "Do you need me to come with you?"

"Dennis is taking me," Silver said with a sigh.

Dennis Denby was the latest in a long line of escorts. He was thirty years old, blandly good-looking, the son of a well-known producer and his socialite wife. Dennis, who ran his own advertising agency, was quite amusing and very ambitious. He was also reasonably adequate in bed. However, he did have one major drawback. From the age of twenty-one, Dennis had systematically bedded every married woman over thirty-five in Hollywood. It seemed to be an obsession with him, and Silver was not sure she liked being on the end of a very long assembly line.

They had been dating for several weeks, and he was certainly a personable escort. The problem was she found she couldn't really take him seriously.

"I thought you'd be bored with him by now," Nora remarked intuitively.

Silver laughed. "When the plate is empty you pick up the crumbs." With a knowing nod she added, "Especially when one is hungry."

Nora squinted with amusement. Silver Anderson's sexual appetite was legendary, dating back to times when it wasn't fashionable for a woman to demand equal rights in bed. Silver had always defied convention when it came to the male sex. If she ever wrote her autobiography it would be a regular *Who's Who* of famous and attractive men — although she was proud of claiming never to have slept with anyone to further her career.

"Who am I to say how hungry you are?" Nora remarked cynically. "But licking the plate is a bit much!"

Silver laughed wickedly. "It's not the plate I lick!"

Nora was the only one who could criticize and get away with it. Silver enjoyed the feisty honesty of her publicist, whom she also regarded as a good friend.

Growing up in show business, Silver had never had time to make friends. Hundreds of acquaintances, and now that she was a star again — thousands. None of them cared about her as a person; all they were interested in was getting close enough to bask in the stardust — hoping that a little of it would rub off on them. Dennis Denby was a perfect example. He *adored* going out with her. He revelled in the attention, the photographers, the fans.

He didn't love her. That was okay, she didn't love him either. They were both using each other for their own purposes.

Silver tried to remember the last time she was in love, and couldn't. It was years since she'd experienced the exhilarating flush of being with someone just because . . .

She was forty-seven years old. Too experienced, too wise, too famous.

*

Wes Money did not know how he ever got into the position of having to take Reba Winogratsky, his landlady, out on a date. *Just luck, I guess*, he thought, as he struggled into his only suit, and tried to hide the frays around the collar of his one white shirt.

Last week, Reba had turned up alone. No Mexican maid or fat son in tow. She had collected the back rent he owed, prowled around the house, and then sprawled on his couch and confided what a bastard her husband was. It seems she had caught him in bed with his secretary, and all hell broke loose.

"I am taking that scurvy son of a bitch for every dime he ever made," she announced. "I am gettin' me the best shit-hot lawyer in America!"

"Good idea," Wes responded, wishing she'd remove her waxed legs and vindictive expression from his couch.

"The man's a cockroach!" she declared. "Lower than a cockroach!" And angry tears rolled down her over-rouged cheeks.

Naturally, good old Wes Money had to console her. And somehow that consoling had ended up with him on top of her investigating the private parts of his landlady, who drove a new Mercedes, only wanted cash, and called her husband a scurvy son of a bitch cockroach.

He wouldn't have minded, but he didn't even get a rent rebate. Just an invitation to the opening of a new restaurant she had invested in. Reba, he discovered, had a passion for cash and sex. In that order.

He should never have started with her. Too late now.

She arrived, dressed for the occasion in a tighter than tight green lurex dress, hooker ankle-strap stiletto heels, and a silver mink jacket. Her dyed red hair was teased into a bird's-nest, and her leathery face and flinty eyes were inexpertly loaded with the best Elizabeth Arden had to offer. She smelled of Blue Grass.

"Hello, sailor," she said, with a crooked leer, and he detected an excess of whiskey on her breath.

"Hello, Reba," he replied, and wondered how he was going to extract himself from *this* one and still run a month late on his rent.

Chapter 23

The studio audience buzzed with anticipation. Jack Python was back in stride, and they loved him. Unlike Carson and Letterman and Merv, he did not sit behind a desk; he operated from a square table for two, just him and his guest – a probing, hour-long confrontation. Unlike Donahue he did not roam through his audience with the hypnotizing speed of a tornado. He took it easy, sometimes loosening his tie (he always wore one) or taking off his jacket. He made his guests feel comfortable. So comfortable, in fact, that sometimes (most times) they forgot about the eager, intent audience, and the intrusive cameras, and chatted as if it was just Jack they were talking to.

He drew them out gradually, carefully. And because he only had one guest a week, he was able to read every piece of research, and decide which questions he wanted to ask. No researchers pointed Jack Python in the direction they wanted him to go. He did it his way.

Today he talked to a bespectacled film-maker who rarely did interviews. The man was a genius, an autocrat and an egomaniac. Layer by layer Jack exposed him, and the reasons he was the way he was became clear.

The audience hardly dared to breathe. They devoured the one-to-one conversation. Jack Python brought them truth, and they respected him for it. He was the perfect American combination: brains and looks. All the Kennedy brothers had possessed it, and Jack Python had been told that if he wanted it, a political future lay ahead. With his amazing popularity and keen awareness he was a prime candidate for an electoral position. He had already been approached by a group with the money to back him should he ever express a desire to run for the Senate.

"That's crazy!" he'd said at first. But when they explained

where his popularity could get him, he hadn't been so sceptical. Hence his all-out effort to clean up his act with the ladies, just in case he wanted to give it a shot.

The show was nearly over. Jack observed "wind up" signals from his producer, and he gently cut off his guest, who was revealing more than he'd come out with in almost ten years of analysis.

Spontaneously the audience began to applaud. A genuine wave of real appreciation. The applause signs hadn't even been raised.

Jack thanked his guest, who was determined to keep talking. They shook hands. Camera one panned back and the lights lowered. As the credits ran, the two men were shown in silhouette.

The show was over.

Jack wanted to get up and race for the shower, only it was never that easy. Extracting himself from the guests was the most difficult part. For an hour he had been their sympathetic, interested, questioning friend, drawing things out that they might never have talked about before – especially not in public. Now it was finished, and with few exceptions they always seemed to need to keep talking.

The women were the worst. Most of them wanted to end the conversation in bed, and once upon a time so be it. Usually he was very careful, and his only slip with a guest, since being with Clarissa, was with a small, rounded movie actress who had such a puppy-dog desire to be loved that he hadn't had the heart to say no. She apologized throughout their lovemaking for everything about herself. Then she fixed him a dish of nourishing lentil soup, and sent him back to Clarissa with the promise that she would never tell.

Fortunately she kept her word, and was now married to a dog trainer. It seemed a suitable match.

Jack's producer, Aldrich Pane, came to the rescue as usual, giving Jack the signal to vanish while he brought the guest down from the Python high.

Jack didn't hesitate. Straight to his dressing room, under the shower, a release of all thoughts.

Half an hour later he was dressed, refreshed, and sitting in the control room watching a tape of the live programme. Aldrich usually joined him, and they had their own private wake if the show was bad, and a celebration if it really took off.

The most important element was the guest. If the guest worked, the show did. If the guest was a dud, everything collapsed.

Tonight was a gem, which pleased both men. It meant an excellent rating for the week. Usually they were somewhere in the top ten.

"Betcha we'll be in the big five," Aldrich said, beaming happily.

Jack agreed. Finding the right guest to carry an hour was never easy, and when it worked as well as it had done tonight it was a good feeling. Especially when he was right, which had just been proven. None of the production team had wanted the reclusive, bespectacled film-maker: they had all claimed he wouldn't talk. What a joke! It had been difficult to shut him up.

"I'll see you tomorrow," Jack said, striding out to his car.

Aldrich waved goodbye. They made a good team. Aldrich had all the patience Jack lacked, and Jack was the driving force. When *Face to Face with Python* went on the air, Jack had insisted on bringing Aldrich in as producer. They had worked together on *The Python Beat* in Houston, and Jack knew he was the right choice. Aldrich moved with his wife and children to Los Angeles, and years later the weekly hour-long programme was hotter than ever.

Driving back into Beverly Hills on the freeway, Jack pushed a tape into the deck and listened to his personal assistant, Aretha, reading off some of his mail. She had the most delightful sing-song voice, and a smile to match. He had found Aretha when he was working in Chicago. At the time she was making coffee around the studio and not much else. Jack spotted potential, and wangled her a job as production assistant. When L.A. happened, he called and asked if she was interested in being his right hand. "Jack, honey, I'd be anything for you," she enthused, and caught the next plane out. She was black, weighed two hundred and twenty pounds, and everyone loved her. Including Jack. He called Aldrich and Aretha his two A's, and swore he'd never get through the day without them.

The traffic was heavier than usual, and by the time he reached Hollywood he was wiped out. He called Clarissa on the car phone and told her he was running late. "Did you watch me?" he asked, anxious for her opinion if not her praise.

"Why should I watch you?" she said, quite seriously. "I'm seeing you soon."

One of the things he hated about Clarissa was that she took no interest whatsoever in his work. She *knew* he liked her to watch. Was it a conscious effort to annoy him that she never did?

"Listen, I'm kind of tired," he said. "I'm going to sleep at the hotel tonight."

Her voice sharpened a fraction. "If you want."

"Yeah. I'm not much company."

"Very well."

There was no *I'll miss you — I'll massage your back — I'll look after you.*

Was *that* what attracted him to Clarissa? Her aloofness. Her undemonstrative attitude. Or did he just like being with her because she was an Oscar-winning actress and not some Hollywood bimbette?

He shook his head. Ecstatically in love he wasn't. The truth was he never had been. He was thirty-nine years old with everything going for him. He had experienced one short marriage which had scared him to death, and legions of women. And yet he just didn't know.

Love.

It probably didn't even exist.

Chapter 24

"Good evening," said Dennis Denby.

"Good evening," sneered Vladimir.

Dennis raised a quizzical eyebrow. "May I come in?"

Vladimir allowed him to do so reluctantly. Vladimir was very possessive about Madame Anderson, and this one did not strike him as one of Madame's better escorts. Vladimir had preferred last month's, a caustic New York man-about-town who cracked incessant jokes, and tipped handsomely.

Dennis Denby walked into the library and began to pour himself a drink.

Following him accusingly, Vladimir edged him out of the way. "My job," he said, taking over. Not that he wanted to make Dennis Denby a drink, but his familiar way in Madame's home infuriated Vladimir.

Dennis walked to the nearest mirror and inspected himself. He was nice looking, if somewhat slight. Beverly Hills born and bred he had manners, style, and a rakish way of dressing. Tonight he wore a canary-yellow jacket over a pin-stripe shirt, and black silk Italian trousers with patent leather shoes. On anyone else the outfit might have looked odd, but Dennis managed to carry it off with great aplomb.

"Will you let Miss Anderson know I'm here," he said to Vladimir as the houseman handed him his drink.

Vladimir wondered if Dennis Denby travelled both roads, and decided he did. Poor Madame. She probably didn't suspect. Maybe he should drop a gentle hint – although Madame's escorts barely lasted longer than a month, so this one's time was almost up. "I vas just going to do so," Vladimir said, the sneer fixed firmly on his face.

Dennis decided to say something to Silver about her houseman. The man had an attitude problem. Trust Silver to employ a Russian.

*

Reba insisted on driving.

"I see you've still got your friend's Mercedes," Wes remarked dryly.

Reba extracted a piece of gum from the glove compartment and stuck it in her mouth. "I'll let you in on a little secret, Wesley," she said confidentially. "This car belongs to my husband. I didn't wanna tell anyone, cos – well ... y'know, what with me goin' around collectin' rent an' all. But yup, it's the scurvy bastard's set of wheels, an' now, goddamn it, it's mine." She chewed gum and went red in the face. "Just let the shithead try t'get it back from me an' I'll crush his balls in the blender."

Wes went pale at the thought. "Has he moved out?"

"You betcha ass he has."

"So you're alone?"

She shot him a suspicious look as the powerful car careened down Pico away from the beach. "No, Wesley, I am not alone. I have a son and a maid and a German Shepherd. I am *certainly* not alone. And the last thing I need is a roommate."

"I wasn't offering," he said quickly.

She continued to chew gum. "Maybe, maybe not. I know I'm a catch — what with all the alimony I'll be gettin' an' everything. Not to mention the car an' the house." She paused reflectively. "I'll be very . . . sought after."

"I'm sure you will," he said. *And not by me.*

Taking one hand off the wheel she patted his knee. "That's not to say I don't like you. Only I can't reduce your rent — I need the money — so don't even ask."

"I didn't."

"I'm tellin' you just in case."

He decided to develop Herpes. Again. Preferably tomorrow.

To change the subject he said, "What does your old man do, anyway?"

The car roared down Pico. Silence for only a moment. "He's in the Mob," Reba said, adding spitefully, "an' any time the cops want me t'sing — I'm ready."

Wes almost choked. A moonlight flit was definitely in order.

*

The great car discussion went on outside Silver's house. Should they take Dennis's car, a snappy Porsche? Or would Silver's white Rolls-Royce be more suitable? They decided on the Rolls, with Dennis driving.

Silver wore a red Adolfo suit with a beige lace blouse. Tasteful rubies adorned her ears and throat, and for a change of look she featured a chic short wig.

"I wish you'd told me you were wearing yellow," she said, a trifle irritably.

"We don't clash," observed Dennis. "We complement."

"Hmmm . . ." She narrowed her eyes. "Yellow photographs better than red. Are we getting used to seeing ourself on the cover of the *National Enquirer*?"

Dennis laughed self-consciously. She was right, he *had* given some consideration to the way his outfit would photograph. The paparazzi adored and worshipped Silver Anderson. Every time she appeared anywhere they whipped themselves into a frenzy. If he was beside her he certainly wished to stand out, not fade into the background like most of her previous escorts.

The restaurant they were going to was called the Garden of Delight, and it was owned by the lover of Fernando, Silver's hairdresser, and two lesbian friends of his. Silver had agreed to appear as a favour. She knew her being there on opening night would guarantee the place maximum publicity and possible success.

Ah . . . power . . . She did so enjoy it.

*

"There's a rumour," Reba confided, "that Silver Anderson's gonna turn up tonight."

Wes didn't believe it for a moment. Why would Silver Anderson honour a gay hang-out like the Garden of Delight with her presence? He eyed the crush in the pink and white candy-striped room. "I doubt it," he said.

"Anyway," Reba said accusingly, shrugging off her mink jacket, "I thought you was gonna get me her autographed picture for my little boy."

"Next time."

Reba flung her mink jacket at him as if he were her personal maid. "You don't even know her," she remarked scornfully. "Check that in, an' be sure t'get a ticket. I don't wanna lose it *thankyouverymuch*."

He fought his way through fag city to the door, where a girl in black leather accepted the jacket and handed him a numbered claim-check. "Silver Anderson's coming here tonight," she confided excitedly. "Don't you just *a-dore* her in *Palm Springs*?"

"Never miss it," he lied, and considered ducking out. Why was everyone telling *him* about Silver Anderson? As if he cared. Although he *had* been in her bedroom, and if this group knew there'd be mass heart failure.

By the time he got back to Reba she was guzzling cheap pink champagne while talking to an undersized man with a huge buoyant quiff of silver hair and matching eyebrows. "Boyce," she said, a perfect Miss Manners. "Meet Wesley."

"*Looove* your frayed collar," Boyce trilled, "*Very Miami Vice*."

"*Looove* your hair," Wes responded, quick as a flash. "*Very* Grecian Formula."

Boyce tossed his head like a frisky pony, and turned away.

"Don't be rude," Reba whispered furiously. "He lives with Silver Anderson's hairdresser."

Wes slapped his forehead in mock horror. "Oh! Jesus Christ! Why didn't you tell me before?"

Reba's mouth tightened into a thin scarlet line.

*

Smile fixed firmly in place, Dennis on her arm, Silver navigated her way through the crowds towards the bar.

The sea of people parted. She was the Queen. They were quite prepared to pay humble homage.

The photographers fought hard for their shots, elbowing and kicking everyone out of their way as they surrounded the star.

"Gangway. Gangway, *please*!" yelled Boyce, who had met Silver once before and was so overcome by her proximity he thought he might faint. He looked desperately around for Fernando, his roommate.

"This place is impossible," Dennis whispered in her ear. "Shall I phone Spago for a table?"

Smiling at her adoring fans, she acknowledged them with a regal wave.

"Silver!" a very young man in a diaphanous caftan screamed. "You're beautiful! We love you! We worship you!"

"Yes, do," she hissed to Dennis. "One drink and we're out of here."

Fernando materialized and all but threw himself at her feet. "You came!"

"Of course I did, darling. You know I wouldn't let you down. I must warn you though, I can only stay ten minutes."

"You're such a loyal person." Fernando's eyes filled with tears of joy. He had produced Silver Anderson, and now – however long she stayed – he would be a hero.

Dennis slipped away to call Spago and warn them of Silver's imminent arrival. The crowd pressed around her. The photographers continued to fight and struggle.

"Gangway!" Boyce pleaded desperately. "Miss Anderson is getting crushed. *Please!*"

Silver's smile became a touch tight around the edges. She didn't notice any security, and Fernando and Boyce were hardly a pair to make one feel secure.

"Silver! Silver! Silver!" The opening night mob swayed with joy as they pressed closer and closer. Over the din the paparazzi's curses flew through the air.

"Don't worry," Fernando said in a panicky voice. "Once we get you to the bar you'll be safe."

Safe? *Safe!* Wasn't she safe now?

Silver began to steam. She was too kind-hearted, that was her trouble. And why hadn't Fernando been *prepared* for her appearance?

A bizarre face straight out of a Fellini movie bobbed in front of her. She couldn't make out if it was a man or a woman. The voice was distinctly deep as it murmured, "You beautiful bitch-goddess. Sing for me! I beg you!"

And then the pushing and the shoving and the quest to get close to her and touch her became seriously dangerous. Fernando's yells of panic filled the air, and a fight started with one of the photographers and a group clad in chains and leather.

Silver felt a clutch of fear. She was going to be loved to death! Oh God! Where was Dennis? And why was she here?

*

Wes smelled trouble before it took place. When you worked bar you knew how to gauge a room. You always had one eye on the something that could happen, and the other on the nearest exit.

"Shit!" he muttered to no one in particular. He was caught up in the crush himself, Reba was nowhere in sight, and when the fight started he knew this was not the place to be. Bad enough for him, because when blows got traded he always managed to catch one. Even worse for Silver Anderson, who was well and truly trapped unless somebody did something fast.

With a weary sigh and a quick scan of the crush he realized he was the only one *capable* of doing anything. The poor woman was on her way to getting trampled underfoot.

"Shit!" he repeated, and moved into action. "L.A.P.D." he shouted authoritatively, causing a minor lull, and giving him enough time to grab Silver's arm and mutter hoarsely, "If you want to get out of here *fast*, come with me and don't waste time asking questions."

He had to hand it to her. She was with him from word one, as he propelled her through the seething mob towards the back exit, giving nobody any time to do anything about it.

They hit the back exit door, and burst out into the parking lot.

"Where's your car?" he asked urgently.

Wordlessly she pointed at the white Rolls parked at the front. He bundled her into the passenger seat, grabbed the keys from a bemused attendant, leaped in himself, and they were on the move just as the crowd and the fight and a hysterical Fernando came pouring out of the door after them.

Chapter 25

For weeks Heaven had been placing phone calls to the great Antonio. Okay, she knew he was a world-famous photographer and all, but *he* had approached *her* at Silver's party, she hadn't asked *him* to do anything. *He* was the one with all the brilliant ideas – telling her she was *young* and *now* and had such a *fabulous look* and he simply *had* to photograph her.

Bull.

Shit.

Another phoney – and she had met enough of *those* along the way. Only this one wasn't going to get off the hook so easily. He had made her a promise, and she was going to see he kept it, however long it took.

Since the party, Eddie had been a complete minus. He was embarrassed because she'd caught him with star-worship in his eyes as he rubber-necked all over the place. And he was pissed off because Antonio hadn't asked *him* to pose. Now he was trying to be Mister Cool again, and he couldn't wait to crow about Antonio not calling her back. "I guess you're not the new Madonna after all," he sneered.

"He's only going to photograph me, not sign me to a record deal," she snapped.

"Yeah. When?"

"Soon."

"You said that last week."

"So?"

He was also pissed off because she wouldn't sleep with him again. Once was enough. She hadn't enjoyed it *that* much, and who needed the hassle of worrying about getting pregnant? At least she wasn't a virgin anymore. No one could tease her about *that*.

One day she hopped into George's car, a slow-moving Chevrolet, and drove over the Canyon to Antonio's studio on Beverly Boulevard. She skipped school to do so. School was a drag anyway; she often took a day off and hung out at the movies or one of the big shopping malls. Once, she had driven over the hill into Hollywood and spent the entire day in Tower Records on Sunset. What a treat! Until two dorks tried to sell her drugs and get her to go to a motel with them. "Bug off," she had told them, which made them pursue her even more.

Heaven liked to think she knew how to look after herself. Living with Silver from birth to ten (give or take the times she was dumped with nannies or left with a strange assortment of her mother's "friends") had certainly made her grow up fast. Most of the times she was with Silver were the lean times – and Heaven remembered them well. She also remembered the pills and the drugs and the booze and the men. Oh, how she remembered the men. Practically every week she acquired a new "uncle".

And then came the really bad days just before Silver's breakdown. There were no men then, nobody to help them when they were evicted from a cheap London hotel for not paying the bill. Thank goodness for Benjii. He was definitely weird on account of the fact that he couldn't make up his mind whether he wanted to be a man or a woman, but he was *very* kindhearted, and took them both in without a murmur.

It was Benjii who told her she had a well-known uncle in America. He helped her locate him, and Uncle Jack came rushing over to rescue her. Life changed after that. With Silver she had lived all over the place and learned to look after herself. Uncle Jack took her to her grandfather's in California, and all of a sudden she was living in a proper house with proper mealtimes and a housekeeper to wash her clothes and make her bed. There was also a school to attend every day. It was all very strange, and took a lot of getting used to. Grandfather George was okay – but it was obvious to everyone that he lived in a world of his own. Uncle Jack was a hunk. He attempted to spend time with her – only it was never enough. Realizing he was very busy, she tried to understand.

Silver never reclaimed her. Heaven could have bet on *that*.

The old Chevrolet chugged grudgingly over the Canyon, slowing everything down behind it. She was only supposed to drive the car to school and back, and she fervently hoped it wouldn't behave like Eddie's Mustang and break down. Uncle Jack had promised her a car for her seventeenth birthday. Who could wait that long? She'd better get her act together and start scoring money of her own. Antonio was the key. If he photographed her then she'd be known, and maybe one of the creeps at the record companies she'd been sending her tapes to would actually *listen* to them.

Unfortunately, Antonio was not at his studio. "He's out on a location shoot," a bored receptionist told her. "You should really call first before coming here."

"I *have* called," Heaven pointed out. "Ten times!"

"Make it eleven," said the receptionist. "Antonio is a very busy man."

Heaven returned to the Valley, dejected but not deterred. She would get to him. Eventually. And when she did, things were going to happen.

Chapter 26

A thousand thoughts went through Silver's head. This man driving her Rolls could be a murderer, a kidnapper, a fan (God forbid!) . . .

She glanced at him sideways. He had an interesting profile, masculine and rugged. And the air of authority he had shown when rescuing her from the crush and spiriting her outside was quite . . . hmmm . . . dare she think it? Horny.

"May I ask exactly who you are?" she demanded haughtily.

"Just call me Robin Hood," he replied.

"Robin Hood stole from the rich and gave to the poor. Is that what *you* intend to do?"

He lightened his foot on the accelerator. "Oh, that's nice," he said. "Really nice. You do a good deed and get kicked in the balls."

She thought she detected the slight trace of a rough English accent. Maybe he was a reporter. She gave him a penetrating look. There was something vaguely familiar about him. "I'd like to know who you are," she repeated crisply. "And exactly where you think you are taking me."

He glanced at her. She liked his eyes – they were knowledgeable eyes, *horny* eyes.

"Listen, lady," he said. "You looked like you might be in a small spot of trouble – like getting crushed to death – y'know what I mean?"

"Maybe," she allowed.

"So I thought I'd do the Good Samaritan bit an' get you out of there." He swerved the powerful car over to the side of the road. "I can always take you back if you like."

"That won't be necessary," she said quickly.

He set the car in motion again. "In that case I'll take you home – an' maybe you'll give me cab fare to get back to my date, who is probably screamin' thief on account of the fact that I ran off with the keys to her car, *and* the ticket for her mink jacket."

"Did you leave your wallet behind along with your girl-friend?" she inquired tartly.

"Naw. I never carry a wallet."

"Where *do* you keep your money?"

"Wherever it'll do me the most good."

She began to laugh. "Who *are* you?" she asked for the third time.

"Just call me Wes," he replied. "An' don't bother with the introductions 'cos I already know who you are."

"*Really?*" Her sarcastic tone was lost on him. "In that case you are one up on me. I'm famous, you're obviously not. What do you do . . . Wes?"

He was enjoying himself for a change. Having a conversation with a woman for a change. Christ, she smelled good. "What perfume are you wearing?" he asked.

"Giorgio. Do you like it?"

"If I don't get asphyxiated by the fumes."

She laughed again. "What *do* you do?"

The Rolls was a dream to drive. He felt quite at home behind the wheel. "A little bit of this, a little bit of that."

She hoped he wasn't an actor.

He read her mind. "I'm not an actor."

"How did you know what I was thinking?"

"It figures." He turned on Fairfax, and headed up towards Sunset.

"I presume you know where I live," she said acidly.

"Yeah, only you'll have to direct me once we get into Bel Air. I always get lost."

"Exactly *how* do you know where I live?" she persisted.

"I bought a stars' map. You were on it."

"Nonsense."

He shot her another glance. She looked different from the night of her party. Then it struck him. "You've cut your hair," he remarked.

His face was definitely familiar. "Do I know you?"

"Not exactly."

"Are you a fan?"

"Are you kidding?"

She was perplexed. Here she was, hurtling through the night in her car exchanging light banter with a complete stranger (although a familiar one), and she wasn't the least bit apprehensive. In fact, she was enjoying herself. "I suppose I should thank you," she said. "It could have been a nasty situation."

"I can see the headlines now," he said. "Five hundred faggots on top of Silver Anderson. Star gives in to the pressure."

She couldn't help being amused. "The gay population does not like being called faggots," she chided. "It's not a very nice expression."

"Excuse *me*."

She tried to decide what to do. Should she allow this refreshingly unimpressed man to drive her home? Or should she have him pull over to the side and get the hell out of her car? She was quite capable of driving herself. And maybe she *should* go back for Dennis. Poor Dennis. He must be frantic.

*

Sometimes Vladimir invaded Madame's bedroom when he knew she was safely out for the evening. The maids, her secretary, her new assistant, and Nora Carvell had all gone home.

Vladimir danced into Madame's private domain and ran the water in her luxurious jacuzzi tub. He stripped off his clothes, went into her dressing room and selected a short curly wig which he placed on top of his wheat-coloured hair. Next he played with a selection of her cosmetics and created a face for himself. When he was finished he had conjured up a great illusion. From a distance he had the Silver Anderson "look" down pat.

*

"Tell me," Silver asked. "Where *have* we met before?"

"I was at your party," Wes replied truthfully.

"Oh, of course." She decided she must have noticed him across a crowded room and had been attracted to him even then. Because there was no denying it, she *did* find him extremely attractive. Dennis Denby was a baby in bed. This one looked like a man. "Who were you there with?"

"Rocky."

Ah . . . he must have been with the Sylvester Stallone group. She relaxed. "Well, Wes. Since we're old friends, you can take me home and I'll give you a drink. I think it's the least I can do. Without your quick action I don't know what would have happened."

He heard a definite invitation in her voice. *Don't tell me I've scored again*, he thought. Only this time it was *bingo* all the way home.

Chapter 27

"Show me a strong woman an' I'll show you a dyke," Howard said to a room full of his key executives – two of them women. They exchanged looks of fury, but neither of them spoke up. It was difficult enough holding down a top job without making waves. Everybody knew Howard Soloman was coked up half the time; it was best to ignore his sexist remarks.

"I don't think she's a dyke," the moon-faced head of production said. "I think she just needs to get laid!"

Guffaws all round. They were talking about the Swedish star of an Orpheus film currently shooting in Brazil. She was causing a lot of problems, and because of her the movie was behind schedule.

Howard stood up, indicating that the meeting was over. "Listen," he said expansively. "If she doesn't get her act together soon I'll just have to go down there an' shove my cock in her mouth – that'll shut her up once and for all!"

More guffaws. More frozen looks between the women.

"I'm only joking, girls," Howard said affably, patting one of them on the behind.

He waited until his office cleared then buzzed his secretary. "Any calls?"

"Orville Gooseberger about the lunch date you've postponed three times. Mannon Cable – he mentioned Las Vegas last week-end and said you would know what he was talking about. And Burt Reynolds's agent."

"Okay. Okay. Hold all calls again until I tell you."

"Yes, Mr Soloman."

Howard went into his private bathroom and locked the door. Removing his stash of cocaine from its hiding place, he laid a small amount on a square-cut flat mirror. With a shaking hand he snorted first one nostril and then the other. Christ! Zachary K. Klinger was coming to town and he was a wreck. Only temporarily, though. Two minutes later and he was back in control, feeling like he could kick ass from here to Boston and back. Picking up the phone next to his john, he summoned his secretary. "Book me a table at Morton's for tomorrow night. Eight people. Make sure it's the front table. Tell 'em I'm bringing Zachary Klinger with me."

"Yes, Mr Soloman."

"And phone Fred, the jewellery store on Rodeo, and ask Lucy to pick out something nice for my wife. In fact tell her to pick out a couple of pieces, and maybe she can stop by the office tomorrow."

"When tomorrow, Mr Soloman? You're busy all day."

"Schedule something. It's important."

"Yes, Mr Soloman."

"Did you get that script over to Whitney Valentine?"

"Yes, Mr Soloman."

"When?"

"This morning, Mr Soloman. Just as you requested."

Hanging up, he opened the medicine cabinet and swallowed some Maalox. Goddamn production meetings, they always upset his stomach. He didn't know why, because he was born to run a studio – nothing fazed him – even the Swedish cunt in Brazil who was costing him fortunes.

Taking a deep breath, he pressed the button on his private line and called Whitney. Nothing had taken place between them yet. They had experienced one lunch and that was it. Sometimes, he decided, the waiting was even better than the happening.

Nobody answered Whitney's private line, which meant she was out. He imagined her riding along the beach on her horse, hair flying, long limbs gleaming. Or maybe she was swimming in the ocean. No luxurious pools for Whitney – she was an outdoor girl.

Now, if he wished to locate Poppy, he would know *exactly* where to look. The Bistro Garden. She lunched there almost every day at her own special table, holding court among her circle of designer-clad friends. And later – Saks, Magnin's, Lina Lee, Gucci. She could be tracked down easily at any of those establishments.

Poppy had once told him that being the wife of a studio head was not easy. There were charities to belong to, people to impress, and rigid standards to uphold.

Poppy's commandments were: Thou shalt not be –

> *Too fat*
> *Poorly dressed*
> *Badly seated in a restaurant*
> or
> *Ignored by those who matter*

The list of Those Who Matter changed weekly depending on a variety of things.

Poppy always managed to know.

Howard had no desire to locate his wife. He would see her later for dinner. He would make love to her if he felt like it, or if just imagining what Whitney was like in the sack got him hot enough.

Zachary K. Klinger was coming to town, and he had to be ready for him.

*

Mannon Cable had always wanted to be a father, so when Melanie-Shanna hit him with the news that she was pregnant, he was delighted. For about sixty seconds. And then the implications set in. How *could* he have a baby with Melanie-Shanna?

131

Whitney was the love of his life, and Whitney was the only woman he wanted as mother of his children.

"Are you sure?" he'd demanded.

She had looked at him strangely. "Yes, I'm very sure. The doctor has confirmed it."

He didn't know what to say. For once in his life he was speechless. How could he mention divorce now? And an abortion was out of the question. Mannon had very strong views on that subject.

"Aren't you pleased?" she asked.

"Yeah," he replied, desperately trying to summon up the right degree of enthusiasm. "Thrilled."

The next day he met with his lawyer and asked for advice.

"Well," his lawyer had said. "If you don't want her to get rid of the kid, you're stuck. You'll have to wait out her pregnancy, and then stay around until the baby is a few months old at least. If you leave her before that the publicity will slaughter you."

Glumly Mannon had to agree. He could see the headlines: *MANNON CABLE AND STRANGE LOVE TRIANGLE! SUPERSTAR DUMPS PREGNANT WIFE FOR WHITNEY!*

Oh yeah. The tabloids would have a grand jerk-off at his expense.

There were also Whitney's feelings to consider. How was *she* going to react to this latest turn of events? It wasn't exactly going to make her think he was pining away for her. They hadn't spoken for a while. He had planned that the next time they did he would be a free man.

"Financially this is quite a blow," his lawyer had said grimly. "Are you *sure* you don't want her to have an abortion?"

He was sure.

They took a trip to New York, where he had to finish dubbing his last film. Melanie-Shanna was full of plans. "We'll decorate the second guest room," she said. "Yellow will be the perfect colour. Or blue?" She couldn't make up her mind. "What do you think, Mannon? Yellow or blue?"

He shook his head, not wanting to get involved. The further away he stayed from this pregnancy and the resulting baby, the better.

Chapter 28

Once inside her house, Silver was able to get a better look at Wes, and she liked what she saw. He was tall — she preferred big men. His hair was longish, brownish, not styled and sprayed like a lot of men around today. His eyes were extraordinary — sludge with touches of a murky seaweed green. He was distinctly masculine, and she felt the juices rising like they hadn't risen in a while. Certainly not for Dennis Denby, who was about as exciting and unpredictable as bacon and eggs for breakfast.

"Fix yourself a drink," she said, giving him an encouraging push towards the bar in the den. "I'll be right back."

"Can I make you something?" he asked politely.

"Vodka," she said over her shoulder as she mounted the grand front staircase. "Lemon twist, no ice."

Ah, maybe she'd remembered he was a barman. It certainly sounded like she did.

Choosing a Baccarat glass, he poured in an inch of vodka, added another one for good measure, and picked a slice of lemon from a small silver dish, expertly skewering it to the side of the glass. For himself he poured a cold beer. Best to make sure everything was primed and ready to go.

Luxuriating in the centre of Silver Anderson's large jacuzzi tub, Vladimir presented a strange and wonderful sight. He sat ramrod straight, naked, bewigged, and fully made-up, while the water bubbled and jetted around him. Clamped around his head were the headphones of a small Sony Walkman. The music reaching his ears was an early Silver Anderson album, and he sang along, mimicking her voice to perfection.

So intent was he that he failed to notice Silver enter her own bathroom and stand transfixed. "What *the hell* is going on here?" she said in complete amazement.

He did not hear her.

She stepped forward and ripped the headphones from him, flinging them across the room.

"Madame!" he shrieked in horror, and stood up.

"Vladimir?" She couldn't believe what she was seeing.

Uttering a stream of Russian curses he tried to cover his most personal items with his hands. The effort was ineffectual, as Vladimir was hung like the proverbial bull.

"God!" Silver flung him a towel and said icily, "Get out of my bath and *cover* yourself."

"Madame! Madame!" he wailed. "Vill you forgive me for this? Vat can I ever do to beg your forgiveness?"

"You can take off my wig for a start. And get *out*."

Vladimir was almost weeping. "Is Madame firing me?"

Silver caught sight of herself in one of the many mirrors and was immediately distracted. She had come upstairs to prepare herself for what she hoped might be a rather interesting evening – not to argue with her obviously deranged houseman. "We'll discuss it tomorrow," she said coldly. "Kindly get this bathroom cleaned up. Now! And then go to your quarters and stay there."

He hung his head in shame as she swept out.

* * *

                    *

Wes was disappointed to note that she had not changed when she returned to the bar. He had hoped for the filmy black negligee, sheer stockings, garter belt (*Down boy, down – not yet – don't blow it*) and high-heeled mules. Instead she was still wearing her fashionable red suit and unrevealing lace blouse.

"Whew!" she said, uncharacteristically flushed. "I just had the most *bizarre* experience. Hand me my drink. I need it."

He gave her the glass of vodka and waited for an explanation.

Flopping down on the couch she sipped the clear alcohol. "Vladimir, my houseman, is crazed!" she announced. "Quite obviously certifiable."

Wes remembered her houseman well – a bossy Bolshoi with an eye for the waiters. "What happened?" he asked expectantly.

She kicked off her shoes and savoured the moment. "He was in *my* bath. Wearing one of *my* wigs. A lot of *my* makeup. Singing one of *my* songs in *my* voice!"

Wes started to laugh. "What?"

She couldn't help smiling. "You heard."

"Was he dressed?"

"Unfortunately not."

They both began to laugh.

"He looked ridiculous," she spluttered. "And when he stood up in the bath with the bubbles all over him —"

"And the makeup and the hair?" Wes joined in.

"Yes. Yes. It's a sight I'll never forget."

He was as caught up as she was in just imagining Vladimir — the star of such a scene.

"What did you *do*?" he roared.

"I was too amazed to do anything!" she retorted. "Oh God! It was so . . . so . . . *funny*!"

Her laughter was catching — he couldn't stop either. This was not the cool bitch-goddess the newspapers and magazines wrote about with such awe — this was a warm and amusing *woman*.

"I guess he'll be looking for another job tomorrow," Wes said at last.

"Not necessarily," she replied. "I might just keep him around for the *entertainment* value!"

More laughter, interrupted by the persistent buzz of the front gate.

Silver frowned. "I don't know who this can be. Will you answer it for me?" She picked up the intercom phone and handed it to him.

"Silver Anderson's residence," he said smoothly.

"Dennis Denby," said an aggravated voice.

He covered the mouthpiece with the palm of his hand. "Dennis Denby," he repeated.

"Oh, no! I suppose you'd better buzz him in."

He gave her a little eye contact. "Do I have to?"

She responded nicely. "I think we'd better, don't you?"

All of a sudden it was *we*. He wasn't being dismissed.

Dutifully he pressed the intercom while she slipped her shoes back on. And a minute later, a red-faced Dennis Denby arrived at the front door. He clutched Silver, glared at Wes, and said, "Thank God you're all right!"

She disentangled herself from his grabbing hands. "I'm perfectly fine, Dennis." She indicated Wes. "Thanks to Mr —"

"Money," Wes supplied obligingly.

Silver raised an amused eyebrow.

"It's an old English name," Wes explained airily.

"Most unusual," she remarked.

"Yeah . . . well . . . most things about me are unusual."

She smiled. "They are?"

"So I've been told." The woman had dynamite eyes – kind of probing and sexy. And Wes knew he wasn't misreading the message in them.

Dennis couldn't help noticing the interaction going on between them, and he asserted himself immediately. "Well, it was very obliging of Mr er . . . Money to bring you home. Although it really wasn't necessary. Everything was under control."

"Whose control, Dennis?" Silver inquired caustically. "Were *you* controlling the crowd when I was about to get crushed to death?"

"Don't exaggerate, dear," Dennis said in a condescending tone.

He had made two fatal mistakes. One was calling her dear – a patronizing term she hated, although she often used it herself. And two was doubting her ability to judge a situation. "You really are stupid, Dennis, *dear*," she said. "You honestly had no idea what was going on, did you?"

"I was calling Spago," he explained, oblivious to her insult. He looked at his watch. "And there's a table waiting for us now." Turning to Wes he added, "So . . . Mr Money. If you'll excuse us."

"Mr Money will *not* excuse us," Silver said crisply. "Because we – you and I, Dennis, *dear* – are not going anywhere. In fact" – she took him by the arm and led him out of the room – "you are going home, and *I* am finishing my drink with Mr Money, who *did* have the presence of mind to see what was going on, and got me the hell out of there before I was bloody trampled underfoot!"

"Silver!" Dennis protested. "Why are you mad at me?"

"I am not mad," she replied, propelling him towards the front door. "I am merely bored."

He rallied desperately. "You can't stay alone in the house with this . . . this *person*. Who is he? What do you know about him?"

"That he has balls, Dennis, *dear*. Which is more than I can say for you! Goodnight!"

She closed the front door on his objections, and returned to the den.

Wes faced her. "Uh huh," he said, "we've had the crazy Russian and the uptight boyfriend. What next?"

She smiled, slowly, seductively. The smile America loved to hate. "I think something'll come up, don't you?"

Who was he to argue?

Chapter 29

Jade fell into the rhythm of Los Angeles easily. She had thought she would hate it, but after a month in the city she decided she loved it. There was so much to do, and gorgeous weather to do it in.

With her books, records and possessions around her, the apartment soon felt like home, and the only downer was Corey. He was weird – something was going on in his life and he obviously had no intention of sharing it with her. She had only seen him a couple of times. "I'm real busy," was his explanation. "What with the new job and settling in and everything."

He might be settling in but she didn't even know where or with whom. When she questioned him he was evasive. "Am I ever going to see where you live?" she asked him pointedly one day.

"Sure," he replied cheerily. "Very soon."

Whenever she mentioned Marita, he clammed up. "What about little Corey Junior?" she asked, referring to her eighteen-month-old nephew.

"He's in Hawaii."

"When are we going to see him?"

"Soon."

Everything was "soon". And Corey was a pain. She called and complained to her mother. "He's going through a bad time," her mother said sympathetically. "Leave him alone, he'll come to you eventually."

So she did. And he didn't.

The good news was that Cloud Cosmetics had hired Antonio

to do the photographs for the print ad campaign. A top video director, Shane Dickson, was to shoot the commercials, and she had been busy with hair, clothes, and makeup tests. The look had to be perfect.

Working with Antonio was always a joy. Not only did they have fun, but his photographs were a stunning visual treat. He combined the style of Norman Parkinson with the gloss of Scavullo and the sharpness and originality of Annie Leibovitz.

Jade found herself hanging out with him and his artistic group of friends more and more. They went to great restaurants, fun parties, and usually ended up on Friday and Saturday nights eating and dancing the night away at Tramp — a private club.

Getting out was excellent therapy. For years Mark Rand's contract had been exclusive. Now she was a free agent again.

She tried not to think about Mark. Every time he came creeping into her thoughts she blanked him out. The affair was well and truly over. *Finito.*

Good.

On her travels around town with Antonio and his friends several propositions of a sexual nature came her way. A sallow-faced producer with bad teeth and hollow eyes made her an offer she could easily refuse. A permanently stoned Puerto Rican told her she was the sexiest woman he'd ever seen. A French hustler in baggy jeans and designer sweatshirt informed her he knew everyone and could make her a star.

Men. She had had enough for a while. And then she met Shane Dickson, and she thought — *Well, maybe not quite enough* . . . She needed *someone* to take her mind off Mark.

Shane Dickson was short, surly, dark-haired and bearded. She liked the fact that he didn't fall all over her like most men did. For a while they circled around each other. He conducted her tests with a detached, professional air. He wanted a certain look for the series of commercials, and he didn't plan to shoot one foot of film until he got it.

Eventually he asked her out to dinner so they could talk about what they were trying to achieve. He took her to Nucleus Nuance on Melrose, and spoke about commercials being the true art form of the cinema. "In a two-hour movie you have time to screw up, get back on track, screw up again. In a commercial or a video you're going for gold in two minutes flat. There's no room for mistakes."

"Are you married?" she asked. Her skin was tingling, every nerve alert. It had been a long time between men, and she needed to feel wanted again.

"Yes," he replied, reaching for her hand across the table. "But my wife and I are separated. She just doesn't understand me."

Were men actually still using that line? She couldn't believe it.

He invited her back to his apartment — an invitation she declined. One married man in her life was enough.

And then, late one afternoon when she'd just returned from an all-day shoot and wanted nothing more than food and sleep, Mark phoned. "I'm in town," he said. "As a matter of fact, right now I'm standing in the lobby of your building. I have to talk to you, Jade. May I come up?"

Chapter 30

Whoever said all cats are alike in the dark must have been deaf, dumb, and blind. From her low moans of ecstasy to her litany of husky requests (Silver was not backward in telling him what she enjoyed), and her expensively perfumed flesh — everything was different. Try driving a Bentley after a succession of worn-down Toyotas.

Wes shifted position, allowing Silver to mount *him*. She had the tight, compact body of a teenager. Taut breasts, firm thighs (not rock hard like his Swede) and a flat stomach. She enjoyed sex with a gusto he was unused to. Reba lay on her back like a skewered fish. Other women talked dirty just for effect. When Silver said, "Fuck me hard, Wes," she meant it. And he did it. And they both got off on it.

She lowered a hard-nippled breast to his mouth while riding him fast. He sucked obligingly. She even tasted different.

He felt the ultimate trip beginning. Thoughts flashed through his head – it had all happened so quickly.

Exit Dennis.

Conversation.

Nothing heavy.

"Let's go upstairs."

Her invitation.

His acceptance.

Once in the bedroom he went for the clinch.

She returned his kiss with teeth and probing tongue and an encouraging stroke of the frothing hound. "I'll be right back," she had said.

This was hardly the time to tell her he was a busted-out some-time barman who lived in a run-down house in Venice and got it on with a variety of unattractive but very grateful women.

When she came back into the bedroom she looked quite different. Gone was the short thick hair – a wig, he realized – and in its place was her own shoulder-length dark hair. She had also removed her heavy false eyelashes, and now she appeared younger and softer. She wore a silk kimono.

"This is the real Silver Anderson," she'd said without a trace of embarrassment. "I hope you're not disappointed."

Disappointed? He was pleasantly surprised. Taking her hand he'd guided it to where it would do her the most good. "Do I feel like a disappointed man?"

She'd laughed, low-down and dirty. "You feel like a man – that's enough for me."

And they set sail.

He climaxed with a ball-busting jolt which shuddered through his body like a fast-moving express train. "Jesus H. Christ!" he groaned.

She was tight, holding him a steady captive. "What's *he* got to do with it?" she asked breathlessly.

*

Humiliated, Vladimir cleaned up Silver's bathroom and fled from the house to his private retreat above the garage. How could he have been so careless? He shook his head. No, no, not careless, just caught. Usually when Madame went out she was gone for at least three hours. This time she had returned within the hour.

Too bad, Vladimir. You should have been more careful.

He was sure that she would fire him. The next morning there would be a curt dismissal from her personal assistant, and a severance cheque from her accountant's office.

He was mortified. How he wished he could close his eyes, then open them and find the whole episode no more than a bad dream.

Before Silver, he had worked for a gay television producer who lived high in the Hollywood Hills. And before that, a retired couple who presented ideal domesticity to the world, and behind closed doors entertained their gay and lesbian lovers at non-stop weekend orgies.

Ah, Vladimir knew plenty. As a houseman he was privy to an Aladdin's cave of secrets. Only what could he do with them? And who would believe him?

Silver Anderson was going to miss him, he was positive of that. For three years he had served her faithfully. He knew her likes and dislikes. He gauged her moods and never disturbed her solitude. He protected her privacy, made sure her house was in impeccable order, and was discreet about her men friends.

Opening his closet he peered mournfully at his clothes. He possessed two suits, a brown one and a blue. Several shirts, a few sports clothes, and a black rubber diving suit. Not that he indulged in underwater pursuits – the rubber suit was a gift from a former friend – a six-feet-four black jock, who *loved* playing water sports. Vladimir had lived with him for two months somewhere between the gay producer and the ideal Hollywood couple. He preferred living alone in his own part of the fabulous mansions he serviced.

Lovingly he fingered the material of a floor-length purple beaded dress nestling in the back of the closet. One day Silver had given him a trunk-load of old clothes to be picked up by a charity organization. Upon perusing the contents, he had come across the dress. Naturally he kept it. Why not? It fitted him perfectly.

He pulled a suitcase from beneath the bed, and in a desultory fashion began to pack. When he was fired he would depart swiftly in a dignified manner. After all, by birth he was a Russian, and he had his pride.

*

Wes leaned across a sleeping Silver to reach his pants, dumped unceremoniously on the floor, and from the back pocket he recovered a crumpled pack of Camels, and lit up. Dragging reflectively on the cigarette, he wondered what was going to happen next. Laying the Big Star was one thing – mission accomplished – although it hadn't really been a mission – more a mutual attraction which led to great sex. So what was the next play to be? He was hardly in a position to entertain her at Chasen's, and somehow grabbing a bite at Kentucky Fried Chicken did not appear to be her scene.

Wes had a problem. He had just made love to a very famous lady indeed, and if she'd enjoyed it half as much as she seemed to, then they were on for more than a ten-cent ride.

What was he going to tell her? The truth? Or lie just a little.

He blew smoke rings towards the ceiling, and studied Silver Anderson in repose. She looked good, the old broad – and he'd had 'em at all ages. Some women after sex looked like they had just gone seven rounds with Joe Frazier – especially the over-thirty-fives. Well, Silver Anderson was certainly no juvenile, but she sure held up in the trenches.

As if she sensed his eyes upon her, she opened hers. For a moment he thought she was going to say "Who are you?"

She didn't. She gave him a long, appraising stare, stretched in a very feline way, and stepped from the bed nude and proud of it.

He could tell she reckoned her body was something special the way she strutted to the mirrored bathroom door. Who was he to argue?

Taking another drag of lung-cancer-inducing smoke, he got out of bed and followed her.

Chapter 31

The production meeting was well underway. Once a month Jack and his team met specifically to discuss suitable guests for the upcoming shows. There was a bulletin board with suggestions, ideas, and a list of what Aldrich called "the current hot hundred". The list was comprised of personalities from every field: politics, theatre, music, sports, movies, publishing, and so on. Since the show only aired for twenty-six weeks a year, there were only twenty-six guests required, and the struggle by publicists to get their clients a spot was competitive and vicious. Bribes were often offered. Bribes were always turned down. *Face to Face with Python* could sell a movie or a book or an event quicker than any other show on television. The bookings were done four weeks in advance, allowing Jack plenty of time to study the material on each guest.

"Why can't we have Mannon Cable?" Aretha demanded. Nobody was surprised: she demanded it every month because she knew Jack and Mannon were close friends.

"Not again," Jack groaned. "I've told you enough times, he always turns me down."

"Bet he wouldn't if *I* got hold of him," Aretha joked in her sing-song voice. "Poppa! That man'ud have the best time he ever had in his whole damn life!" She beamed happily at the thought. "Yessirree!!"

"I'll tell him," Jack dead-panned.

"You *always* say that," Aretha chided. "How come he appears on Carson all the time, and *you* can't get him?"

"Because I don't really want him," Jack replied lightly. "We know each other too well and too long. It wouldn't work."

"Yes it would," she sang. "Stand back an' watch our ratings *riiiiiise!*"

"Let's get serious," Aldrich interrupted. "Eddie Murphy is a definite yes. Diane Keaton won't commit. We can get April Crawford if we want her. And do we go for Fonda or not?"

"We're getting too show-bizzy," Jack complained. "There has to be balance between entertainment and information. Put April Crawford on hold. Fonda's overexposed right now. How about Mailer? There's that new biography on him; it's interesting. I did a three-minute segment with him in Chicago years ago – now might be the right time to talk to him again."

"I'd sooner see Prince," sighed Aretha. "What a guy! A touch petite for me – heck, I can overcome *that*! He has such adorable buns!"

Aldrich ignored her. "I'll get one of the researchers onto Norman Mailer," he said. "See what he's up to."

"Do that." Jack pushed away from the conference table. "We can talk again on Monday. Right now I've got to see a man about a house."

Both Aretha and Aldrich raised eyebrows and voices and chorused as one, "A *house*?"

He grinned. "Don't worry, nothing serious. I thought it might be relaxing to take a summer rental at the beach."

"Very relaxing," murmured Aretha sarcastically. "All those steamy teenage bodies parading up and down your front lawn and frolicking in your pond!"

"Trancas," Jack said. "Away from the madding crowd."

*

It took him an hour to drive there from the television studio. And that was on a quiet Friday afternoon without much traffic. By the time he found the turn-off, parked his Ferrari, and walked down a series of stone steps hewn into the side of a mini-cliff, he wasn't so sure this was such a sensational idea.

When he entered the house he changed his mind.

The rental agent let him in. She was a divorced woman in her forties who had dressed for the occasion in a jersey suit too tight for her spreading curves. Half a bottle of Estée wafted from her excited body. It wasn't every day she got to show a house to Jack Python.

She greeted him effusively. He was twice as handsome off the little screen as on. His direct green eyes sent her into an absolute tizzy.

"Are you alone?" she asked, when she'd recovered her composure.

"Yes," he replied. "Why? Shouldn't I be?"

"No, no, it's just that . . ." She trailed off. Most celebrities travelled with an entourage of yes-people, and she was surprised that Jack Python obviously preferred solo. "Do come in," she gushed, remembering her manners. "The owners are out for the day. They're leaving for Europe in three weeks, and they wanted me to assure you that all their personal items – clothes, etcetera, will be packed and put in storage. Right now the house has a lived-in feel. However, I'm sure you understand. Actually, I always think –"

Jack moved past her into a glorious circular glass-walled living room. Outside was a huge deck, with steps leading down to a deserted cove, and the Pacific Ocean in all its glory.

For a man who had never been house-hungry he fell in love instantly.

The rental agent launched into her hard-sell routine, completely wasted on Jack, who wasn't listening as he strode to the glass walls and discovered they folded back to create a completely open environment.

He walked out onto the deck. It was a clear, windy day with high rollers and a very blue sky.

"This location is absolutely private," the realtor said, following him outside. "As a matter of fact I've been here several times, and I've never seen another soul."

He noticed a sunken hot-tub, a barbecue pit, and table tennis all set up.

"No tennis court?" he joked.

"Actually," the woman said anxiously, "the owners are considering building one." She laughed nervously. "Not before their trip though."

He gazed out at the blue sea. The waves and the soothing sound of the surf were almost hypnotizing. "How long will they rent it for?" he asked.

"It's a six-month rental," she replied. "With an option to buy if they decide to stay in Europe."

"I'll take it," he said decisively.

"Mr Python, you haven't even looked around."

"I've seen everything I need to see."

"You're a very impetuous man, and a clever one. This is the best house in Trancas. I've already got two couples thinking about it – their cheques are only phone calls away."

"And mine" – he slid his chequebook from his jacket pocket – "will be with you any second. The house is rented."

Driving back to Beverly Hills he felt elated. His first house! Only a summer rental, but he had a feeling he might go for the buy if the couple stayed in Europe and decided to sell.

Driving directly to the Beverly Wilshire, he showered and changed clothes. Clarissa had finished her movie and taken off for New York. She had wanted him to accompany her. He had made "too much work" noises, so she had gone without him.

Before leaving there had been a confrontation, something he had been unconsciously avoiding for months. They had attended a screening at the Academy, and stopped by the party at Tramp afterwards. The paparazzi trailed them with gusto. Unfortunately there were three of his former girlfriends present, all well-known females who greeted him warmly, while the paparazzi struggled to capture every moment.

"I can't stand this," Clarissa said angrily. "The trouble with you, Jack, is that you attract too much attention."

"*Me?* How about *you? You're* the one with the Oscar on your shelf."

"I don't court publicity."

"Neither do I."

"Nonsense. You love every moment of it. You revel in it."

"That's absolute bullshit and you know it."

They were in the car, driving back to her house. It was raining, and the streets were slick.

"I've been thinking," she said slowly.

"What?"

"I want to get married."

The Ferrari hit a puddle of water and skidded. A car coming towards them sounded its horn. It took all his concentration to get the Ferrari under control.

Clarissa was unfazed. "I'd like a baby," she said.

He swallowed hard. Marriage was bad enough, but now she wanted a baby too!

Measuring his words carefully he said, "We've never discussed this."

"I know," she replied flatly. "I think you should consider that we've been together over a year. Either our relationship is going somewhere, or we may as well end it."

"Are you giving me an ultimatum?" he asked tightly.

146

Her long face was ghostly pale in the night light. "I am saying we can't drift along anymore. I want a commitment."

He was stunned. Miss Independent all of a sudden wanted a commitment!

"I've never considered marriage," he said truthfully.

"I'm well aware of that," she replied. "Neither of us has. We're both loners —"

"You've never complained," he interrupted.

"I'm not complaining now," she said evenly. "I'm merely suggesting a change." Turning away from him she stared out of the side window at the relentless rain. "Between us we have no family. I think I want to start planting roots."

He stifled an insane impulse to laugh. She sounded like she was planning a garden!

"*I* have a family," he protested. "My father, and Heaven."

"Your father lives in a world of his own, you've often told me that. As for your niece . . ." She shrugged. "You pay her no attention."

"They're still family."

"That's not what I'm talking about, and you know it." She lapsed into silence for a moment, and then said quietly, "I'm not asking you to make up your mind right now. Tomorrow I leave for New York. I won't come back until you tell me what you've decided."

One thing about Clarissa, she didn't mince words.

He had no idea what he was going to do. With Clarissa in the East he was enjoying his freedom. Good behaviour had gone on far too long. He needed a break — and a weekend with Mannon and Howard in Las Vegas was just the way to celebrate.

Chapter 32

Howard had use of the company jet. He saw no reason why it couldn't take him to Vegas and back, and *then* go to New York and pick up Zachary Klinger, who was coming out to the Coast to torment him. The man was driving him crazy. He had already cancelled two proposed visits at the last minute. Zachary K. Klinger, Howard realized, liked to keep people on their toes.

When Mannon suggested Las Vegas, Howard jumped. He needed the break. Oh, how he needed it! A weekend away from Poppy was better than ten days at the Golden Door.

Poppy was not so thrilled. "Baby Roselight and I will come with you," she said firmly.

"No way," Howard countered. "Your luggage will ground the plane!"

"Don't you *want* us?" she pouted.

"I do, sweetheart," he lied. "Only you'll be bored, and I just won't have the time to spend with you."

"Why not?"

"Because it's a business trip, puff-pie. I keep on telling you that."

"What sort of business do people get to do in Las Vegas that they can't do in L.A.?" she asked suspiciously.

"How many times must I explain it to you?" Swallowing his aggravation he told her – yet again – why he and Mannon were going. He had concocted a highly original story about an old and infamous gambler who lived just outside of Vegas and refused to travel. Mannon wanted to meet him with a view to filming his life story. For Orpheus, of course. Poppy knew Howard had been trying forever to get Mannon to commit to a project for Orpheus. She bought the story. Finally.

"I'll miss you," she said tearfully, as if he were going for two months instead of two days.

"Me too, sugar-lips."

"What'll I *do* all day?"

"Spend money."

She seemed to like that suggestion, and cheered up considerably, enabling him to escape from the house without further hassle.

He snorted coke in the back of the limo on the way to Burbank airport, and by the time he boarded the company jet he was in fighting shape.

★

"Have a safe flight," Melanie-Shanna said softly.

Mannon had to admit that when it came to choosing women he certainly had an eye. He didn't know if it was Melanie-Shanna's pregnancy or what, but she looked a picture of glowing health as she bade him goodbye from the door of their Sunset Boulevard mansion.

For a moment he forgot Whitney. "What'll you get up to this weekend?" he asked, the first time he had bothered to inquire.

"I don't know − this and that. I thought I might go nursery shopping."

"Good idea." He kissed her on the cheek.

She responded by turning her face towards him and kissing him on the mouth.

He savoured her cherry-fresh breath, then pushed her gently away. "Don't make me miss the plane," he joked.

"I thought planes waited for big stars like you," she said wryly.

Her eyes needed him − their message was loud and clear. He hesitated: it was weeks since they'd made love − now that she was pregnant it just didn't seem right. "Gotta go, kid," he said decisively. "Have fun."

She watched him stride towards the stretch limousine, climb inside, and vanish from sight.

Her movie star husband was off for the weekend and she would miss him. She would also spend most of her time worrying about what he was up to. When it came to movie stars women had no shame. The unspoken message was always there. *I'm available if you want me.*

Melanie-Shanna walked back into the house and hoped that he didn't.

The phone was ringing. Before she could reach it their Mexican housekeeper picked up.

"For you, missus," the woman said.

Melanie-Shanna took the phone and wondered who it was. She didn't encourage friendships, preferring to be available for Mannon at all times. When he first brought her to Hollywood, the Beverly Hills wives had rallied round — inviting her to this luncheon, that charity event, this celebrity fashion show. She declined all invitations politely, and eventually they left her alone.

"Hello," she said tentatively.

"Hi, sweetie," said the unmistakable voice of Poppy Soloman. "Now I *will not* take no for an answer. The husbands have deserted us, and you and I are going to have lunch at the Bistro Garden tomorrow, followed by a *tiny* little stroll down Rodeo."

"Oh, Poppy, I don't think —"

"I told you, dear, I am not allowing *any* excuses. We're having lunch, and that's that."

*

"Welcome aboard," greeted Howard.

Mannon grinned, all thoughts of Melanie-Shanna and her appealing freshness forgotten. "It's a pleasure to be flying with you, Mr Soloman."

"May the trip last all weekend," said Howard. "Do I need a touch of R & R!"

"Who doesn't?" agreed Mannon, flopping into a leather armchair.

The interior of the jet was decorated like a luxurious conference room — all leather and brass, with polished tables and a curving bar. There were two attractive stewardesses — an Australian girl, and an English redhead. They both wore tight beige gaberdine skirts with matching belted jackets, and a little insignia on the right-hand breast pocket that read KLINGER, INC.

"Can I get you anything, Mr Cable?" asked the Australian.

"What did you have in mind?" Standard responses came easily to Mannon. He loved double entendres.

"Vodka. Scotch. Rum. Perrier. Soda. 7-Up. Coca—"

"Hold it!" he laughed. "A scotch on the rocks'll do me fine."

She smiled — "Yes, sir" — and walked away.

Mannon watched her ass. Beneath the pristine gaberdine lay great promise.

"Where's Jack?" Howard asked.

Mannon stretched. "I don't know. Is he late?"

Howard checked his watch. "A few minutes, he's probably on his way. He had to go see a house or something."

"A house?"

"Yeah – you know. One of those buildings with four walls an' a window."

The Australian stewardess delivered Mannon's drink with a linen napkin and a silver dish full of nuts. Curbing an impulse to pinch her ass he asked, "What's Jack looking at a house for? He's not going legit, is he?"

Howard pulled a face. "Whadda *I* know?"

"Universal is pitching a script for me to do with Clarissa," Mannon said casually. "I'm not sure she'd be a laugh a minute to work with. What do *you* think?"

"I think you should do a film for Orpheus," Howard said self-righteously. "Jesus! Don't you have a loyal bone in your body?"

"Come up with something, friend, and I'll consider it."

"You fuckin' actors," spat Howard. "When you're on the way up you'll grovel for a walk-on. When you make it you're impossible assholes. And when you're stars you're so full of shit it comes pourin' out every time you open your goddamn mouths! Don't forget, I remember you when – *friend*."

Mannon laughed. "And I remember *you*."

Jack kept them waiting twenty minutes, and then he came bounding up the outside steps into the plane. "Traffic," he said, before anyone could complain.

"What's all this crap about a *house*?" Mannon asked.

"I saw it. I liked it. I rented it."

"Let's get this show on the road," Howard said impatiently. "We've waited long enough to make this weekend. If we don't get our ass in gear we're gonna spend it sittin' on the goddamn plane!" He picked up the intercom and spoke to the pilot. "All aboard. Let's fly!"

Chapter 33

They circled each other like suspicious tigers. Jade hadn't wanted to see him, yet when Mark announced he was down-stairs in the lobby, it seemed too petty to say he couldn't come up. So she let him. And here he was. Mark Rand. English asshole.

She had wanted to remember him as he was in her bathroom the last time they met, but it was not to be. Mark looked good. Very good. He was wearing an impeccably cut blue blazer, a Turnbull & Asser white shirt open at the neck, a thin lizardskin belt, and blue slacks with a knife-cut crease. His brown hair was appealingly ruffled, and he had a slight tan.

"It's so *good* to see you," he said enthusiastically, wandering around the apartment inspecting her books and paintings and ornaments.

She had not had time to plan for this meeting, and wasn't quite sure how to handle it.

"You moved so swiftly," he continued. "When I came back to talk to you, you were gone – just like that."

"When *did* you come back, Mark?" she asked, curious to know how long it had taken him.

"After we . . . er . . . had our fight, I returned to England." He paused at a table set with her collection of glass decanters and bottles of liquor. "Do you mind if I pour myself a drink?"

"Go ahead," she said coldly, not about to do it for him. "Please make it a short one, I have an appointment."

He looked at her with honest eyes. "I promise not to keep you, Jade. I'll say what I have to say and be on my way."

His crisp English accent was a turn-on – it always had been. She stared at him warily as he poured scotch into a glass and added a touch of soda.

"May I get something for you?" he asked politely.

"No, thank you," she replied, equally formal.

"Well ..." He sipped his drink. "When I returned, you were gone. No forwarding address, everyone sworn to secrecy about your whereabouts." He allowed himself a tiny smile of triumph at his own cleverness. "But I found you."

"I can tell," she remarked, concentrating on his crooked teeth in the hope they would take her mind off the rest of him. She felt uncomfortably warm.

"I heard about the contract with Cloud Cosmetics. Quite a coup. Congratulations."

"Thank you."

His grey eyes sought out hers. "I miss you very much, Jade." His English accent dripped sincerity.

Oh damn! Why didn't she just admit it? He was a lying, cheating sonofabitch, but she missed him too.

Her jaw tightened in a determined thrust. She had to get rid of him before she did something she would regret.

"When we parted I flew straight to London," he continued. "On the plane over I thought about everything and I was deeply ashamed of the way I'd tried to deceive you."

"If this is an apology I accept it," she said, jumping up from the couch. "The thing is, Mark, I've got a date, and if I don't get ready ..." She trailed off, waiting for him to take the hint.

"I'm divorcing Fiona," he announced dramatically. "I have already consulted my lawyer, and we are proceeding immediately."

It was a bombshell. For six years she had heard nothing but *when the children are older*. What caused *this* sudden change of heart?

"I realize asking you to forgive me is not enough," he said gravely. "I can't expect you to resume our relationship the way it was. This is my pipe of peace. When I'm divorced, I would like you to be my wife."

She was speechless. This was the last thing she'd expected.

Laughing self-consciously he said, "I know this is a surprise, and I don't expect you to make an immediate decision. I just want to be sure that you realize how very important you are to me, and that I love you very, very much."

Oh God! Mark, full of sincerity with his crooked English teeth, tousled hair, and "little boy lost" stance, drove her crazy.

Come clean, Johnson. You're infatuated with this guy. You want to jump his bones. Why hold back?

She took a deep breath. "This is a little too much for me to digest in one sitting," she said, striving for a light-hearted approach. "Why don't we talk tomorrow when I've had a chance to . . . uh . . . think this over?"

He nodded, and raised a quizzical eyebrow. "This *is* a proposal, Jade. I have come to you hat in hand, so to speak. Please don't punish me for the past, let's think about the future. *Our* future," he added pointedly.

She walked him to the door.

"I'm staying at the L'Hermitage," he said. "Maybe you might care to visit me later, after your . . . date."

"I'll call you," she said.

He held her shoulders and gazed into her eyes. "I know I've been foolish. I'll never risk losing you again. Am I forgiven?"

She *wanted* to forgive him, only something held her back. She wasn't going to be sweet, wonderful *trusting* Jade anymore. She was going to check his story out before she committed herself.

He leaned close to her. He smelled of peppermint breath spray and Hermès aftershave. "Cancel your date," he said urgently. "We've been apart too long. I want to touch you . . . stroke your glorious body. I want to make love to you, Jade. You must feel the same way." Pulling her to him he began to kiss her.

For a moment she allowed his insistent lips to press against hers, his familiar tongue to invade her mouth. Hard against her thigh she felt the pressure of his desire. She wanted to say — *The hell with everything, Mark is back, and I'm glad*.

But she didn't. She had her pride. He wasn't going to walk into her life just like that and take over.

With supreme willpower she disengaged herself. "Please, Mark, go back to your hotel. We'll see each other tomorrow."

He was disappointed, but determined to behave like a gentleman. "For breakfast?"

"Lunch."

"Where shall we meet?"

"I'll come to your hotel."

"Who's your date with, Jade? You know I'm an extremely jealous man." He smiled when he said it, but she knew he was in agony. Mark was unreasonably possessive.

"Just a friend," she said lightly.

"Why can't you cancel it?"

"Don't push me."

"I miss you."

"Tomorrow."

She closed the front door on him. Her head was spinning. For six *years* she had waited for this moment. Now that it was here she wasn't sure *what* she wanted . . .

She paced restlessly around her apartment. There was no date arriving to take her out. Shane had wanted to see her, but she had begged off, claiming exhaustion. On impulse she called Antonio. He had mentioned something about going away for the weekend. She wouldn't mind going with him. Anything to get away from Mark while she thought things out.

Antonio was still at his studio.

"Where are you off to?" she asked.

"Las Vegas, *bella*. You want to come?"

She didn't hesitate. "Definitely."

Chapter 34

The ride back to reality took Wes twenty minutes. That's how long it was between Silver Anderson's Bel Air mansion and his run-down house on the Venice boardwalk. Silver had loaned him what she referred to as her "spare car". It was a snappy red Mercedes Sports 350 SL. A classic model. "Nobody uses it," she had said airily when seeing him off the morning after their night of passion. "Why don't you return it around eight tonight, and we'll have dinner at the house?"

She certainly wasn't backward in coming forward. He liked the fact that she didn't leave him hanging. She was obviously used to calling the shots, and enjoyed doing so.

"I'm not sure I'm free for dinner," he'd said lazily.

Her eyes challenged his. "Make yourself free."

"I just did."

He gave her his phone number at her request, and took off in the red Mercedes. What a trip! He had a feeling he had fallen into one peachy scene. Only how to proceed? When she found out he was nothing more than a broke barman she was not exactly going to be thrilled to death. Right now she had no idea who he was or what he did. And how to keep it that way?

Parking her Mercedes in a side street he walked briskly to his house. Silver obviously trusted him. She had lent him her car, hadn't she? If she thought he was a bum she wouldn't have done that. Although what did a car mean to Silver Anderson? Probably nothing. She was insured if he did a quick vanishing trick. All rich people were insured. And she was probably loaded.

He felt a building excitement. Maybe he'd just lucked into a whole different lifestyle.

There was a note tacked to his front door. It was short and to the point:

PAY UP OR GET OUT BY NOON TOMORROW.

Reba, venting her fury at being dumped last night. He wondered if she'd recovered her precious mink jacket for which he still had the claim check. Poor old Reba, she must be boiling.

"Is this your dog?"

Wes turned to confront his nextdoor neighbour, the uptight female who played classical records all night and drove him crazy with the noise. She was a skinny little thing, plain, with her scraped-back hair and granny glasses. She wore no makeup and looked about twelve in her baggy pants and tee-shirt. He had tried to talk to her several times – well it was only neighbourly to be friendly, wasn't it? Every time he made an attempt she had ignored him.

"You should be ashamed of yourself," she continued hotly, not waiting to find out if it was his dog or not. "The poor animal sat outside your door howling all night. That is, until *I* took it in. He had a nasty cut on his front paw which I cleaned and bandaged as best I could. You'd better take him to a vet."

Wes checked out the dog sitting patiently beside the girl. It was the same dog that had been following him around for a while – ever since picking him up on the beach one day. It was a mutt, a mongrel with stupid trusting eyes, and he'd thrown it a few bones once in a while – just to get it off his back. "It's not *my* dog," he denied vehemently. "Never set eyes on it before in my life." He had no intention of acquiring any vet bills.

"Liar!" she accused. "I've seen this dog with you on many occasions."

"How many?"

"What?"

"Okay, okay. So it's followed me around sometimes, but it's not my dog. You can have it. It's a stray."

The girl was busting with fury. "You bum! How can you give your dog away? How can you be so . . . so . . . *uncaring*?"

He caught sight of her nipples – erect under the skimpy tee-shirt. If you did the old secretary trick – took off the glasses and let the hair loose – she might be quite pretty. "Who, *me*? You're the one with the crappy loud music all night long so that nobody gets any sleep."

Glaring at him she said, "The last thing *you* do is sleep. You're never home."

"Have you been spying on me?"

"I've got better things to do with my time."

The dog whined pathetically, and lifted its bandaged paw.

She calmed down. "Look," she said. "I took a day off work to wait for you. I thought it was your dog; you say it's not. Why don't we get together on this and take it to the vet?"

"Go ahead. I'm not stoppin' you." He indicated the note on his door. "I have problems of my own to take care of."

She glanced at the note then back at him. "Oh, you can handle our dragon landlady, I've seen you do it before."

"It seems you know a lot more about me than I do about you."

"I'm observant."

"So I've observed."

She didn't crack a smile. But she did remove her glasses, and he noticed that her eyes were ever so slightly crossed, giving her a rather appealing look. She was extremely young. And on closer inspection quite pretty, as he'd suspected. She made him feel ancient. He watched her twirl her glasses in child-size hands.

"If I take the dog to the vet will you pay half?" she asked tentatively. "And if we keep it, then maybe we can split the cost of its food."

"Something tells me you're not exactly flush," he remarked. She fidgeted. "Not exactly."

"I wasn't really thinkin' of getting a dog."

"Half a dog," she corrected.

Shit! Why was he such a sucker? "Okay, okay," he said, giving in.

Her face registered relief.

"What's your name?" he asked. "I suppose that now we're partners in a dog I should know."

"Unity."

"Wes." He held out a friendly hand. "And what'll we call the mutt?"

The shadow of a smile flitted across her face. "I think we should."

"Should what?"

"Call our dog Mutt. It suits him perfectly."

He laughed – she was a funny little thing, but quite spunky. "You're on. While I live here we'll share the do– Mutt. Right?"

She nodded. Little did she know he would be moving out at any moment.

★

Silver greeted everyone on the set with unusual friendliness. Purring her way into the makeup chair, she leaned her head back, closed her eyes and murmured, "Make me divine!"

"Hmmm," commented Raoul, her makeup artist. "*Somebody* had a wonderful time last night, and it wasn't me."

She giggled girlishly. "Do I look haggard?"

"Quite the opposite actually."

Another giggle. "Great sex is better than sleep any day."

"Mr Denby living up to his reputation, is he?"

"You've *got* to be joking."

"Not a new one?"

"A real man."

"Oooh, I *love* real men!"

"Don't we all. And there aren't too many of them around."

"*Tell* me about it."

By noon, news of Silver Anderson's new lover had swept the sound stage. Everyone wanted to know who it was, only after her initial chat with Raoul she wasn't talking.

"I'm *so* sorry about last night," Fernando fretted, as he fussed with her hair. "It was an absolute *mob* scene. Boyce was awfully upset."

"I survived," Silver said dryly.

"So I heard!" Fernando pushed for information. "Anyone we know?"

"Ouch!" She pulled away from his teasing brush. "More care if you please."

"Sorry!"

"So you should be."

She stared at her reflection in the mirror as Fernando darted around her like an exotic plumed cockatoo. Wes Money. An unusual name. An unusual man. He wasn't in awe of her, not one bit. She adored that. Not like Dennis Denby, who was a waste of time.

Wes Money. What did he do? Where was he from? Was he married? Divorced? Did he have kids?

Last night was not a fact-finding mission. It was a night of hot sex, lustful sex. She smiled at the memories, still so very recent.

In the morning there was no time for talk, she had an early call and had to rush. Tonight she would find out about him.

Nora turned up for lunch. "I think I missed a page in your book," she said acidly.

Silver blinked. "What are you talking about?"

"Cut the crap. Who is he? And what does he want?"

Silver picked daintily at a chef's salad. "Does nothing escape you? Are there no secrets anymore?"

"Once Raoul knows, you may as well take out a full-page ad in *Variety*. Everyone is aware you got *schtupped* last night. And the big question is, by whom? Because it's common knowledge poor old Dennis didn't get lucky."

Silver smiled. She adored the attention and speculation her love life received. "Let them all keep guessing," she said. "I met a new man, with the emphasis on *man*!"

"Big cock, huh?"

"Nora!"

"Don't act shocked with me. I've seen a few in my time – before I changed tracks, of course."

"His name is Wes Money."

"And does he have any?"

"*I* don't know."

"Shall I give him the Dun & Bradstreet treatment?"

"I'm not planning to *marry* the man."

"Is he an actor?"

"Don't be ridiculous."

Nora chain-lit a cigarette. "What'll I tell the news hounds?"

"Nothing."

"They'll drive you crazy."

"There's nothing unusual about *that*."

Indulging in a coughing fit, Nora said, "You love it, doncha?"

Silver beamed. "I've been all the way to the bottom. And now I'm right back at the very top. Why *shouldn't* I love it?"

Chapter 35

The Forum Hotel accommodated Jack, Howard and Mannon in great style. They were given the Presidential six-room suite, which sprawled across the top floor of the hotel replete with terraced bedrooms, a sunken living room, an eight-seater jacuzzi, and a small screening room.

"I like it," Howard announced. "I want to run the studio from here and never leave."

Mannon threw himself down on an oversize fur-covered couch. "Not bad," he agreed. "If we don't have enough beds, this'll do!"

Jack wondered why he was there. In the plane, all the way to Vegas, Howard and Mannon had talked nothing but women. One might think they were a couple of out-of-towners on their first night away from their wives. Howard Soloman – the head of Orpheus Studios. And Mannon Cable – superstar. And all they had on their minds was getting laid.

Jack knew for sure he'd outgrown them long ago, and it didn't bother him one bit. What *did* bother him was that he'd agreed to come on this weekend. It was his own fault. He should have know what to expect.

Howard was bounding around like a tennis ball. "I love it!" he kept on exclaiming. "This is sensational! No phone calls. No wives. No pain." The phone rang and Howard automatically grabbed it. "Yeah?"

Jack thought of Clarissa. He wondered how she was. He wasn't sure if he missed her or not.

Howard spoke rapidly and hung up with a smile on his face. "That was Dino Fonicetti," he said. "He and Susanna wanna throw a party for us tonight. Whaddya say?"

Dino Fonicetti was the son of Joseph Fonicetti, who owned the Forum Hotel. He was married to Susanna, daughter of Carlos Brent – the legendary singer.

"Sure," said Mannon at the same time as Jack said, "No."

"What's with the no?" Howard yelled excitedly. "We came here to party, didn't we?"

"*I* came here for a break," Jack said determinedly.

"I can recall when the only break *you* cared about was between some bimbo's legs!" Howard laughed at his own humour. "You don't wanna party, don't do it. Mannon an' I will show 'em. Right, Mannon buddy?"

Mannon nodded agreeably.

Jack wondered what would happen if Mannon ever suspected that Howard planned to hit on Whitney. He wouldn't be so amiable then. "I'm going to take a walk," he said. "Maybe I'll lay fifty bucks on black, lose, and go to bed. I've put in a heavy day."

"So what was *I* doin'? Lyin' in the sun?" demanded Howard indignantly. "My day was a crap-shoot from start to finish. However, *I* am ready to roll – all the way."

"Have a good time," smiled Jack.

"Yeah," said Howard. "We'll tell you what you missed in the mornin'. Y'can cry in your orange juice!"

*

From the moment they set off, Jade had her doubts about why she had wanted to accompany them. Antonio had a new boyfriend, a dapper interior designer whom he couldn't keep his hands off. And along for the ride was a sulky male model with a waist-length mane of hair. Jade wasn't sure who *he* belonged to, but he was Danish and didn't speak any English, so she didn't let it bother her. After all, he wasn't *her* responsibility.

Las Vegas was not her kind of town – she knew it the moment they arrived. Gambling had never interested her, and the heat on the streets was suffocating. The hotels were all glittering gambling palaces, the people tourists, and the noise of whirling slot-machines non-stop. She hoped Antonio wouldn't be insulted if she hopped on a plane back to L.A. early in the morning.

Yeah. Just in time to keep your lunch date with Mark. Who are you kidding?

Antonio had arranged rooms in a hotel called the Forum. Talk about bad taste. The place was a salute to it! In her room she found a vibrating bed, thick-pile gold carpets, a mirrored ceiling, and porno movies on the closed circuit television.

"Later we party," Antonio advised. "My friends, Dino and Susanna, they have the hot party."

Jade almost yawned in his face. Exhaustion had set in. Two days in bed, sleeping, might be the perfect way to spend the weekend. "I may pass on that," she said.

"You may not!" exclaimed Antonio. "You come here for fun. *Bene.* Fun you shall have!"

*

"Good evening, Mr Python."

"Hiya, Jack!"

"Hello, Jack Python."

"I know you."

"God! You're better lookin' off than on!"

The greetings and comments surrounded him until he felt he was drowning in a sea of flattery.

"Do you like Bette Midler?"

"Is Meryl Streep tall?"

"Does Dustin Hoffman smoke?"

"What's Ann Margret really like?"

The questions came at him from all sides, until a fixed smile slid into place on his face and stayed there as he searched for the nearest exit.

"Hi. I'm Cheryl. Wanna have a nice time?"

"Try my room, 703, in ten minutes."

"I'd really like to sleep with you. I'm a big fan."

"Wanna get it on, TV star?"

The women were not shy. They were aggressive with their come-ons. A tiny blonde, with huge boobs hardly concealed in a shiny blue cocktail dress, trailed him relentlessly. Finally he had to turn on her and say, "Listen. Don't follow me. I *am not* interested. Okay?"

"Who d'y think you *are?*" she shouted belligerently.

"I know who *I* am," he muttered, and pushed through swing

doors to the peace and quiet of the vast swimming pool.

The outside area was deserted. It was past ten, and the sun-bathers and swimmers were long gone. He gazed up at the sky. The stars were out with a vengeance. Tomorrow was going to be a scorcher. Mannon had said something about taking a boat out on Lake Mead.

What was he doing here? In theory it sounded great – a weekend with the guys. But he'd already realized he wasn't one of them anymore. He had other things on his mind, and getting drunk and getting laid just for the sake of it had lost its appeal. Maybe he should alert Aretha to send him a fast telegram saying his presence was urgently required back in Los Angeles. Not such a bad idea.

*

"Hiya, beautiful."

"Want a drink?"

"How about dinner?"

"Do you live around here?"

"Mama! Mama! I died an' went to pussy heaven!"

Jade ignored the remarks. She was used to getting attention. New York had taught her how to deal with it. Just ignore the suckers and they'll soon go away.

However, in Las Vegas they did seem a touch more persistent.

She whirled on one man who made a particularly obscene remark. "Dream on, asshole!"

"Right between your legs, baby!"

She hurried away. Taking a walk around the casino to get the feel of the place was not such a good idea. In Vegas, a woman alone at night obviously spelled available. She followed the SWIMMING POOL sign, and walked outside.

*

"I love giving head," the expensive hooker in the filmy chiffon dress whispered into Howard Soloman's ear. "It's my favourite sexual act. How about you?"

Howard, who had no idea the woman was a hooker, nodded happily. "If you wanna give it, who am I to stop you?"

The woman smiled. Her teeth weren't great, but the rest of her was verging on perfect. Long legs, big bosom, long hair. "I like a man who folds easily," she said, leaning all over him. "And you're *sooo* attractive. Exactly my type."

163

Howard felt the old one-eyed snake stir. This broad was something else. She had been coming on to him from the moment she sat down next to him at Dino and Susanna's party. "You're not an actress, are you?" he asked suspiciously.

"No," she replied with a scornful toss of her head — although if the truth were known she was a better actress than most of the flibberty little bits of fluff she saw on television. "I'm in real estate," she added. "What do *you* do?"

Was she putting him on? Perhaps. Perhaps not. After all, he wasn't a famous *face*. "I'm a businessman," he said guardedly. Better she didn't know too much about him.

"I *looove* a man who handles things," she purred. Her expensively manicured hand moved onto his thigh. "Why don't we go somewhere private?"

Howard agreed readily. He didn't find time to play around in Hollywood. Oh sure, he could always use the never-ending supply of actresses looking for a part — but he didn't like the thought of a woman sleeping with him just because of what he could do for her career. And if you got laid in Hollywood, the whole town knew about it the next day. A lot of men simply didn't care, they just went for it and the hell with the consequences. One well-known producer regularly checked into The Beverly Hills Hotel for an afternoon tryst with his various paramours. Once, his wife was attending a charity function in the Coterie Restaurant, but that didn't faze the producer; he still checked in with a top-heavy redhead, and waved a greeting to his wife's friends at the same time. That was called *chutzpah*.

Howard didn't have the nerve — Poppy would kill him. "Excuse me a minute," he said. "I'll be right back."

Dino Fonicetti was talking to a group of people. Howard drew him to one side and indicated the woman. "Do you know her?" he asked.

Dino looked across the room. Did he know her? Oh, yeah, he knew her, she was the perfect sexual partner for some of his more important guests at the hotel, and he paid her handsomely to entertain them. "Yes. She's very nice. Very respectable. Not a spinner."

"Spinner?" This was a phrase even Howard hadn't heard.

Dino chuckled. "You know, a spinner. A broad who spins from one guy to the next."

Howard laughed too.

"You're not leaving, are you?" Dino asked.

Howard winked. "I'll be right back." He indicated Mannon, who was playing poker with a tableful of high-rollers. "Tell him I'll see him later, or in the morning."

Dino nodded understandingly.

*

"Don't we know each other?" Jack asked.

Jade, sitting on the edge of the diving board, sighed with annoyance. She'd had it with the never-ending pick-up factor. *"Go away."*

"Huh?"

"You heard."

She hadn't even looked at him. He persisted. "Hey – I'm not trying to hit on you. I remember you from . . . uh . . . Silver Anderson's party. My name's Jack Python."

She didn't exactly jump, more a slow turn. She knew who he was all right.

He decided maybe Vegas wasn't such a dead loss after all. He'd been watching her for ten minutes, and he recalled her leaving Silver's party very well. She had been with Antonio's group.

"We never met," she said, recognizing him immediately.

"You *were* there," he stated.

"So was half of Hollywood," she pointed out.

"Can we have a drink and discuss it?"

She began to laugh. "*Mr.* Python. Have you any idea how many times I've been asked that tonight? I'm *surprised* at you. Couldn't you have come up with a more original approach?"

Smiling the Python killer-smile, he said, "Tell me an original approach and I'll use it."

"How about . . . what's a nice girl like you doing in a sleazy city like this?"

He nodded. "That's good. It's got impact. Let me try it." He took three steps away from her and then strode briskly back. "Excuse me – Miss?"

She played the game. "Ms., if you don't mind."

"Uh . . . Ms.?"

"Yes?"

"What's a nice girl like you –"

"Woman," she interrupted.

"Woman?"

"Girl is a patronizing term."

"Come on – *you* told me what to say."

165

"Just checking to see if you're smart enough to change it."

"Hey — watch the insults!"

Getting up, she said, "Don't sweat it, Mr, Python. I can't have a drink with you anyway." She took the sting off her words with a dazzling smile. "I do enjoy your show, only my mother warned me never to talk to strangers, and let's face it, you may be famous, but you're still a stranger."

She walked briskly away before he could answer, and vanished into the hotel.

Once inside she stopped to think. What was a man like Jack Python doing picking up girls — women — out by the pool of the Forum Hotel at ten-thirty at night? He was dangerously good-looking. Too dangerous for her. She had enough involvements right now, and certainly did not need a one-night stand with a man who had a stud reputation. Besides, she had made a strict rule to always steer clear of well-known men — they had egos the size of Atlanta. And that's the last thing she needed.

★

"Take it off, Howard," crooned the woman.

"What off?" gasped Howard. He was marooned among her long legs and big breasts and mass of hair, naked as a bare-assed baby, and just as happy.

"Take off the rug, it's inhibiting you."

"What rug?" he asked indignantly.

"*This* rug!" she said with a triumphant tug at his prize thatch of hair. She whirled it in the air and threw it on the floor.

"Shit!" he exploded.

She bounced on the bed, large breasts jiggling. "I get off on bald men," she explained. "It's sexy. Let's do sixty-nine."

"I'm *not* bald."

"Gettin' there."

"Thank you *very* much."

"Let's do sixty-nine."

"No."

"Why?"

"Because . . ."

"What? You don't like to eat pussy?"

He didn't answer.

She shrugged, and her large breasts heaved. "Your loss," she said, thinking of the female lover she would get it on with later.

★

Mannon Cable won fifty thousand dollars. The party was going strong. He shook the women off like aggravating bugs, and retired to the suite – alone. Jack was in the living room fixing a drink. The door to Howard's bedroom was firmly closed.

"You know something?" Mannon said, "I think I'm getting too old for catting around."

"Want a shot?" Jack asked, pouring himself a scotch.

"Brandy."

"Coming up."

"This place is loaded with hookers. Who did Howard end up with?"

Jack found a bottle of Courvoisier. "I never made the party. I took a walk instead."

Mannon clicked the television on and ruminated. "I've got a beautiful wife, and a beautiful ex-wife. I came here to get laid, but quite frankly – who needs it?"

"You're asking *me*?" Jack said, handing him his brandy. "Let's take the plane back tomorrow."

"What about Howard?"

"What *about* him? He's over twenty-one. I think he'll make out."

Mannon held the brandy glass between his hands and swirled the amber liquid. "It's strange, isn't it? Once we would have given our right arms for this kind of set-up. Now we've got it, who wants it? Who needs it?"

Jack laughed. "Howard."

"Yeah. You can take a kid out of Colorado –"

"But you can never take Colorado out of a kid!" Jack finished Mannon's sentence, and as he did so Jade's coffee commercial appeared on television. "Hey –" he exclaimed. "*That's* where I know her from."

"Who?"

"The girl on television."

They both stared at the set. Jade in a supermarket, buying a jar of coffee. She wore shorts and a tee-shirt and looked like every man's fantasy of the girl next door with her hair piled on top of her head. Next shot. Jade at home – drinking the coffee. Dissolve . . . She's dreaming . . . Jade on a Caribbean beach swaying from the sea in a white bikini, her body tanned and supple, her copper hair long, tangled and wild. She strides from the sea, an Amazon princess. What a body! The camera pans in for a close-up of her face. What a face! *"My place or yours?"* she asks with a long and challenging look straight at the camera. Fade out.

Jack was mesmerized by the commercial. "I think I'm in lust," he dead-panned. "Have you any idea who she is?"

"I thought *you* knew," Mannon said.

"I *want* to know. She's here in the hotel – I just saw her."

Mannon was amused. "Is this love at first commercial? Should we alert Clarissa?"

"Aw . . . get lost!"

Howard emerged from his bedroom and staggered in, hairpiece in hand. He wore a white hotel bathrobe and looked like a beaten man. Two prominent love bites decorated his neck. "Drink," he requested hoarsely.

Jack handed him the bottle of scotch.

"Cigarette," he mumbled.

Mannon handed him a half-full pack of Marlboros.

Howard took a deep breath. "I think I'm having a wonderful time," he said, his voice heavy with exhaustion. "She's got a pussy like a vacuum cleaner. Wake me if I'm not dead in the morning."

And with that he reeled off.

"Viva Las Vegas," said Jack dryly.

Chapter 36

Reba turned up at noon. She let herself in with her pass key, and stood, arms akimbo, a furious expression on her heavily made-up face, at the end of the bed where Wes lay snoring.

He did not stir, in spite of her malevolent glare, which could have cracked paint.

She kicked the end of the bed. "You *shithead*!" she shrieked.

He opened one eye and smelled trouble. Best to face it head on. Sitting up quickly he said, "Jesus! Am I glad to see *you*. I couldn't figure out what happened last night. Once I got Silver Anderson home I came racing back to find you, but you'd gone." He stared accusingly. "Why did you leave without me?"

She opened her mouth like a surprised fish. This was not what she'd expected to hear at all.

"Reba, Reba," he continued, warming to his theme. "You *ran out* on me. I was stranded. I had to stay at a friend's house, and get the bus back this morning."

Frowning, she tapped extremely long fingernails on the end of the bed. "*I* didn't know you were comin' back," she said. "I thought you'd run off an' dumped *me*."

He managed to look hurt. "You thought that?"

"That's what it looked like, didn't it?" she answered defensively.

"It may have looked that way, only surely you know me better? I had your car keys, the claim check for your jacket. I *broke my neck* gettin' back." He paused, careful not to lay it on too thick. "How *did* you get home?"

"I always carry a spare set of keys for the car," she admitted.

He stretched out and yawned. "I'm just glad you're okay. That mob scene was a joke. I had to get the poor bitch out of there before things got out of control."

Reba sat on the end of the bed. "I guess I owe you an apology," she said lamely. "I didn't believe you even knew Silver Anderson."

"I told you I knew her. We're old friends."

She perked up. "I'd love to meet her."

He dodged that one. "So would half the world."

"Maybe we could all have dinner," she suggested hopefully.

Reaching for a cigarette he said, "Maybe." He threw her a stern look. "What was the welcoming note on my door when I got back this morning? What kind of crap was *that*?"

"Oh." She looked embarrassed. "You *do* owe me, Wesley."

"And I'm gonna pay you. Next week. I don't appreciate being threatened with eviction."

She licked her scarlet lips flirtatiously. "Would I do that to you?"

He played along – after all, he didn't want to find himself out on the street, did he? "I don't know *what* you'd do to me, given half the chance."

Laughing lasciviously, she edged along the bed. "Wanna find out, Wesley?"

"I can't, darlin'," he said, quickly. "I gotta see a man about a job. Y'want your rent, don't you?"

She stood up. "It's not that I'm pushin' you, Wesley. Only now that I'm about to be a single woman, I can't let my finances lag behind."

"I quite understand," he said gravely.

Pursing her lips she said, "Well, next time there's some sort of an event —"

"You'll ask me."

She preened coquettishly. "I'll have to see."

"Yours truly will be waitin'."

Her voice took on a businesslike tone as she prepared to leave. "Please telephone me as soon as you get my money."

"I don't have your number. You want to give it to me?"

She thought about that one — and decided against it. "Don't worry, I'll drop by next week."

"Can't wait," he said, with a friendly wink.

As soon as she left he reached for the Yellow Pages and called up the nearest locksmith. There was no way Reba Winogratsky was going to come and go as she pleased in *his* house. Who the hell did she think she was, letting herself in and standing over him while he slept, like a wronged wife?

Screw *her.*

It was over.

*

"Your behaviour was quite reprehensible," Nora said sternly. "However, after a day of thought, Miss Anderson has decided to keep you on." Dragging on her cigarette she added, "Why, I don't know."

Vladimir, head bowed, allowed relief to flush his cheeks. "Madame Silver is very kind," he murmured.

"She sure is," agreed Nora. "I hope you appreciate it."

"I do."

"You'd better."

"I do, I do." He backed gratefully out of the room.

"You're on parole," Nora called after him. "So watch it, sonny!"

He didn't reply.

Nora buzzed the bedroom. "All done," she said.

"Thank God!" replied Silver. "I do *so* hate scenes."

"Are you coming down, or shall I come up?"

"Neither, Nora dear. I'm going to soak in a long hot bubble bath. Wes will be here at eight. Thanks for doing the dirty work. I'll see you at the studio."

"Don't you want me to stick around and meet the new Boy Wonder?"

"Not necessary," Silver replied crisply. "And he is *not* a boy, Nora. He is a man."

"How old?"

"I haven't asked him."

"Fifty? Sixty?"

"Don't be ridiculous."

"Nineteen? Twenty?"

"Cradle snatching is hardly my style."

"Give me a clue."

"Good*night*, Nora."

Talk about being dismissed! Nora gathered her purse, and a stack of photographs Silver had autographed. She was tired after a long day. How come Silver never got tired? With a shake of her head she set off to her apartment in West Hollywood and a quiet TV dinner.

Upstairs, Silver relaxed in a Calèche-scented tub. A Frank Sinatra tape serenaded her. She loved Frank. He was a survivor, just as she was. He would be a performer until he dropped, and so would she.

*

Getting dressed was a problem. He couldn't wear the same suit again, and it was his only suit. He couldn't wear his one white shirt either, it didn't smell too fresh.

Wes inspected his closet. A depressing experience. He possessed two pairs of worn jeans, a pair of black gaberdine pants with a dodgy zipper, two blue shirts — both with frayed collars to match his white one — several unexciting sweaters, a leather bomber jacket and one sports jacket with old-fashioned large lapels. A fashion plate he wasn't. Usually he just stuck anything on and didn't give it a second thought.

A date with Silver Anderson required second thoughts.

He checked the time. It was a quarter to seven, and she had told him to be at her house by eight. She had also said they were staying in, which meant tonight he didn't have to sweat it. Tonight the jeans would pass muster, and maybe a blue shirt (if he could only hide either the missing button on one, or the gravy stain on the other) and his well-worn leather jacket. Of course, tomorrow was another matter. If indeed there was a tomorrow.

He showered, found a small shaker of Jean Naté talcum a

girlfriend had left behind, and liberally tossed the powder over his body. Underwear presented no problem because he never wore it.

A quick shave, on with the chosen outfit, and he was ready.

*

Silver could not make up her mind what to wear. Should she be casual? Dressy? A cross between the two? Finally, after discarding several outfits, she settled for black silk jersey floppy pants, and a black sweater with Joan Crawford shoulders. She doused herself with scent, and wore her dark hair drawn tightly back.

When she was satisfied with her appearance, she swept downstairs and surprised Vladimir in the kitchen.

He jumped to attention. "Yes, madame. Vas there something you needed?" Her visits to the kitchen were not a frequent occurrence.

She tried to forget she had seen him naked, in all his Russian glory. Oh God, banish the very thought! "Yes, Vladimir. I'd like a glass of Cristal. And I'd like you to set the dining room table for two – use the best cutlery and china. Then I want you to phone Trader Vic's and order dinner for two. Have them deliver it, and when it arrives lay out the dishes on the hotplate in the dining room, and go to your apartment. In other words – get out until the morning. I don't want you hanging around."

"Not even to clear up, madame?"

"Didn't you *hear* me, Vladimir?"

"Yes, madame."

She left him to organize everything while she selected more Sinatra to put on the elaborate stereo system, and lowered the lights – all the better to flatter her complexion.

It had been a long while since she'd felt like this about a man. Wes Money had her juices flowing. She couldn't wait to see him.

*

Just as he was leaving there was a knock at his front door. He hoped it wasn't Reba – he wouldn't put it past her to return.

"Yeah?" he called out.

The lock was safely changed, so at least there was no way she could come marching in.

"Are you busy?"

He recognized his neighbour's voice. *Don't tell me she's going to drive me crazy too*, he thought.

"I'm just on my way out," he shouted back.

Silence. She must have taken the hint. He turned off the television in the bedroom, grabbed the keys of Silver's Mercedes from the dresser, and set off.

Leaning against the wall outside was Unity with their newly acquired dog. "Hi," she said.

"Hello," he replied.

She had let her hair down. It was soft and brown, and curled around her heart-shaped face. She was getting prettier every visit.

"I took Mutt to the vet," she said.

"That's nice."

"Don't you want to know what he said?"

"What did he say?"

"He looked at his paw, cleaned it, and put another bandage on."

"Is that all?"

"Yes."

"Great. You'd already done that, hadn't you?"

"Yes, but we had to make sure."

"How much?"

"Your half comes out to nine dollars."

"You mean he charged you eighteen bucks just to look at the dog's *paw*?"

"And a flea bath."

"What's with the flea bath? I never agreed to that."

"He had to have it. The poor dog was crawling."

Wes shook his head. He was down to about fifty bucks, and now he had to shell out nine of them because the dumb dog had fleas. Jesus! If there was an award for sucker of the year he'd win it for sure.

Reluctantly he dug into his bankroll, peeled off a five, and four grubby one-dollar bills.

She accepted the money before springing the next bombshell. "I bought him a collar and lead," she announced.

"You're a generous little thing, aren't you?"

"I guess you don't want to pay half?"

"Look," he said patiently. "I am broke. Busted out. I would like to help you, but nine bucks for a dog is about as far as I'm prepared to go."

"What about its food?"

"Jesus!"

"You promised you'd pay half."

"How much?"

"Your split is a dollar fifty-seven. I got a bag of Gravy Train – I think it will last the week."

"If it doesn't," he said fiercely, groping for more money, "the mutt goes hungry."

She accepted two more dollars from him, and began to search for change.

"Forget it," he said grudgingly. "Put it towards the collar and lead."

"That'll give you a five percent share," she said gravely.

He couldn't help laughing. The dog began to bark. Gingerly he patted it on the head.

"Did you work things out with our dragon landlady?" she asked.

He nodded.

"I told you it would be easy for you."

"Yeah, well y'just have to know how to handle her."

"And I expect you do."

Was she giving him a jab? He couldn't tell. God, she was young. Too young to even know how to jab.

"How old are you?" he couldn't help asking.

"Older than I look," she replied mysteriously.

Since she looked about twelve that didn't help much. "Lucky you. I'm about ten years *younger* than I look."

She almost smiled. He couldn't tell what was going on behind her John Lennon specs. "Well, I gotta get goin'," he said. "See you."

He strode briskly away, leaving her standing outside his front door, a rather forlorn little figure. Didn't she have any friends?

What did he care whether she did or not?

Come on, Wesley, Get your ass in gear. The star is waiting.

Chapter 37

In the Bistro Garden, an elegant Beverly Hills restaurant, the hum of conversation was muted as the rich and famous checked each other out. Poppy Soloman had a table in the tree-shaded garden. She had invited two other women apart from Melanie-Shanna, and while she waited for her guests to arrive, she sipped Perrier with a slice of lime, and inspected the other diners.

There was a well-known producer – well known for his shoplifting proclivities.

There was his wife – an English rose from whom the bloom had long since faded.

There was a young screen writer – whose main claim to fame was his perpetual state of inebriation.

There was a teenage actress who had slept her way *down* the ladder.

Scattered among them were the stars, the true royalty of Hollywood. Poppy counted two retired greats, and a semi-retired almost-great. She also spotted Chuck Nielson with his agent. They exchanged waves.

Melanie-Shanna arrived before the other two women. She was flushed and full of apologies. "Am I late? I'm so sorry. I do hope I haven't kept you waiting."

Poppy tossed back her long blonde hair. Her thick tresses were her best feature, and she always made sure her hair was clean and shining and smelled of deliciously expensive shampoos and conditioners. "You're not late," she said, consulting a diamond-studded watch. "As a matter of fact, you're exactly on time."

"Thank goodness!" sighed Melanie-Shanna.

Poppy summoned the waiter with an authoritative gesture. "What would you like, dear?"

She quickly looked to see what Poppy was drinking. "The same as you, please."

"No, no. You must have something alcoholic. I'll join you in a minute." Poppy clicked her fingers at the waiter. "Bring Mrs. Cable a Mimosa."

Melanie-Shanna hesitated for only a second, then asked, "What's a Mimosa?"

"Champagne and orange juice," Poppy replied patronizingly, as if everyone should know. Before she married Howard, and got herself an education, she'd had no idea either.

Melanie-Shanna looked apologetic again. "Mannon doesn't like me to drink."

"A Mimosa is hardly a drink. You'll love it." Poppy stared critically at her luncheon guest. The girl was pretty enough in a very Texan sort of way. She had wonderful hair and skin, widely spaced eyes, and a body men watched. However, she was not Whitney – who apart from being dazzling was also a big star. Things like that made a difference. Poppy wondered where Mannon had found this one. It seemed every time he went on location to Texas he came back with a wife. "You know, dear," she said, "we've never really had an opportunity to *talk* before. I want to hear *all* about how you and Mannon met."

Melanie-Shanna shrugged. "The papers were full of our story. I thought everyone knew."

"Not *me*," said Poppy. "I never have *time* to read the news-papers, what with my charity work, catering to Howard, and watching Roselight. She's such an *active* little girl, just like her daddy. You must come over and see her one day."

"I'd like that."

The waiter placed a Mimosa in front of Melanie-Shanna. She sipped it delicately, and wished she hadn't come. Ladies' lunches always made her feel uncomfortable, as if she had a run in her tights or chipped nails.

"Good," Poppy said brightly. "Here are the girls."

The "girls" were two women of indeterminate age, although both would never see fifty again. Ida White was the fourth wife of super-agent Zeppo. She was put together with cement to hide the joins, and had pale skin, dramatically white hair pulled back in a tight chignon, an Yves Saint Laurent ensemble, and a blank stare. Rumour had it that Ida was permanently stoned, preferring the land of la-la to life with her womanizing husband.

Zeppo was an infamous Hollywood character known for his sharp tongue and two-inch cock, which – at one time or another – he had offered to every actress in the Western world.

The second woman was the wife of Orville Gooseberger, the producer. She was big and matronly, with the requisite facelift, frosted hair, and a very loud voice. Her name was Carmel, and her husband was even larger and louder than she.

"Does everyone know each other?" trilled Poppy, in between accepting hair-crushing kisses and cries of "You look *wonderful*!" from each of the women.

"Melanie, dear," continued Poppy (she loved playing hostess, it made her feel so important and busy) "this is Ida – you know, Zeppo White's wife. And I'm sure you've met Carmel Gooseberger. Her husband's the producer." Poppy made sure she gave everyone billing. "Girls," she said happily, "we have *finally* managed to get Mannon's wife *out*. Can you imagine? She never goes *anywhere*. We simply *have* to befriend her."

"I knew Mannon when he was getting under a hundred a picture," boomed Carmel.

The stoned Ida rallied. "He was adorable then. So . . . so witty . . ."

"And quite a ladies' man, I hear," giggled Poppy. "I'm too young to remember, but the rumours! Oh dear me!"

Melanie-Shanna smiled politely. She knew about Mannon's past reputation – they didn't have to stick her nose in it. After all, it was a long time ago, before Whitney. She swallowed hard when she thought of her predecessor. Last week she had gone to Mannon's bedside drawer, searching for aspirin. And there, face up, was a framed photograph of Whitney and him together. Just the two of them, in muted colour, standing with their arms around each other, a faraway look in their eyes.

Her immediate reaction was to smash the frame to the ground and rip up the picture. She *hated* Whitney Valentine Cable. If Whitney wasn't around, Mannon would be hers. For in her heart of hearts she knew he still belonged to his ex-wife.

The waiter delivered drinks to the table, and Poppy raised her glass of Perrier. "Now that we're all here," she said gaily, "I'd like to propose a toast."

Ida picked up her double vodka. Carmel lifted white wine. Melanie-Shanna reached for her second Mimosa.

"To us," announced Poppy. "Just because we deserve it!"

The ladies drank.

"And to Melanie." Poppy was on a roll, and wasn't about to quit. "Because we want her to feel she's one of us."

They made an incongruous quartet. Melanie-Shanna, so young and pretty, and obviously painfully out of place; Poppy, designer-labelled to the eyebrows, but not quite chic – her hair style put paid to that; Ida, totally out of it; and Carmel, old enough to be Melanie-Shanna's and Poppy's mother.

"I nearly fucked Mannon once," recalled Ida, a faraway look in her eye.

"Shush!" said Poppy warningly. "Melanie doesn't want to hear about *that*."

"Zeppo was his agent," Ida continued, oblivious. "We were all on location. I wasn't married to Zeppo then, but he was after me all right!"

"Zeppo was after everything that drew breath," Carmel remarked loudly.

"So was Orville," retorted Ida, with a spark of clarity. "I can remember when no actresses would step into his office because he insisted they give him a blow job under the desk."

"*Really?*" Poppy gasped.

"The Screen Actors Guild had to step in," Ida added. Her thoughts drifted. "I nearly fucked Mannon once."

"Well, you *didn't*," roared Carmel, "so *do* get off the subject."

Poppy giggled. She adored these two Hollywood old-timers – one never knew what was going to come out of their mouths next. And in their own way they were important women. At least their husbands were important, which made them important by association.

There is a certain kind of woman in Hollywood who believes that because she is married to a famous/rich/powerful man everyone loves her, and she is one of the queens of Hollywood.

Sure everyone loves her, while the marriage lasts. When the divorce comes – forget it. Suddenly the invitations cease and the loyal friends vanish. Sad but true. The friends stick with the famous/rich/powerful husbands. Some friends.

Ida and Carmel were two such women. Fortunately for them their marriages had lasted, sparing them the humiliation of being cast aside.

Chuck Nielson, sitting across the restaurant, had one eye on Melanie-Shanna and one eye on his agent, Quinne Lattimore. His concentration wavered between the two.

"Chuck, are you *listening* to me," Quinne asked irritably.

"Yeah," Chuck replied. "Only I gotta take a leak. I'll be right back."

He had noticed Mannon's wife rise to go to the ladies' room, and he was conveniently there when she came out. "Hello, pretty lady," he said.

She looked startled and flushed and exceptionally fuckable.

"Chuck Nielson," he reminded.

"Yes, I know."

"When are you coming to visit me at the beach?"

"What?"

"The beach. Malibu. Remember? I invited you down."

"Oh, yes."

"Don't go wild with excitement."

"We'd love to come."

He raised an eyebrow. "We?"

"Mannon and I."

Chuck grinned boyishly. "You don't have to bring him, y'know."

She edged away.

He stopped her with a hand on her arm. Whitney was giving him a hard time and he needed to teach her a lesson, bring her into line. She was too independent by far. If he started an affair with Mannon's new wife it would drive Whitney crazy.

"Take my number," he urged, handing her a packet of matches with the number scrawled inside. "Call me."

Melanie-Shanna smiled vaguely; she didn't know what else to do. Mannon would be furious if he found out about this. "Excuse me," she said, pulling free.

"Call me," Chuck repeated, as she hurried back to her table.

"Well," Poppy said, savouring every word. "I see our local beach stud has you in his line of fire. How incestuous!"

"He was just inviting Mannon and me to his house in Malibu," Melanie-Shanna explained lamely.

Poppy grinned knowingly. "I bet he was!"

"*Really.*"

"That man is a rutting dog," Carmel announced. "Orville had him in a film once. He laid every woman on the set, including his co-star."

"And who might that be?" Poppy asked anxiously, never one to miss out on good gossip.

"I don't know. One of those flat-chested little popsies with

179

goo-goo eyes. They all look the same to me. She married a vet or a dog trainer or something – I can't remember which."

Poppy's eyes gleamed. "You must know some *outrageous* stories."

Ida knocked over her glass of vodka and pretended not to notice. "*I* know the best stories," she said in her strangely flat voice. "*I* know everything."

"You should write a book," Poppy gushed.

"I will," Ida said vaguely, "when I find the time."

Chapter 38

They were headed in one direction all night. Bed.

The champagne was cold.

The food delicious.

The conversation light.

Sex was on both their minds.

After dinner Silver suggested that they have brandies upstairs.

Wes grabbed a bottle of Courvoisier and two glasses, and followed her up the winding staircase.

It wasn't long before they were rolling around on her California King without a care in the world.

Silver Anderson, in bed, did not have any inhibitions. From experience Wes knew that after thirty, most women (he could only think of one exception – a tall thin porno star who swallowed men whole) had the most incredible hang-ups about their bodies. *Am I too thin? Fat? Floppy? Have I got stretch marks? Do my breasts sag?* God almighty! They carried on and on and on.

None of that from Silver Anderson. She wasn't twenty-two, and didn't give a damn. She had a compact, sinewy body, with firm breasts and hard nipples. Her bush was a little sparse, which was the only disappointment as far as he was concerned – he liked them with an abundance of hair down there. It didn't matter, though, and it certainly made it easier when going down on her. He didn't end up with a mouthful of annoying little pubic hairs which were impossible to get rid of.

Silver *loved* getting head. She didn't mind giving it either. Some women thought they were doing you the favour of all time. Not Silver. She got down and boogied with a good solid beat.

Tonight she gave him another ball-busting climax, and after a few minutes' recovery time he began to repay the compliment. Only he was in no hurry, and she didn't object.

He laid her out, put pillows under her ass, spread her legs, and went to work. Eating pussy was not one of his favourite things, but he tackled the task gamely. Tongue probing, pushing, exploring. Going for the gold, and finding it.

She responded nicely, with just the right amount of moans and groans.

Usually he didn't offer this service. In fact he could only remember doing it to two women before: his steel-thighed Swede, and the one love of his life — Vicki. Well, you had to keep *something* special, didn't you? He wouldn't have gone down on Reba Winogratsky for a thousand big ones. Maybe two thousand, but that was a lot of bucks.

Silver climaxed with abandon, thrusting her pelvis towards him until he was almost suffocated by her juices. He felt the throb, and knew it was a job well done.

He rolled away from her and dived into the bathroom, where he took a mugful of tap water and swished it around his mouth. Then he peed, and returned to the bedroom.

Silver was sitting up in the rumpled bed with the sheet tight to her chest. She had a smile of pure satisfaction on her face.

He grinned at her. No need for words as he bounded into bed beside her, reached for cigarettes for both of them, lit up, and handed her one.

They puffed silently, perfectly in tune. And when she was finished with her cigarette she reached for his balls under the covers, and kneaded them gently.

Not again! he thought. And rose to the occasion.

This was better than conversation any day!

Chapter 39

The yacht on Lake Mead was a rather grand affair with two decks and a uniformed crew. It belonged to Joseph Fonicetti, but he hardly used it, so his son, Dino, usually commandeered it at weekends.

This particular weekend Dino and his wife, Susanna, were hosting a luncheon with a somewhat disparate group of guests.

There was Howard Soloman, extremely hung over, with red-rimmed eyes, and a turtleneck to cover his scars of battle.

There was Mannon Cable, with his cobalt blue eyes, dirty blond hair, and sly, self-deprecating humour.

There was Jack Python, looking uncomfortable.

And three of Susanna's girlfriends. Two divorced, and one still searching for a victim. On a scale of ten, they ranged from a three to a six and a half.

There was Dee Dee Dionne, a beautiful black chanteuse, who was Carlos Brent's current lady friend. She wore dark glasses and sat watchfully in the background.

There was Carlos Brent himself. He was Susanna's father, and a true legend in his own lifetime.

And Carlos Brent's assorted entourage.

There was Antonio, with his decorator boyfriend, and long-haired Danish friend.

And there was Jade Johnson.

Quite a group.

Jack had only stayed to see Carlos Brent. He wanted him for his show, and going through intermediaries was never satisfactory. When he spotted Jade, he knew fate had a hand in things somewhere along the line, and he was glad. Quickly noting who she was with, he detected no competition. Clarissa was in New York. He deserved a break, didn't he?

Without hesitation he started to move towards her, only to be short-stopped by Antonio, who wanted to show off their acquaintanceship.

Jade smiled at him across the deck. A good sign. At least he wasn't losing the Python touch.

"Who is she?" he asked Antonio, pointing her out.

"You don't know Jade?" the photographer said in surprise. "How can that be?"

"Who is she?" Jack repeated.

The hunting look in his eye was duly observed by the wily Italian, and his *bella* Jade could do worse than Jack Python.

"She is Jade Johnson. The most famous model of all. Forget Jerry Hall, Cheryl Tiegs and Christie Brinkly. *This* is the one."

Jack felt like an idiot. Of course. He knew her name. *And* her image. Only she managed to look different in everything she did.

Putting on his glasses, he rubbed the stubble around his chin. Jade Johnson. A famous lady in her own field. She must think he was a grade A schmuck going for a quick pick-up. No wonder she hadn't responded.

Jade Johnson. He had heard her name a hundred times. Shaking his head he smiled to himself. She presented a challenge. It had been far too long between challenges.

Susanna Brent's girlfriends could not believe their good fortune. They were three Beverly Hills princesses with tight asses and hungry eyes. Susanna had invited them to Vegas for a reunion of sorts – they had graduated from high school together over twelve years before. "Maybe you'll find some hot guys in Vegas," Susanna had promised temptingly. Hot guys were one thing – but Mannon Cable and Jack Python, both within reaching distance! They were in heat!

Naturally, it was Howard who did the chasing. Howard, sweating in his turtleneck sweater, dropping names, *and* his pants if they would let him. On this weekend away from home ground he had gone pussy crazy!

Susanna's trio of girlfriends were not interested. None of them wanted to be actresses. The term *studio head* did not impress them. And Howard, with his insane mugging and overpowering approach, scored a zero.

Mannon began telling jokes, and soon drew an attentive audience. Carlos Brent strolled over and started to top each one of Mannon's stories with a better one of his own. The two men enjoyed each other's celebrity.

Jack edged over to Jade, who was leaning over the rail studying the cool green water.

"Searching for sharks?" he asked casually.

She straightened up and faced him. Up close, in the strong daylight, she was staggeringly good-looking. Her very lightly tanned skin was soft and luminous, her gold-flecked eyes fascinatingly direct. The best thing about her, though, was her strong square jawline – which took the edge off perfection and made her vulnerable, strong, and just a touch aggressive, all at the same time.

He curbed a wild impulse to reach out and touch.

She pushed a hand through a tumble of shaggy copper hair and looked around at Dino and Susanna's guests. "If I was searching for sharks, I'm sure there are better places to look than in the water. Yes?"

He liked the way she said "yes" at the end of a sentence.

"You see that man over there." She indicated Howard, who had now moved on to Carlos Brent's girlfriend and was promising her stardom.

"What about him?" Jack asked curiously.

"When I first came out to Hollywood – I guess it must be ten years ago. Anyway, he was an agent then, chic in his gold chains and perfect suntan. God, he gave me a real hard time. Chased me around the couch in my hotel suite, and badgered me day and night to go out with him. Antonio tells me he's the head of a studio now. I'm in shock. The man is a moron! Do you know him?"

Jack considered his reply carefully. It was not going to do him much good if he admitted he was spending the weekend with Howard the moron. And he had to agree that if you didn't know Howard, he *could* come across as an asshole. Choosing to shift focus he said, "What were you doing in Hollywood then?"

"A screen test. The usual bullshit. Ten minutes in town was enough to convince me that I didn't want it. I like to be in control of *my* life."

A woman who thought along the same lines as he did. He liked her style. "Hey – I'm sorry for not knowing who you were last night," he said apologetically.

"It's not required knowledge," she joked. "A good model sells a product, not herself."

"And you're the best, I hear."

"Who told you that?" She paused. "Ah . . let me see, could it be the great Antonio by any chance?"

"God, you're quick!"

"Only when I'm running away from Howard whatshisname! Or maybe we should just call him Moron Numero Uno." She tilted her head. "Do you think I'm being too cruel?"

"He's not such a bad guy once you get to know him."

"Ah *ha*! So you *do* know him."

"Guilty, I'm afraid."

She thought he had the sexiest eyes she had ever seen. They were an incredible green, with a deep intensity she could easily get lost in. "I hardly ever watch your show," she blurted foolishly, just so he wouldn't think she was impressed.

He regarded her with cool amusement. "I didn't ask you, but go on, make me feel bad."

"I didn't mean to do that –"

"Oh yes you did."

She laughed. "I didn't. Really."

Their eyes met and stayed locked together just that moment too long.

She felt a jolt of electricity and so did he. Neither of them could ignore it.

"What are you doing tonight?" he asked.

She didn't hesitate – sometimes she liked to take risks. "We're having dinner, aren't we?"

He liked a direct woman.

He liked everything about her.

Chapter 40

Immediate problem: make a score. He had to pay Reba, and support his half-share in a dog, and eventually he was going to have to take Silver out, although *in* suited him just fine, and he wasn't pushing.

Another night of unadulterated lust. And very nice too. Somewhere along the way she had asked him what business he was in. Casually he had replied, "Liquor." She hadn't pushed it. Probably thought he owned Seagrams!

Now he was driving back to Venice in her 350 SL, early a.m., and feeling no pain.

She likes me! She likes me! he thought, feeling like Sally Field when she gave her Oscar acceptance speech.

If he played it right he could be moving in any day now. He strongly suspected that Silver quite fancied the idea of having a man about the house. She had dropped a few not so subtle hints about the way everyone took advantage of her, and how nice it would be to have someone she could trust to look after her affairs. This, after two nights of passion. Things were looking good.

However, it did not solve the pressing problem of scoring bucks.

Usually, when he needed money, he went to work. Tending bar on a good week – with a touch of petty larceny on the side – he could pull in eight or nine hundred. Just the kind of money he needed now. Only he couldn't take time off right at the beginning, she wasn't *that* hooked. His only alternative was Rocky, who could probably point him in the direction of something seriously illegal. He didn't have much choice.

Taped to his front door was an envelope. Not Reba again!

He ripped it open and read the childish scrawl, bad spelling and all.

MUTT AND I THAWT YOU CAN COME
TO EAT WITH US TONITE. I WILL
COOKE. 7 OCKLOCK. LOVE FROM
UNITY.

What brought that on? He couldn't go. Silver had already
booked him.

Happiness was being in demand.

*

"Poppy Soloman called," Nora said, in between bouts of
coughing. "She wants to have a dinner for you. She said you'd
discussed it."

"You sound terrible," Silver scolded. "Aren't you planning
to *do* something about that cough?"

" 'Twasn't the cough that carried me off, 'twas the coffin
they carried me off in!" joked Nora, with a macabre grimace.

"*Most* amusing," said an unamused Silver.

They were in her dressing room at the studio. It was the
lunch break, and Silver rested on a couch, her legs up, her head
supported by two large pillows. "I'm exhausted!" she announced. "Pass me my vitamins, for God's sake."

Nora duly obliged. Silver gulped the mixed vitamins down
by the handful. Then she yawned, a long-drawn-out self-satisfied
yawn.

"I presume last night was another winner," Nora said acidly.

Silver closed her eyes. "Mmmmmm . . ."

"When do I get to meet Mister Wonderful?"

"Soon."

"When?"

"How about Poppy Soloman's dinner?"

"I don't think she's planning on inviting *me*."

"Tell her you're part of the deal. You know I like to have
you around."

"I get overtime for attending dinners," Nora rasped.

"Good. Charge it to the studio."

"Don't think I won't."

A knock on the door announced lunch. A tray for Silver.
Grated carrots, sliced peppers, raw broccoli, and thinly sliced
cucumbers on a plate.

She looked at it with distaste. "What I wouldn't give for a
big fat juicy hamburger!" she sighed with longing.

"Shall I order you one?" Nora asked.

"Are you mad?"

*

Rocky knew just the trouble Wes could get into. He had heard there was a very special collection to be made which would pay big. "I don't wanna have anythin' t'do with it," Rocky said. "There's warring factions out in the hills of Laurel Canyon. It's not serenity city, but if you wanna score fast, I'll give you the man to call."

If Rocky didn't care to be involved it had to be heavy, and usually Wes liked to steer clear of any whiff of trouble. He went for it, though – there didn't seem to be much choice if he wanted fast bucks.

*

"I'm going back to the office," Nora said. "Are you cozying with Stud of the Year tonight?"

"I see no reason to quit while I'm on a winning streak, do you?"

The older woman shook her head. "Where do you get the energy? Sex every night. Work every day. And interviews in your spare time. Which reminds me, I want to go over next week's schedule with you. *Bazaar* wants you for the cover, and –"

Silver waved her away. "Not now, Nora. I'm hardly in the mood."

If Silver didn't want to talk covers, she must be *really* hooked. "Later?"

"I shall be busy later. *Very* busy."

*

The deal was this. A certain bad-boy rock star and his fifteen-year-old girlfriend were holed up in a remote house high in the hills of Laurel Canyon. They owed. And they owed big.

"These people don' wanna pay," explained the black dude to whom Wes had refused entry to Silver's party. He was a short man, with a toothy grin and huge white-framed sunglasses. "You wanna go get the green stuff. We grateful. We pay big."

The meet was taking place in the back of the man's limo at the bottom of the multi-storey parking lot in the Santa Monica shopping mall. They were separated from the driver by a thick tinted glass window.

When Wes had called, the man had suggested they get together at once, and arranged the rendezvous, which Wes just managed to arrive at by noon.

"What's the big fuss?" he asked; there didn't seem to be anything complicated about picking up some money.

"You wan' the truth, I give it to you," the black man said. "This boy a bad one. He beat up on my las' delivery man. He steal my coke. He keep my money."

"Yeah?"

"This not good scene fo' me. *No trouble* is my motto. I don' wan' no connection to this bad boy. None at all."

"You're tellin' me he's not going to greet me with a kiss and a fistful of dollars. Right?"

"Maybe. Maybe not. I don' pay no thousan' for nothin' easy."

"I figured that."

"This famous bad boy – he collect guns. His sweetie-box – she only fifteen. We don' want no duckin' an' divin' with this couple. So we sen' you in for pick up. You fuck up – no connection."

"And what makes you think he'll hand over the money to me?" Wes asked cynically.

"He say he will now. He ready." Taking a silk handkerchief out of his top pocket, he wiped his face. "You carry a piece?"

"Whoa!" Wes said quickly. "I'm not gettin' into any of *that*."

The man made a face. "I don' care personally. Jus' for your own protection. You want the job? You carry a piece. Insurance, thas all."

Staying silent, Wes thought it out. On the one hand it seemed fairly straightforward. On the other it stank stronger than a dead catfish.

"I don't get it," he said at last. "Why would you pay a thousand for this pick-up?"

"Don' give me no D.A. questions. You do it or no?"

So it wasn't the smartest move in the world; even Rocky had turned *this* one down. But he had luck on his side. Wes Money always made out – somehow.

"I'll do it," he decided.

"Tonight."

"Not tonight."

"Nine o'clock on the stroke, or no deal."

Shit! He could call Silver and tell her he'd be late. Better still, he could turn this offer down and ask *her* for money. Just a loan. Nothing serious.

Sure. And it would be goodbye Wesley without a second thought.

"Money up front," he said.

"No problem."

Now he was more suspicious than ever. What kind of a schmuck parted with money *before* the deed was done?

The man handed him a small snub-nosed revolver, and a crisp packet of new hundred-dollar bills.

"Aren't you worried I'll tango out of town with this?" Wes joked.

"You'd be motherfuckin' crazy to do that to me," the man said, removing his shades and staring.

"Wouldn't think of it," Wes said quickly.

The man passed him a slip of paper with an address written on it. "Nine o'clock. They be expectin' you. Then you bring package to me here. I be waitin'."

Wes nodded. And with gut instinct he knew he was making a wrong move.

Chapter 41

A strong blast of the white powder into each nostril made Howard Soloman feel like a real man. He was on a roll. Vegas was the best time he'd had in a while.

Leaning back against the cool marble of the bathroom wall he allowed the full drug-induced sensation to take over his body. By the time he was ready to rejoin the party he was fucking invincible!

He determined to tell Mannon Cable where his loyalties lay. How dare he refuse to do a film for Orpheus. Shithead actor. Stars or not they were all shitheads. Mannon was his friend. You made certain moves for friends. And goddammit, signing a deal with Orpheus should be one of them.

Conveniently he forgot he was hellbent on getting Mannon's

ex-wife into the old sackerooney. Exquisite Whitney. He got hard just thinking about her. Which made him think of Poppy, for whom he had a permanent soft-on!

Howard laughed aloud, leaned over the basin, and splashed cold water on his face.

He was at another party, a Saturday night after-the-show bash for Carlos Brent.

Carlos hadn't done a movie in ten years, and Howard planned to nail him. Okay, so Carlos Brent had made a few flops in his time — singing was his forte, not straight drama. Howard's brilliant idea was to offer him a *musical*! Shit! What an idea! The kind of musical they used to make way back in the forties with John Payne and Betty Grable. Nostalgia time. Everyone would love it!

Howard was at a loss to figure out why nobody had thought of it before. The idea screamed BOX OFFICE! He would get a young hot-shot director/writer. One of those boy geniuses just waiting for a big budget. And an experienced producer to keep a steady eye on things. Orville Gooseberger would be ideal. And Whitney Valentine for the female lead!

Howard was so excited he had to take a quick pee before rejoining the party.

He had just come up with the project of the year!

*

"I hate some of your movies, they're so masculine. And you play a real macho sexist pig!" So spoke one of Susanna Fonicetti's girlfriends, hoping this negative approach would impress Mannon Cable so much that he would whisk her off to his hotel suite for further discussion.

He blinked his impossibly blue eyes and winked. "Let me tell you something, darlin'. You're absolutely right."

"On the other hand," she added quickly, "in some of your films you really are quite wonderful. The quintessential golden-haired hero riding in from the west."

"You gotta make up your mind, sweetheart," Mannon drawled. "What am I? The macho sexist pig? Or the golden fuckin' hero?"

"You're both," she stated dramatically, convinced that he thought she was the most intelligent woman who ever drew breath. "And you're magnificent!"

"And *you're* full of it, sweetheart. Excuse me." He ambled off in search of Carlos. Swapping dirty stories was a lot more fun than swapping conversation with the ding-bats floating around Vegas.

For once in his life Mannon did not feel horny. He felt home-sick. Away from home he was on show. *Come see the movie star. Watch him walk, talk, eat. Try and get him to fuck.*

Damn it, he was fed-up with the attention. He felt like he was in a sideshow – only *he* was the main attraction.

"Are you all right, Mannon?" Susanna Fonicetti, née Brent, appeared at his side. She was the typical Beverly Hills daughter of a great superstar. Hollywood kids turned out one of two ways. They either dropped out completely, or went with the lifestyle all the way. Susanna had gone all the way. She was the seed of Hollywood royalty and she knew it. Oh, how she knew it!

"I'm fine, darlin'," he said, with a big grin. "Where's your daddy?"

Susanna giggled. "The way you say that makes me feel about fourteen!"

"You don't look much older."

"Flatterer!"

She took him by the hand and led him to a corner table where Carlos held court. The entourage scattered, giving Mannon room to sit down.

"Did you hear the one about the Porsche and the rabbit?" he asked Carlos.

Carlos roared. "Did I *hear* it. *I* made it up, for crissake!"

*

The candlelight in the small Italian restaurant cast a warm glow. The conversation too, for Jack found Jade to be an informed talker and attentive listener. They covered everything from Reagan's politics to idle gossip. And also ate a hearty meal which consisted of thinly sliced mozzarella cheese and tomatoes to start with. And delicious medallions of veal, accompanied by a side order of pasta in a delicate cream sauce.

"Dessert?" Jack asked, when the trolley came around.

Jade grinned. "Why not?"

The waiter pointed out the various delights, and she picked chocolate chip cheesecake.

"I'm a chocolate freak," she admitted guiltily. "Complete with withdrawal symptoms and all."

He laughed. "I can relate to that. Ice cream is my downfall. Show me a carton of Häagen Dazs and I'm anybody's!"

The waiter kissed his fingertips. "We have the best ice cream," he announced. "Made on the premises. We have vanilla, cherry, rum, banana, strawberry –"

Jack stopped him. "You've hooked *me*," he said. "Bring a dish of banana."

"With hot chocolate sauce?"

"The works."

"Nuts?"

"Everything!"

"And two cappucini?"

"I think I'll live dangerously and have a plain coffee with Amaretto on the side," Jade said.

"Make that two." Jack smiled across the small table at her. "I knew you'd make me live dangerously – one way or the other."

She smiled back. "Is an Amaretto all it takes?"

"That and a back rub." He regarded her closely. This was the most enjoyable evening he'd had with a woman in a long time. He hadn't realized quite how serious Clarissa was. She would slit her throat rather than eat a meal like this. Not only was she a vegetarian, she also wouldn't touch sugar or alcohol, which made culinary activities somewhat boring.

"I hope you're having a good time," he said, meaning every word.

"I'm having a lovely time. You're great company." And indeed he was. Even if he hadn't been, just looking at him was a treat. Those eyes. Those penetrating green eyes. And the way he smiled, and his jet black hair which hit the back of his collar in exactly the right place. She had seen a lot of good-looking guys in her time, mostly models, and mostly gay. Jack Python was different. He was amusing and smart, with a cynical edge. And he was making her forget Mark Rand with a vengeance.

The coffee and Amaretto arrived, along with Jack's ice cream. She leaned across the table and stole some of his chocolate sauce. "Mmmm . . ." she murmured, licking her lips. *"Fan-tas-tic!"*

"Are you involved with anyone?" he asked abruptly.

She paused before answering, because she wasn't quite sure if she was or not. Mark Rand wanted to be back in her life. She hadn't said yes or no, just run for cover. She was supposed to be thinking things over – and yet here she was, having a perfectly wonderful evening. What kind of answer could she give him? It wasn't that simple.

"I don't know," she said softly.

193

He stared at her quizzically. "You don't know?"

She picked up her glass of Amaretto and tipped it into her coffee. "Uh . . . it's complicated. I *was* involved, *very* involved. Now I'm not so sure."

"Anything you want to talk about?"

"I don't think so."

They lapsed into silence.

'And you?" she said, breaking the pause in conversation.

Okay. What did he tell her? That he was supposed to be considering getting married. That would go down well.

"I guess I sort of see Clarissa Browning," he said guardedly. "We've been together over a year. She's in New York at the moment."

She sipped her coffee. This wasn't exactly fresh news; Antonio had filled her in before the date. "Oh," she said, and added as an afterthought, "She's a magnificent actress."

"That she is," he agreed. And they looked at each other, and the look could burn bridges.

"I want to sleep with you," he said.

She was completely lost in his eyes. "I know."

"Well?"

"I don't think we're the perfect couple – what with our commitments and all."

He stared at her intently. "Do you want me as much as I want you?"

The "yes" slipped from between her lips before she could help herself.

Chapter 42

Okay, Wes knew it was some kind of set-up, only he couldn't figure out the angle.

He called Rocky and questioned him.

"Don't involve me," Rocky said. "I only gave ya the connection to help out. My advice is watch your balls, an' tread carefully at all times."

That made him feel very secure.

Next he called Silver at the studio.

A raspy voice answered the phone with a not too friendly "Silver Anderson's dressing room. What do you want?"

"I'd like to talk to the lady herself."

"She's on the set. Who is this?"

"Wes Money. It's important."

"I'll have to take a message."

Shit! He had really wanted to explain things to her personally.

"Go ahead – shoot," said the raspy voice.

"Can you tell her somethin' came up – business-wise – and I'll be running late tonight. I'll try to be with her by ten-thirty."

"Got it."

"Say I'm sorry, it's unavoidable."

"Right."

"Tell her if I could have changed it I would."

"What is this – a continuing saga? I'm taking a message not writing a book!"

"Sorry. Oh, the name is Wes Money. M-O-N –"

"I know how to spell money."

"Thanks."

"I'll give her the message."

He rubbed the bridge of his nose. Funny thing, whenever he was uptight or tense his nose always gave him trouble. Usually he got a dull ache right by the break.

He had sealed the thousand dollars in an envelope, and now he had to decide where to hide it until this job was done. There was no safe place – break-ins were common along the boardwalk.

He waited until he heard Unity return from work, and knocked on her door.

She was fastening an apron around her tiny waist as she opened up. "You're too early," she admonished. "Dinner won't be ready for an hour. I'm fixing stew."

He loved stew! It was his favourite meal. In fact it was the *only* meal his mother had ever cooked.

"I can't make it over for dinner," he said regretfully, remembering her note.

She didn't look him in the eye. "That's okay," she said, and he sensed her disappointment.

"You didn't give me much notice, did you?" he complained.

"I asked you. You can't come. I understand," she said flatly.

"Remember me next time," he urged.

"Sure," she replied unenthusiastically.

The dog appeared and wagged its tail. Wes leaned over and patted it. "How's the paw?" He glanced around her side of the house. Same rented furniture, dismal prints on the walls, cramped little kitchen. Reba's taste was up her ass. "What kind of job do you do?" he asked.

She was busy peeling carrots. "I'm a waitress in a bar."

"No kiddin'! I work bar on occasion."

"Yes?" she said, completely uninterested. "Where?"

"Around. I pick and choose. How about you?"

"Hollywood Boulevard. Tito's."

"I don't know it."

"You don't want to."

He pulled the envelope of money from the pocket of his leather jacket and hoped he could trust her. Since he had no choice he asked her anyway. "Can you look after this for me? Just for a couple of hours?"

"What is it?" she asked suspiciously.

"My life savings," he replied sarcastically. "What else?"

Smoothing down her apron she glared at him, her slightly crossed eyes giving her a vulnerable look.

"Seriously," he said. "There's some important documents I can't leave in the house. So if you wouldn't mind . . ." He trailed off.

"I'm going to sleep early," she said, taking the envelope from him. "If you're any later than ten you'll have to pick it up in the morning before I go to work."

"What time's that?"

"Tomorrow my shift is eleven till three. I'll be leaving here at nine-fifteen."

"Perfect." Silver usually booted him out at seven, when she left for the studio. He could collect his money at eight a.m. if he got held up tonight. "I'd appreciate it if you could do me this favour," he said.

She nodded, put the envelope on the side, and continued peeling carrots.

"Okay," he said, backing towards the door. "Enjoy dinner. Oh, and Unity?"

"Yes?"

"Do me another favour. Don't let the envelope out of your sight."

★

"Your boyfriend phoned," Nora said. "He sounds a real charmer."

"What did he want?" Silver asked, trying to conceal her sudden interest.

"Your body. He says you're the best lay he's ever had!"

"Thank you, Nora. I already know that. What did he *really* want?"

"He's running late. Cannot be with you until after ten tonight."

"Damn!"

"What?"

"I hate being kept waiting. You know that."

Nora lit up her forty-fifth cigarette of the day. "He said it was business."

"What kind of business does he have to do at night?"

Nora shrugged her shoulders. "Ask *him*, not *me* – I'm only the message taker."

"I'll do that." She swooped into a large Gucci tote bag for her telephone book and handed it to Nora. "Get him for me, will you?"

Nora backed up. "I'm here to look after your publicity not your lovers. Where's your assistant?"

"For Christ's sake, Nora. Each one is worse than the last. I fired the last one, you know that."

Grumbling, Nora looked up Wes Money's number. "I should be getting double pay. I'm doing two jobs."

"I'll buy you a present," Silver said graciously.

"Make it a condo in Miami. I think I'll retire."

Nora punched out the number, and waited. An answering machine picked up. She passed the phone to Silver.

"This is Wes. I'm out. I'll be back. Leave your name, number and time of call. Go for it . . . NOW!"

Perfect timing. The bleep sounded immediately.

"Wes." She hated machines, she felt so stupid speaking into them. "Er . . *Why* are you running late? It's really *most* inconvenient. Phone me at home before you come over."

"That'll tell 'im," remarked Nora sarcastically.

"Kindly shut up, dear," said Silver grandly, and swept back to the set.

*

Wes took Sunset all the way in from the beach. He drove Silver's Mercedes, and stayed in the right-hand lane and under the speed limit. It wouldn't do to get stopped while he was carrying. He sweated at the very thought.

Jeez! What had he got himself into, and why?

He knew enough to realize if you carried you'd better be prepared to use. And he had no intention of doing that. In and out. That was his plan. If the guy gave him any trouble he would back gently off and split fast.

Laurel Canyon wound its way off Sunset into the hills, and meandered all the way over to the Valley. The house Wes was looking for was located halfway up, along with several other homes on a private road. The numbers were listed on a row of mailboxes, and a sign read PRIVATE PROPERTY. STAY OFF. ARMED PATROL. BEWARE OF DOG.

Talk about a warm welcome!

It was dark up in the hills and he had to shine a flashlight outside the car window to be sure he was at the right place.

Turning up the side road, he drove slowly, looking for the correct number. When he found it he idled past, just to get the lie of the land. There was one more house after it, and then the hills grew wild and steep.

He turned his car around with difficulty, all the while planning, thinking. He didn't want to drive up to the front door, park the car, and present himself just like that – a sitting target if things went wrong. He had to be in a position to make a fast getaway if the need arose – which he hoped it wouldn't, but you could never be too careful.

He drove two houses down. Each home had its own private driveway snaking up into the hills. None of the residences was visible from the private road. They all seemed to have these long, winding paths to negotiate.

On impulse, he drove up the wrong one. It was not your manicured Beverly Hills type driveway. This was pure country, with overhanging trees, and a lot of wild bush.

He reached a ranch-style residence with several cars parked outside. Switching off his lights, he turned his car around, and headed back to the main private road. Halfway there, he pulled the Mercedes tight into the side, killed the ignition, and got out. Pocketing the keys he checked his watch. It was five of nine. The man had said to collect at nine o'clock prompt. He was running on time.

On foot he moved swiftly, having had the good sense to wear comfortable sneakers.

Down the path, up the private road, until he reached the right number, and yet another sign warning of armed patrol and dogs.

Feeling a shudder of apprehension, he made his way up the steep incline towards collection point. Shit! This whole cloak-and-dagger bit was like something out of a James Bond movie!

The house, when he reached it, was silent. Only one light shone in an upstairs room. A silver Maserati, a black Jeep, and an old blue station wagon were dotted around outside. A coyote howled somewhere in the hills.

With trepidation, he approached the front door. *This is a piece of pussy*, he thought.

The hairs on the back of his neck told him it wasn't.

He groped for the gun. It nestled in his pocket like a security blanket. Not that he would ever use it. As the man had said, just insurance in case of trouble.

What trouble?

Confidently he rang the bell. It was nine o'clock exactly.

Silence. Nothing. Nobody answered.

He rang again.

Repeat performance.

Stepping back he glanced up at the lighted window. No sign of movement there.

Shit!

Drawn like a magnet he reached forward and tried the front door.

It opened. Just like that. Deep down he had known it would.

Inner voices screamed – *Don't go in, schmuck! Get your ass in gear and vamoose!*

Far off in the distance he heard police sirens. They harmonized with the mournful howling of the lone coyote.

As he entered the house he thought about Silver. Her throaty laugh, expensive skin, hot, throbbing –

Jesus! He had known it was a set-up.

Sprawled halfway down the stairs was the body of a man. Blood dripped from him like a faucet, forming a pool on the hall carpet. He had been shot in the head.

Drawn unwillingly, Wes stepped farther into the house, chills coursing through his body.

Face down, half in and half out of a room, lay the body of a female — a fan of yellow hair spread out and spotted with blood.

He felt the bile rise to his throat, and as he turned to run he glimpsed a shadow with a raised arm, and a lead pipe heading in his direction.

"Oh, *Jesus Christ — no —*" he began to say, raising his right arm to protect himself.

It was too late.

Blackness descended.

Wes Money was temporarily out of the game.

Chapter 43

Somewhere between the restaurant and the hotel, Jade changed her mind. Deeply attracted as she was to Jack Python, one-night stands were not her style, never had been. Besides, there were too many complications. She hadn't made up her mind about Mark. And Jack had admitted he was deeply involved with Clarissa Browning. Nothing was ever easy.

When she told him, he took it with a philosophical shrug. "I guess our timing is off, huh?"

She touched her hand to his cheek lightly. Somehow she felt they were intimate strangers. "Something like that," she said softly.

He understood perfectly. And they parted good friends with no mention of further meetings.

The next day, on the flight back to Los Angeles, Antonio was dying to know everything.

She was noncommittal. "We had dinner. We talked. He's a terrific guy."

"*And, bella?* You make love with him?"

"It's none of your business," she said firmly.

Antonio sulked. He hated being left out of anything.

She thought about Jack Python quite a bit on the way home. And then she thought about Mark. And she realized it wasn't over. Not yet anyway.

Mark had left several messages with her answering service. There was also a call from her brother, Corey, which made a pleasant change. She telephoned him first.

"What's up, bro?" she asked cheerfully.

"Nothing." He sounded wistful. "I was thinking about you. Thought I might take you out to lunch."

She glanced at the time. It was almost six on Sunday evening. "A little late for lunch," she said lightly. "How about dinner?"

"Can't do it. I'm all tied up."

You're always tied up, she wanted to say. *Don't you remember how close we used to be?*

"Where are you going?" she asked, a trifle stiffly.

"There's this party . . . business."

Sometimes he really pissed her off. If *she* was going to a party and knew he was alone, she'd ask him to go with her. But no such offer was forthcoming.

"You know something? I still haven't seen your house *or* met your housemate," she said, and before he could answer she continued with, "Look, I know you think I don't approve. And I have to admit that I *was* upset when you told me about you and Marita splitting. However, I love you, and whatever you do . . . well . . . it's your life. When can I meet her?"

"Who?"

"Your housemate, densehead!"

A long pause. He obviously wasn't insane about the idea.

Too bad. She had waited long enough. She might as well get a look at the woman who had broken up her brother's marriage.

"I'll tell you what," she said. "Why don't I take you both out to dinner next week? My treat. How about Friday night?"

He was silent.

"Can I get an answer around here please?" she persisted.

"Let me check. I'll call you tomorrow," he finally said.

Anyone would think she was inviting him to a funeral!

"Promise?"

"I promise."

Hanging up, she put a little Bruce on the stereo. Springsteen always cheered her up; he could do no wrong.

Then she realized she was going to have to do something about Mark, and reached for the phone again.

"Lord Mark Rand checked out at noon," said the hotel operator.

"Are you *sure*?"

"Quite sure, madame."

"Did he leave a number where he can be reached?"

"One moment please. I'll find out for you."

He certainly hadn't hung around waiting for her. What enthusiasm. What tenacity. What a bastard!

You're being unreasonable, Johnson. You were the one who took off.

The operator came back on the line. "No referral number."

"Thank you." She put down the phone, and wondered where he was now. She'd played games with him. He was merely returning the compliment. English asshole. He knew she hated playing games.

★

Jack couldn't fault Jade for changing her mind. After all, it was a woman's prerogative, and he had always tried to be a gentleman about such things. Only it didn't alter the fact that he still wanted her. And when Jack Python wanted, he usually got.

He returned to the empty suite, and placed a call to Clarissa in New York. She was staying with a girlfriend in the Village. Not for Clarissa the large hotel suite or penthouse apartment. "I enjoy living among ordinary people," she had told him. "Nobody takes any notice of me in the Village. I can wander around and not be bothered."

Sure she could. Because nobody recognized Clarissa off the screen.

She answered the phone herself.

"Hi, babe," he said. "I was just sitting here thinking about you."

Her voice sounded muffled. "Who is this?"

Christ! You go with a woman for over a year and she doesn't even recognize your voice!

"Phil Donahue," he said dryly.

"Oh, God. Jack. It's two-thirty in the morning here. Where *are* you?"

"You'll never believe this."

"Try me."

"Las Vegas."

"Are you drunk?"

"When have you ever seen me drunk?"

"You must be if you're in Las Vegas."

"I am sober. And missing you. I'm calling to say hello."

"You *are* drunk. And you've woken me. Really, Jack, you can be very thoughtless at times. A broken night's sleep disturbs my bio-rhythms."

"Spoken like a true Californian."

"What?"

"Nothing."

"I'm going to *try* to get back to sleep. Call me tomorrow if you want."

Hey – give the lady the prize for Ms. Romantic of the year.

He poured himself a brandy. Thoughtfully he sipped it, took a cold shower, and went to bed.

Some nights you just couldn't win.

*

Failing in the pursuit of the prettiest of Susanna's three friends, Howard settled for a short redhead with enormous silicone boobs and a silly smile. When he got her back to the suite and undressed her, even *he* was turned off by her two jutting great globules of flesh. They felt like movable cement before it hardens, and looked like a couple of giant melons with a cherry on top of each.

"I'm fighting a cold," he announced, with a phoney sneeze. "You'd better go home."

"Let me fight it with you," she begged. "I've got the cure of the century!"

"No," he insisted. "I feel sick. I think I've got a temperature."

Dressing reluctantly, she confided she was working on a screenplay with a friend. "Can I send it to you?" she asked hopefully.

Trapped again. "Yeah, of course."

As soon as she left he tracked down the woman from the night before. An answering machine picked up, but she called him back five minutes later.

"Come over," he said. "Let's continue what we almost didn't finish."

She hesitated. "I'm busy."

"What could make you un-busy?"

She decided he could take the truth. "I get a thousand bucks a night. Last night was on the house – the hotel picked up the tab. How about it, sport? I take American Express."

He was outraged. "Are you a pro?"

"No. I'm Mary Poppins. Can't you tell? Do you want me to come over or not?"

He slammed down the phone. Howard Soloman didn't sleep with hookers. Howard Soloman had never paid for it in his life!

God damn Dino Fonicetti. Who did he think he was dealing with?

*

Mannon went back to Carlos Brent's magnificent house after the party. The entourage trailed them, plus they picked up a few strays along the way.

Carlos took him on a tour of the mansion, which had sixteen bedrooms, a full recording studio, two Olympic-sized swimming pools, and its own golf course.

"This is just my little ole hang-out," Carlos boasted. "My *real* home is in Palm Springs. I'd like you and your lovely wife to come and stay with me for the weekend sometime soon."

"Sounds good to me," Mannon said agreeably.

"I've seen that wife of yours on television. She's some gal!"

When was Melanie-Shanna on TV?

"Whitney Valentine Cable," mused Carlos. "What a pretty lady!"

Mannon scowled. "We're divorced," he said.

Carlos looked amazed. "Any man who lets *that* filly go, has *got* to be *insane!*"

Mannon nodded. There were some statements you just couldn't fight.

*

The Klinger plane took off from Las Vegas earlier than expected. All three passengers were aboard, and anxious to get back to L.A.

Chapter 44

There was a blue haze somewhere in his head. And a pain of ferocious intensity. And when Wes opened his eyes he had no idea where the fuck he was.

Oh shit. He had to quit with the one-night stands. Waking up in strange women's beds was getting to be a drag.

Only he wasn't in a bed. He was on the floor. And clasped in his right hand was a gun. And . . . oh shit . . the blue haze lifted, and he knew he was in big trouble.

Trying to coordinate his body with his mind, he made an effort to rise, first dropping the gun to the floor.

He was in the entry hall of the Laurel Canyon house, and his companions were the same two bodies that had been there before.

Vomit threatened, and he staggered into a nearby toilet and threw up. Blood trickled into his eye from a gash on his head, and he realized a rapid exit was in order. For some unknown reason he had been set up, and he did not care to wait around to find out why.

A fast look at his watch told him only seven minutes had elapsed since he'd arrived at the house, which meant he must have a skull made of fucking concrete.

There was an eerie stillness. A loud silence screaming GET OUT.

Still feeling disoriented and sick he picked up the gun. It had his prints on. Whoever hit him over the head had wanted it that way.

Was it the murder weapon?

Probably.

We want no connection with this bad boy an' his sweetie-box.

Sure. No connection. Murder the two of 'em, then send the

schmuck in to take the blame. Schmuck gets caught red-handed and the man walks away with no connection.

Fuck!

They had bought him for a thousand dollars. The perfect patsy. Who was going to believe Wes Money's side of the story?

His heart was beating so fast and so loud he hardly dared to move in case it exploded. Grimly he tried to remember every murder mystery he'd ever seen. *Prints. Get rid of all the prints.*

He shoved the gun into his pokcet. It was no good trying to clean it now. The gun was important evidence, and he had to dispose of it properly, to be absolutely sure it could never be connected with him.

Frantically he raced into the toilet again, grabbed a handful of tissues, and cleaned anything he might have touched.

GET OUT! GET OUT! GET OUT!

The front door was still ajar. He made sure he wiped the handle. And the buzzer. And – *shit!* He heard the sound of a car approaching, and threw himself bodily into the shrubbery.

His heartbeat alone was enough to give him away.

Within seconds a police car appeared at full speed and screeched to a stop outside the open front door. Wes could make out two officers inside, neither of whom seemed ready to leave the safety of their vehicle.

It figured.

Set the schmuck up.

Send in the cops.

Schmuck discovered with murder weapon in hand. What would it matter that he had been beaten unconscious? He was holding the fucking murder weapon, for crissake. Book him and throw away the key!

With a supreme effort he tried to breathe slowly, evenly. Once they ventured inside the house, the whole area would be alive with cops. He had to get out fast.

Random thoughts raced through his head. If only he could get rid of the gun it would be a big help. But how could he risk it?

Sweat mingled with the blood dripping into his eye as he slowly crawled along the damp earth, hidden by the thick trees and bushes which tangled with his face and hair and body – scratching and tearing at his skin.

Wes Money had never been a religious man. Only now it seemed quite apt to say his prayers, and he did so with fervour.

One of the cops got out of the car. He was big and burly, the way policemen are supposed to be. He said something to his partner, but Wes couldn't hear what it was. Fortunately he was on his way, putting distance between himself and discovery.

The other cop got out of the car, and the two of them had a short discussion before drawing their weapons and approaching the front door of the house. They had their backs to him.

With perfect timing he judged it was safe for him to rise, slide into the shadows, and jog sharply away from the scene of the crime.

He ran down the driveway as if the devil were pursuing him. Along the private road. Up the other driveway where he had prudently parked the Mercedes. A feverish grope for the keys. Into the car. Start the ignition. *Not too fast. Don't attract attention.*

His breathing was laboured, and his throat felt like he'd just vacated a burning building. A sharp stitch dug into his side, and his head hurt like hell. He hadn't realized he was in such lousy shape.

Slowly he coasted down the driveway to the private road, only just stopping himself from flooring the gas pedal. When he hit Laurel Canyon he made a sharp right turn, and allowed himself to breathe. Clumsily he took the gun from his pocket and stuffed it under the passenger seat. There was other traffic going down the hill, and he slid in between a Honda and a Jeep. Again he allowed himself to breathe.

Halfway down, coming from Sunset, were two police cars, one behind the other. With sirens screaming and red lights flashing, they roared up the hill.

Along with the other vehicles, he pulled the Mercedes over to the side and allowed them clear passage. Breathing heavily he took a Kleenex from the glove compartment and mopped his head. The blood was drying now, congealing in a mass.

He wanted to throw up again, but he didn't dare.

He was safe. Temporarily.

Only what the fuck did he do now?

*

Angrily Silver glanced at the clock again. It was past nine. She was not used to being kept waiting, and certainly not by the likes of Wes Money.

In a sudden fury she called Dennis Denby.

He was home. She would have been most surprised if he wasn't.

"That table at Spago, Dennis," she purred. "Is it ready and waiting?"

Dennis, who had been trying to contact her ever since the gay restaurant débâcle, did not hesitate. "For you, Silver, beauty, anything is possible."

"Pick me up in fifteen minutes," she commanded.

He was one minute late, which was admirable considering he'd had to get rid of a lady friend (the forty-five-year-old raven-haired wife of a director who was secretly into boys), call Spago and request an immediate table. Not easy, but for Silver Anderson they complied. And dress. He wore a white sports jacket from Bijan, Italian trousers, and a light pink cashmere sweater.

"You've forgiven me!" he exclaimed, kissing her hand, a gesture he had seen George Hamilton employ with great success.

"I was never mad." She looked elegantly casual in a suede jacket and pants, her own hair scraped back, a full studio makeup still in place.

"You never returned my calls," he pointed out.

"Dennis, dear, you must realize that I don't even have time to go to the bathroom!"

He understood. Silver was a very busy woman.

On the small hill outside the fashionable Spago, photographers and fans stood in a huddle waiting for a celebrity arrival. Since the celebrities always used the back entrance, the chances of catching a good shot were remote.

Silver chose to have Dennis drive her Rolls. The fans gathered at the entrance to the parking lot and called to her longingly. She gave them a queenly wave, and swept into the restaurant the back way with Dennis trotting obediently behind her.

Before reaching their table – ready and waiting – they went through a parade of smiles and kisses and fond greetings. Spago, with its laid-back atmosphere, mind-blowing pizzas and incredible array of desserts, was celebrity hang-out numero uno. And Wolfgang Puck – the chef and owner – along with his darkly dramatic wife, Barbara, made sure everyone felt comfortable and at home.

"I absolutely *adore* the glorious flower arrangements here," Silver remarked, when safely seated.

"So do I," agreed Dennis.

"And it's such a *fun* place."

"I agree," agreed Dennis.

When did he ever not? He was her yes-man. She could do with him whatever she wanted.

Not so Wes Money. There was something about him . . . an unknown quality . . . a lurking danger.

She shivered excitedly. And he was not used goods either. Well, not by anyone *she* knew. It was quite possible that half the women in the restaurant had romped in the hay with Dennis.

Tonight she would teach Wes a lesson. Let him know exactly *who* he was dealing with. She had left explicit instructions with Vladimir that if Mr Money called, he was to inform him that she was out, and to phone back the next day. Alternatively, if he arrived at the house, Vladimir was to send him on his way.

Let Wes know she was not *completely* at his beck and call just because he had a hard cock and a persuasive tongue.

She smiled at the thought of both pieces of his anatomy.

"What are you smiling at?" Dennis asked anxiously.

She picked up a piece of bread, looked at it longingly, and put it down again. "Nothing that would interest you, Dennis, dear. Shall we order? I'm famished."

*

The men's room in a gas station on Sunset supplied Wes with an image which frightened the shit out of him. He was wild-eyed, wild-haired, with scratches all over his face. His clothes were dirty and torn, and there was a nasty spongy spot on the top of his head where he had been hit.

Better than being dead, with a bullet through his skull.

He felt the bile rise again, only this time he could supply nothing but dry heaves.

Quickly he cleaned up as best he could. The result was not Paul Newman. Face it – he looked fucked.

Searching through his pockets for a pack of cigarettes he came up with two unexpected items. A large glassine envelope filled with a white powder that looked suspiciously like cocaine. And a wad of used thousand-dollar bills totalling twenty-two thousand.

Shit! Part of the set-up. They had wanted him pegged as a dealer.

Swearing viciously, he stuffed everything back in his pocket. Just in time, as two Mexicans entered the can, unzipped, and began to relieve themselves.

He hurried out of there, and went over to a pay phone. His

first thought was to call Rocky. Just how much did his good friend know?

For a moment he played with the quarter. Should he? Shouldn't he?

A hooker drifted by in orange fishnet stockings and little else. "Wanna visit love city?" she drawled.

He ignored her. Maybe it wasn't such a smart move to contact Rocky. After all, *he* was the one responsible for getting him into this mess in the first place.

And then he thought about going home. Was it safe?

Sure it was safe. What could they do to him now?

They could come searching for their money, that's what. It was hardly loose change. They could come to reclaim their cocaine – there must be at least fifteen hundred bucks' worth.

He had no intention of parting with either. This money he had *really* earned. *And* the thousand stashed with Unity.

No, going home tonight was not the best idea in the world.

He thought of alternatives. And then he thought of Silver Anderson. Nobody would come looking for him at her house. With Silver he'd be safe.

Chapter 45

"We're having a dinner for Silver Anderson," Poppy announced, as she brushed her long hair in front of her dressing table mirror.

Howard, who had returned from Vegas earlier in the day, and was sitting up in bed surrounded by papers, documents, and unanswered memos, looked at her as if she had gone berserk. "Why? You hardly know her."

Poppy continued to brush her luxuriant blonde tresses. "Politics, sweet-buns. There may come a day when you want her in one of your movies. A touch of social intercourse never did anyone any harm."

"Willya talk English, for crissake?"

She leaned closer to the mirror and inspected her pampered skin. "I'm going to give the dinner in the back room at Chasen's. Who would you like me to invite?"

Knowing Poppy, she already had the guest list planned. "I don't care. How many people you got in mind?"

"Eight couples. I'd like your input on this, Howard."

A dinner party for Silver Anderson. Cross brother Jack off the list for a start. Mannon would be okay, but if they invited Mannon he couldn't invite Whitney, and he really wanted to see her.

"I don't know. You're the social queen. You'll come up with a good group."

Just the answer she had been hoping for. She put down her hairbrush and dipped her fingers into a pot of expensive cream, which she then proceeded to massage gently around her eyes. "Well," she said, "with us, and Silver and her escort — I do hope it's Dennis, he's so charming — that makes two couples. And then I thought the Whites, and the Gooseberegers. Maybe Oliver Easterne, and Mannon and Melanie, and —"

"I'd sooner you invited Whitney," Howard interrupted. "I'm still thinking of using her for that script you suggested."

Poppy finished patting in the cream. "Whitney is still seeing Chuck Nielson," she informed him. "You know you don't like him. And I've already mentioned the dinner to Melanie. I can't very well *dis*-invite her. I suppose having Mannon *and* Whitney is out of the question, isn't it?' She turned around and looked questioningly at him.

He pulled the collar of his pyjama top up. Cleverly he had concealed his Las Vegas love bites with a stick of makeup he had found on Poppy's dressing table. He could hardly wear a turtleneck to bed. "No way," he said shortly.

"Oh, dear . . ." Her little-girl voice wavered. "I hope I haven't made a boo-boo."

He hated it when she came out with baby talk. "So we'll give another dinner," he said magnanimously. "Big deal. You can plan a special night for Mannon and whatever her name is."

Poppy thought about it, and decided it wasn't such a bad idea at all. She could gain a reputation for throwing chic little dinners — maybe once a week — and everyone would fight to be included.

"Delicious!" she exclaimed, jumping up and hurrying to his

side. She knelt on the bed, completely messing up his profusion of papers. "Who's a clever boy, then?"

He peered down the décolletage of her rose pink peignoir. Perkily waiting were a perfect pair of 36B tits. *His* tits. He had paid for them. They were nothing like the Vegas redhead's monstrosities. They were lively and upright. Not too big and not too small. Just right, in fact. Before having them done, Poppy had consulted him on his preferences. "A perfect handful," he had said, and she had obliged.

"I'm in the mood, Howie," she whispered coyly.

I'm not, he wanted to reply. Only he didn't. He bundled his papers to the side, switched off the light, and reached for one of his possessions. A perky 36B possession.

*

"I had lunch with Poppy Soloman yesterday," Melanie-Shanna informed Mannon.

He paused, mid press-up, and said, "What did you do that for?"

"She invited me."

"Oh yeah, and what did she want?"

"Just to be friendly."

"Sure!"

"No, really."

"Everything Poppy Soloman does has a purpose."

"If there *was* a particular reason for inviting me, it never came up."

"It will."

"What do you mean?"

"You'll see."

He resumed a punishing set of press-ups, and then moved over to his Nautilus machine, where he proceeded to work on his arms.

Melanie-Shanna watched him pensively. He was so handsome, and she loved him so much. And yet every day – in spite of her pregnancy – he drew further and further away from her. Nothing she could say for sure, just a feeling.

"Was Vegas fun?" she asked brightly.

"Hell, no. I hated it."

Then why did you go?

She couldn't ask him. Mannon did what he pleased, and she never questioned.

"I went shopping with Poppy after lunch," she volunteered. He had lost interest. "Good," he said vaguely.

"She took me to Giorgio, and I opened a charge."

"Glad to hear it."

She wondered how glad he would be when he found out she had spent several thousand dollars. Poppy had encouraged her. "Spend his money, for God's sake!" she had urged. "What do you think he *makes* it for?"

So, for the first time in her marriage, Melanie-Shanna had spent without asking.

Mannon heaved and grunted as he worked up a sweat. His muscles rippled.

"Poppy's invited us to a dinner she's having for Silver Anderson," Melanie-Shanna said.

"Poppy this and Poppy that. I thought you hated lunch and shopping and all that phoney crapola."

"It wasn't phoney. I enjoyed it. I met some very interesting women."

"Who?" he demanded disbelievingly.

"Ida White . . Carmel Gooseberger."

Mannon burst out laughing. "Those two old mares! Jesus, kid, you're really mixing with racy company. Those broads are so jaded they wouldn't blink an eyelid if Reagan streaked across Rodeo and lit a fart!"

Melanie-Shanna pursed her lips. Sometimes Mannon treated her like an idiot, and it was beginning to gall. Everything she did he sneered at and criticized, and she'd had enough. At lunch the women had been discussing a recent scandalous divorce. The wife was demanding *and* getting half of everything the billionaire husband possessed. Poppy had winked gaily. "California law So fair. I *love* it!" And then she had leaned conspiratorially towards Melanie-Shanna. "You didn't sign a pre-nup, did you?"

"What's that?"

Poppy had laughed loudly, and explained it to her.

Now Melanie-Shanna realized her strength, and if Mannon didn't change his attitude, she was certainly going to change hers, and stop him treating her like a doormat

Chapter 46

"Madame Anderson is out," Vladimir said firmly, on the speaker to the front gate.

"I know that," Wes replied evenly. "But I have her car, and she asked me to return it."

"Ah . . ." sighed Vladimir.

"Ah . . ." copied Wes.

A pause, while Vladimir considered what to do. Madame hadn't mentioned her car. She would obviously want it back. Vladimir was also curious to see the man who had ousted the awful Dennis Denby from her bed. Pressing the buzzer to open the gate, he marched to the front door. When Wes drew up in the zippy red Mercedes, Vladimir was ready.

Wes pulled the car to a stop and jumped out. "Evenin', mate," he said to the houseman, attempting to push past him and enter the house.

Vladimir pulled himself up to his full height of five feet nine inches, and blocked the way. He was shocked at the man's unruly appearance.

"Excuse me, *sir*," he said grandly. "Madame Anderson left instructions that you are to telephone her tomorrow. Tonight she is out."

"Is she now?" Wes sized up the situation. An unthreatening gay butler. No problem. "I guess I'll just have to wait for her. She won't mind."

With no further ceremony he shoved past Vladimir, who was outraged, and headed for the library, and the bar, where he proceeded to pour himself a much-needed drink.

Vladimir stomped in after him, his authority questioned, his face turning a dull red. "Vat do you think you are doing?" he demanded. "You can't come in here vithout Madame Silver's permission."

Wes took a long gulp of straight scotch. It hit his belly with a warm spreading sensation. He threw the houseman a threatening glare. "Who says?"

"*I* say." Vladimir peered at the invading stranger. There was something disturbingly familiar about him. "I am in charge. You vill please leave."

Wes flopped into an armchair. Frankly, he didn't need this crap. He was all washed out. "I ain't goin' nowhere, sunshine. Don't get your balls in an uproar. Just lie back an' enjoy it."

"Vat?" steamed Vladimir.

"Relax. Hang loose. Go with the flow."

Vladimir felt a migraine creeping up on him. He would get the blame for this. He knew it. Madame Silver was going to be furious and she would fire him, the firing he had nearly got after the bathroom incident. He didn't know what to do. Physical action was definitely out of the question. This man looked positively *violent*. Definitely rough trade.

Running his hands through his wheat-coloured hair, he tried to decide how to deal with this uncomfortable situation.

Wes leaned back in the chair and closed his eyes. "I feel like shit," he mumbled. "If you're smart you'll just leave me alone. Stay out of my way an' everything'll be cool. I'll fix it with your boss. Don't sweat it." He was drifting into a light sleep, and he had no strength left to fight it.

Vladimir stared.

And stared again.

His memory was trying hard, but he couldn't quite come up with where he had encountered this unruly person before.

Almost . . . almost . . .

The knowledge eluded him.

*

"So, Dennis?" Silver said belligerently. "Why do you accept defeat like a bull with no balls?" She had demolished half a bottle of champagne, picked at a lobster salad, tasted dessert (the apple pie and caramel sauce was to die for!) and was now in an argumentative mood.

"*Moi?*" asked Dennis, a slight lilt to his voice.

"Do you swing both ways?" she asked suspiciously. She had never thought that of Dennis before, but tonight there was an air about him.

He reacted strongly. Too strongly?

"Are you drunk?" he shouted. "How *dare* you. How can you

- of *all* people - accuse me of having homosexual tendencies? Surely you know me better than that?"

"Calm down, Dennis," she said soothingly. "Some of my best friends are gay. It's just that I do not wish to sleep with them."

"I'm extremely insulted," he said sternly. "How would you like it if I asked *you* the same question?"

Her eyes drifted around the restaurant. Dennis Denby bored her. Everything about him was bland. His face, his clothes, his conversation. "Let's change the subject," she said mildly.

"Why?" He glared at her spitefully. "Have I hit upon something? Do you swing both ways?"

Icicles could have formed on her smile. "Get the check. You're taking me home. And if we're both terribly fortunate, we'll never have to see each other again."

★

Vladimir did not dare disturb Madame Silver at the restaurant. He did the next best thing, and disturbed Nora at her apartment.

"What do you want?" she asked irritably, interrupted in the middle of *Cagney and Lacey* and a chicken sandwich.

Vladimir explained his predicament.

Nora was torn. She was enjoying the programme, and her chicken sandwich was delicious. However, the idea of getting a peek at Silver's new boyfriend was certainly tempting.

"Are you telling me the guy just walked in the house and fell asleep?" she asked incredulously.

"Madame Silver vill blame me," Vladimir said mournfully.

What the hell . . . She clicked off the television, clicked on the tape machine, and with a large bite of her chicken sandwich under her belt, set off.

Vladimir greeted her at the door.

"Is he still asleep?" was her first question.

"Yes," hissed Vladimir, still furious at this gross intrusion by such an uncouth-looking man. At least Dennis Denby was well dressed and seemed prosperous. *This* one appeared to have crawled off the street. Sometimes Vladimir thought Madame Silver employed exceptionally bad taste.

Nora hurried inside, making her way straight to the library. The sight of Wes, sprawled out snoring peacefully, brought her to a full stop.

"Is this the specimen?" she said loudly.

Vladimir, hot on her heels, nodded. "Vill you get rid of him before Madame returns?" he requested hopefully.

Wes, oblivious to the conversation going on around him, slept on.

Nora stepped closer. This big, distinctly masculine, grubby-looking character was not what she'd expected at all. This guy looked like he'd been digging ditches, and that wasn't Silver's style. Or was it?

She adjusted her glasses and blew cigarette smoke in his direction. " 'Scuse me," she said in her smoke-encrusted voice. "This is not a hotel."

He opened one sludge-coloured eye and peered up at her. " 'Ello, darlin'," he said, reverting to his childhood English cockney. "Wanna give me a back-rub?"

Vladimir clicked his tongue in disgust.

Wes yawned and stretched, throwing his arms wide. "I know *you* would," he said to Vladimir. "Only I'm not givin' *you* the chance."

Nora frowned. He was not your standard Beverly Hills bachelor by any means. Nor your Hollywood stud. She had a feeling she had seen him somewhere before. "Have you and I met?" she demanded.

He stretched again, very slowly. Then he stared at the two of them – Silver's butler and the old publicity broad. He had a hunch they were of a mind to throw him out.

"Where's Silver?" he asked, playing for time. "She told me to meet her here, an' now she's on the missin' list."

"*When* did she tell you to meet her?" said Nora.

"Last time I spoke to her."

"And when was that?"

Jeez! He needed this scene. He stared the dyke down. "I don't think that's any of your business."

"*Everything* Silver Anderson does is my business," she replied tartly. "And I suggest you shift your fat ass before Miss Anderson comes home and finds you here."

It was the "fat ass" he took exception to. Who did the old bag think she was dealing with? What right did *she* have to throw him out? The only person who could do that was Silver.

"Go whistle up Liberace's ass," he said insolently.

Nora was startled. "What?"

"You heard."

"Unless you get out of here *now*, Mr . . . Money," Nora said slowly, emphasizing every word, "I shall call the police, and they will evict you in a proper manner."

He stood up. "Y'can do what y'want. Silver invited me. An' here I stay until *she* tells me to get out."

"You're giving me no choice," Nora said sternly.

He was unmoved. "Go ahead. The *Enquirer*'ll love it."

"Yes. I suppose that's the sort of scumball you are. Anything for the money. Am I getting your number?"

"You're gettin' on my tits, old lady. I don't appreciate bein' threatened when I'm an invited guest."

Vladimir watched the heated exchange like a spectator at Wimbledon. He loved every minute of it! Wait until they heard about this one down at Rage. Better than Dennis Denby any day.

"Mr Money," said Nora, very, very slowly. "Are you going to leave quietly, or am I going to telephone the police?"

"Why don't you call Silver an' save us all a lot of bother?" he suggested.

The idea *had* crossed her mind – although she would sooner see him dragged off in chains. Instant hate had taken place.

"If you insist," she said stiffly. Turning to Vladimir, she instructed him to call the restaurant where Silver was dining.

Meanwhile, Wes picked up his glass and strolled over to the bar. He needed a refill. He was handling this much more calmly than he felt. His stomach was churning, his head still aching. What if Silver *did* tell him to get lost? And the last thing he needed was the cops.

He poured a steady stream of scotch into his glass. His legs felt like two hollow pipes. If he drank all night there was no way he could get the slightest buzz on. Pleasure was out.

Then three things happened all at once. Vladimir held the phone aloft and announced, "Madame is on her way home."

Silver herself burst into the room, flushed and slightly tipsy, with Dennis one step behind.

And Nora, with a sudden start of recognition as she watched Wes pour his drink, stared at him closely and exclaimed, "*Now* I know where I've seen you before. The night of Silver's party – you were one of the barmen!"

"Yes, yes!" agreed Vladimir, almost jumping up and down with excitement. "I remember too!"

Silver looked at Wes.

Wes looked at Silver.

There was a dramatic silence.

Chapter 47

"I'm renting a house at the beach for the summer," Jack said.

Heaven, who had been gazing idly out the window of his Ferrari, jumped to attention. "A beach house! Wow! Is it near Muscle Beach?"

He laughed. "No. It is not near Muscle Beach. It's in Trancas. And it's remote and quiet and — well, I love it."

What kind of a place was *remote* and *quiet*? — somewhere dull. Why couldn't Uncle Jack rent right in the heart of Malibu where all the interesting people were?

"I want you to come and stay," he said. "Maybe bring a girlfriend if you like."

She fidgeted on the hot leather seat. "It sounds awfully . . ." Searching for the right word she came up with ". . . lonely."

"Not at all. There's shops and restaurants just a short drive away. And I want you to stay when *I'm* there. We'll keep each other company."

God! She had seven girlfriends who would adore to keep Uncle Jack company. For an older man he sure had fans. "What about Clarissa?" she asked. "Will she be there?"

"I don't know," he replied honestly. There were decisions to be made, and he wasn't in the mood to make them.

"Hey, Uncle Jack, I think I'll love it!' she decided. "When can I come? And for how long?"

"All summer if you want."

"What about grandpa?"

He smiled. "I don't think he'll notice, do you?"

She smiled back. They both understood about George.

Sometimes she felt very close to her uncle. Tonight was one of those times. He had called late Sunday afternoon and said, "I just got back from Vegas, and I feel like grabbing a Chinese feast. Do you know anyone with the same urge?"

"Me! Me!" she had replied, standing Eddie up, but who cared?

"I'll pick you up in an hour."

True to his word he was there within the hour, and drove at breakneck speed to Madame Wu's on Wilshire, where he had pre-ordered a great Chinese meal. Now he was taking her home, and she wished he wasn't. She would give anything to live with him permanently.

"How's your music going?" he asked casually. They had covered school, home life and boyfriends at the restaurant.

"Okay," she replied listlessly. Frankly it was going nowhere. Just the occasional school party gig, and nothing else. "I've sent my tapes to all the record companies. All they do is send them back with a shitty form letter." She gazed at him hopefully. "I wish you'd come and *see* me next time I perform."

He nodded, knowing full well he had promised many times before, only something always came up. He made a mental note to definitely do it. Heaven was important to him, and he was going to have to make more time for her now she was growing up.

"You've never even listened to one of my tapes," she added reproachfully.

"Why don't you give me one? I'll play it on the drive home."

"Promise?"

"Would I lie?"

She didn't think so, but he had certainly never gone out of his way to take an interest in what she did.

George was locked away in his workroom when they arrived home.

"I won't disturb him," Jack said. "I'll call him about you coming to stay with me."

"Promise?"

He kissed her lightly on the cheek. "What is it with you tonight? Don't you believe *anything* I say?"

She laughed self-consciously. "Just making sure."

He was gone before she could find a tape to give him

Halfway across the Canyon, listening to a soulful Billie Holiday on the car radio, Jack realized he'd forgotten to get Heaven's tape. Not that he really wanted to hear it. What if she sounded awful? He wasn't about to take the responsibility of telling her. Maybe she sounded like Silver. God forbid! His sister's voice did not thrill him. It reminded him of his mother, and the way she had deserted him when he was a kid. The same way Silver had deserted Heaven.

His thoughts moved on to Clarissa, still in New York. Did he miss her? He still couldn't decide.

Then he thought about Jade Johnson, and what might have been if she hadn't changed her mind so swiftly. One night of great sex. Maybe more . . .

How could there be more until things were resolved with Clarissa?

He shook his head, turned the addictive Miss Holiday up loud and clear, and headed for the hotel suite he called home.

Chapter 48

Wes did not like confrontations. Never had. Especially when he wasn't looking his best, and he knew the image he presented was pure shit.

Silver stared him down. She was angry — little glints of light caught the reflection in her eyes and bounced right off him. But she was cool. Didn't give in to pressure, handled the whole thing with style.

"Hello, Wes," she said calmly, and turning to Nora she added, "I didn't know we had a late meeting?"

Nora knew her moods as well as anyone, and prepared for flight.

Silver then iced Vladimir with a glare. "What are *you* doing here? I didn't ring."

"Madame Silver —" Vladimir began valiantly. "This man is an intruder. I —"

"Good*night*, Vladimir. You may go to your quarters. I won't be needing you again tonight."

He slunk from the room.

Nora cleared her throat. "I guess I'll be going home."

"Good," said Silver shortly.

"Vladimir called me," Nora began to explain. "He thought there was a problem . . ."

Silver waved a dismissive hand in her direction. "Remind me to add a security bonus to your pay-cheque."

Nora was affronted. She had only been trying to help. "I'll tell City Television," she rasped. "*They* pay me, not you."

Picking up her purse she followed Vladimir from the room. Silver Anderson was treading on dangerous ground. No wonder she had wanted to keep Wes Money to herself; the man was nothing but a cheap hustler – a barman! And when word got out – and it was only a matter of time before it did – the whole town would be laughing.

Dennis Denby stepped forward, determined to assert himself. "Who exactly *is* this man, Silver?"

She'd forgotten he was behind her, trailing her like an eager puppy dog. "Dennis, *dear*," she said graciously. "I know I invited you in, but now I'm inviting you *out*. Please be understanding about this. I promise I'll telephone you tomorrow." As she spoke, she edged him from the room.

"What's going on?" he whined. "I thought we had something together."

Kissing him lightly on the cheek, she continued to edge him towards the front door. "Whoever said we didn't?"

Reluctantly he allowed himself to be shepherded out. "Is anything going on between you and that man?" was his final plaintive cry.

"Don't be so silly," she said firmly, closing the door on him.

She paused in the hall before returning to the library and Wes, trying to gather her thoughts. Nora's words had not escaped her attention. *Silver's party . . . one of the barmen.* And Vladimir's excited confirmation.

Goddammit! Why hadn't he told her?

And if he had?

She shook her head – if he had she would have sent him on his way without a second glance.

Marching into the library she confronted her latest lover. Hands on hips she raked him over with a very cool expression indeed. "Well?" she demanded icily.

Slowly, deliberately, without rising, he lit a cigarette. "I'm getting really fed up with bein' treated like a piece of shit around here," he said.

"*You're* fed up!" she raged, pacing up and down in front of him. "How the *hell* do you think *I* feel?"

"About what?"

"God! Don't pretend there's nothing happening."

He blew smoke in her direction and stood up. "I think I'll go," he said. "I've heard of warm welcomes, but this is ridiculous."

Taking in his dishevelled appearance she snapped, "You look like a tramp."

"Sorry about that, *Madame* Silver," he said sarcastically. "I wasn't plannin' on gettin' beat up before I came to see you."

She regarded him warily. Even in the state he was in there was something about him. A masculine, strong quality.

She knew she should tell him to get out — out of her house *and* out of her life.

Why?

Just because he was a barman? Who said that Silver Anderson had to follow rules? She could do whatever she pleased.

"I wish you'd been honest with me up-front," she said edgily.

"Why?"

"Because then I wouldn't have had to be humiliated in front of the people who work for me."

"*Are* you humiliated?"

"Yes, I am."

He tested the water. "*How* humiliated?"

She heard the humour in his tone and was not amused. "Fuck you, Wes Money," she said, stalking to the bar.

"Promises! Promises!" Beating her to the bar, he positioned himself behind it. "And what can I get for Madame? A glass of her favourite bubbly? A vodka martini? Or let me suggest one of my specialities — a strawberry daiquiri with just a hint of Bénédictine? Oh, and I give great nuts!"

He had her with that one. She couldn't conceal the glimmer of a smile.

"You look terrible," she said crossly.

"I had a hard night."

"A shower will help."

"Is that an invitation?"

"You know, I really do not appreciate you just turning up here uninvited."

"You *did* invite me."

"And you cancelled."

"Postponed."

"I don't like being kept waiting."

"Sometimes it's worth it."

"When?"

"Shall we put it to the test?"

Later, much later, after hot sex and a cool shower, while Silver slept, Wes crept downstairs and switched on the television in the kitchen. He opened the fridge and dug into a plate of cold cuts while searching for a news channel with the remote control.

When he found one he almost choked. The murders were a big item. A pretty blonde news reader told the story:

> "Heavy-metal singing star Churnell Lufthansa, and his fifteen-year-old girlfriend, Gunilla Saks, were found shot to death in a remote Laurel Canyon hideaway late last night. No murder weapon was found. The police have no suspects at this time. Churnell Lufthansa climbed to fame in the late sixties with his band the Ram Bam Wams. He was known for —"

Abruptly he switched off, hardly wanting to hear the details, as long as *his* name wasn't included, and he didn't see how it could be.

Quickly he picked up the phone and punched out Rocky's number. Several rings, and then Rocky's unmistakable pugilistic voice.

"Where the fuck are ya, man?" Rocky demanded.

Wes spoke carefully. How did Rocky know he wasn't at his house? He hadn't said anything. "I'm home," he said guardedly.

"Naw!"

"Why wouldn't I be?"

"Because they're fuckin' loo —" Rocky stopped.

"Lookin' for me?" Wes finished the sentence for him.

"I guess." Rocky's voice was sulky. He didn't want to have this conversation.

"What's the scam, my friend?" Wes asked, knowing he wasn't going to get a straight answer.

"Ya dumb fuckhead!" Rocky exploded. "Waddya havta ice 'em for?"

"Huh?"

"Ya heard me, birdbrain."

"Shit!" Wes said disbelievingly. "You don't think *I* did it, do you?"

"Word is out that not only did ya do it, but y'ran off with fifty thou in cash, an' plenty of the white stuff."

"That's bullshit!"

"It's on the street. They're lookin' for ya."

"Where?"

"Everywhere."

"Who's they?"

"The big boys."

"Shit!"

"So . . . where are ya?"

Rocky's attempt at casual was pathetic. Not only were they looking for him, but there was probably a price on his head. One that Rocky wouldn't mind collecting.

"Arizona," he said quickly. "I came here for my health."

"And you'd better stay there." Rocky paused, then all in a rush said, "Hey — what's ya number? I'll call ya if I hear anything."

"Don't call me, I'll call you."

Thoughtfully he replaced the receiver. If he'd gone home tonight there was a likelihood he would have joined Churnell Lufthansa and Gunilla Saks in the Garden of Eden. And he wasn't ready to start fertilizing tomatoes. No way.

He opened up the fridge again and took out a cold beer, wiping the top before putting it to his lips because someone had once told him dogs peed on the side of cans.

Okay. What was he going to do?

Alternatives.

New York. He had a few friends scattered around.

Too goddamn cold.

Not as cold as ten foot under.

Florida and Vicki.

There was no going back. She was probably fat and married now, with two kids and the picket fence she had always dreamed about.

Okay. He had no family. *So what the fuck was he going to do?*

Silver entered the kitchen silently. She glided on high-heeled mules, a peach robe wrapped around her nakedness. "Hmmm . . ." she murmured. "And what do we have here, a compulsive eater?"

Automatically he reached for the curve of her ass and

scrunched a handful. "You're hot stuff," he said, charm on automatic pilot.

"So I've been told."

"Yeah? Who told you that?"

"Half of America."

"Crazy people."

"Don't be so rude!"

"Maniacs!"

"Watch it, barman."

"No. *You* watch it."

Pulling her close to his chair he parted her robe. Then he pressed his mouth to her thatch and inserted his tongue.

Obligingly she spread her legs, allowing him free access.

Eating Silver Anderson was no hardship. Half the turn-on was the realization that he was tonguing one of the most famous women in America.

She arched her pelvis back with great agility, enjoying every minute of his expert attention.

After a very satisfying orgasm she smiled and said, "A first, Mr Money. Nobody's ever done that to me while I was standing."

"You've led a sheltered life," he remarked, helping himself to a piece of Sara Lee chocolate cake from the freezer.

"You'll break your teeth," she warned.

He flopped into a chair. "Listen – if your pussy didn't do it – chocolate cake's a breeze!"

"You crud!"

She could be very girlish, old Silver Anderson. He found himself laughing with her. And then she was on her knees giving him a little lip.

Whew! If anyone had told him he could get it up again tonight he would have said they were crazy! But up it came. Eager as a housewife at a swap meet.

She knew her stuff. He nearly zoomed through the fucking ceiling! And he certainly forgot all his troubles.

Temporarily.

When it was over she smiled at him. "You're keeping me up," she said succinctly.

He grinned. "Who's keeping *who* up?"

"You're a bad influence. I need my sleep. I'm not nineteen, you know."

"Jeez! You must be kiddin'!"

"Funn*ee*. I'll look like a hag on the set tomorrow."

"*You* could never look anything but beautiful."

"Flatterer."

"And you love it."

"I can't deny it, barman."

"Wanna get married?" He blurted it out before really thinking what he was suggesting.

She raised an amused eyebrow. "I *beg* your pardon?"

He might as well go all the way. "I thought we could hop a plane to Vegas an' just do it."

She wrapped her peach robe tightly around her and began to laugh. "Why on *earth* would I marry *you*?"

Everything fell on top of him. He was too tired to take any more crap. "Yeah," he said bitterly. "Why would y'wanna marry me? I'm all right to screw the ass off – but marriage? You're right, rich lady – I'm just a bum. I'll take your money and scam out of your life quicker than a wino with ten bucks. *Fuck* it!"

Getting up from the table he paced around the room completely naked. Turning on her angrily he said, "I've never asked anyone to marry me in my life. And waddya do? Huh? *Huh?* You laugh in my face like I'm some kind of pet fuckin' joke! Well, let me tell you this – I don't *want* your money, I'm not *interested* in your fame. I just kinda thought we'd have a good time together. You enjoy me. I enjoy you. Why not go all the way?"

She was caught off guard. This was the last thing she'd expected. Wes was furious, like a big caged animal. And he looked so funny as he marched up and down her kitchen with his highly impressive credentials swaying in the breeze.

Marriage. Hmmm . . . Each time she did it, it was a terrible mistake.

Marriage. Hmmm . . . It might be kind of fun. And front page news, of course.

Wes grabbed another can of beer from the fridge, and pressed it open so violently that a fine spray flew all over the floor.

"I don't know a thing about you," she pointed out reasonably.

"I'll tell you whatever y'need to know."

"How *kind* of you."

He ignored her sarcasm. "I'm free, white, and over twenty-one. I'm also broke, and in a spot of trouble with some characters who think I owe them money – only I don't. There are no strings attached to me. I've got no social diseases. I won't be your go-fer, but I'll look after you and watch out for your interests. I'm no fuckin' genius, but I'm street smart and sharp – y'can learn a lot from me."

She went on to say something. He held up his hand and stopped her. "I don't want anything you've got. Not your house, your cars, your money. I'll sign any goddamn paper your lawyer puts in front of me."

"If you're broke, perhaps you can give me some kind of indication about what you intend to live on?" she asked acidly.

He swigged from the can of beer. "I don't mind you payin' the bills. I got no macho problem about *that*."

She began to laugh. "What a relief!"

Walking over to her, he grabbed her around the waist, and pulled her towards him. "I think we'd be a pretty steamy combination, don't you?"

"I've got everything to lose and nothing to gain," she protested feebly.

He rubbed the scar above his left eyebrow with one hand, and cupped her tight ass with the other. "Yes you have. You got me. And y'know somethin', rich lady?"

It was ridiculous, but she felt the heat of desire creeping up on her again. Her voice was husky. "What?"

"I'll make you the happiest broad in Hollywood."

Somewhere in the Midwest . . .
Sometime in the seventies . . .

The girl grieved for her father and his lady friend in a proper manner. She was taken in by a neighbouring farmer's family, while the entire community speculated on who could have committed such a hideous crime — setting a man's house on fire and incinerating everyone and everything in it.

"They said he was crisp as a burnt chicken," the girl heard the woman of the house confide to a friend. Good, she thought. I hope he suffered. I hope he died a thousand deaths.

Nobody suspected her of the crime. In fact, for the first time in her life she received love and sympathy from most of the people around her.

The farmer and his wife had four children of their own, and it was understood right from the start that her stay with them was only temporary. She shared a room with the two daughters and kept to herself. The sisters — one seventeen and one almost eighteen — regarded her as an unwelcome intruder. Although she was younger than them and in a lower grade at school, they knew her reputation as a loner, and thought she was odd. Their names were Jessica-May and Sally, and they thought and talked about nothing but boys.

"I think Jimmy Steuban's cute," Jessica-May would say.

"I like Gorman," Sally would join in. And then they would discuss the pros and cons of both boys for hours at a time.

Occasionally they would both stare at the girl and demand belligerently, "Who do you like?" When she didn't answer they would dissolve into fits of giggles and whisper among themselves.

The farmer's wife was a kind woman. Her husband was a brusque man with bright red hair and matching beard. Their two sons, ten and twelve, were little rascals, up to tricks day and night. The girl settled into family life, and waited for the sheriff to find one of her brothers or sisters to take her in. She had no regrets about what she had done. Her father and his painted whore deserved it.

Money in the farmer's household was short, and it wasn't long before the girl was asked to contribute to the family income by getting a job. She worked weekends as a box girl in the town's only supermarket. Her sixteenth birthday came and went. She didn't tell anyone. There was nobody who really cared.

At night, in the room she shared with the two sisters, she would lie in bed and gaze at the ceiling for hours on end wondering what was to become of her. She had no intention of staying in the town, and secretly she started saving the tips she got at work. With her sixteenth birthday behind her, her body began to fill out at last. Her breasts grew, and her waist narrowed. Suddenly she looked like a woman, and the boys at school took a lot more notice of her than they ever had before. One boy in particular, Jimmy Steuban, started to follow her everywhere. He was seventeen, with black hair and an athletic build. The girl tried to ignore him, because she knew Jessica-May liked him. But he was very persistent — always asking her for a date, and hanging around outside her place of work.

One night she let him walk her home. He grabbed her in the bushes near the farmhouse and tried to kiss her. She screamed so hard he ran like a frightened moose.

But he didn't give up, and against her better instincts she started to like him back, and before long they were girlfriend and boyfriend. Jessica-May was furious. Every day she pleaded with her mother to get rid of the unwanted boarder.

"She has nowhere to go," the kindly woman pointed out. "No kin that anyone can find. We're God-fearing people. We must keep her till she's at least seventeen."

Jessica-May got angrier, and did everything she could to make life difficult for the girl. She put dead mice and cockroaches in her bed, messed up her school books, cut the buttons off her clothes, and generally bad-mouthed her. She elicited the help of her sister, Sally, who joined in gladly. Both of them wanted to see the back of her.

Jimmy Steuban was her only solace. He treated her nicely. Took her to the movies and on picnics, and talked to her as though she was a decent human being. When he finally tried to make love to her, she found that she couldn't say no. So she allowed him, one cold night in the back of his father's rusty old Ford, to remove her blouse and then her flimsy bra. He touched her breasts reverently, and spoke of how much he loved her. Then he lifted her skirt, pulled down her panties, and thrust his manhood into her.

230

She was rigid with fear and anxiety, expecting it to be like it was with her father. Only somehow, with Jimmy, it was different, and she found herself relaxing and responding with more feeling than she'd ever had in her life.

"You're terrific!" he gasped. "I really love you!"

She really loved him too. And over the next few months they made love and plans on a regular basis. "What if I get pregnant?" she asked him nervously one night, although deep down she was sure that she couldn't, after what had happened.

"I'll marry you," he said gallantly. "We'll live in a castle, and I'll be your prince!"

Six weeks later she discovered she was pregnant. She told Jimmy, who told his father. Two days after that Jimmy was sent out of town, and she never heard from him again.

Jessica-May and Sally crowed the news from the rooftops. Shortly after, she was sent to a home for unwed mothers fifty miles away. The home was run by nuns —strict, unsmiling women, who demanded respect and obedience at all times. The sixty pregnant girls had to rise at five a.m., do two hours of penance on their knees in a freezing cold chapel with a concrete floor, and then housework until noon, when they were given a plate of soup, a piece of stale bread, and a cup of milk. The afternoon was study time, because most of the girls were under eighteen. Bed was seven p.m., and once every two weeks a florid-faced, bull-necked doctor arrived to examine them. The doctor had his own examining room in the house. Some of the inmates christened it the torture chamber.

The girl dreaded his visits. She never slept the night before his always punctual arrival. He drove a dusty sedan, and was usually accompanied by a sour-faced nurse, who preferred to spend her time drinking cups of herb tea with the nuns. The doctor didn't seem to mind. As girl after girl presented herself to him he always said the same thing. "Clothes off. On the table. Legs in the stirrups."

He never looked at their faces or knew their names. He called them by numbers, and when one of them was carted off to the hospital and gave birth, he crossed her off his list, and added a different name in front of the number.

The girl drew number seven. It wasn't her lucky number. She had never been to a gynaecologist, nor even heard of them — but a fat redhead confided that this was not the way it was supposed to be.

First the doctor drew thin rubber gloves onto his bony hands. Then he dipped his index finger into a jar of Vaseline, and plunged straight into whoever was on his table. He stayed inside a good five minutes,

231

sometimes ten, probing, pushing, hurting — for he was never careful. Sometimes he bent his head down, grabbed a torch, and peered inside for a very long time. Once he arrived with a hat that looked like a miner's, a flashlight perched on the top. This contraption enabled him to look and feel at the same time. Occasionally he forgot to put on his gloves. The worst times were when he inserted a wooden speculum and forced the labia wide. The girl had to stop herself from screaming because it hurt so much, and when she mentioned it he'd said, "Don't be such a stupid child. You let your boyfriend get inside and have a good time. If you hadn't, you wouldn't be in this mess today."

The breast exam came next. A long session of fondling, pinching and squeezing.

Businesslike, when he was finished, he would say, "Off the table, let me look at you." And whoever was in the room would have to endure a lecherous once-over from the rheumy-eyed doctor. Once a month he took a Polaroid picture. "For my files," he always said.

"Dirty old man, he should be struck off or whatever they do to filthy old perverts," said one eighteen-year-old. But everyone found out that complaining got them nowhere. The nuns thought the good doctor was a saint, and would hear no ill of him.

The girl endured her pregnancy as she had endured the rest of her life. She kept to herself and remained silent.

"Fuckin' stuck-up bitch!" said a skinny brunette. "Think you're too bloody good fer us, doncha?"

She didn't think. She knew. One day she was going to leave her humble beginnings far behind and make something of herself.

When her baby was born, shortly after her seventeenth birthday, it was put up for immediate adoption. She suckled the infant for a mere six days, and then it was taken from her.

"Sign this," said a big nurse with pop-eyes and a hairy chin.

"I don't th —"

"You have no choice."

She signed, and was sent from the hospital to a foster home. While there, she learned that Jimmy Steuban had gotten Jessica-May pregnant and that they were to be married immediately. No exile for Jessica-May — far from it. The wedding was a lively affair, with four brides-maids and a two-tier cake. The girl read a report in the local paper. And there was a picture of the happy couple. Jessica-May wore a white dress her mother had sewed for her. And Jimmy Steuban looked fine — if slightly uncomfortable — in a rented tuxedo.

The girl waited until she was eighteen before doing anything about it. She waited quietly and patiently. Then one night, when the moon

*was full and shining like a beacon, she borrowed her foster brother's
bicycle, stole a can of gasoline from the local gas station, and rode
seven miles to the tiny house where Jessica-May and Jimmy Steuban
lived with their new baby.*

*Quietly, methodically, she shook the gasoline around the house.
Lighting the first match was easy . . .*

BOOK THREE

Hollywood, California
August 1985

Chapter 49

Poppy Soloman had changed her outfit five times. She was in a panic and simply could not make up her mind. Should she wear the Valentino? The Chanel? The Saint Laurent?

She stamped her foot and let out a blood-curdling yell of frustration.

Howard came running into her dressing room from his bathroom. He wore boxer shorts, his usual manic expression, no toupee, and a dribble of white powder between his nose and his upper lip. "What the fuck happened?" he shouted excitedly.

Poppy, clad in nothing more than sheer beige panty-hose and a magnificent diamond necklace, her long blonde hair swept up in an elaborate style, pouted. "Baby can't decide what to wear!" she wailed.

"Jesus *Christ*!" he roared. "I thought you were being murdered!" He waved lethal-looking scissors in the air. "I nearly cut my friggin' balls off!"

"What were you doing with scissors near your balls?" she asked curiously.

"Trimmin' the grass," he replied sarcastically. "What do you *think* I was doing?"

Poppy sighed. She was in no mood for one of Howard's silly outbursts. "You've got to help me, sweet-buns." She picked up a deep pink Bill Blass creation from the floor. "Tell me *truthfully* which dress you like best."

"Pick the most expensive," he said sourly.

"I don't keep the receipts in my head," she replied tartly. "Now, please be sensible and cooperate. Otherwise we'll be late."

"You can't be late for your own dinner party," he pointed out.

"Exactly!" she agreed.

Twenty-five minutes later, after he'd had to endure a mini fashion parade, the choice was made. An exquisite Oscar de la Renta short silk jacket in a kaleidoscope pattern of shimmering beads over a black velvet long dress. It had cost him nearly six thousand bucks, and she'd never worn it!

"Thank you, honeybunch." She gave him a hug, and then noticed that he was still in his undershorts. "Get dressed, Howard!" she exclaimed crossly. "If you make us late I'll kill you!"

Muttering ominously, he locked himself securely in his bathroom. Poppy could drive a man nuts! This dinner party had changed dates, venues, and guest lists ten times. Now it was all set. An intimate little sit-down for seventy-five people, and it was tonight. Although why *they* should be the ones giving an exclusive wedding dinner in the upstairs room at the Bistro for Silver Anderson and her mystery bridegroom, was beyond him, He hardly *knew* Silver, and she and Poppy were certainly not close. Of course, he had realized two minutes into his marriage that Poppy combined the most ferocious qualities of a social climber and a star fuck. Personally he didn't give a rat's ass. Whatever made her happy.

Reaching for his rug he plopped it in place, securing the two clips that held it in position, then combing his own hair over the join.

The buzzer on the telephone next to his toilet signalled. He picked up the receiver and snapped a no-nonsense "Yes?"

"Mr Klinger for you, Mr Soloman," said the housekeeper.

Why was Zachary K. Klinger calling him at home on a Saturday night? The man was an erratic prick. Seven times he had threatened to fly out to the Coast for a meeting, and seven times he had cancelled. Good. Howard didn't need him. He was doing very nicely without Zachary K. Klinger looking over his shoulder. Orpheus was in good shape. Three movies in production, and three more just about ready for preproduction, including Howard's brilliant idea – the old-fashioned musical starring Carlos Brent, with Orville Gooseberger producing, and Whitney Valentine even now reading the script, a remake of an original classic.

"Hiya, Zachary," he said, in the friendliest tone he could muster, waiting for the latest cancellation. Zachary was supposed to be arriving on Monday.

"I'm surprising you, Howard," Zachary said. He spoke in a

sinister whisper, sounding very much like Marlon Brando in *The Godfather*.

"I know, I know," Howard replied easily. "You can't make the meeting on Monday. It's okay, Zach." He used the nickname with confidence. "We all understand. Everything's buzzin' along without you."

"I'm here," Zachary announced with no preamble. "I'd like to meet tonight."

"You're here?" Howard repeated hoarsely. "Really?"

"Flew in fifteen minutes ago."

"You did?" Howard felt sweat break out all over his body. He didn't need this kind of surprise. Months of farting around, and now the asshole had to appear on the night of Poppy's big dinner for Silver Anderson. "Jesus, Zach. I wish you'd given me some warning."

"Why?" Zachary asked mildly.

Howard knew the unruffled voice was a front, concealing unbridled fury. When Zachary K. Klinger wanted something, a person didn't argue. The stories about him were legendary.

"Uh . . . my wife, Poppy, she's giving this uh . . . black-tie dinner. It's for Silver Anderson." He laughed nervously. "Broads! If I backed out of this one she'd be at Marvin Mitchelson's before breakfast!"

"No problem at all," said Zachary understandingly.

Howard breathed again.

"Fortunately, I always keep a tuxedo on both coasts," Zachary continued. "Which means I'll be able to join you. What time? And where?"

For a split second Howard was speechless. *What time? And where?* Poppy had spent three days seating this dinner. *Three fucking days!* Zachary K. Klinger's appearance was going to throw her into a tizz she might never recover from. And he, Howard Soloman, would feel her wrath for weeks, months, maybe even years!

"This is great news, Zach," he managed. "Will you be coming alone?"

"Yes."

"Fine, fine. It's at the Bistro. Eight o'clock. Black tie, but you already know that, don't you?"

"Yes, I do." A pause. "And, Howard?"

"What, Zach?"

"I don't like being called Zach. My name is Zachary, or Mr Klinger. Make your choice and stick with it."

The line went dead in Howard's hand. *"Shit!"* he screamed. Poppy would never give him head again!

*

Nervously Heaven peeked at the third contact sheet handed to her by one of Antonio's assistants. She could not believe that the image she saw in stark black and white was herself. The photographs were staggering.

"You like?" asked the assistant, a butch-looking female.

"Sensational!" breathed Heaven. "Is this really me!"

"Yeah. Antonio's hot stuff with a camera. As long as he has someone to work with – an' you've got it."

"Do you think so?" Heaven asked modestly.

"Just look at the pix. You give out attitude. The camera can play with you and have a good time."

She gazed reverently at the contacts. It was true. The success of the photographs was *not* just due to Antonio. Her personality shone through her eyes and gave the pictures real life. With a little help from a makeup artist, a hairdresser, and an incredible stylist. They had all done their bit.

She was glad she'd persevered and not given up on Antonio's promise to photograph her. It had taken some doing, but she had finally got herself in front of his camera – and the results were brilliant! She was sure he'd enjoyed the session as much as she had. He'd played loud rock music, and encouraged her to move to the beat and have fun.

When signing the release she had made one stipulation – she had asked him to make sure that wherever he placed the photos, there was no mention of Silver Anderson being her mother.

"Bene," he had said, and that was that. She trusted him.

Wow! Silver would freak out when she saw these pictures!

"What's he going to do with them?" she asked Antonio's assistant.

The girl said, "No idea. Feel relieved that he likes them. He's *very* particular."

"Can I order some?"

"You *are* joking, aren't you? Antonio *never* gives out prints. Sorry."

Heaven wondered if she could steal a contact sheet. What was the point of *doing* the pictures if she couldn't get hold of any?

"Well" – the assistant relented a bit – "I'll ask him what plans he has. Call me in a couple of weeks."

Reluctantly she left the studio half excited and half let down. At least it was a *positive* move. How many other girls of sixteen got to pose for the great Antonio? And how many other girls got to spend the summer at the beach with their famous uncle? She was elated about *that*, even though Jack's house was definitely in the wrong direction. Santa Monica was where all the action was. Still . . . it was probably a brilliant house and she couldn't wait to see it. It was dynamite of him to invite her — she knew how busy he was.

Her mother hadn't even called to find out what she was doing for the summer.

Her mother . . .

Sometimes she wondered who her father was, and if she had known him would he have cared about her? Or would he be just like Silver?

She was frightened to ask his identity. Anonymity was better than more rejection.

Stopping at the big Rexall drugstore on the corner of La Cienega and Beverly, she stocked up on suntan oils, and began to feel excited. At six o'clock that evening Uncle Jack was picking her up, and her summer at the beach would begin. As Jack had predicted, Grandfather George had hardly reacted at all. In fact, he had seemed quite pleased. Now she could look forward to six weeks of total freedom! Ah, if only she could get her career going everything would be perfect.

Driving over the hill she thought about Eddie. He was such a dork. She didn't like his guitar playing anymore, and she didn't like him. Perhaps this was the break they both needed.

The rambling house was empty when she got home. Her grandfather was in his workroom, and the housekeeper was out. She called a couple of girlfriends, found out nothing new, and began to pack.

What to take for six weeks at the beach? Bikinis, shorts, tank tops, tee-shirts and pants. She came across her long army coat hanging in the closet. A few months ago it was her favourite garment, but after Silver's party she'd never worn it again. Dragging it out she slipped it on. Hey — this was a definite *look* —why had she abandoned it?

Because it reminded her of dear mother. Her caring mother who recently got married for the *third* time, and did not even bother to inform her. Like the rest of America she had read about Silver Anderson's latest wedding in the newspapers.

She spun in front of the mirror, and the huge coat encircled her. Hardly right for the beach. Too hot.

She thrust her hands in the deep pockets and came up with a crumpled napkin. Written on it was ROCKY and a phone number.

For a moment she gazed at it blankly. Rocky? And then she remembered. The dude from Silver's party. The one behind the bar with a friend in the record biz. She had forgotten about him, what with meeting Antonio and the quest to get him to do the promised photos.

On impulse she dialled the number.

No answer.

Carefully she folded the napkin and stuffed it in the side of her suitcase. Rocky. She would give him a call and see if he *did* have a friend in the music industry. After all, she was going to be seventeen soon. She wasn't getting any younger.

Chapter 50

Wrapped in a soft leather Donna Karan dress, Jade arrived at the Ivy restaurant before her brother. She couldn't believe he hadn't changed the date as he had been consistently doing for weeks now. Since dinner never seemed to work out, she had finally pinned him down to a lunch. She was pleased, but also apprehensive. What if she hated his new girlfriend? What if the girlfriend hated her?

A Bloody Mary seemed like a good idea. She ordered one and sat back. A man at a nearby table smiled. She nodded distantly. Because her face was so familiar people always thought they knew her. Commercials did that for you. Wait until the Cloud Cosmetics campaign hit an unsuspecting public. It was going to be an all-out push to make Cloud bigger than Revlon and Estée Lauder put together. And *her* image was going to be on every television commercial, in every print ad, featured on the cover of every brochure – there would even be billboards across the country.

Cloud Cosmetics was already a famous and successful international company. Now the name Jade Johnson would be synonymous with Cloud. For she was not only the face to launch the new products, she was also the personality to sell them. There was a cross-country tour planned, personal appearances, and a host of other things. Mark would never have allowed her to sign such a deal. "It's too public," he would have proclaimed. "Hang onto your privacy, it's one of your most precious possessions."

And thinking of Mark, she realized that if he'd wanted to pique her interest, he'd certainly done a good job. But then he always *had* been a *clever* English asshole.

Since turning up at her apartment and the subsequent phone calls, she had not heard a word from him.

Isn't that what you wanted, Johnson? You ran off to Vegas fast enough.

She wasn't certain. Maybe he *was* divorcing Lady Fiona. Maybe he *had* changed.

Sure.

"Jade?"

She glanced up and exclaimed, "Beverly! I don't *believe* it!" Pushing away from the table she leaped to her feet and hugged her old friend Beverly D'Amo.

Beverly was a very tall, black, exotically beautiful model turned actress. She had jet hair hanging in a thick plait past her waist, and cheekbones that could cut glass.

"Believe it, J.J.!" yelled Beverly. "What the fuck you doin' here, girl?"

Several people turned to stare. Beverly's language never *had* been lady-like.

"I called you," Jade said. "Your answering service told me you were in Peru or somewhere."

"I was doing a movie, babee. A real-life DRAMA! She*cit*! I got the runs the moment I arrived, an' spent most of my time visiting the can. Two minutes on the screen and two months in the crapper!"

Jade smiled. "Nothing changes. Still the same old Bad Beverly."

"Yeah. This may be hot-shot city, babe, but the *Brrr*onx is in my blood."

"You left the Bronx when you were fifteen," Jade pointed out.

"So . . . I can have my roots, can't I?"

Grinning, Jade said, "Why don't you just sit down, shut up, and order a drink."

Beverly grimaced. "I can't. I'm having lunch with my agent. A power lunch, my dear. We have my *career* to discuss, you know." She waved across the room.

Jade shook her head. "You're so full of it! But I still love you. Can we have dinner?"

"Not tonight we can't. Tonight I am attending a very chic little dinner party for Silver Anderson. Just seventy-five of her *very* closest dearest friends!"

"And you're one of them, I presume."

Beverly let loose a wild, high-pitched Eddie Murphy type laugh. "Don't even *know* the bitch! But hey, J.J., I'm a party animal, you remember that, don't you?"

How could she ever forget? She had started modelling with Beverly, and for a while they were known as the Terror Team, because of all the practical jokes they played. Jade had nothing but warm memories of the wild and wonderful Ms. D'Amo. "How about tomorrow night?" she suggested.

"Babee, you're on. We'll go cruising. Where's His Lordship?"

"Dead."

"He deserves worse."

"Oh. So you knew about him too?"

"*Everyone* knew about him. His prick stood at attention whenever you left the room."

"Thanks for telling me."

"We'll talk tomorrow. I've got gossip comin' out my ears!"

"Can't wait."

"Call me in the morning. See ya!"

Jade watched Beverly slink across the room and settle at a table, her loud laughter ringing across the small, intimate restaurant.

Sipping her drink she waited patiently — brother Corey and friend were late. Signalling the waiter she ordered another Bloody Mary.

Corey walked in twenty minutes later, with what she had learned to recognize as his guilty face. When they were kids he employed it every time he did something naughty.

"What's up, bro?" she asked, determined not to comment on his tardy entrance and spoil their lunch.

His greeting was strained as he glanced anxiously around the restaurant. A pretty blonde girl approached their table, and Jade steeled herself for the introduction.

The girl walked briskly past. Behind her was a very handsome young man, slight of build, with dark curly hair, and a dimpled chin.

Corey put his hand possessively on the young man's arm. "Norman," he said in a strained voice, "I'd like you to meet my sister, Jade."

Norman had an open smile, and a gold Rolex on his wrist. He extended a friendly hand and introduced himself. "Norman Gooseberger," he said pleasantly. "Delighted to meet you. I'm the mystery roommate. I'm sorry it's taken so long for us to get together – but *you know* your brother."

She had thought she did. Suddenly she wasn't sure at all – for it was quite obvious that Corey and Norman were much more than mere roommates.

Chapter 51

They entered the Bistro like couple of the year. Which, of course, they were. Silver Anderson and her new husband, Wes Money.

The photographers skulking around the entrance went beserk when they drew up in a sleek limousine. Silver wore a shimmering long gown of gold and a big smile. Wes wore a recently purchased tuxedo and a white silk shirt with diamond and gold studs – a wedding present from Silver.

He was unused to the sudden rush of photographers, and nearly tripped. Grabbing Silver firmly by the arm he pulled her inside, his expression grim.

"What's the matter?" she asked, with an amused smile.

"Those people are animals," he complained. "Don't pose for 'em, it just encourages the sleaze-bags."

"Charming! What a delightfully *visual* word."

"Believe me, it sure describes *this* group."

She adjusted the top of her dress before ascending the staircase to the upstairs room where the party was taking place. "Get used to it, darling," she said casually. "Wherever Silver Anderson goes, the press follows. Sometimes it's fun, most times it's not. I just bare my teeth and take it in my stride."

"*I* don't," he said grimly.

"You soon will."

"Care to put money on it?"

"We'll see."

They had been married for exactly five weeks. The wedding had taken place in Las Vegas. Quick, quiet, and very secret. So secret, in fact, that the press had no smell of anything going on, and Silver, unrecognizable in a long blonde wig and dark glasses, had completely fooled the old couple in the wedding chapel. Only later, when checking the register, had they noticed her name. By the time the wire-services and television crews were alerted, Silver and her new bridegroom had flown to a remote hideaway house in Hawaii, loaned to them by the executive producer of *Palm Springs*. There they stayed for several delicious weeks, shut off from the outside world, quite content to just relax and get to know each other. What they actually did most of the time was make love. A lot. As Silver later remarked to Nora in a confiding moment, "It was the perfect honeymoon. Sex, sleep, sex, food, and sex, sex, sex!"

Nora, as usual, marvelled at the woman's energy.

Once Silver made the decision that, yes, she *would* marry Wes, everything fell into place like a perfectly planned chess game. She told only Nora, her lawyer, and the producer of *Palm Springs*. Together they eased the way for a publicity-free union. Not easy, but possible. Especially as Wes had never been publicly connected to her, and nobody knew who he was anyway.

Naturally they all tried to talk her out of it. She listened to one minute of *Who is he? You know nothing about him. He could be after your money*, etcetera. Then she told them, very politely, to kindly butt out of her personal life. Which they did. Albeit reluctantly.

Prudently she did have her lawyer draw up a document excluding Wes from sharing her wealth. He signed it quite happily.

"Do you have any family you wish to tell?" she had asked him shortly before the ceremony.

He'd shaken his head. "Nope. I come to you free and clear of any mothers, fathers, sisters, brothers, children or ex-wives."

"Hmmm . . . You also come to me free and clear of any worldly goods."

"I've got a few things – nothin' I'm in the mood to collect right now. I can get 'em when we come back."

Their timing was perfect. One more day's work, and then Silver was on hiatus from her television show for three months. She had been considering doing a Movie of the Week – fortunately nothing was signed.

Several days after he proposed, they did the deed, and Silver Anderson became Mrs Wes Money. Actually, Wes Money became Mr Silver Anderson, because that's the way it goes in Hollywood. The famous name is the one everyone knows. So limo drivers and doormen and porters all referred to him as Mr Anderson. What did he care? He was safe. He was no longer a nobody – overnight, Wes Money had become a somebody.

Now they were back in L.A., still comparative strangers, although he *did* know her favourite food was golden caviar – which he hated. Her favourite booze, champagne – which gave him ferocious hangovers. And her favourite sexual position – anything, anytime, anywhere.

The whole scenario was like some kind of wild fantasy. He kept on thinking he was going to wake up and find himself lying on the floor in the hall of the Laurel Canyon house with the cops right outside and the murder weapon clutched in his hand.

Jesus! Every time he thought of that little nightmare he got the chills. But he had outsmarted them all the way down the line. First – he had escaped before discovery. Second – he had married well. They couldn't try to pin anything on him now, he was no longer Joe Schmuck. And let them whistle for their money. As far as he was concerned they could all eat shit. He had nearly been tricked into oblivion, and they could damn well pay for it. The money and cocaine were stashed in a safe-deposit box at the bank. It was his insurance in case Silver ever threw him out.

"Poppy, darling – this is Wes," Silver said, between cheek kisses which missed by half a mile. "I want *you* to be the first to meet him."

Wes took in a short blonde with silicone tits (he could always tell), fabulous real diamonds (he could always tell) and a self-satisfied smile.

"So *you're* the mystery man!" she exclaimed in a breathy voice. "How *exciting*!"

He nearly choked on her perfume.

"*Do* meet my husband, Howard Soloman." She pulled at the sleeve of a short man with obvious shoe lifts and a rug. "Howard, poppet. Say hello to Wes."

Howard Soloman winked at him, just as Silver said, "Congratulate me, Howard. I've done it again!"

"Congratulations, kiddo," Howard said amiably. An out-of-control muscle twitched on his cheek. "Nice to meet you, Les."

"Wes."

A lone female photographer stepped forward and took their picture.

"C'*mon*," said Wes forcefully. "No pictures."

"Don't worry" – Poppy dimpled nicely – "it's only George's girl."

"Who's George's girl?" he muttered to Silver.

"George Christy, darling. He writes the wonderful back page in the *Hollywood Reporter*."

"They allow photographers into these things?"

"Only the key ones. Oh look, there's Dudley. He's so wonderful. I adore him. Did you see him in *Ten*? Such a *funny* man."

For the next-half hour it was "spot the stars". It seemed everyone from Johnny Carson to Kirk Douglas had turned out to inspect Silver's latest husband.

Wes tried to maintain an aura of cool as he said hello to Jacqueline Bisset, Whitney Valentine Cable and Angie Dickinson. Three women he had lusted after forever.

And then came the men. He actually got to meet Carlos Brent. He had grown up *fucking* to the records of the legendary Carlos Brent. What a night *this* was going to be!

*

Poppy took the news of Zachary K. Klinger as an extra guest extremely well. She moved Howard's place card from his seat of honour beside Silver, and cleverly replaced him with Zachary.

Then she switched place cards with Whitney Valentine Cable, and put herself the other side of the new guest. Howard and Whitney she relocated on table number two. Had it been anyone else but Zachary K. Klinger she would have screamed for days. As it was she felt quite elated. Getting Zachary K. Klinger was a hostess's coup.

Meanwhile, it was past eight-thirty, and Zachary had failed to put in an appearance.

"Where is he?" she hissed at Howard. "I'm going to have to seat everyone in fifteen minutes."

"Go ahead, he'll be here." Howard spoke in a carefree manner, but oh . . . was he going to get it if Zachary didn't show.

He eyed Whitney, who was standing across the room, positively glowing in a strapless lime-green dress. He was purposely staying away from her until dinner when he would be sitting next to her. Maybe by this time she had read the script and wanted to do it. How could she *not* want to do it with Carlos Brent starring and Orville Gooseberger producing? The lady was going to move into heavyweight country, and *he* was responsible. He hoped she would be suitably grateful.

Mannon Cable made an entrance. Late, of course. The bigger the star, the later the entrance. Once the guest list passed thirty people, Poppy had decided it was perfectly proper to invite Whitney *and* Mannon. "After all," she had said, with a great deal of logic, "if one stopped inviting people because they were once married to other guests . . . well, in Hollywood, you'd end up with no one!"

Very true.

Mannon waved at Howard. Howard waved back. If he *did* have an affair with Whitney, and Mannon found out . . .

It didn't bear thinking about.

*

Zachary K. Klinger greeted his driver curtly, and stepped into the back of a maroon Rolls-Royce. The Rolls, although several years old, was in pristine condition. Zachary rarely visited California, but believed in keeping a car and chauffeur in every major city across the world. He was rich enough to have dozens of cars wherever he wished. In fact, his riches enabled him to do whatever he damn well pleased for the rest of his life.

Sighing, he leaned back against the plush leather upholstery. Money. It could buy him anything and almost anyone. Except . . .

with nagging realization he knew the old cliché was true – money could not buy the happiness he so fervently desired.

*

"Enjoying it?" Silver gave Wes a sly smile. She was loving every minute of the attention.

He nodded. To tell the truth, he was quite bemused. All these people, all these well-known faces. He knew for a fact that if he wasn't Mr Silver Anderson, they wouldn't give him the time of day. Rich folks lived life different. They only wanted to mix with other rich folks. Wes knew this. He had stood behind enough bars in enough fashionable establishments to observe the way things were.

Famous people were exactly the same. Show a star another star and they'd break bones to be together. Unless they were deadly rivals, in which case icy politeness ruled.

Jeez! If this lot only knew who Wes Money *really* was.

Fortunately, the supermarket rags had managed to find out nothing. He was a complete mystery man.

Nora had released a statement on Silver's behalf. It was short and to the point:

SILVER ANDERSON, STAR OF *PALM SPRINGS*, MARRIED RECENTLY FOR THE THIRD TIME. HER NEW HUSBAND, WESLEY MONEY JUNIOR, IS A BUSINESSMAN.

Wes had exploded when the announcement appeared. "What the *fuck* is this *junior* crap?" he'd demanded.

"Nora's idea," Silver had replied. "And I must admit, it does give you *some* sort of background."

"You want a background, you should've married Teddy Kennedy!"

She had smiled. "Just a touch too plump. I do so *hate* love rolls, don't you?"

He had to admire Silver. She didn't give a damn about anything or anybody. She was a tough, gutsy broad who did what she wanted, and to hell with criticism.

"My life hasn't always been easy," she had informed him one balmy night on their lust-filled honeymoon. "Four years ago I had a nervous breakdown. I thought it was all over."

"Yeah?" He wasn't interested in talking pasts. He couldn't imagine Silver anywhere but at the top. And once they were married he couldn't imagine himself being anywhere except by her side.

This was not love. This was good times.

*

Poppy fussed among her guests as they began to sit down at their various tables. She wanted Howard. She wanted his blood. Zachary K. Klinger had failed to show.

Just as she was about to start screaming – discreetly, of course – Zachary K. Klinger walked through the door. She recognized him at once, and wasted no time in hurrying over. "Mr Klinger," she gushed. "This is *such* a pleasure! I am delighted you made it."

"Who are you?" he asked, in his sinister rasp.

"Why, I'm Poppy Soloman." She smiled sweetly. "Your hostess."

He looked her over. He was a big, well-preserved man in his late sixties, with exaggerated strong features – and behind his steel-rimmed glasses, cold, opaque eyes. He made her feel immediately uncomfortable.

"Why don't I find Howard for you," she suggested.

"Yes. Why don't you?" he said, taking a cigar from his breast pocket and lighting up.

How rude, she thought, *and before dinner, too.* Perhaps she had made a mistake seating him next to Silver; the man obviously had no manners.

She grabbed Mannon, on his way back from the men's room. "Have you seen Howard?" she asked anxiously. And then, as an afterthought, because she was nervous, she introduced him to Zachary. The two men had never met. They shook hands and tried to out-grip each other.

"Howard's in the john," Mannon informed her.

"Can you get him for me?" she pleaded.

"I'll find him myself," Zachary said, staring piercingly at Mannon. "We'll talk later. I want you for Orpheus. When you hear what I have to offer, you'll jump."

"I never jump," said Mannon easily – his ease belied by his mouth, which set into a thin line.

"Never known an actor who didn't," said Zachary, with all the confidence of a man used to getting his own way.

"Well, I guess you're looking at him," replied Mannon.

"I don't think so." Zachary set off to find Howard.

251

Mannon was not pleased. "What a jerk," he said derisively.

"I'm certain he's not," Poppy said quickly, not quite sure why she was defending a man she had taken an instant dislike to.

"Grow up, Poppy. These guys that come walking into a business they know nothing about are all uniform jerks. You can take everything they know about the film industry and shove it up Howard's ass – *and* you'll have room for an agent or two."

"Mannon!"

"Believe me. I've been around."

He stalked off to his table, which unfortunately was the same one Zachary would be sitting at.

*

Locked safely in a booth in the men's room, Howard snorted the magic white powder. With a sigh of deep pleasure he felt the effect almost immediately. Nothing like it. Instant head honcho of the jungle. King Kong with concrete balls! Infuckingvincible!

He sailed out of the booth and bumped straight into Zachary K. Klinger.

"Mr K. You made it!" he exclaimed.

"Was there any doubt in your mind?"

"Never. *Ne-ver.*"

"When I say I'll be somewhere, I'm there."

"Sure you are." *When it suits you.* Howard walked over to the sink and began to wash his hands.

"I just talked to Mannon Cable," Zachary said, in his heavy whisper.

"Good."

"I want him for Orpheus."

Glancing in the mirror Howard noticed a dusting of white powder beneath his nose. Quickly he wiped it away. "I've tried to get him. The trouble is he's always tied up on some other project."

"I want him," Zachary repeated.

Howard wondered if old Zach ever cracked a smile. Probably not.

"I'll give it another shot," he said.

"You'll do more than that," Zachary retorted sharply.

"What?"

"I have a proposal. When he hears it, he'll be ours."

"Don't get too excited. Mannon's a lot pickier than everyone seems to think."

"Money talks."

"To some people."

"To everyone."

"Like I said — we'll give it another try."

As he walked towards the door, Zachary blocked him. "I don't believe in tries. I believe in certainties. I want Mannon Cable and *I will have him*."

"If you say so." *Shit*, Howard thought. *The old guy thinks he's Harry Cohn and this is the 1950s. No way, José.*

*

"Well?" Silver whispered, reaching for Wes's thigh under the table. "Are we having a good time?"

He didn't go overboard on this new, semi-patronizing attitude she was adopting. Benevolent keeper, showing her new pet off to the crowd.

"It's all a crap shoot, Silver, and you know it."

Giggling girlishly she said, "Don't I just. Some of the women can't keep their eyes off you. They're all *dying* to know where I found you."

"You didn't *find* me anywhere. Let's get it straight, I rescued you from a bunch of fags who were out to rip you to shreds. Remember?"

"How could I *ever* forget. The thing I liked about you — even then — was your forcefulness."

"Silver, dahling!" Carmel Gooseberger descended on them, a nightmare in huge yellow frou-frous. "Is *this* the bridegroom?"

"Yes," said Silver. "Wes, meet Carmel Gooseberger."

He shook the large woman's hand.

"I know, I know," boomed Carmel, in an extremely loud voice. "Wesley Money, Junior. I think I know your father."

Wes looked alarmed. "You do?" he asked, remembering a shifty-eyed English pimp whom he hadn't seen since he was eight, and a pot-bellied American stepfather who had only been in his life for five minutes.

"Yes," nodded Carmel. "It's the San Francisco Moneys, isn't it?"

Silver kicked him under the table.

"Sure is," he agreed.

"What a family! Ah yes, I remember them well. It was quite a few years ago. Orville and I had just started going out together, and I was in San Francisco on location — I used to be an actress, you know."

Silver leaned forward glowing with amusement. "Go on, Carmel. Confess. You had an affair with Wes's father."

Carmel laughed in a loud and bawdy fashion. "If I did, dahling, you're the *last* person I'd tell."

"What won't you tell Silver?" Carlos Brent flashed a smile as he sat down at the table, accompanied by Dee Dee Dionne.

"Carmel claims to have slept with Wes's father. She was cheating on Orville at the time." Silver spoke with obvious relish.

"I reckon Carmel humped every good-looking cat in this town before Orville found her an' took her in off the street," Carlos said, with a big grin. "Am I right, gorgeous?"

"Stop!" roared Carmel, loving every minute of it. "You're so *bad*, Carlos."

"You can't fool us, sweetie," he joked. "I got in line once, but the line was so long I didn't have the strength to wait!"

"You're ruining my reputation," shrieked Carmel, patting her frosted hair, frou-frous heaving above a mammoth bosom.

"*What* reputation?" cracked Carlos.

The wisecracks continued as the table filled up. Mannon and Melanie-Shanna came over, and Orville Gooseberger, who had an even louder voice than his wife.

Silver was in fine form. Glittering like a Queen. Accepting compliments and congratulations as her due. Many years before, she and Carlos Brent had indulged in a short and passionate affair. Someone had tipped the press off that they were going to get married, and Carlos had blown a fuse – thinking Silver was the culprit. They had parted acrimoniously. Now, years later, she felt very secure with her hot career, and her horny new husband.

Poppy hovered, waiting for Zachary to emerge from the men's room so she could guide him to his seat. Howard was settled at his own table, with Whitney on one side and Ida White on the other. Ida was looking particularly glassy-eyed. Poppy hoped she'd last through the dinner. Ida had been known to go to the ladies' room at parties and fall into a blissful, drug-induced sleep. No one was sure what she was on, but whatever it was it certainly kept her floating, her head calmly above water – only just.

Zachary appeared, and Poppy grabbed him. "You're at my table," she cooed, and then proceeded to name-drop. "You're sitting with Carlos Brent, Mannon Cable, Silver Anderson – you do know this party is for her?" Without waiting for a reply she rushed on with, "Oh, and Orville Gooseberger. *Quelle* character! Quite a group for one table, don't you think?"

"Am I next to Silver Anderson?" he asked curtly.

"As a matter of fact, that's *exactly* where I've seated you."

Zachary nodded his approval.

Proudly, Poppy led him across the room. Several people tried to greet him, but Zachary gave the word *ignore* new meaning.

They reached the number one table, and Poppy began to introduce her most important guest.

Silver had a glass of champagne halfway to her lips when she looked up and saw Zachary.

The colour drained from her face.

Zachary K. Klinger was "The Businessman" from her past.

Zachary K. Klinger was Heaven's father, although he didn't know it.

Zachary K. Klinger was the hate of her life.

Chapter 52

"It's amazing!" Heaven exclaimed for the tenth time. "I totally, like, *love* it!"

She was referring to the beach house, which she had explored several times.

Jack loosened his tie and removed his jacket. He had been in a meeting with his accountant all afternoon and felt a strong need to flake out.

"And my room is just brilliant!" she continued. "It overlooks the beach and the ocean. I can just sit at my window all day and stare!"

"Sounds good to me. Do you want to stare in the fridge and see what the maid got in for us? I left a note for her to stock up at the market."

"I'm *starving*!"

"You're always starving! Whenever I see you I get this feeling you don't eat between my visits."

"I don't."

"You're a funny one."

She giggled happily. "I'll check out the food situation. Do not go away!"

As she rushed into the kitchen, he wondered what he had gotten himself into. Who would ever have thought he'd be living in a house *and* looking after a kid. Jack Python – surrogate father!

He kind of liked it.

Clarissa was still in New York. Because she had time between films, she had decided to do an obscure off-Broadway play for a limited run. They spoke on the phone every few days, but it was definitely a relationship that had gone off the boil. He knew she was waiting to see what he planned to do about her ultimatum. And quite frankly, the more he thought about marriage, the more he loathed the whole idea. Who needed it?

Silver had just married again. Silver could do what she damn well liked. He cared about *her* the way *she* cared about Heaven. Zilch feelings.

"I found potato salad, coleslaw, chicken and ham," Heaven announced triumphantly.

"Or we could go out," he suggested.

"Let's stay in."

"You don't have to twist *my* arm."

Much later, after food and unpacking and calling all her friends – including Eddie – Heaven fell into a happy sleep while Jack prowled around the house. He wasn't at all tired. Grabbing a sweater he decided to take a walk along the beach.

The dull realization hit him that he had to go to New York and settle things with Clarissa. They were either on or off. He *definitely* did not want marriage. She did. Either she was prepared to go on with the relationship the way it was, or it was over.

Decision made, he felt better. He would tell Heaven to have a girlfriend stay with her, and as soon as that was arranged, he'd take the next flight into New York. The show was on a six-week break, so it was the perfect time to sort things out.

In a way he hoped Clarissa would tell him it *was* over. Being with her was not exactly a laugh a minute. She was a broody, intense woman, simmering with secrets. She never revealed herself to him. There was always that guarded quality as if there were an unseen wall between them. The only time she really laid herself wide open was on the screen.

If he was really truthful with himself he would admit that the real appeal of Clarissa was her enormous talent.

He jogged back to the house and watched a late night movie. Lana Turner in her prime. A sexy, ballsy broad. They didn't make 'em like that anymore.

By one a.m. he began to fade, his eyes closed, and he drifted off to sleep.

Tomorrow he would work things out.

*

Back in the city, in her apartment on Wilshire, Jade sat alone on the terrace with a pack of Camels, a glass of wine, and a small dish of yoghurt-coated pretzels. She had *A Star is Born* on her stereo — the Streisand/Kristofferson version of the movie was one of her favourites.

The lights of Los Angeles were laid out like a glittering patchwork quilt. She never tired of watching them sparkle. *Hmmm*, she thought, *I'm turning into a loner. I like my own company a lot more than the party circuit.*

Well, that's what happened when there was no one in particular she wanted to be with. Besides, she enjoyed her own company, and never felt lonely. Ever since she was a child she had been self-sufficient and able to entertain herself. Whereas Corey had always needed friends over.

Corey —

My brother —

Is gay.

Subconsiously she had tried to stop herself from thinking about it all day. After lunch, which turned out to be a stilted affair, she had bolted from the restaurant fast. Without thinking, she'd gotten in her car and headed for the nearest shopping mall, which happened to be the Beverly Center. Once there, she had toured the shops with a dedication bordering on the obsessive.

One leather jacket, two pairs of Levis, a silk shirt, three pairs of stiletto-heeled shoes, four hard-cover books, an assortment of makeup, and a heavy glass ashtray later, she had driven home, where she showered, watched a tape of *Hill Street Blues*, and mindlessly ate a can of cold baked beans, a bar of chocolate and an orange. She smoked three cigarettes — a habit she had given up six years ago – and now she was sitting on her terrace *finally* thinking about Corey.

The revelation was an enormous shock. Not that he'd said anything. It hadn't been necessary. Just watching him with Norman Gooseberger the picture had become excruciatingly clear, and she knew immediately why her brother had been avoiding her.

Desperately she had tried to act normally, but it was difficult when all she wanted to do was scream at him – *Why? Why? Why?*

Polite conversation took place. *Have you seen this movie? Been to that restaurant? Tried this hotel?*

Norman seemed nice enough. His father was Orville Gooseberger, the well-known film producer, and his mother – to quote him – *gives great charity.*

"How did you two meet?" she'd found herself asking.

And Norman replied. Corey had nothing to say. It seemed they had worked together in the San Francisco branch of Briskinn & Bower, the big publicity firm. When Norman was transferred back to Los Angeles, he'd asked his father – who owned a chunk of B & B – to arrange for Corey to be transferred too.

She didn't want to know any more, hardly caring to hear the details.

Now, sitting quietly on her terrace, she began to wonder. Had Corey always been gay? Or did Norman bring it out in him?

She remembered how when he was a teenager he had always been inordinately shy around girls. One day her mother had voiced a mild doubt, swiftly forgotten, because the very next week he had started steady dating a girl named Gloria, with big breasts and sturdy legs. Were he and Gloria making out? She had asked him once, but he never replied. And then she had taken off for New York and her career, and only saw him on her occasional visits home.

When he met Marita, the entire family had been delighted, once they got over the shock of her being Hawaiian. Their wedding was old-fashioned and lovely, and they both seemed very happy. A year later, when the baby was born, everyone felt Corey was settled for life.

Now *this* bombshell. Her mother would have a nervous breakdown.

She reached for another cigarette. Some of her best friends were gay.

Jesus Christ, Johnson. What kind of a bigoted thought is that?

She hated herself for it, but she couldn't control the shock and disappointment she felt. And she was angry too.

Why hadn't he told her?

Because, asshole, he knew you'd react just like this.

Shut up.

It's true!

Guilt crept up on her. Was Corey doing it to spite her? Beautiful, successful Jade Johnson. Always the centre of attention. Always the star of the family. Was Corey striking back in the only way he could think of?

Drawing deeply on her cigarette, she realized *she* was the one who would have to tell their mother.

Why?

Because she has to know.

Why?

Oh, fuck off!

The phone interrupted her argument with herself. Since the answering machine was still on she let it pick up. First the message, then the bleep, followed by the unmistakable tones of Lord Mark Rand. English jerk-off artist.

"Jade?" he asked. "Are you there?"

When she said nothing he left his message, sounding embarrassed, as most people are when faced with speaking to a machine.

"Er . . . I'm in town."

Obviously.

"Please telephone me at L'Ermitage."

Oh, great! A repeat performance.

"This is Mark."

As if I don't know.

"Er . . . call me. Please."

He hung up.

She sighed. She wasn't ready for him. Not now.

Yes she was. She just wanted to curl up in his arms and shut out the world.

With a sigh of resignation, she reached for the phone.

Chapter 53

Silver managed a frosty smile. She was outraged, furious, *incensed*. What was Zachary doing at *her* wedding dinner? Who *the hell* had invited him?

She had gone over the list of guests several times, making sure there were no enemies included. Poppy had been most obliging, crossing off a ridiculous actress made of silicone, and a glassy-eyed producer who everyone knew was certifiably insane, but put up with anyway because he continued to produce movies, even though none of them ever made any money.

"I don't think we should invite riff-raff," Silver had remarked mildly, and the two offenders' names were struck through with a heavy felt-tip pen.

Now Zachary K. Klinger was present. And not only was he present, he was sitting down beside her.

The smile was fixed on her face like a frozen mask. *Poppy Soloman knows! Poppy Soloman did this on purpose! I'll get the bitch for this!*

"Good evening, Silver," Zachary said.

"*Zachary!* How *lovely* to see you. What a surprise! I'd like you to meet my husband, Wes Money, Junior."

"Will you cut out the Junior," Wes muttered irritably.

Zachary ignored him, concentrating only on Silver. "Congratulations on your success," he said.

"Thank you," she replied, anxious to excuse herself and rush to the ladies' room just to make absolutely certain she looked her best. Not that she cared what Zachary thought. It was just that after sixteen years one didn't want to be caught looking anything but perfect.

"You haven't changed," he said.

Nor had he, only she wasn't about to flatter him. His hair was completely grey, and there were more lines on his face, that was all. He had never been handsome, but he radiated power, and it was that which had attracted her to him in the first place.

When they first met, he was an important and extremely rich man. Since their last encounter he had become a legendary business tycoon and billionaire.

"Well!" Poppy exclaimed, as a delicate avocado and papaya salad was served. "Isn't this *fun!*"

*

"When are you goin' to dump the bozo?" Howard asked, with a knowing wink.

Whitney flashed her famous teeth. "Don't be bad, Howard. Chuck is an excellent actor, and extremely misunderstood."

"The guy is a stoned beach bum who is not worthy of you."

He liked that. The "not worthy of you" exhibited a great deal of class.

Whitney held her smile steady. "I'm not planning to *marry* him."

Howard wanted to say — *Just hump his ass off, huh?* But that wasn't classy, not classy at all. And above all he wanted her to regard him as a man of style.

"Have you read the script?" he asked.

She nodded, all teeth and hair and sparkling aquamarine eyes. "Yes, I have."

"And?"

"Zeppo has asked me not to discuss it with you."

"What?" He was outraged. "Since when has Zeppo been your agent?"

"Do I hear my name?" Zeppo White asked. He was sitting next to Beverly D'Amo, who was keeping him royally entertained with stories of her exploits in Peru.

Whitney widened her eyes. "I was just telling Howard that you're my agent now."

"How'd he take it?" snapped Zeppo, blinking rapidly several times. He was a small nut of a man, with a shock of bright orange hair, alarmingly styled in some kind of crazed pompadour. His reputation was fierce.

"I don't know," smiled Whitney. "How *did* you take it, Howard?"

"When you get bitten by a snake, you look around for someone to suck out the poison."

She continued to smile. "Yes?"

"And if I'm very lucky, you'll suck it for me, won't you, Whitney?" Not too classy, but funny all the same.

She laughed. Zeppo laughed. Beverly laughed. Ida White looked vague, but laughed anyway.

"I wouldn't put all your money on it if I was you, Howard," teased Whitney.

"Dirty talk! I love it!" exclaimed Beverly. "I thought you warned me to behave myself tonight, Zeppo."

"I wouldn't ask you to do the impossible, kiddo," Zeppo replied with a jaunty wink.

*

"Did you know that my wife died several months ago?" Zachary said, staring intently at Silver.

She sipped champagne, refusing to return his gaze. What did he want from her? Was she supposed to say she was sorry? Silver Anderson was not a hypocrite and refused to act like one.

"This means I'm free at last," he said pointedly.

She thought she might laugh in his face. Free. Sixteen years later. So what?

"How nice for you," she replied coolly.

He continued to stare at her, waiting for a more positive reaction. Didn't she understand what he was telling her? Finally they could be together, for over the years Silver was the only woman he had thought about and always wanted.

She was the perfect match for him. The Queen to sit beside him on his throne. Now that his wife was dead there was nothing to prevent their union.

"I have an interesting proposition for you," he said.

She appeared bored. "Really?"

"Perhaps you can meet me at my hotel tomorrow."

"I don't think so."

"It's to your advantage."

"I *don't* think so."

"A business meeting. That's all."

Arrogant bastard. Did he really imagine he could walk back into her life and take over? "I would hardly suspect it to be anything else," she said icily.

He lowered his voice, so only she could hear his harsh whisper, determined to get to her. "Don't flatter yourself, Silver. You're too old for me now."

His words stung like a sharp slap. How dare he talk to her like that. HOW DARE HE!

Lowering her voice to match his, she said, "You were *always* too old for *me*, Zachary."

He laughed without humour, remembering her weak spot. "Dear Silver, you never could take criticism, could you?"

Unable to control herself, she said, "Shove it, Zachary *dear*, right up your decrepit *old* ass."

*

"How're you doin'?"

Melanie-Shanna, on her way out of the ladies' room, jumped. Chuck Nielson loomed in front of her, stoned eyes and boyish grin.

Pulling herself together she asked him evenly, "Do you follow me every time I go to the bathroom?"

"Only when I know you want me to."

His come-on was out in the open. Usually it worked. Tonight it didn't.

"You're on the wrong track, *Mr* Nielson," she said. "And if you don't get off it, I'll tell my husband."

"Hey – hey – hey! Back off, beautiful. I'm only makin' polite, not grabbing your gorgeous body."

She looked him straight in the eye. "Don't. Okay?"

He threw up his hands. "You got it, babe."

She hurried past him, back to her place at the table next to Mannon. It crossed her mind that maybe she *should* tell Mannon, if only to see what he would do. Then she thought, no, why cause unnecessary trouble, she could deal with it herself. All her life she had been dealing with it . . .

*

For the first time in Silver's company, Wes was bored. Mixing with the movers and shakers from the other side of the bar was not the trip he had imagined it to be. Here he was, surrounded by the rich and famous, and once he got to talking to them, he realized they were just as boring as the rest of the population.

Carlos Brent was no great wit. Orville Gooseberger talked too much and too loud. Ditto the wife; *nobody* could shut her up. Mannon Cable was broodingly quiet, and Melanie-Shanna Cable – although a knock-out to look at – didn't open up her mouth all night.

Which left Dee Dee Dionne, who was quite charming; Zachary K. Klinger, who monopolized Silver from the moment he sat down; and their hostess, Poppy Soloman – a supercharged bundle of nerves.

Without exception, everyone had one eye on the door to see if anyone they should know about was exiting or entering. Wes caught on fast. He'd be mid-sentence and their eyes glazed over while their attention wandered. It could make a person feel very insecure. Especially as nobody seemed to give a flying fart what anyone else had to say.

Silver seemed well taken care of with Zachary Klinger whispering away in her ear, so after the entrée Wes excused himself, and took a walk around, mentally counting the stars. He hadn't met Whitney Valentine Cable, and since she was the best-looking female in the room, he thought it might make life worthwhile. He caught himself staring as he hovered near her table.

She smiled at him, brilliant white teeth flashing.

He walked over and proffered his hand. "Wes Money."

What a smile she had!

"I know. Congratulations."

"Thanks."

"Have you met Chuck Nielson?"

Yeah. He had met good old Chuck when he'd sold him cocaine at Silver's party. Only he was just a barman then, and who remembered barmen? Certainly not anyone at *this* dinner.

"Hey, man." Chuck gave him a bone-crushing handshake. "You an' Silver are gonna make each other very, very . . ." He trailed off and looked to Whitney for help.

"Happy," she said, her dazzling smile still going strong.

Ida White leaned back in her chair and placed a thin, blue-veined hand on his arm. "I hope you're going to be good to Silver," she remarked, nodding her own confirmation. "We all love her, you know. She's one of us. If you can –"

"She's a pro," interrupted Zeppo, spitting out each word like machine-gun bullets. "The important thing in Hollywood is to always act like a professional, and Silver does that better than anyone. Except perhaps Elizabeth Taylor, Shirley Maclaine . . . there's still a few of 'em left. Anyway, Silver has class."

"Yes," agreed Wes. "She sure does."

"The woman's a star," Zeppo added. "One of the last of the truly *great* stars. You see 'em running around in tee-shirts and sloppy clothes with straggly hair. All the young actresses today look like somebody's maid."

"Thank you!" interjected Whitney.

"Not you," Zeppo barked. "You look okay, kiddo."

"And how about me?" demanded Beverly.

"You're an original, but you can all learn from Silver," Zeppo continued, warming to his theme. "Star quality! She had it the first time I saw her nearly thirty years ago. And she's *still* got it."

For the next fifteen minutes he continued to sing her praises. Chuck got up from the table. "Wanna smoke?" he asked Wes. Wes nodded, and they headed for the door.

"Let's take a walk, it's hot in here," Chuck suggested.

They went down the stairs and out to the street, where Chuck lit up a joint, drew deeply, and handed it over.

Wes did not wish to look unappreciative, so he took a drag, then passed it back.

"This is grade A shit," Chuck stated proudly.

"Yeah," Wes agreed. He'd had better, but what did a permanently stoned, out-of-work movie actor know?

"Zeppo White's a fucking bore," Chuck remarked sourly.

"What does he do?" Wes asked.

Chuck turned on him in surprise. "Are you shittin' me, man?"

He shrugged. "I'm not in the business."

"Yeah, well Zeppo would have a cardiac arrest if he thought there was someone around who's never heard of him."

"I'm that someone."

Chuck began to laugh. "He's an agent. He's *the* agent, or at least he thinks he is."

"Is he *your* agent?"

"I wish. But Zeppo only wants 'em when they're ridin' high. Right now he's Whitney's agent. An' don't think the little turd hasn't tried to fuck her, because he has."

Wes couldn't conceal his surprise. "Zeppo White has fucked Whitney Valentine Cable?"

"Naw . . . just tried to. Bad enough."

"He must be at least *seventy*."

"So? You think it stops poppin' when you pass sixty-five?"

*

"I wish you'd leave me alone." Silver's voice was tightly coiled. "What are you doing here anyway?"

"I told you," Zachary replied patiently. "It's been sixteen years and I've never forgotten you. Now that I'm free, I want you back."

She snorted with laughter. "How flattering!" And then she added sarcastically, "But I thought I was too *old* for you, Zachary. And you're *certainly* too old for me."

Ignoring her sarcasm he said, "I want you, Silver. This time for keeps."

She could not believe the nerve of the man. Not to mention the conceit. "It may have escaped your notice," she said coldly, "but this is my *wedding* dinner. I just got married."

"And how much do you think it will cost me to get him out of your life? He looks like he comes cheap."

"You *bastard*! As far as you're concerned money buys everyone, doesn't it? You always thought that."

"Shall we put it to the test?" he asked mildly.

With an exasperated sigh she got up from the table. Wes was nowhere in sight, which infuriated her. She swept off to the ladies' room.

Poppy, who was not completely insensitive to atmosphere, jumped up and followed her.

★

Mannon noticed Chuck was on the missing list and took the opportunity to stop by the next table and greet his ex-wife.

"Hello, Mannon," Whitney said guardedly.

"You're looking well," he replied, equally guarded.

"So are you."

They hadn't spoken in months. It made the situation awkward, but Mannon plunged in anyway, although he was sure half the people at the table were trying to overhear, especially Zeppo, who never liked to miss a thing.

"There's something I want to talk to you about."

She played with the base of her wine glass. "What?"

"I can't go into it here."

"Why not?"

He indicated the rest of the table. "Why do you *think* not?"

"Hello, Mannon," said Ida White, catching his eye.

"Mannon, my boy," greeted Zeppo. "I hear you're considering the role Reynolds turned down." He wagged a warning finger. "You shouldn't do it. No way."

"I'm not planning to."

"Good, good."

In the distance Mannon saw Chuck. His fist itched to connect with the slimy creep's jaw.

Whitney sensed trouble and quickly said, "It was nice seeing you." She turned away in the hope that he would leave.

Chuck approached the table. He looked good until you put him next to Mannon, and then you realized he was just a poor copy.

"Hey — it's my ole buddy," he exclaimed. "How're ya doin'?"

Mannon did not consider them friends, although they had once been close. He did not even consider that he had to be civilized to the prick, so he ignored him.

Chuck took this as an insult. "What the fuck's the matter with *you*?" he demanded belligerently. "Don't come sniffin' around Whitney if y'can't even say hello t'me."

Mannon began to walk away.

Chuck went to stop him with an angry hand on his shoulder.

"Oh, no," sighed Whitney. She knew what was going to happen, and there was nothing she could do to stop it.

Mannon spun around, removed Chuck's hand and shoved him hard.

Chuck kept his balance and automatically struck out. A punch which Mannon countered with style and grace, while his right fist did just what it had been wanting to do all night, and smashed into Chuck's jaw.

*

"I've made a boo-boo, haven't I?" asked Poppy.

Silver, busy applying a liberal amount of lip gloss as she peered in the mirror, said, "I don't know what you're talking about."

"Zachary," persisted Poppy. "I shouldn't have put him next to you."

Silver thought about her reply. It was unlikely anyone knew about her affair with Zachary. Sixteen years was a long time, and they had been very discreet because of his marriage. Obviously she had misjudged Poppy. Seating Zachary beside her was probably supposed to be an honour – he *was* the most influential man in the room.

"Don't worry about it," she said dismissively.

Poppy confirmed what she was thinking. "I had no idea you two even *knew* each other."

"Oh, we're old adversaries," Silver said vaguely. And then, realizing she should tread carefully, she added, "I've always found men like Zachary Klinger to be ego-inflated bores."

"I agree," said Poppy, patting her elaborate upswept hairstyle. "I can't stand him. He's so pompous. I should have given him to Howard's table, they deserve him."

"Quite!" agreed Silver.

"Maybe he'll leave soon," Poppy said hopefully.

"If he doesn't, *I* shall."

Poppy saw her entire evening falling to pieces. "You can't do that," she said in an alarmed voice. "You're the guest of honour."

Silver licked her lips, squinted slightly, and took a step backwards to admire the overall effect of her makeup repairs. "Yes I can, Poppy," she said sweetly. "And I will."

Before Poppy could plead and beg, which she was fully prepared to do – *anything* to save her party – Melanie-Shanna came rushing into the ladies' room, tears streaking her pretty face. "I hate her!" she shrieked. "I hate that woman!"

"What woman?" Silver and Poppy chorused as one.

"That bitch – Whitney Valentine. She's *ruining* my life!"

Poppy had never perceived Melanie-Shanna as anything but a docile little mouse. The anger she was exhibiting was a revelation. Not such a quiet one after all.

"What has Whitney done?" inquired Silver, only mildly interested in gossip unless it was directly related to her.

Before Melanie-Shanna could reply, Ida White and Carmel Gooseberger barged through the door, both talking at once.

"Poppy!" Carmel boomed excitedly. "Don't you know there's a *fight* going on?"

"Blood!" exclaimed Ida in her deep, flat voice. "Everywhere!"

It was getting too crowded for Silver; she edged her way towards the door.

"A fight?" wailed Poppy. "At *my* party."

"It's that bitch's fault," yelled Melanie-Shanna. "That *fucking bitch*! I'd like to break every bone in her body!"

Chapter 54

Regrets were immediate:

Ms. Jade Johnson regrets. Making love with the English asshole one more time was a grave mistake.

She stared at him, asleep in her bed. He lay on his back with his mouth slightly open, a whispery snore escaping from between his lips.

It was seven o'clock in the morning and she was awake and alert, already reviewing the activities of the night before.

Why had she called him?

Because it seemed like a good idea at the time.

Naturally he'd been delighted to hear from her, and arrived at her apartment in what seemed like minutes, although half an hour probably elapsed.

She had turned off all the lights and decorated the place with small votive candles. Springsteen made beautiful background on the stereo. A bottle of chilled Russian vodka and two shot glasses stood on a table by the bed. She greeted him in an oversize black tee-shirt and nothing else except Opium scent.

He started to talk the moment he walked through the door.

She wasn't after conversation. Silencing him with a finger to his lips, she drew him towards the bedroom.

It didn't take long for him to get the message.

The sex was okay. It was not sensational. If she wanted to be *really* truthful it was pretty damned ordinary. What were the words of that old song? *The thrill is gone. The thrill is gone. I can feel it in your arms, see it in your eyes . . . the thrill is gone.*

Shutting the bedroom door behind her, she padded on bare feet into the kitchen, and switched the kettle on.

At least she knew. It was over. As far as she was concerned there were no doubts about *that*.

*

"I've got to take a quick trip to New York," Jack informed Heaven. "Can you arrange for a girlfriend to stay here with you?"

"When?"

"As soon as possible."

She thought about who she could invite, and rejected every possibility. Some of the girls at school were okay, but she really didn't have much in common with any of them. Eddie was her best friend, only since Silver's dumb party, where he had trailed after her mother like some moronic fan, she had gone right off him.

"I'll get someone over," she promised. "Just tell me when you're going."

"How about tomorrow?"

She nodded. "Terrific." And she thought — *I'll stay here alone, I don't mind.*

"Good, that's settled. I'll only be away for a couple of days."

She rather liked the idea of being by herself. Maybe she *would* have Eddie down and they could do some rehearsing. Lately their gigs together were pure garbage. Either he'd lost his touch or she was just bored with screaming out rock and roll.

Uncle Jack had *still* not heard any of her tapes. It pissed her off. But . . . he was an okay dude — at least he *cared* about her, which was more than she could say for her mother.

One day, when she was rich and famous and no longer treated like a dumb kid, she was going to confront Silver Dearest, and ask her plenty.

Like — *Who is my father?*

Like — *Why don't you give a damn about me?*

Like — *Why did you shove me out of your life as if I didn't matter?*

Anger and frustration welled up inside her. What kind of crap was it not to know the identity of your own father?

*

Mark emerged from the bedroom at nine-fifteen, tousled charm on full wattage.

Jade sat in the kitchen, clad in jeans and a shirt, legs on the table, watching *A.M. Los Angeles* on television. She had a cup of black coffee by her side, and a cigarette (her new favourite habit) smouldering in an ashtray. She was thinking about Corey. Their lunch had been an uncomfortable experience for both of them, and now that she'd had time to mull things over, she knew she had to call him.

"Good morning, lovely lady," Mark said, bending to kiss her, clad only in a pink bath towel knotted tightly around his waist, a look not suited to his skinny physique. He had spindly arms.

"Hi." She tried a friendly smile. It wasn't going to work — she never *had* been able to hide her feelings.

"What's the matter?" he asked, immediately sensitive to her restless mood.

Fixing him with a look, she said, "It's over, Mark. This time it's *really* over."

He preferred not to deal with her statement. "Why are you smoking?" he asked sternly. "You gave it up years ago."

"How's Fiona?" she asked. "Is *she* upset about the divorce?"

Mark considered her question. He was smart; he never liked to get himself caught in any traps. "She's had an extremely bad case of the flu," he explained seriously. "It dragged on. Almost turned into pneumonia."

"Most unfortunate."

"Yes, very. Naturally, I wasn't able to broach the subject of divorce."

"Naturally."

He gave a deep sigh. "Is that why you're cross with me?"

He was so English and refined. *Cross with me*. How quaint!

"I had no idea Fiona wasn't aware of your divorce plans," she said truthfully.

"Ah, but I'm going to tell her on my next trip home."

"Will that be soon?"

"Very."

"Not on my account, I hope."

He sat down beside her, and as he did so the towel parted, and she couldn't help noticing his aristocratic balls blowing in the wind.

"I *am* going to tell her, Jade, darling. And you and I *are* going to be married."

"There's only one small snag."

"What's that, sweetheart?"

"It's *finito*, Mark. Last night was the proof."

Tapping his fingers on the table, he was unsure of how to handle her. "You didn't have an orgasm, did you?" he asked at last.

Typical! Change the subject. He was so full of shit.

"The sex was great," she lied. "Don't you see? It makes no difference. We're history."

"Never," he insisted adamantly.

"Believe it." She was equally adamant.

"When Fiona and I are divorced you'll feel differently," he said confidently.

"*No*, Mark."

"*Yes*, Jade."

There seemed no point in continuing the argument. She didn't have to. Mark Rand was *definitely* history.

Chapter 55

Wes scooted from the house before anyone was up. He had told Silver the night before that he might go out early, and she had said, "Whatever you do, don't wake me. I need plenty of sleep to recover from *this* débâcle."

He was forced to admit that it had turned out to be *some* party – what with Mannon Cable and Chuck Nielson getting it on like they were the star players in a bar-room brawl. And Poppy Soloman having hysterics. And when the main event was over, Whitney Valentine and Melanie-Shanna Cable had indulged in a most unladylike screaming match. Wes couldn't help noticing that when Whitney Valentine got angry her tits swelled like a couple of melons, and her nipples headed straight for the entire male population's eyeballs.

So this was Hollywood high society. Not quite as boring as he had thought.

Naturally, he had gotten involved. Well, he had to, didn't he? Nobody else was doing anything about the battle of the movie stars, and Mannon Cable was beating the bejesus out of his new friend, Chuck Nielson, who was too stoned to defend himself. There was blood pouring from his nose, and he was reeling all over the place, while Mannon seemed intent on beating him to a pulp.

"For God's sake, somebody *do* something," Whitney had pleaded. That's when Wes moved into action, with the help of a waiter or two. They pulled Mannon off with difficulty as Chuck sprawled groaning on the ground.

By this time Poppy had emerged from the ladies' room to view the demise of her wonderful party, and was yelling furiously at a bemused Howard Soloman. But the real surprise was Melanie-Shanna Cable, who hadn't said a word all night.

She followed Poppy from the ladies' room, walked straight over to Whitney Valentine and shouted, "Leave my husband alone, you sex-crazed bitch! He's not yours anymore. Just remember that, or you'll be sorry!"

Whereupon Whitney had responded with a pithy "Fuck you, cunt! Don't you *dare* speak to me like that."

And they almost came to blows, only Mannon grabbed Melanie-Shanna and practically carried her off without a backward glance.

"Makes *Dynasty* look positively tame," crowed Carmel Gooseberger, loving every minute.

The party — as the saying goes — turned out to be a blast.

Silver was strangely quiet on the drive home, which surprised Wes. Usually she liked discussing every moment of the excitement.

"What's the matter?" he asked.

"I'm exhausted," she responded.

I'm exhausted was her favourite expression — she used it constantly. It hadn't taken him long to learn that she was only exhausted when it suited her.

No longer confined to the Mercedes, he took Silver's Rolls on his morning trip. He had decided to visit his former home, pack up his possessions, and officially move out. By this time it had to be safe. He was Mr Silver Anderson now. He was untouchable.

*

As soon as Wes left the house, Silver awoke. She had hardly slept all night, and felt dreadful. Reaching for the phone, unmindful of the early hour, she contacted Nora.

"Guess what?" she stated dramatically.

"He ran off with all your money," yawned Nora.

"Don't be facetious."

"How was the party?" Nora was miffed she hadn't been invited, but wise in the ways of Beverly Hills hostesses, she knew that *some* hostesses refused to accommodate the star's entourage. And as Silver's P.R., that's what she was regarded as. If Silver had *really* wanted her there she would have been included, but obviously that was not the case. Since Wes Money's entrance into her life, Nora's presence was no longer required at every event.

"I'm sure you'll read all about it," Silver said dryly.

"Does that mean you can't be bothered to tell me?"

"It means, my dear, that *my* party ended up being a fist fight between Mannon and Chuck. And a verbal battle between Whitney and Mannon's present wife – who's *not* the mild-mannered creature she appears to be."

"No kidding?"

"The *real* shock of the evening was my dinner companion."

"Who was it, the Ayatollah?"

Silver laughed ruefully. "Just as bad. Zachary Klinger."

Nora knew when she was needed. "I'll be right over," she said.

*

Parking Silver's Rolls in a side street, Wes reflected that it might have been a mistake driving it into the seedier reaches of Venice. What if it got damaged?

No big deal. Silver would just buy another one. He had to learn to think rich. All his life he'd counted dimes, now he could relax and stop worrying. He was married to a wealthy woman! Hey – shout it out!

He walked briskly along the boardwalk towards his old house. It was a bright Californian day, early, but already hot, and a few serious skate-boarders were in action – girls in tight shorts and minuscule tank tops, and a few guys wearing even less. They were in pursuit of the perfect tan, and what better way to get it?

Wes could think of a better way. Lying out beside Silver's luxurious swimming pool with Vladimir serving him piña coladas, and a portable colour television at his elbow.

It seemed funny, approaching his old house. Actually, it gave him a shudder or two. He had no desire to resume his former lifestyle; the present one suited him just fine.

He groped for his front door key, fitted it in the lock, and was surprised to find it didn't work.

Sonofabitch! Somebody had changed the lock.

Why was he surprised? Reba Winogratsky wanted her rent. She wasn't going to allow him to walk in and cart off his stuff without paying. Good old Reba!

He knocked on Unity's door. Once he picked up the thousand bucks she was holding for him he would have to pay a good chunk of it straight over to Reba. Well, that was the breaks. It wasn't like he needed it desperately.

Nobody answered, so he knocked again.

A drag queen flung the door wide. A six-foot drag queen with crew-cut hair, and the remnants of last night's makeup smeared across his face. He wore a flowered bedspread and dusty pink toe-nail polish on inordinately large feet. "What the hell do you –" The voice changed. He liked what he saw. "Hel-*lo*. Are you visiting or staying?"

"Looking for Unity."

"Sounds *divine*. Is it a new religious cult?"

"What?"

"Do I have to join?"

"Unity. She lives here."

The drag queen batted sturdy false eyelashes that had lasted through the night. "You remind me of my first lover," he said coyly. "*Très* butch."

Wes sighed. Fags loved him. He brought out their animal instincts – or so he'd been told on more than one occasion. Patiently he said, "I'm looking for a girl called Unity. She lives here, or used to. Where is she?"

"Oh. *Her*. I think she did a moonlight disappearing act and stuck the landlady for the rent. This place looked like a *prison* when I moved in. Brown peeling paint and –"

"Do you know where she went?"

The drag queen shrugged. "Search me." A ribald laugh. "Please!"

"Have you got a phone I can use?"

"Ring my bell any time! Only how do I know you're not going to rob and rape me?"

Wes levelled him with a steely stare. "You'll just have to live in hope."

*

Over coffee, Silver and Nora discussed the ramifications of Zachary K. Klinger being in town.

"He makes me sick!" Silver exclaimed. "Sitting next to him was a terrible ordeal – I don't know how I did it."

"Does Wes know about you and Zachary?" Nora asked.

"Certainly not. Nobody knows. Only you."

Nora, the perennial cigarette stuck to her lower lip, nodded. "If I were you I'd leave it that way."

Silver got up and paced the room. She was clad in a pale lilac tracksuit, with her hair pulled back and no makeup. Nora was constantly amazed at how good she looked unadorned. If she wasn't so vain, and cared to tackle a non-glamorous role, she would probably surprise a lot of people.

"The good news is that Zachary knows nothing about Heaven," Silver said, as if to reassure herself.

Nora decided to step onto dangerous territory. "Why is that

such good news? Surely the child asks you who her father is?"

"She never asks. And if she does, I'll tell her it's none of her business," Silver snapped unreasonably.

Nora sniffed her disapproval. They'd had this discussion before, and Silver always firmly maintained that it was her privilege to keep the knowledge of who Heaven's father was to herself.

"I fail to see what you gain by *not* telling her Zachary Klinger is her father. The man's a billionaire with no children. You're denying her the right to inherit an enormous fortune."

"He humiliated me," Silver said stubbornly. "I will *never* give him the satisfaction of knowing that *my* humiliation resulted in *his* becoming a father."

Sometimes Nora wished she had not been made privy to Silver's big secret. She was the only person to know the truth, and it was a burden – for she understood only too well that it was completely unethical *not* to inform Heaven. With a heavy sigh she reached for the coffee pot.

Outside the room, Vladimir strained to hear every word. Ever since the threat of dismissal when Silver discovered him in her bath, he had decided to take out a little insurance. His six-figure policy was a thick notebook filled with gossip about his famous employer. He noted her moods, phone conversations, purchases, clothes, and he had a whole section on her new husband – the ex-bartender. Now he had the most interesting and explosive material of all. Zachary K. Klinger was Heaven's father! This information must be worth a small fortune! And Vladimir knew exactly how to get it.

Chapter 56

Breakfast at the Beverly Hills Hotel at eight o'clock in the morning was not exactly the ideal way for Howard Soloman to start his day. But breakfast it was, at Zachary K. Klinger's command.

Howard awoke late, threw himself in the shower, cut himself shaving, dressed too quickly, and with a fast snort of cocaine to see him on his way hurried from the house.

Fortunately, Poppy still slept. She had kept him up half the night talking, and he couldn't take a repeat performance. Personally he had enjoyed every minute of Mannon beating the shit out of that slime-bucket Chuck Nielson. Poppy had been destroyed. "It *ruined* my party," she moaned all night long.

"It *made* your goddamn party," Howard had assured her. "People'll be talkin' about it for weeks."

The parking valet at The Beverly Hills Hotel took his car, and he rushed inside aware that he was ten minutes late, and if he knew old Zach like he thought he did the old bastard was bound to be a stickler for punctuality.

Zachary sat in the Loggia, the garden part of the Polo Lounge, and acceptable to be seen in only for breakfast and Sunday lunch. The big man's salute to California was no tie. He wore a grey suit and white shirt. Howard had thrown on a white sports jacket over a loose-knit sweater and dark pants – all the better to conceal the lifts in his shoes.

"You're late," Zachary greeted him.

"Traffic," Howard replied airily.

"Isn't your house close by?"

What is this, a fucking inquisition? "How'd you sleep, Zach . . . er . . . Zachary?"

"As well as can be expected."

A waitress appeared with coffee and began to pour him a cup.

"Ah," Howard said, making a face. "Nothin' like the old caffeine to get you off to a racin' start. Right, Zachary?"

"It's bad for your heart."

"It is?"

"My doctor only allows me to drink decaffeinated products."

"Really?" Howard took a sip and burnt his tongue. Maybe the goddamn caffeine was responsible for the wild heart palpitations he had been getting on and off for the past few months. He was certainly due for a complete physical. "Do you get a check-up once a year?" he asked curiously.

"Every three months," Zachary replied.

Howard noticed the older man was drinking a glass of water with a slice of lemon, and on the plate in front of him was a plain bran muffin. "I gotta re-think my eating habits," he announced as the waitress handed him a menu. Without bothering to look he ordered scrambled eggs with smoked salmon, and hash browns on the side.

His eyes hurt. Maybe he needed glasses. Had to go see the optician too. He hoped he remembered to tell all these things to his secretary. She was a lovely girl with a milky complexion and dangerous lips. Once Poppy saw her she would be fired like all the rest. Poppy liked his secretaries to resemble Hulk Hogan on a bad day.

"How long are you staying in L.A.?" he asked, hoping the answer would be five minutes.

Zachary extracted a very long Cuban cigar from a thin leather case, and lovingly caressed it. "It depends on *you*," he said.

Howard made a gesture of compliance. "I'm all yours. Although it would have been better to take this meeting in my office, where I've got all the facts and figures."

"I already have that information."

Howard didn't want to get into *that* one. He knew that Zachary had spies everywhere. What did he care? As long as the studio was making money, everyone should be happy.

"Then you've heard about my plans for *Romance*, with Carlos Brent starring and Orville Gooseberger producing? It's gonna be a big one, Zach, uh, Zachary. It's gonna make us millions."

"I read the script."

Howard was surprised. Even *he* hadn't read the script. He liked to concentrate on story outlines, and this one was sensational, better than the original. "Great, huh?"

"Expensive."

"It takes money to make money."

"I know that."

The waitress delivered Howard's food. As she set it before him, Zachary lit his cigar, and the expensive fumes drifted lazily over Howard's plate. He needed this. Didn't the old fucker have any manners?

"Bad for you," Howard said, indicating the cigar and trying to make a joke of it. "Worse than caffeine. What does your doc say about *that*."

"I listen to my doctor when it suits me to listen to him," Zachary replied reasonably. "I pay him to tell me so much, and when I've heard enough I make my own decisions. I carry that policy through in every one of my business dealings."

Howard sensed a zinger was on its way, and he wasn't wrong. "An example." Zachary paused. "I pay you a great deal of money to run Orpheus for me. But ultimately, *I* make the final decisions. I do what *I* want, when *I* want."

"Sounds good to me." Howard winked, falsely jovial. "As long as we agree."

· Zachary didn't crack a smile. He smoked his cigar, and watched two girls in tennis clothes settle at a nearby table. Howard enjoyed girl-watching, but Zachary stared at them with such intensity that even *he* became embarrassed.

"I want Silver Anderson for the female lead in *Romance*," Zachary said, still staring at the two girls. "I want Mannon Cable for the reporter in *The Murder*, and Whitney Valentine Cable for his sidekick. And I want Clarissa Browning to do a cameo as the victim."

Howard began to laugh. "What is this? Some kind of *joke*?"

"I haven't finished," Zachary said coldly. "You will offer them each exactly double the money they made on their last project. And if they have participation deals, you will double their points." He paused, and dragged his eyes away from the two girls, who had noticed his relentless stare, and were fidgeting uncomfortably. "No negotiations. These offers are to be made to their agents immediately – in writing."

Howard felt the muscles in the back of his neck turn to steel, and a dull flush of anger suffuse his face. "You're not serious?" he asked tightly.

"Yes. Very serious," Zachary replied, perfectly sanely. "Why? Don't you feel that having Mannon Cable, Silver Anderson, Clarissa Browning and Whitney Valentine Cable is good for Orpheus?"

"Well, sure," Howard replied, trying to figure out how to handle this maniac who knew fuck all about the movie business. Humour him, that was the way to go. "Only I don't think Clarissa Browning would ever consider doing a cameo."

"You think not? I disagree. A week's work at double the price of her last film. She won her Oscar four years ago, and hasn't been in a moneymaker since. She'll do it."

"Mannon won't," Howard argued sourly.

"Yes he will. The money will lure him. *And* the opportunity to work with Miss Browning."

Howard decided there was no point in mentioning Whitney – she would do whatever came along – but Howard wasn't sitting still for Silver Anderson. "About Silver. She's too old," he stated brutally.

"And how old is Carlos Brent?" Zachary replied, with a great deal of logic.

"I dunno – fifty-five, six."

"He's sixty-three. Silver Anderson is in her forties. They'll suit each other admirably."

"She's a daytime television star," Howard objected vehemently.

"She's a *star*. That's all that matters. And *I* want her." Zachary blew cigar smoke in Howard's face, and rose from the table. "I'll expect you back here at four o'clock, in my bungalow, with the letters of intent to go to each artist's agent. I wish to look them over before they're delivered." He stared at the two girls in tennis garb once more, then back at Howard, who sat helplessly surrounded by cigar smoke and congealing eggs. "Excellent party last night," he said casually. "Have someone at the studio send your wife flowers from me."

With that he walked off, leaving Howard a seething, infuriated wreck.

Chapter 57

Once Wes revealed that he was the tenant from next door and needed to contact their landlady so he could get into his house and pack up his belongings, the drag queen – whose name was Travis – realized exactly who he was and fawned accordingly. "You're married to Silver Anderson," he said reverently, allowing his flowered bedspread to slip off one shoulder.

"Yup," agreed Wes, reaching for the telephone and calling Reba.

"Wesley?" Her voice was a mixture of surprise and disbelief. "Stay where you are. I'll be there in twenty minutes."

Travis made him a cup of overly strong black coffee served in a mug with MAKE MY DAY OH PLEASE MR EASTWOOD! emblazoned on the side. Then he stared at him with an awestruck expression and asked breathlessly, "What's Silver Anderson *really* like?"

Wes parried questions until Reba's arrival. She was accompanied by a male, baby-faced streak of lightning, wearing blue jeans with a worn patch at the crotch, and a string vest. He looked like an eighteen-year-old hooker plucked straight from the cruising end of Santa Monica Boulevard. Travis fell instantly in lust.

"Oh, Wesley, Wesley, Wesley," Reba greeted him, with her usual hungry expression. "You moved right up, didn't you? Surprised us all, I can tell you."

"I surprised myself too," he admitted truthfully.

"You promised me a picture," she reminded him reproachfully.

"Oooh . . . *I* want a picture," interrupted Travis. "Signed if you please. To Travis. With love and admiration, Silver Anderson."

"Can I get a picture, too?" the street hustler mumbled.

"Shut up," said Reba sharply. "I'm payin' you to be my bodyguard, not to horn in on my conversations."

Wes raised a quizzical eyebrow. "Bodyguard?"

"You think you're the only one who's important?" she sniffed. "I'm havin' problems with my divorce. I need protection."

Her protection and Travis were falling in love, exchanging long looks of serious intent to commit a sexual act.

"Why did you change my locks?" Wes asked.

"You'll see," she replied mysteriously. "C'mon."

He bade Travis goodbye.

"Don't forget my picture," Travis reminded him with a pout. "And remember — any time you want to bring Silver over, she's *always* welcome" — a flirtatious tilt of the chin — "and so are you . . ."

Wes concealed a grin at the thought of Silver anywhere near this neighbourhood.

He followed Reba next door. She produced a bunch of keys and gained entry, then stood back and allowed him to walk in first. Understandable. The place was a wreck, and she wanted him to get the full impact. Someone had gone over his house with a thorough and not too gentle hand.

"What were they lookin' for, Wesley?" she asked, picking up a small lamp that seemed to have survived the search and placing it back on a table.

"How would *I* know?" he replied irritably. "I only live here."

"Lived," she corrected, producing a large notebook from her purse. "I suppose you've already moved to Beverly Hills or Bel Air, or wherever Silver Anderson resides."

"You got it."

"Nice of you to contact me before," she said reproachfully.

"I'm here, aren't I?"

She began ticking off items in her notebook. "You owe me three months' rent. Breakage on several items —"

"*I* didn't break anything," he objected.

"Whoever came in did."

"Am I supposed to be responsible for burglars?"

She pursed her lips. "Yes."

"You can whistle for it, Reba."

"Don't act like a cheapskate. You're responsible for everything that happens in this house while you're the tenant. It's the law, you know."

He kicked at a bunch of clothes strewn on the floor, then bent to pick up scattered photographs from his short career as a singer. The room stank of stale cigarettes and dirty clothes, a far cry from Silver's Bel Air palace. He wanted to get out as fast as possible, and with that thought in mind he grabbed an old duffel bag and began stuffing in anything salvageable.

Reba leaned against the wall watching him. She had left her "protection" outside. "You were never the perfect tenant," she said, with a sly smile, "but you an' I — we always understood each other, didn't we, Wesley?"

"I guess," he agreed.

"An' we had good sex, didn't we?"

He knew better than to argue with *that* one. "The best," he replied warily.

She licked her lips, coated with jammy scarlet lipstick. "Is that what Silver sees in you?" she asked. "Is it the sex?"

He shrugged non-committally, and speeded up his packing.

Reba cleared her throat and suggestively fingered the top button of her blouse. "I wouldn't say no to one last fling, Wesley," she announced. "Would you?"

"C'mon," he chided. "I'm a married man."

Ignoring that piece of information she began to unbutton. "You an' I, we were always special together."

Yeah, he thought, *about as special as a corn-beef sandwich.*

She nearly had her blouse off, revealing a pink Frederick's of Hollywood push-up bra. He held up a warning hand. "Enough, Reba."

"Don't enough *me*, Wesley. You know you're horny. And I'm better than your fancy movie star any day."

It occurred to him that he didn't have to be nice to her anymore. He did not need Reba Winogratsky. She was his past. Just as the run-down house was, and hustling petty scams to make a buck, and working bar. He was a free man!

With a feeling of triumph he reached into his pocket and took out a stack of bills — he had visited his safe-deposit box the day before and taken out enough cash to pay her just in case Unity wasn't around with his thousand bucks. Good thinking. "How much do I owe you?" he asked, businesslike and brisk.

She paused before unclipping her Frederick's special. "I'll tell you when we've finished."

Shaking his head he said, "No you won't, darlin'. Because we ain't even gonna start. I owe you money, that's all. The rest is not for sale."

*

Mannon regarded Melanie-Shanna warily as she entered the breakfast room. She looked calm enough in a flowing house-dress, her auburn hair tied sedately back.

She sat down opposite him at the table, and reached for a piece of toast.

"'Morning," he said.

She mumbled a reply.

Mannon regarded her quizzically. He'd had no idea he'd married such a wild-woman. Last night she'd surprised the hell out of him, and everyone else in the vicinity of her whip-lash tongue. He'd had to practically drag her out of the Bistro before she went for Whitney's throat. The two of them were all set for a cat-fight.

Driving home, she'd let him have it, mouthing off about Whitney full-throttle. The force of her fury really turned him on, and once they reached the privacy of their bedroom he had silenced her with the best lovemaking of their marriage. It had been several weeks since he'd touched her, and now he wondered why. Whitney was making it with Chuck. Why shouldn't he enjoy himself with his wife? Even if he *was* planning on divorcing her.

"How do you feel?" he asked.

"Fine," she replied, eyes downcast.

The housekeeper waddled in with a plate of home-made pancakes — Mannon's favourites. He looked over at Melanie-Shanna. "Did you tell her to make these?"

"No."

It seemed quite obvious she was not in a talkative mood. Last night she had accused him of still being in love with Whitney. True. But he wasn't about to admit it. He'd denied it vehemently.

Mannon was between movies. He had just finished shooting a tough, lean Western. And his next film was not due to start for several months. For the first few weeks he always enjoyed the rest, and then he got stir-crazy if the break lasted too long.

He could work non-stop if he wanted to. His ego did not require that kind of boost. It was important to be prudent, and he chose his future projects with a great deal of care. He was right at the peak of his career, and that's exactly where he planned to stay.

This morning he felt pretty damn good. The thud of his fist connecting with Chuck Nielson's dumb-ox features had delighted him. What a victory to knock the asshole on his butt in front of a roomful of the industry. Especially in front of Whitney.

Chuck Nielson was an unprincipled prick. He deserved it. You didn't screw another man's wife and get away with it — especially when that other man was your ex-best friend.

"What are you going to do today?" he asked.

Melanie-Shanna refused to look at him. She stared out of the French doors at a vast expanse of lawn, leading to a kidney-shaped swimming pool. "I don't know," she said.

"Well." He rose. "I'm playing tennis, so I'll see you later."

She waited until he had left the room before untensing her muscles. It took a great deal of effort even to be civil to him. He had allowed her to make a fool of herself in front of everyone last night, and every time she thought of her behaviour she cringed,

Mannon Cable. Big movie star. Big lover. So what? When he made love to her last night she *knew* for sure he was thinking of Whitney. And she hated him for it. *Really* hated him.

*

The telephone began ringing in the Soloman household from eight-thirty on. First Roselight's nanny took care of the calls, and then Poppy's own personal secretary, who arrived at nine-thirty.

Poppy did not emerge from her bedroom until noon. She kissed her little daughter, who was playing with a Cabbage Patch doll, one of twelve Roselight had received the previous Christmas from Howard's business associates, and proceeded into her pastel office, where her secretary sat watching *As the World Turns* on a portable Sony television.

"Don't I give you enough to do?" Poppy asked tartly.

"So sorry, Mrs Soloman," said the woman, turning the television off with a guilty start and replacing it on Poppy's side of the huge ornate double desk.

Poppy liked to be referred to as Mrs Soloman – English style. Not for her the free and easy first-name camaraderie of American workers. She and Howard had spent their honeymoon in London at the Savoy Hotel, and she had never got over the dignity and respect of it all. She was Mrs Soloman'd all over town, and loved evey minute of it.

"Messages?" she said irritably, not in a good mood at all.

"Mrs White called at eight-thirty. Mrs Gooseberger at nine. Army Archerd at ten – he'd like you to return his call."

Poppy listened, trying to decide who to call back first. There were seven more messages, including columnist Liz Smith in New York. Who to talk to? Liz or Army? Better see what Carmel had to say. Poppy dreaded the older woman's pronouncement of "Disaster of the Year".

Carmel Gooseberger did not say "Disaster of the Year" at all. Carmel Gooseberger said, "Poppy! Darling! One of the best parties I've ever been to. I adored every minute. Did you *hear* Mannon's wife? My God, I never realized she could *speak*, let alone come out with words even Orville never uses! And did you *see* Silver and Zachary Klinger? I don't know if I was the only one to notice but –"

An hour later Poppy got off the phone. From the big mouth of Carmel Gooseberger to the hills of Beverly, Bel Air and anyplace else where you couldn't buy a house for less than a million bucks – her party was a hit! A smash! A rip-roaring success!

She phoned Howard to give him the good news, but he was in a meeting. Shame. Last night she had really steamed into him, claiming everything was his fault. Poor Howard. Sometimes she knew she was too rough on him, only a little aggravation did him good, kept him alert. And he needed to be alert with that snake Zachary Klinger in town.

She wondered if Howard might feel like buying her a cabochon ruby and gold necklace she'd had her eye on in that divine new jewellery store Tallarico.

Ten minutes later she decided he would. After all, a hit party created *great* public relations, and she deserved a prize.

Without further ado she slipped into a simple Karl Lagerfeld suit, and Christian Dior sunglasses.

On her way out of the house she noted twelve flower arrangements lined up in a row, awaiting her inspection before being placed in the perfect spot. She plucked the small white envelope from the most extravagant basket, ripped it open and read it quickly.

> You give great party. Can you join
> us for dinner Saturday?
> Silver and Wes

Poppy felt a small glow of pleasure. *Yes, thank you, Silver. Howard and I will be delighted to join you.*

Smiling with satisfaction, she hurried out to her car.

Chapter 58

Howard hit the office like a mini-tornado after the meeting with Zachary. He shut himself in his private bathroom, telling his secretary, "No calls. I don't care if it's the friggin' President!"

She knew when to leave him alone, and went back to reading a riveting article on herpes.

Howard took off his jacket and rinsed his face with cold water. His heart was racing, and so was his mind.

JUST WHO THE FUCK DID ZACHARY KLINGER THINK HE WAS DEALING WITH?

Howard Soloman.

He was Howard Soloman.

He was nobody's office boy, and he refused to be treated like one.

What was this "I want" shit, "pay 'em double" crap? Was Zachary Klinger serious?

Yeah, unfortunately the dumb bastard was. And Howard Soloman was supposed to follow through.

Well, screw that. Howard Soloman did not jump rope for anybody.

He sat on the closed toilet seat, head in hands, and tried to think clearly.

Zachary Klinger paid him a vast amount of money to run Orpheus, and in the year he had been in power he had done exceptionally well. When Zachary brought him in, the studio was in deep shit. The asshole before him had been running up astronomical overheads with no product. Howard had stepped in, and within months made it an efficient operating company. He had pared overheads to the minimum, cut off the blood-suckers and go-fers on the payroll, and bought money-making outside product for distribution. Not to mention getting three pictures into production, and at least two dozen development deals.

So he didn't have major superstars or world-renowned actors working for the studio. Big frigging deal. He had pictures that were going to make money. And wasn't that the whole idea?

Now Zachary Klinger flies in and wants to play Father Christmas. *Pay 'em double. Give 'em points.*

Howard had to turn this to his advantage or get out. There was no choice, otherwise he could end up looking like paid schmuck of the year.

*

Chuck Nielson had a black eye and a split lip. "I'll sue that sonofabitch!" he yelled when he awoke in Whitney's bed.

"Up and out," she said, matter-of-factly. "Today I've got two interviews, and a meeting with my new publicity people. I don't think you should be here."

"What new people?" he demanded disagreeably. "And why *shouldn't* I be here?"

She hated it when he questioned her. After all, they weren't married, and she saw no reason why she had to answer all his never-ending queries. The trouble with Chuck was that his once very successful career had ground to an inexplicable and sudden halt, and it was driving him crazy. It was also driving her crazy. She was definitely considering Zeppo White's advice. "Get rid of him, kiddo. He's an albatross around your neck. Dump the putz."

It had to be done. And the sooner she did it, the better she would feel. But it wasn't going to be easy. Chuck was like a big, excitable puppy one minute, and a jealous, aggressive nut the next.

He was jealous of her career – which was about to take off again nicely, thanks to Zeppo.

He was jealous of Mannon.

In fact, he was insanely jealous of everyone and everything around her.

Fortunately, they did not live together as such. She spent time at his home on the beach. He stayed the occasional night at her house on Loma Vista. She wasn't locked into anything. Thank God!

"You shouldn't be here," she said patiently, "because it will be boring for you."

"Yeah, you're right," he admitted. "Who's the new P.R.? And why? I thought you were happy with the one you've got."

"I am. Zeppo wants me to have a new image, so I'm going to Briskinn & Bower."

"What new image?"

"More serious."

He hooted with laughter. "Serious? *You*?" he sneered derisively.

Her mouth drooped with displeasure. Chuck had no confidence in her ability as an actress. He hadn't actually said so, but she knew it, and it irked her.

Zeppo was right. The time had come to disassociate herself from Chuck Nielson.

★

The cocaine blazed a trail. A trail of clear, clean thoughts. A lucid path through the machinations of Zachary K. Klinger.

Howard released himself from his bathroom a new man. He was moving into turnaround. Taking a crazy situation and making it work for him.

He buzzed his secretary.

She entered his office looking like a ripe kumquat, all quivering lips and an ample bosom encased in angora. "Yes, Mr. Soloman?"

How come Poppy had let this one through the net? And then he remembered that his regular girl was on vacation – this morsel was only a temporary replacement.

"Get me a list of the agents for Silver Anderson, Mannon Cable, and Clarissa Browning." No need to ask about Whitney: she was represented by Zeppo White – a legend in his own eyes.

"Yes, Mr Soloman."

"Are you an actress?" he couldn't help asking.

She nodded.

Well, act on this, he wanted to say. He had a hard-on. Must be the challenge of outwitting Zachary.

Taking a packet of toothpicks from his desk drawer, he broke one in half and vigorously attacked his gums. Add dentist to his medical requirement list. He was sure he had a loose crown and a cavity. Who had the time to go?

The secretary got him the list within minutes. He studied it carefully.

Clarissa Browning was with Artists, a large corporate outfit. Her representative was Cyrill Mace, a shrewd, no-nonsense type of man.

Mannon Cable paid his ten percent to Sadie La Salle. Ah, Sadie . . . the queen of the lady agents. She was always a pleasure to deal with.

Silver Anderson employed Quinne Lattimore. Small potatoes.

It was just past ten o'clock. He summoned his secretary again. "Get me Sadie La Salle," he commanded. "And after that I want to speak to Cyrill Mace, Zeppo White and Quinne Lattimore, in that order. I'm not accepting any incoming calls – including my wife – in fact, any of my wives."

The secretary nodded. "Yes, Mr Soloman," she said obediently.

*

"I think" – Whitney's striking face was very serious – "that the public perceives me as altogether too frivolous."

"Why do you say that?" asked Bernie Briskinn, the senior partner at Briskinn & Bower. He was old Hollywood, with a moon face, thick lips, and a black patch covering one eye. Rumour had it he had lost his eye in a skirmish with Humphrey Bogart over a woman.

Whitney gestured impatiently. "I've shown too much, too many times."

"Ever done *Playboy*?" Bernie asked anxiously. He was nearing seventy, but still interested.

Norman Gooseberger cut in. "I think Whitney means that she's travelled the scanty-outfit-decorative-role path as opposed to . . . uh . . . nude shots."

Whitney's face lit up as she smiled at the dark-haired young man who was so obviously on the ball. "Exactly," she said. "I wouldn't dream of posing nude. I never have."

Bernie Briskinn looked disappointed.

"I understand the problems you have to overcome." Norman said, taking over the interview. "And I'm sure Briskinn & Bower can satisfy you in every way."

"Yes?" breathed Whitney.

"Certainly," replied Norman, with confidence.

"Oh, that's wonderful!" she sighed.

Bernie Briskinn sucked on his false teeth. He was merely a figurehead, but never failed to attend first meetings with beautiful actresses.

"How do we begin?" Whitney asked eagerly.

Norman was quick to reply. "First of all we drop the Cable from your name. It always reminds people of your former husband, and there's no need for that now. And then we cut the hair."

"What?" Her voice filled with panic.

"The hair is going to keep you exactly where you are today. So it's goodbye Cable and goodbye hair."

"How about breast reduction surgery?" she asked sarcastically.

"Not necessary," Norman replied with a cheerful grin.

Bernie chimed in. "Thank God for that!" he said.

Norman was hitting his stride. "You have your own identity," he said enthusiastically. "And before we're through with you that identity will be as a strong and beautiful *actress*. Right now, with all due respect, you are viewed as a lightweight. When Briskinn & Bower have finished with you – well . . . dare I say it? Producers will think of you at the same time they think of Jessica and Clarissa and Sally."

Whitney glowed. "Really?"

"Don't forget, Jessica Lange started out sitting in King Kong's paw, and Sally Field was Gidget. If it can be done for them . . ." Norman trailed off as if he were personally responsible.

Whitney was visibly excited. Bernie Briskinn nodded approvingly. Orville's boy was a winner. He had the gift of conviction, and in the P.R. business conviction was better than gold. Bernie was glad he'd hired him at Orville's insistence five years ago. Relatives usually turned out to be duds. This one was a winner. "We'll talk price with Zeppo," he said. "Norman will handle your account himself. He's one of our best. And I'm always available. Any time you want me. Any time at all . . ." He sucked on his false teeth again and buried a fart in her white couch. "Welcome to Briskinn & Bower, Whitney, dear. You won't be disappointed."

*

In the space of two hours Howard was whistling. Not quite *Dixie*, but he had done a certain amount of creative manoeuvring, and saved his ass from mooning Hollywood.

Sadie and Zeppo were easy to deal with. They understood power, money, and deals. They understood "jerk me off a little and I'll do the same for you". Offering them a deal on the one hand, and a kickback to him under the table on the other, made sense to both of them. Sadie seemed to think she could convince Mannon as long as the script of *The Murder* was halfway decent. Zeppo said of Whitney, "She'll lick your balls, Howard."

He should be so lucky.

"As part of the deal I want to be there when you tell her," he insisted.

"We'll do it together," Zeppo promised – and called him back with the news that they could do it at six o'clock, when Whitney was free.

With Cyrill Mace he played it straight. No creative moves with Cyrill. Just an out-and-out straight-up offer.

"Send over the script, and the offer in writing," Cyrill said. "Are you feeling all right, Howard?"

"Generous and well," Howard replied. "I need an answer within twenty-four hours, otherwise the offer is withdrawn."

"A week."

"No way."

"Clarissa's in New York. It'll take a day to get the script to her. Then she's got to read it."

"For this kind of money she doesn't have to read. She's ten minutes on the screen, for crissake. I'll give you forty-eight hours."

"Three days."

"You got it."

Howard phoned Jack for extra insurance, telling him the deal, and urging him to talk Clarissa into it. When Jack informed him he was on his way to New York, Howard knew the timing was perfect, and messengered a copy of the script over for him to deliver personally.

Which left Quinne Lattimore – an honest, middle-of-the-road agent, with about as much fire as a stagnant pond. Howard trod carefully with Quinne. It was the honest sons-of-bitches who tripped you up every time. City Television, he had found out, were paying Silver Anderson far less than she deserved. Quinne had negotiated a contract that, quite frankly, stank. Howard decided to double the amount she received for six weeks' work on *Palm Springs*, and try to get her on her hiatus. It was still play money, although it caused Quinne to almost choke with excitement.

By the time the offers were all written up, Howard felt confident about the structure of the deals. He had what was on paper, and he had his special arrangements with Sadie and Zeppo. They would both throw back half of their commission on the money above the established price their clients would receive. It suited everyone. Mannon and Whitney would have raised their going price by double the amount. Sadie and Zeppo could look forward to larger commissions in the future. And Howard got the stars *and* an added bonus. The kickback money was destined straight for his numbered Swiss bank account.

It wasn't stealing from Orpheus. It was creative operating – Hollywood style.

Chapter 59

The moment Jack left the beach house, Heaven sprang into action. She had already invited Eddie, who was on his way. It seemed the perfect time to call the guy from Silver's party, the one with all the contacts in the record business. She had tried him several times before with no luck. He had a stupid answering machine with some dumb voice on it. She refused to talk to answering machines.

"Yeah?"

At last! He actually picked up the phone himself.

"Rocky?" she asked tentatively.

"Who wants him?"

"Uh . . . is he there?"

"Do you have a name?"

"Heaven. But . . . uh . . . he probably won't remember my name. Tell him we met at Silver Anderson's party a few months ago. He asked me to call him. It's . . . uh . . . it's like business."

A long pause. Then, "Hey, *I* remember you. The baby fox in the long coat. Y'wanna be a singer. Right, chicken?"

"Am I speaking to Rocky?"

"The one an' only."

"Why didn't you say so?"

"Back off, baby. I don' havta say nothin' to no one. What's the deal?"

"You told me you had connections," she said stiffly.

"Are y'on a buyin' spree?"

"You said," she repeated slowly, "that you might be able to help me with my career. You know, your friend in the record business . . . you wanted him to hear my tapes."

The dime slid into the slot. Rocky remembered. She was a pretty one. And young – just the way he liked 'em.

"How come it took ya so long t'call me?" he asked.

"I've been busy. School . . . y'know."

"Yeah. I get the action."

A silence.

"Can you help?" she asked impatiently. "I've got my tapes, and Antonio has taken some brilliant pictures of me. You said you're the kind of guy can make things happen. Can you, or not?"

"Don' challenge the great Rocky, baby fox. He can do anythin'."

"Then let's get going. I'm ready."

*

"Mr Python. How nice to see you again."

Jack checked out the stewardess. Nice legs. Nice ass. Nice smile. He was feeling uncomfortably horny. Clarissa had been away too long, and apart from the night he nearly connected with Jade Johnson in Las Vegas, there had been no one. Jack Python had been boringly faithful. Talk about changing one's way of life!

He felt good about the fact that he *could* do it. It certainly proved he had willpower.

"Can I get you anything?" asked the stewardess.

He remembered flying with her several months before. She had inviting eyes.

"I'd like a Jack Daniels."

She smiled. "I'd like a Jack Python."

"Huh?"

"Just joking, Mr Python."

But she wasn't, and they both knew it.

There was a rainstorm pummelling New York when they landed. A representative from the travel agency met him at the airport, spiriting him to a black limousine waiting curbside.

He had not told Clarissa he was coming. All his life the element of surprise had worked in his favour. He wanted her unprepared reaction to his sudden visit.

*

Eddie was fully impressed. He tried not to look it, but he was. And how!

Heaven couldn't help grinning to herself. Let him eat his heart out. Eddie was no longer number one on her hit parade.

He did look good though, with his black leather jacket, tight jeans and slicked-back hair. Real fifties. He carried an overnight bag and his guitar. "I hadda leave your number with my mom," he announced reluctantly. "I told her there's a whole group of us stayin' over. She'd freak out if she thought it was just you an' me. Y'know what moms are like."

"As a matter of fact, I don't," Heaven said pointedly. "And aren't you a little *old* for your mom to be keeping such a close watch on you?"

"I guess I gotta put up with it until college," he complained.

All her friends took it for granted they were going to college. She had no intention of doing so. Why waste another three years of her life being ordered around by dumb teachers?

She was thrilled she'd finally made contact with Rocky. At least it was a start. He might be all talk, and then again he really *might* have connections in the record industry. It was worth a shot.

She had asked him over. He'd said he would try and make it. She couldn't wait!

Eddie stripped down to shorts and a tank top. He was tall and lanky, with an athlete's body. Most of the girls at school thought he was the babe of all time. Heaven couldn't care less.

They sat out on the circular deck with a portable tape machine and a couple of beers. Eddie nursed his precious guitar, and Heaven held a sheaf of papers to her bare stomach. She wore a bikini and a Bruce Springsteen bandanna. The papers were scribbled all over with the lyrics of her latest songs.

Eddie strummed a few chords, and she began to hum.

"Uh . . I've got a couple of slow songs I wanna try," she said, after a few moments.

He groaned. Eddie only liked rock and roll. He didn't understand anything else.

"Just ease me along with a little background," she pleaded. "And then I've got some other stuff you'll love."

She started to sing, a low sound at first, as she wasn't used to hearing herself without a rip-roaring background, and it seemed strange.

> Baby
> I never told you how I felt before –
> Because
> Baby –
> You always make me wait for you –
> Because
> Baby
> Don't you know I love you
> Don't you know I want you
> Don't you know I need you
> Because
> Baby –

Her voice strengthened and began to soar. She sounded like a cross between Carly Simon and a less sophisticated Annie Lennox from the Eurythmics. She combined innocence and knowingness, and her voice had a wonderful husky quality.

She did not sound anything at all like Silver Anderson, although it was obvious she had inherited her mother's talent.

Even Eddie was forced to admit reluctantly that she was good. "I hate the song, but you're singin' fine," he said, bursting into a lively rendition of *Blue Suede Shoes* on his guitar.

She didn't mind that Eddie couldn't appreciate her slow songs. *She* knew they were right.

"One more time," she said forcefully. "I want to tape it, and I want it to be perfect."

*

There was a young actor in the off-Broadway production Clarissa was appearing in who played her lover. Naturally, she had felt an immediate urge to put him at his ease – even though he was living with one of her best friends. "What Carole doesn't know, will not hurt her. And we need this closeness for our performances," Clarissa explained logically.

He struggled weakly, gave in, and found it was so good for his performance that doing it every night seemed only fair to the audience. Clarissa agreed.

When Jack arrived at the theatre he was informed that Ms. Browning could not be disturbed before the show. It was a strict rule.

"I think I'm an exception," he said confidently.

When he entered her small dressing room with a pass key and the script of *The Murder*, he found Clarissa bent double over her dressing table, and a skinny bare-assed actor servicing her doggy-style.

His eyes met hers in the dressing table mirror. Her deeply intense gaze was completely devoid of any emotion.

Without a word he threw down the script and left.

Chapter 60

"Quinne's dropping by." Silver stretched and smiled as she lay out by the pool. "He says he has something important to tell me."

"Quinne's your –"

"Agent." She finished the sentence for him.

"Is he good?" Wes asked, reaching for an open can of Coca-Cola.

"I wouldn't be with him if he wasn't, would I?"

Shrugging easily he replied, "I know fuck-all about the film business, but isn't Zeppo White supposed to be the best agent around?"

"Ah . . . Zeppo." Silver popped a white grape in her mouth and savoured the taste. "When I was planning my comeback in America, Zeppo White would not even answer my phone calls."

"I bet he's sorry now."

"*Naturellement*. All the big agents are sorry. Quinne was there for me and I'll never forget it. He was the only one who knew I could do it."

"Does he renegotiate your contract every season?"

Giving him a penetrating look, she plucked another grape from the glass dish. "For someone who knows nothing about the biz, you've certainly picked up a phrase or two . . ."

"I was talking to Chuck Nielson. He was thinking of signing with Quinne."

"And did he?"

Wes shook his head. "He said going with Quinne Lattimore is like admitting defeat."

"Hmmm . . . for someone like Chuck it probably is. Once you fall from Sadie La Salle's favour . . ."

"Who's she?"

"The hottest *female* agent in town. I was with her once, long ago and far away. And before you ask, she *also* didn't answer my calls when I was desperate."

"Desperation breeds contempt."

"You're telling me! *I* lived through it." She sat up and reached for a huge straw hat. Her eyes were already covered by black wraparound sunglasses. She did not believe in allowing too much sun to reach her face. It dried the skin, causing premature lines and wrinkles.

Her body, in a strapless pink swimsuit, cut high on the thighs, was beginning to tan nicely.

"A weekend in the Springs might be nice," she murmured. "Now that I'm a free woman we must take advantage of it. Once I go back to work, the schedule is pure murder."

"You work very hard, then."

"Like a dog!" she exclaimed, obviously loving every minute of the pressure.

"Why?"

She stretched a smooth leg out in front of her. "To make the bucks, darling. To keep us in the style you are soon going to become *very*, *very* accustomed to."

Laughing, he caught hold of her slim ankle. "I'm used to it already."

She twisted towards him. "I know. Luxury *is* irresistible, isn't it?"

He allowed his fingers to tip-toe up her leg, pausing on her inner thigh, where he began slow stroking.

"I like it," she said, her voice husky.

His fingers crept between the flesh of her leg and the elastic of her swimsuit.

She sighed with pleasure.

Just as he was about to go for the gold, Vladimir appeared.

Vladimir had developed a habit of ignoring him whenever possible. The Russian houseman had decided he knew exactly who Wes Money was. A con man, a hustler, and a paid stud – in that order.

"The phone, madame," Vladimir said, handing her the instrument. "It's Miss Carvell."

She reached for the receiver. "Nora. What are you up to?"

"Fending off investigative reporters," Nora replied grumpily. "Everyone wants to know more about Wes. If we don't give 'em something, they'll *really* start digging."

"Let them," Silver said defiantly. She turned to Wes. "Do you have anything horrible to hide, darling?"

He indicated the telling bulge in his brief swimsuit. "Only this."

She laughed delicately.

Vladimir, standing in the background, glared.

Wes gave him a look. "We don't need anything," he said. "You can go."

"I'm vaiting for the telephone," Vladimir replied stiffly. "I only bother Madame vith calls she vishes to receive."

Wes glanced at Silver, who was busy chatting to Nora. "Piss off, Vlad," he said in a low voice. "When we want you I'll give you a shout. Until you hear me calling – stay in the kitchen, or wherever you hang out, and don't bother us. Have you got that?"

Vladimir blushed a deep scarlet. "I obey Madame's vishes –" he began.

"You obey *mine*, or you're out on your ass," Wes interrupted sharply.

Vladimir backed off, vanishing into the house without another word.

Wes concentrated on Silver. "Hang up," he said.

"I'm speaking to Nora –"

He started to stroke her thigh again. "I *said* hang up."

She giggled girlishly. "Nora, I have to go now, a minor emergency. I'll call you back."

His fingers began serious exploratory work.

She lay back in the hot sunlight and spread her legs, murmuring, "Easy access."

"C'mon." He pulled her to her feet. "Show me how to switch the jacuzzi on."

"I don't want to get my hair wet," she objected.

"I don't think I care."

"Wes! You're incorrigible!"

Is that what they call it? he thought with a grin.

She threw two levers, and the jacuzzi bubbled to life.

He took her by the hand and led her down the steps into the steaming water. She still had on her hat and sunglasses, but he didn't care. He was suddenly as randy as a dog after a bitch in heat. Making it in a jacuzzi was a fantasy he had not yet realized.

She sat on the marble seat and began to complain. "This is *not* a good idea. My hair . . . my skin . . . this water is too harsh . . . I . . ."

He silenced her with a kiss, and at the same time he took off her hat and threw it away, while his other hand pulled the top of her swimsuit down and played with a nipple.

She stopped objecting and leaned back.

With both hands he peeled her swimsuit all the way down and off, crushed her breasts together, and tongued both nipples lightly.

"Mmm . . ." she sighed.

Slipping out of his shorts, he manoeuvred her legs until they were wrapped firmly around his waist. And then, without hesitation, he plunged straight in, fighting the water every inch of the way.

"I love it," she gasped. "More, more, give me more!"

The strong jets of water were everywhere. Very slowly he withdrew, and holding her legs apart he positioned her in front of one of the jets.

"*Oh . . . my . . . God!*" she shouted. "Ohhhh . . . *goddamm*it!"

Instant orgasm. Which excited the hell out of him, and he immediately went back for more, catching her in the throes, making her come again and again, and finally letting go himself with a triumphant yell. At which point they both sank under the bubbling water.

Silver was some sport, which really surprised him. She surfaced choking and coughing, her hair plastered to her head, her wraparound sunglasses askew. "You sonofabitch!" she exclaimed, spluttering with laughter. "It just gets better all the time."

He had to agree. And he wanted to pinch himself to see if he woke up. He'd gotten luckier than he'd ever dreamed possible.

"Towel," she commanded.

Quickly he hopped out of the jacuzzi and grabbed a large striped beach towel which he held open for her to step into.

"Thank you," she said formally. "You're very kind."

"And you're some hot broad."

"So eloquent!"

"So full of it!"

Jumping back into the jacuzzi he groped for their swimsuits.

Vladimir, lurking behind a curtain in the living room, watched everything, and as he saw them approaching the house he scurried off to the kitchen and made copious notes. When he was ready to sell his story, he was going to make an absolute fortune!

Chapter 61

Vaguely it occurred to Howard Soloman that snorting cocaine was becoming more than just a habit. He did not feel comfortable unless he knew the soothing white powder was within easy reach.

I can afford it, he thought. *It's certainly no worse than alcohol and much less anti-social.*

The only problem was he couldn't get through the day without it. No problem really — because he didn't have to.

Over the months he had developed several new sources of supply, so he did not need to depend on anyone in particular

It was an expensive habit, but God – it was worth every hard-earned dollar.

The day passed smoothly, thanks to his quick thinking and clever way of dealing with Zachary's cockamamie orders. By four-thirty he had all the offers in writing, and a runner standing by to deliver them to the forewarned agents.

He drove over to Zachary's bungalow at The Beverly Hills Hotel, and sat there cockily while the old man scanned them one by one.

I'm the highest-paid messenger boy in history, he reflected, with a private smile.

Zachary paused when he came to the offer for Silver. "Why so little?" he asked.

"It's double the amount she received for six weeks on her soap. That's more than fair, isn't it?"

"It's pennies compared to the others."

"We're talking big bucks with the others. Quinne'll kiss our ass from here to Australia. And so will Silver, if she's smart. They're not exactly rushing her to do movies, y'know. Sure, she's big on television, but that means cow dung. Look at Tom Selleck. The guy was hotter than she is today. Three movies later and nothin' happened. When they can get it for free, they don't want to pay for it."

"We'll see," said Zachary.

"I hope you're right," Howard remarked cheerfully. His throat was parched. Sitting here for twenty minutes and no offer of refreshments. The old guy was either tight or rude. Probably a combination of both. "Do you mind if I order a drink?"

Placing the written offers in a neat pile, Zachary stood up. "I'm going out," he said brusquely. "Feel free to use the Polo Lounge if you want a drink."

"Good idea. I'll do that." *Take your job and shove it all the way up your constipated asshole, prickface.*

"Before you go, Howard. Two requests."

"Yes?" *Cheap motherfucker.*

"Since I've decided to stay over, I'm free for dinner tonight. May I join you?"

"Absolutely. Wouldn't have it any other way." *Oh, Christ. Poppy will be really thrilled.*

"And please arrange companionship."

Howard looked blank. "Companionship?"

"Two high-class ladies. Discreet, and under thirty." A

301

meaningful break, then, "And they should both have clean bills of health, dated today."

His own stuttering took Howard by surprise, along with the request. "Er . . . c-c-certainly. I'll g-get right on it."

Fuck! Paid messenger was one thing. But pimp, too? Maybe it *was* time to start looking around.

★

"This is the big leagues, kid," Zeppo White said, edging closer to his beautiful client. "I told you I could do it for you."

"What? *What?*" Whitney begged.

"Not a word until Howard gets here. I promised."

"Ha! An agent's promise is like a Bloody Mary without the vodka. It doesn't mean a thing. *And* you know it."

Zeppo displayed a row of flawless false teeth. When he removed them he could give a woman more pleasure than she'd had in her entire life. "Patience, kiddo. Howard can be a mean one."

"Nobody's mean to *you*, Zeppo," she coaxed. "You're too important."

"Flattery'll do it every time," he said, and just as he was about to tell her, Howard arrived.

Whitney tried to compose herself. It had been an exciting day, what with her meeting with the new publicity firm, and now Zeppo White *and* Howard Soloman arriving at her house with something good to tell her.

She knew what it was. They were finally going to confirm that she had the role in *Romance*. Although the script had been sent to her, it was no sure thing. Word was out that Orville Gooseberger wanted an actress who could sing. Well, she could learn, couldn't she?

Howard appeared even more manic than usual. He had stopped in the Polo Lounge and consumed a large piece of chocolate cake (lunch) and two glasses of warm milk (he feared an ulcer.) He had also spoken to the head of publicity at Orpheus. "Get me two hookers for a V.I.P. The expensive stuff. I need 'em tonight, an' they both have to bring doctor's certificates dated today." A pause. "Yeah, yeah. I know it's oddball. Tell 'em to add the doctor's charges to the bill."

That was easy. Now came the difficult part. A phone call to his wife. "Poppy, honey?"

"Our party was a smash, Howard! Rave reviews! What time will you be home?"

302

"One more meeting and I'm on my way."

"Roselight wanna kiss big daddy daddy nighty-night," Poppy baby-talked.

Whew! She must be in a sensational mood. "What are we doing tonight?" he asked.

"Dinner at Mortons with the Whites. I'm going to bask!"

"Add three more."

Her tone changed. "Who?"

"Zachary Klinger and his date, and her . . . friend."

Ominous silence.

"C'mon, Poppy sweetie, it's business." He hated it when she forced him into what she referred to as "poppins talk".

More silence.

Shit!

"You can stop by Cartier tomorrow," he suggested.

A guilty giggle. "I was in Tallarico today."

Trust his wife. She knew exactly when to strike.

Whitney looked quite edible, as usual. She had a healthy glow about her, an outdoor radiance coupled with an indoor sexuality.

"Drink?" she inquired breathlessly.

"Water," Howard replied.

She ran to the kitchen and got it for him. Whitney did not surround herself with servants. It made a refreshing change. Most of the women he knew were all terrified of breaking a nail.

Zeppo beamed. "Well, kiddo," he announced. "I'm gonna let Howard tell you – it's *his* studio."

"I've got *Romance*, haven't I?" she pleaded.

"Better," said Zeppo. "You've –"

Howard cut him off at the pass. "Orpheus wants you for the starring role in a sensational new film, *The Murder*. I may as well tell you up front – we're after Mannon as your co-star, and Clarissa Browning for a cameo as the victim."

"Clarissa Browning!" Whitney whispered reverently.

"Hey – we're not talking *Friday the Thirteenth part fifteen*. This is class," said Howard proudly.

She glanced over at Zeppo as if she did not quite believe him. "Is this true?"

"You're damn right it is. And I got you double money, kiddo."

Howard watched her nipples carefully. They were hardening

before his very eyes. He urgently required the chance to see them unadorned, and decided then and there to add a nude scene to the script.

"Will Mannon *do* a film with me?" she asked both of them.

"The offer is out. I think he'll say yes," Howard replied.

"You bet your bananas," agreed Zeppo.

Whitney smiled, and thought of her humble beginnings.

She was about to achieve more than she'd ever dreamed possible.

Chapter 62

Mortons, a fashionable West Hollywood restaurant located on the corner of Melrose and Robertson, was crowded with Hollywood's movers and shakers. Beverly D'Amo steamed in like she owned the place, exchanging kisses with the maître d', while waving greetings to everyone in sight.

"You sure made yourself at home in *this* city," Jade remarked.

"Girl, I make myself at home just about every place I go. It's the only way to operate. Especially here."

They were given a table at the front, which, according to Beverly, was the only place to sit. "The back of this restaurant is Siberia," she warned. "Land of the under-achievers. Don't even *glance* in that direction."

Jade laughed. She had never understood people's fixation with getting good tables in restaurants.

"You're lookin' hot, babe," Beverly announced. "I wanna hear all about the dead Englishman, an' the Cloud deal. Rumour has it that you've moved into megabucks country. True or false?"

"True, I guess," Jade admitted modestly.

"Fanfuckıntastic!"

"How about you?"

Beverly grinned. "I'm gonna be a movie star. Doncha love it?"

"I think it's great, if that's what turns you on."

"Sure does. I've already made two films – nothing *memorable*. But this week I changed agents an' signed with Zeppo White. He's gonna do it for me. He's a wild character and horny as a sailor, an' I love him! He's a real goer. You've got to meet him, you'll love him too!"

"I doubt it."

"Huh?"

"Hollywood men do not turn me on. They *are* what they *drive*, and they all look like Porsches to me!"

Beverly hooted with mirth. "I don't mean you'll want to *fuck* him. He's like a cute little dog. You'll enjoy watching him get feisty. And apparently he gives great dinner – parties that is."

Beverly paused to swap kisses with a good-looking man in a white sweater and matching pants. From his smooth suntan to his white shoes he was perfection. The woman with him was older and crusty. She dug him in the small of the back to hurry him along. She was not interested in being introduced to a couple of devastatingly beautiful models.

"Penn Sullivan. He's in my acting class," Beverly said knowledgeably as the couple moved off. "And the old broad with him is Frances Cavendish, a casting agent. I bet she'll be casting around in *his* pants tonight!"

"Do you know *everyone* in town?"

"Only the ones who matter."

Jade felt good being with Beverly. A little of the New York excitement rubbed off; she enjoyed swapping stories and hearing all about their old friends. Beverly seemed to know what everyone was doing, and with whom. It certainly took her mind off Mark. He had been difficult to get rid of. And Corey – she knew she had to call him and let him know that however he wished to live his life was his business and perfectly all right with her. After twenty-four hours of worrying, she had finally realized that whatever he did was okay. It was *his* life.

"Now here comes a man I'd like to meet," said Beverly, her voice filled with admiration. "Mister Big. Zachary K. Klinger. He owns Orpheus Studios, you know."

They both watched the large man settle at the front round table with a skinny redhead and a cool blonde.

"I can't believe there's actually someone you haven't met!" Jade said teasingly.

"I'll meet him before the end of the evening," Beverly replied confidently. "I nearly did last night at the wedding party for Silver Anderson. He was at the next table, and just as I was going over, Mannon Cable and Chuck Nielson started to have this amazing fight!"

"You're kidding?"

"Haven't you heard?"

"Beverly, I am not – repeat, *not* – remotely interested in the movie business. Why would I hear?"

"Because, my dear, you have to know what's goin' on."

"Why?"

"Good question."

Beverly continued to chat, but her focus of attention had shifted. Her eyes were now on Zachary Klinger. She wanted him to notice her, and it wasn't long before he did. In fact, he noticed both of them. They were hardly low-key. Beverly was clad in a red body-suit with a purple Claude Montana leather jacket and boots, her jet hair scraped back into one long plait. Jade's shaggy copper hair framed her direct, challenging face. She wore a black jeans jacket over a short knit dress, and lots of silver jewellery.

Most men in the restaurant were trying to cool it, pretending not to notice them. However, there were a record number of trips to the men's room just to check them out.

Zachary stared.

Beverly, who was facing him, stared back.

"A little eye contact?" Jade teased.

"I bet I can get him hard at fifty paces!"

"Trouble is, you'll never know."

"Don't lay money on it."

"Beverly, he's *old*."

"So's Reagan. And I'd jump into bed with him too, if he asked me. I'm into power, girl. It really creams me up."

"You're impossible!"

"I'm truthful." She leaned forward. "The two bimbos with him look like hookers, and – hold everything – here come the rest of his party."

Poppy and Howard Soloman walked in, followed by Ida and Zeppo White.

Beverly was on her feet in a flash. "Zeppo!" she shouted. "It's me. Your new star, babee!"

Zeppo paused, undecided as to whether he should kiss

Zachary's ass, or greet Beverly D'Amo. He chose Zachary. One of the first lessons you learned in Hollywood was whose ass to kiss first.

"Just a minute, kiddo," he said with a distracted wave, hurrying to pay homage to Zachary.

"Who are those two women?" Zachary demanded, ignoring Howard and Poppy, who were both busy apologizing for being late.

"That's Beverly D'Amo," Zeppo said. "Lovely girl. Good actress. She's expensive, but if Orpheus has something for her I'm prepared to talk a deal."

"And the other one?"

"I don't know. Do you want me to find out?"

"Later. Sit down. I'm ready to order."

Across the room Beverly sank back into her chair and watched the action from afar. "Shit!" she exclaimed.

"What's the matter?" Jade asked.

"The little mouse is not coming over. He'll pay for that."

Sipping her wine Jade said, "Don't you think you're taking this all a bit too seriously?"

"Hell, no! Hollywood is a combat zone. And baby – *I* fight to win!"

Poppy's bright eyes darted around the restaurant. She wore her new cabochon ruby and gold necklace like a badge of honour. Howard loved it. He hadn't seen the price-tag yet.

"Thank you for the gorgeous flowers, Zachary," she gushed. "So *thoughtful* of you. I'm *mad* for orchids. How did you know?"

He gazed at her blankly.

Go on, light up a cigar, you ill-mannered pig, she thought. The least he could do was tell her how wonderful her party was.

She glanced around the room again with a feeling of pride. Mrs Howard Soloman. Hostess supreme. Nobody knew what a struggle it had been to get where she was today.

Nobody knew how hard it had been . . .

Chapter 63

At night the pounding of the waves thundered on the beach. Heaven decided she never wanted to be without that sound again.

"How long is your uncle gonna be away?" Eddie asked, comfortably stretched out on the deck listening to an old Elvis album, a can of beer nearby.

She shrugged. "I dunno. He's gonna phone tomorrow. A few days, I guess."

"We should throw a party," he suggested.

She had to admit the thought *had* occurred to her. "Who'll pay?" she asked.

"We'll make it a bottle party. Everyone brings their own."

Hesitantly she said, "Gee, I don't know . . ."

"We could have it out here on the deck an' on the beach. Nobody would havta go in the house." Digging in the pocket of his shorts he produced a sorry-looking joint. "Whaddya say?"

"When?"

"It's too late to get it together tonight. How about tomorrow?"

She was angry that Rocky hadn't shown. Dumb geek. He was probably a loser anyway. "Yeah, let's do it!" she agreed, knowing full well that Uncle Jack would be pissed off if he ever found out.

"Right on! Let's go for it!" exclaimed Eddie. "We'll get the group down, an' some of the other dudes. We can tell the Fish to pick up pizzas. It'll be a full blast!"

"Like no more than fifty," Heaven warned. "And *not* in the house."

"No way," Eddie said adamantly.

*

Jack Python was drunk. Uproariously, rip-roaringly drunk. And he did not care. In fact, he felt great as he sat at a back table in Elaine's and held court. At least he wasn't sloppy drunk, he was talkative and very funny.

Elaine herself watched from afar, as she kept an eye on all her famous clientele to make sure none of them was bothered. Ocasionally she came and sat, tossing back a drink or two and missing nothing.

Jack shared a table with a couple of writers, ace publicist Bobby Zarem, a publisher, and a wicked-tongued socialite. Elaine's mixed group. She enjoyed shaking up her famous singles at a large round table.

Getting drunk, Jack decided, was not the act of a desperately unhappy man. It was an act of celebration. He was out of a relationship he had been reluctantly hanging on to because it was good for his image.

Well, screw his image. And screw Clarissa Browning. Jack Python was back on the field.

He couldn't help laughing.

"What's so funny?" asked the socialite. She had red hair worn in a bun, sharp cheekbones, and dazzling diamonds.

"Just thinking," he explained, reflecting on the irony of it all. *He* was the one with the supposed stud reputation. Clarissa had told him how all her friends warned her he would never be faithful. And *she* was the one screwing around. Unbelievable!

"Thinking about what?" she persisted, determined to attract his interest.

He looked her over, slowly, lazily. She was old money, an heiress to a billion-dollar fortune.

He lowered his voice so only she could hear his reply. "I'm thinking about how I'd like to fuck you."

Billion-dollar heiresses did not have to play games. "What are we waiting for?"

And so, later on, he ended up in the socialite's bed in a Park Avenue penthouse, with the scream of police sirens outside, and the clink of diamonds inside. "I never take them off," she announced with a restless smile.

She was an insatiable woman, but that was Jack's speciality. Once he got on for the ride he never quit until the lady asked him to.

Later, when he awoke, he had a relentless hangover, and a

strong desire to be elsewhere. The woman slept beside him. Red hair, naked white skin, and gleaming diamonds at her ears, wrists, and throat.

Not wanting to wake her, he dressed hurriedly, and let himself out of her sumptuous apartment.

Early morning light filtered through the tall buildings as he walked briskly to the Helmsley Palace Hotel, where he had a suite.

The desk clerk in the private tower section greeted him warmly, as did the pretty elevator operator.

He rode up to the forty-eighth floor thinking of the lucky escape he'd had. If he hadn't flown to New York and caught Clarissa cheating on him, he might never have known. And he had actually given serious consideration to marriage!

Christ! One mistake in his life was more than enough.

"I love your show, Mr Python," smiled the elevator operator.

"Thank you." He smiled back, his hangover receding.

In the privacy of his suite he clicked on the televison, stripped off his clothes, and allowed a cold shower to wash away the faint aroma of Private Collection.

Jack Python was back where he belonged. Single and up for grabs.

*

Found out and unrepentant, Clarissa studied the script of *The Murder*, along with an incredible financial offer, which was really quite ridiculous and very tempting.

She read the script twice. Carefully.

And then she called Cyrill, collect. Clarissa had never been known for her loose purse strings.

"Well?" asked her agent anxiously. "I know it's garbage. However, for five days' work, at that price . . . Clarissa, I have to leave it entirely up to you."

"It's not garbage," she replied crisply. "Not at all. It's a very interesting and provocative thriller, with a fine relationship between the two main characters, and a strong line of humour."

He sounded relieved and surprised at the same time. "Does this mean you want to do it?"

"I most certainly do. Only listen to me carefully, Cyrill. I will not play the victim. I desire the leading role. It's *exactly* the kind of part I've been searching for."

Chapter 64

"Hello," Wes said. "Make yourself comfortable – Silver'll be down in a minute."

"Thank you," said Quinne Lattimore, a stocky man in his fifties, with a florid complexion. He regarded Wes warily. Like all Silver's friends and acquaintances he viewed the new husband with deep suspicion. Who was he? Where had he come from? And what was he after?

"Silver tells me you've got good news," Wes said amiably.

"Excellent," replied Quinne, full of confidence. "I have something to tell Silver that will make her a very happy woman indeed."

Wes drifted over to the bar. Vladimir had already served an English tea, but he felt like something a touch stronger, so he poured himself a hefty scotch, added a couple of ice cubes, and turned to check out the agent.

The man did not look big-time. The man looked comfortable but not affluent. He didn't give off any energy, and he certainly didn't have killer eyes.

Wes remembered his own short career as a singer. The group he was with had an agent who made big promises and never came through. More-successful groups had agents with energy. The big boys had agents with killer eyes. Wes always remembered the look. Zeppo White had it written all over him.

Chuck Nielson had warned him, "Lattimore's nowhere city. Silver can be with whoever she wants. You should get her to change."

Silver made her entrance a few minutes later – hair swept up, makeup perfect, simple lounging pyjamas in gold lurex. She enjoyed creating impressions. Even in her own house, with only her agent for an audience.

"Quinne, darling!" She kissed him on each cheek, European style.

"You look gorgeous as usual," he said. Quinne had always had a little bit of a hidden crush on her.

"I feel outrageously *wonderful*." She reached out her hand for Wes. "It's marriage, you know, it agrees with me. I adore it!"

Quinne chortled uncomfortably.

"Pour me a glass of champagne, darling," she said to Wes, and then lowering her eyes coquettishly she added, "I think I deserve it, don't you?"

He moved into the role of barman easily. It didn't bother him.

Quinne took Silver's arm and led her over to the couch. "Sensational news," he announced, puffed with pride. "Orpheus wants you to co-star with Carlos Brent in *Romance*. It's a definite offer, and wait until you hear what they're going to pay us!"

Silver, who had quite resigned herself to being a television star, and did not consider movies – because they did not consider her – shrieked with delight. "I can't believe it! When did this happen?"

Wes poured the champagne and kept a steady ear on the conversation.

"Today," Quinne said happily. "Out of the blue. Shooting starts in ten days, and the schedule fits right into your *Palm Springs* break."

"I'm *thrilled*!" she exclaimed. "When can I see a script?"

Ambling over, Wes handed her a glass of cold champagne. She looked up at him, glowing with delight. "Did you hear, darling? They want me for a movie!"

"Why shouldn't they? You're a star, aren't you?"

"A *television* star," Quinne said pointedly.

"The biggest female television star in America," Wes replied, equally pointed. "I'm surprised this hasn't happened before. What movies have you suggested her for? It'd be interesting to know exactly who's turned her down and why."

Quinne began to stutter about movies never being their goal, and timing, and how great this deal was.

Silver went to say something, and Wes silenced her with a look. He knew he had the agent on the defensive.

"Were you out hustling this deal, or did it just turn up on your desk?" he asked.

Quinne was a truthful man. It was probably his downfall as

far as his relationship with Silver Anderson was concerned. "I didn't exactly chase after them. I must admit they came to me."

Wes just looked at Silver as if to say – *This is an agent? Agents are supposed to be out there selling. Getting more money for their clients. Hustling. Hustling. Hustling.*

Quinne Lattimore was useless – and by the time he left the house twenty minutes later, they both knew it.

After he'd gone, there was a meaningful silence. Silver walked over the large terrace windows, opened them, and walked outside.

Wes followed her.

"Quinne's been very good to me," she said.

"Do you pay him commission?"

"What kind of question is that? You know I do."

"Then he's been well compensated, hasn't he?"

"What are you suggesting?"

"That we move on up." He put his arm around her. "You're a huge star, baby. You belong with Zeppo White. He can do things for you that Quinne Lattimore can't."

It was the first time since the death of her mother that somebody was telling her what to do, making decisions, and really caring. "Do you think so?" she asked tremulously.

"I *know* so. And I don't want you to worry. I'll take over. Tomorrow I'll go see Zeppo. We'll hand the movie deal over to him, and make a generous settlement with Quinne. You can bet your ass Zeppo'll get you better terms. And then I want Zeppo to check out your contracts with City Television. I don't know what they're payin' you, but whatever it is, I bet it ain't enough."

"Will you really take over everything?" she asked hopefully.

"Why not? I've got nothing else to do."

"The accountants and the lawyers and all the boring stuff I hate, hate, hate?"

He rather liked the idea of being in charge. "Everything, Silver. You just act. I'll look after every single thing." He paused and hugged her tightly. "After all, if you can't trust me, who *can* you trust?"

Chapter 65

The ambience at Le Dôme, on Sunset, appealed to Mannon. The restaurant attracted a mixed clientele of music people, producers, agents, and entertainers. The tables were not on top of each other, and in the back the restaurant divided into several sections so you could always hide if you so desired.

Mannon strode through the bar to Sadie La Salle's table. Sadie was a powerhouse agent. Short, dark, with one hand poised forever near the jugular. A scandal had rocked her life a couple of years before when two murders took place at her mansion. Sadie had survived the storm, and gone on to bigger and better deals.

She regarded Mannon with a critical eye. "You're still the best-looking sonofabitch in this town," she announced, downing a shot of straight vodka. "How would you like to walk away with eight million buckeroonies for one lousy movie?"

He smiled. "If anyone can get me that kind of money, Sadie, it'll be you."

She picked up a script sitting on the chair next to her. "Here's the words. That's the price. It's for Orpheus and they're anxious."

Taking the script from her he said, "Are we talking on the level here?"

"Do I tango with midgets?"

"Sounds good to me."

"Read it. They're going for Clarissa Browning —"

"If Clarissa does it, I'm in," he interrupted quickly.

"Wait, there's more."

"What?"

"They want Clarissa for a cameo, and Whitney for the lead."

He couldn't conceal his surprise. "*My* Whitney?"

"I thought she wasn't anymore."

He leafed through the pages, giving himself time to think. He was being asked to star in a movie with Whitney, for double the money he had received on his last project. So why was he even hesitating?

Because . . . he had always been opposed to Whitney's acting career.

Because . . . Whitney couldn't act.

Because . . . why should he pay half of eight million dollars to Melanie-Shanna when he was planning to divorce her?

"Listen," Sadie said. "You know I never try to influence you in any way, but I've read the script, and it's not bad at all." She paused, and signalled the waiter to get her another vodka. "Plus, this is going to raise your price to new heights. I'm not saying we'll always get this kind of money, but we're in a whole new ball park. And I think I like it."

"The money is acceptable."

She raised an eyebrow. "*Sooooo* glad!"

"I've got to think about it though."

"You have to *think* about eight million bucks? What's the problem?"

"Personal."

She skewered him with a look. "Personal like you married some Texas bimbette on the rebound an' now you want out? Or personal like being close to Whitney is gonna get your hormones workin' overtime?"

He laughed. She knew him so well.

Sadie placed a soothing hand on his arm. "Here's my advice. Take the money an' run. It's 'fuck you' money. I'm tellin' you, the script's okay. It's not *Officer and a Gentleman* but it plays. Whitney will be able to manage it." She shrugged. "And if you don't want to do it, that's okay too. I'm your agent, I can only advise you."

Mannon nodded. Eight million bucks and he was hesitating! Jesus! Had he come a long way!

*

The beach party started at nine o'clock, with a straggle of Eddie and Heaven's friends who toured the house saying "Holy shit!" and "This place is *it*, man."

They were impressed, but only for a short while, then out came the crates of beer and the boxes of pizza, and the grass and the Quaaludes.

315

Heaven enjoyed being the focus of attention. It was *her* party, and she strutted around taking full advantage, all thoughts of keeping them out of the house forgotten. As the evening progressed, more and more people started to arrive. The word was out. There was an open party going on, and everyone wanted to be part of the action.

Eddie got the group together, and they played a set of Elvis Presley's oldies – with Heaven doing the vocals. When she first got into singing she really loved the loud stuff – as far as she was concerned the louder the better. Anything to be totally different from her mother. Silver's voice was powerful and strong. In her time she had been compared to Streisand and Garland. Today, after years of misuse, her voice was thicker, more smoky. But Silver had always remained a traditional singer, excelling at show-tunes and material written by the masters - Sammy Cahn, Cole Porter, and the other great popular song writers of the forties and fifties.

Heaven was certainly different. She skidded out of a ballsy rendition of *Jailhouse Rock* and took a rest.

The party was growing. Young people seemed to have a bush language all their own – news of the party had them arriving from as far away as Pasadena and Hancock Park.

Heaven thought that maybe they should put a brake on it, and cornered Eddie to tell him.

He was stoned, and had a line going with a Pali High senior who looked like a female version of David Lee Roth.

She knew why he was coming on to the girl. He was trying to make her jealous, only she couldn't care less. One thing she had learned from her mother: never expect anything from anyone – that way you can never be let down. Silver taught her that when she was six or seven, and the lesson stuck.

"We gotta push this blast out onto the beach," she warned Eddie.

He regarded her lazily, with blank eyes and slack lips. The excitement of playing for an appreciative and rowdy audience had worn off; now he just wanted to guzzle beer and get laid. "Everyone's havin' a good time," he said, pulling Miss David Lee Roth closer.

A loud crash signalled the demise of a crystal lamp.

"Shit!" Heaven snapped. "Move 'em outside, Eddie, or I'm callin' the party off."

"Whaddya think *I* am, Superman? They ain't goinna take any notice of me."

She wanted to pull his long, dirty black hair and kick him in the crotch. He was the one who had talked her into having this party, and now he was backing off from the responsibility. Goddamn geek! She'd had it with him.

The place was being wrecked before her very eyes. Several guys were playing a makeshift game of baseball with empty beer cans, couples were lolling all over the couches with greasy pizza and burning cigarettes, someone had broken the lock on the cupboard in the bar and was passing out bottles of scotch and vodka, drugs were being used openly all over the place, and a buxom blonde girl was taking it all off to shrieks of delight from the assorted gathering.

Heaven remembered London, six years earlier. She was ten and she'd been around. Silver and she were staying with a woman called Benjii. Only Benjii wasn't a woman, she was really a man. Actually, at the time, Heaven couldn't decide *what* Benjii was – she only knew that Benjii took them in when they ran from a London hotel in the middle of the night because mama – as Heaven called Silver then – couldn't pay the bill.

For two months they put up with Benjii and his parties and his strange friends. Until one night mama just freaked. She ran out on to the little balcony which overlooked the King's Road in Chelsea, ripped off all her clothes, and screamed and screamed. "I'm jumping! Don't try to stop me. I'm jumping!" And stark-naked, she attempted to climb from the shaky balustrade, while a petrified Benjii held her desperately around the waist and shouted hysterically for Heaven to phone the police.

Which she did. Calmly. Until they took her mother away.

After that she curled herself into a tight ball and sat in the corner sucking her thumb, listening to Benjii on the phone telling everyone what had happened.

Heaven felt numb them. She felt numb now.

A feeling of *déjà vu* overcame her. She was in a situation she couldn't control, and all she wanted to do was find a corner and hide.

*

Jack took the last flight out of New York to Los Angeles. He thought about hanging around, taking in some meetings, doing a little business. But Heaven was alone in the beach house, so he figured he'd give her a nice surprise. Besides, he had made love to one of the richest women in New York, and where did he go from there?

Sitting on the plane leafing through a magazine, he came across an advertisement for Cloud Cosmetics. Jade Johnson stared out at him. She was stunning, and not in a Whitney Valentine or movie-starish way. She was pictured leaning against an old brick wall, clad in faded, skin-tight jeans and a washed-out denim shirt casually unbuttoned to the waist. Her breasts were hidden, but if you looked closely you could make out slightly erect nipples through the material, and the faint shadow of cleavage. Clasping her waist was a silver-buckled belt, worn low. And cowboy boots covered her feet.

She looked straight at the camera with a direct and challenging stare. Wide-apart eyes, straight nose, sensual mouth, and aggressive square-cut chin. Her copper hair, shaggy and shoulder length, tumbled around her face.

The copy was simple:

> Smart women
> wear Cloud

Jesus! How had he ever let her slip by? Their dinner together in Vegas remained a memorable occasion.

Jade Johnson.

He was free now.

He only hoped that she was too.

Chapter 66

"Mr White wondered if you ladies would care to join his table," the waiter said.

"No, thank you," replied Jade swiftly, as Beverly snapped a quick "Yes, please!"

The waiter, an unemployed actor, winked at Jade as if she were some out-of-town hick. "Zeppo White. The *agent*," he said knowingly.

"*My* agent," Beverly interrupted possessively.

The waiter was deeply impressed, and wouldn't have minded a lengthy conversation about how one got the infamous Zeppo White to represent you.

Beverly ignored him. "C'mon," she pleaded. "This is business."

"I don't want to sit with a group of people I don't know," Jade objected.

"I'll introduce you."

"Big fucking deal."

They glared at each other. Back, when they shared an apartment over ten years ago, they had always fought. Both spoke their minds and never dodged a confrontation.

"I'm asking nicely," Beverly said. "Like I'm saying *please* and *will you* and this means *a lot* to me."

"Why don't *you* join them, and I'll go home? I've got an early call in the morning. I really don't mind."

"Hell, no."

"Why not?"

"Because if you can't help me out on this, then you're not the friend I thought you were."

"Shit, Beverly. Don't give me that line."

"*Plllleeease?*"

With a sigh of resignation Jade said, "Okay, I'll do it. But it's against my principles to watch you play kissy ass with the rich and powerful."

Beverly grinned triumphantly. "Observe a true professional in action." She rose from the table shrugging off her Montana jacket, causing a man nearby to almost choke on his drink. She was ebony-coiled perfection – beside her even Grace Jones seemed understated.

She undulated over to Zeppo's table, where waiters struggled to fit in two more chairs.

"Beverly, kiddo." Zeppo leaped to his feet, his bright orange hair standing on end.

"Zeppo, babe! Say hello to my best best friend Jade Johnson."

He clasped her hand. "Jade, it's a pleasure. You ever thought of doing movies?"

She smiled politely. "Never."

"Lauren did it . . . Marisa . . . Kim Basinger. You'd be a natural."

"Thank you, Mr White, but I'm not interested."

"Call me Zeppo. All my friends do. And my enemies!" He honked with amusement.

Meanwhile, Beverly lost no time in zeroing in on Zachary. "Mr Klinger," she purred. "I'm a fan. That article about you in *Forbes* last month was a dazzler. By the way" – she extended a friendly hand – "my name is Beverly D'Amo."

Poppy kicked Howard under the table. It was bad enough to be saddled with Zachary and what appeared to be two hookers, but now this black freak, although Poppy had to admit she admired Jade Johnson, whom she had seen on numerous *Vogue* and *Bazaar* covers.

Howard was busy slipping and sliding down memory lane. Beverly D'Amo reminded him of his first wife, the fierce activist to whom he had been married for a fast forty-eight hours. What a panther in the old sackerooney! Je-*sus*!

The two expensive call-girls exchanged bored glances. They had seen it all and done it all. Nothing surprised them. They knew for sure that later the black woman would be joining them for a delicate trot around Zachary Klinger's sexual fantasies.

"Goddamn *hot* in here," remarked Ida White crossly. "And noisy."

Everyone ignored her, including Zeppo, whose hand was busily creeping up Beverly's thigh under the table. She shook it off like an annoying gnat, and questioned Zachary about the stock market.

What an operator! thought Jade. *Nothing changes.* Once, on a cover shoot in Tennessee, Beverly had slept with a local department store owner, his son, *and* his son-in-law. On separate occasions, of course, just because the photographer had bet her a hundred bucks she couldn't do it. Beverly loved to achieve the impossible.

Howard Soloman stared at Jade. "Haven't we met before?"

She nodded, and took a deep breath. "About ten years ago," she said. "I came out for a screen test. You were a studio exec or an agent or something."

Shaking his head sympathetically, he said, "Didn't work out, huh?"

"Howard!" Poppy scolded. "Jade Johnson is one of the top models in the country."

Howard was unimpressed. As far as he was concerned everyone wanted to be a movie star. It was the great American dream.

"Excuse my husband," Poppy said with an ingratiating smile. "He doesn't understand. I'm crazy for the new Cloud ad. Antonio is a *wonderful* photographer. Does he ever – you know – photograph *real* people?"

By the time Jade made her escape an hour later, Poppy was her new best friend.

"I have to be up *so* early," she said as she excused herself.

"Call me," Zeppo said insistently. "I can do things for you."

"Call me," Howard said, "if you ever change your mind about the movies."

"Call me," Poppy said, "we'll have lunch."

"Call me," Beverly said, with a huge wink, "tomorrow for sure."

She rushed out to the parking lot, where Penn Sullivan, the actor Beverly had greeted earlier, and Frances Cavendish, the casting agent, argued hotly while waiting for their car.

Jade caught ". . . I'm not just a piece of fucking beefsteak" out of his mouth, and ". . . If *I* say it's right, *you'll* do it" out of hers.

The two of them got into an old Mercedes, still fighting, and roared off into the night.

Jade found herself alone again.

Naturally.

★

"Sit next to me," Zachary Klinger instructed, when Beverly arrived at his bungalow a few minutes after him. She had left her car with a valet at the front of the hotel. He travelled by chauffeured limousine.

"I'm more comfortable over here," she said, settling into a couch across from him. "Where are your girlfriends? Did you drop them home?"

"I want you next to me," he repeated.

"He who wants might never get," she joked.

"Don't play with me, Miss D'Amo. Tell me what *you* want, and let us not indulge in childish and time-consuming games."

"I want to be a big, big star, Mr Klinger. Bigger than even *you* can imagine."

"Then sit beside me, and we shall see."

"Promises don't interest me."

"What does?"

"Action. Do something for me, and *then* I'll do something for you."

"Agreed. But I need something tonight."

"No can do. You shouldn't have sent your girlfriends home Between 'em they looked like they could do *plenty* for you."

"And they will. Only you must sit next to me and watch.) won't touch you. They won't touch you. Unless you ask . . ."

A definite weirdo. Berverly complied – she had absolutely nothing to lose, and plenty to gain.

*

"I'm tired," Poppy complained.

She was tired. Ha! She sat on her fanny all day, and only moved it out of the house to buy jewellery and have lunch with her cronies.

"I've had a very tough day," Howard said. "*I'm* frigging exhausted."

Poppy giggled. "Are we both too tired to play naughty?"

"Sorry, sweetheart, tonight I'd need Arnold Schwarzenegger to lift it for me."

She giggled again. "You're so funny!"

"I try to please."

"Oh, babykins, you do!"

What had he done right for a change?

They were approaching their house, and he pressed the automatic gate opener, pulling the car to a halt while the massive iron gates swung open.

"Howard?" Poppy asked plaintively. "Do you love me?"

"What kind of a question is that? You know I do." He hated it when things got sloppy.

They were in their own driveway now. "Pull the car over to the side," she whispered. "Park, Howard. Pretend we're in high school."

"What?"

"*Do* it."

Reluctantly he obeyed. Poppy was a woman you didn't fight with, not unless you wanted to be up all night.

As soon as he stopped the car she was on him, burrowing into his lap like a hungry rabbit.

"What are you *doing*?" he blustered, as she went for his zipper

"The thing you like best in the whole wide world, Howie." She reached his shorts, and triumphantly pulled his limp, exhausted penis out into the moonlit front seat.

"Poppy —"

"Be quiet. You know you love it."

Enclosing him with her mouth, she gave him her special kiss-of-life technique. The same technique she had used the first time they became more than just boss and secretary. Somehow she had gotten under his desk and displayed her special talent. Three months later they were married.

"Poppy!" he groaned, as she did the impossible and summoned a dead person back to life.

For the first time in a long while he did not think of Whitney as he fell asleep later that night.

Chapter 67

Rocky had the Sylvester Stallone walk. He had honed his imitation until it was perfection. Slight swagger, macho steps, a forward thrust. He could, if he wanted to, have made a living as a celebrity look-alike. But hey — as far as he was concerned Sylvester copied *him*.

The drive to Trancas was a bitch, and a couple of times he almost turned his Jeep around and headed back to civilization. The Pacific Coast Highway drove him nuts. He always got this insane urge to cross the line and play chicken with the oncoming traffic. It bothered him that one night he might just get stoned enough to do it, and end up in the slammer for sure. Again.

Funny, he'd been living on the edge all his life, and the only thing he'd been put away for was reckless and drunken driving. Six months' hard time just because this old couple broke down on the freeway and *he* was the jerk who had to run into them. If it hadn't been him, *someone* would have hit 'em.

Heaven. A foxy little piece. With her own beach house. Probably some shack, but hey — check it out.

When he found the turn-off there were cars crowding the shoulder of the road, and a lot of noise and loud music coming from the house, which was situated beyond a series of stone steps.

Party time, he said to himself. There was nothing Rocky liked better than to party.

*

Stewardesses always came on to Jack; it was automatic. The one on the flight back was outrageously pretty, a blonde Californian peach.

"How long have you been doing this?" he asked.

"Six weeks," she replied. "It's hard on the legs, but I'm *really* enjoying it. I get to meet so many interesting people." She paused and twinkled, all shiny-bright and eager. "Like you, Mr Python."

"Call me Jack."

"Give me your number and I will," she said boldly.

He reckoned she would last another six weeks on the job before she was either discovered and became an actress, or lured off to get married. She was that pretty.

"What will you do when we get to L.A.?" he asked.

She laughed ruefully. "Flake out."

He had a strong desire to take her to bed. She was so different from the socialite, and very appealing in a one-night-stand kind of way.

Strapped in his seat, with a scotch on the rocks and Jade's picture shut safely in the magazine, he tried to make up his mind whether to come on to her or not.

Christ! he thought, as the 747 prepared to land. *I've been almost faithful for eighteen months. And for what? To catch Clarissa with her talented ass in the air servicing some macho actor. The hell with it.*

He rang the buzzer and the stewardess came running.

"I'll buy you dinner if you're available," he said.

*

Heaven didn't care anymore. She would make up a story for Uncle Jack. Like she invited a couple of people over, and a whole crowd gate-crashed. Which wasn't such a lie, it was the truth.

The trashing of the house was almost complete. Couples were now making out in both bedrooms, and strangers surged everywhere. Someone had turned on the jacuzzi, which was packed with naked bodies.

324

She couldn't see Eddie. She hated Eddie. She would never speak to him again for allowing this to happen.

*

Roaming around, Rocky figured he had fallen into teenage heaven. Baby pussy was knee deep, and he was in love with all the little foxes with their tight fannies and perky tits.

Rocky partied a lot, but usually the parties were full of hard-faced women who pretended to be actresses or models but usually turned out to be hookers on the side. He had lived with a few – more than a few, in fact. Good bodies – money-trap minds. Any money he made was strictly for himself. He had a decent apartment, and a third-hand Merc, which he used when he wasn't in the Jeep. The Jeep was strictly for business purposes only. Like tonight, for instance. He had worked bar at a big party and walked away with three thou in drug sales, *and* a case of the best scotch.

He had not walked away with Silver Anderson – who wasn't even there.

When he thought about his so-called friend Wes Money, and what he had gotten away with, he could hardly believe the jerk's dumb-ass luck. And *he*, Rocky the man, was responsible, for it was he who had taken Wes to Silver Anderson's house in the first place. And not so much as a "thank you" for his trouble. No dinner invite. No "Come by the house." No nothin'

Some people.

Some people were dogshit.

Rocky glowered. And flexed his not inconsiderable muscles. And said, "Yo there, fox-trap," to a fifteen-year-old, who moved away fast.

Conveniently, Rocky forgot it was he who had set his good friend Wes up the Laurel Canyon trap. Not that he'd known the extent of the scam, but he *had* known it was something heavy, and if he'd been a true friend he would never have given Wes the number to call.

Grabbing the attention of a tall lunatic in Levi cut-offs, he asked, "You seen Heaven, man?"

The boy jumped excitedly. "A few of the dudes got Ecstasy. What's this Heaven shit?"

It occurred to Rocky he was wasting precious time. He

had the perfect opportunity to go for sales. Business looked like it could be brisk.

*

The stewardess had peach-fuzz-smooth skin, a glorious mound of apricot pubic hair, and an obliging disposition. Making love to her was like taking a trip through a small-town candy-store.

They were in Jack's suite at the Beverly Wilshire, and it was past midnight. After the event he just wanted to get rid of her.

And then he got an attack of the guilts. She was genuinely nice, and tried so hard to please.

She was also a fan, which he couldn't help being irritated by. "What's it like being Jack Python?" she asked in an awe-struck voice.

What *was* it like?

"Very public," he said at last, which seemed to satisfy her.

"I bet you've met everybody."

"Not quite."

"I bet you've met Paul Newman."

"Yes," he admitted.

"I always buy his salad dressing," she said reverently. "It's excellent. Have you tried it?"

Time to extract himself.

Definitely time.

He was out of practice, and couldn't quite remember how to go about it.

She gave him the perfect cue by sitting up in bed and stretching – bouncy tits glowing with health. "I'm hungry," she said. "Aren't you?"

He was out of bed in seconds. "I've got a great idea."

"What?"

He reached for his pants and pulled them on. "Where do you live?"

"Santa Monica. Eleventh Street. I don't have to be home until later . . ." She gazed at him expectantly.

"Get dressed," he said cheerfully. "We'll go over to Hughes and buy everything in the market. Then I'm going to drive you to your place, and you're going to cook me the best breakfast I ever had."

"I am?" she asked uncertainly, disappointed because room service seemed like a much better plan.

"You *can* cook, can't you?"

"Sort of."

"Let's go!"

*

Making money with the kids was better than raking it in from their rich mommies and daddies. And they knew what they wanted too – a few uppers, downers, ludes, grass, coke. Especially Ecstasy – the new designer drug. Like their Calvin Klein and Guess jeans, they wanted only the best. And Rocky found that quite a few of the little foxes were prepared to barter for their goods.

He was just thinking about taking one grateful teenager for a walk along the beach, when he spotted Heaven, curled up in a corner, ignoring the wild action like it wasn't even happening. With a growl of recognition, he pounced. "I made it!"

She regarded him with huge amber eyes, and dragged herself back to reality. "Like a day late," she muttered.

"Din't wanna miss the party," he said breezily. "This is some heavy place. You got an old man keepin' you or what?"

"I live here alone," she mumbled. She certainly didn't owe *him* any explanations.

He was impressed. "Yeah?"

She stared at him warily. "Have you *really* got a friend in the record business?"

He scratched his armpit. "Yeah. Wanna warble somethin'?"

"If you clear all these total creeps out of my house, I'll play you my tape. Can you get rid of them?"

He looked affronted that she would even consider he might not be able to. "Yer askin' Rocky," he said boastfully. "I've bounced 'em out of bigger parties than this."

*

Jack purchased two hundred dollars' worth of groceries in the market while the blonde stewardess kept on exclaiming, "You're *crazy*. Who's going to *eat* all this stuff?"

"Let me enjoy myself," he insisted. "I never get to do this."

Filling the Ferrari with paper sacks, he drove to her apartment, a modest place she shared with two other stewardesses.

"Shhhh!" she giggled, as he filled the tiny counter space in her kitchen. "It's three o'clock in the morning!"

"I'd better go," he said, when he'd delivered everything.

327

"No, no. I'm going to cook for you, remember? That was why we went to the market."

He kissed her button nose. "I'm not hungry anymore. And I've got a teenage niece alone in my beach house. I've got to be going."

In a way she was relieved. Explaining Jack Python to her roommates at three in the morning was not a simple task.

Understandingly she nodded, and asked very softly, "Will I ever see you again?"

He wasn't about to lie to her. "Tonight was special." Only a white lie. "The truth is, I'm just coming out of a long relationship, and I don't want to make any promises I might not keep." He touched her cheek. "So . . . pretty lady, don't wait for the phone to ring, because right now I'm not the most reliable guy in the world."

"I appreciate your honesty . . . Jack," she said earnestly "Take my number anyway – you never know when you might feel like shopping!"

He grinned.

"And thanks for the groceries," she added.

He left feeling good. It was nice to be able to walk away with a clear conscience.

*

He was doing it! Rocky was clearing them out in clusters. Telling them the party was over and brooking no argument.

Eddie was the only one to give him trouble.

Heaven turned away when Rocky forced him over to a quiet corner and had a word in his ear.

Eddie left shortly after, his face red, his guitar under his arm. *Bye-bye Eddie.*

She was going to tell Uncle Jack she wanted to transfer from her high school. Better still, stay out altogether and become a professional singer – with concerts, and gold records, and personal appearances – the whole deal.

As the last stragglers left she turned to Rocky in the debris of a once perfect house.

"Sit down," she said, determined that *someone* was going to hear her tapes. "And listen."

*

Driving along the Pacific Coast Highway, Jack broke the speed limit with reckless abandon. He let the Ferrari rip, tearing up the road with a cool forcefulness.

The dawn light was breaking, casting a pale glow along the coastline. Traffic was light and he enjoyed the effortless drive. New York seemed like a dream. In. Out. It was almost as if he'd never been there.

Humming softly to himself he arrived at the Trancas house in record time.

*

"This is not bad," Rocky said grudgingly. "Kinda catchy."

She had played him the slow tape of her new song; now she decided to try him with some good old rock and roll.

She put on the fast stuff and waited for his reaction.

While she was busy watching Rocky, lolling in a leather chair smoking a recreational joint, Jack walked in.

Rocky noticed him first. "Hey —" he began, starting to sit up. "Aren't you —"

"What the *fuck* is going on here?" Jack asked coldly.

*The girl ran from her foster home. She ran at night and she ran fast,
having first stolen three hundred dollars from a savings stash she had
discovered hidden behind a sack of flour in the kitchen.*

*She was still only a teenager, but she looked older than her years
and attractive, in spite of cheap clothes and amateurish makeup.*

*It did not take her long to find a job in the city she ran to. Working
behind the toiletry counter of a five-and-dime-store gave her enough
money to rent a room, and just about scrape by.*

*The manager of the store liked her. He was a short man with a
bulbous nose and two fingers missing from his left hand. Middle-aged
and married, he watched her constantly. She hadn't been working there
two weeks when he trapped her in the back room and stuck his hand —
the one with the missing fingers — up her skirt.*

*She shoved him off and told him he was a pig. Her angry words
only seemed to excite him more, and he continued to chase after her.*

*The girl tried to ignore him, but he was persistent, and never seemed
to leave her alone.*

*One day his wife came to the store. The woman was even shorter
than her husband and quite fat. A fine black moustache decorated her
upper lip.*

*The manager behaved himself that day, which was a relief. Only
the next day he was twice as bothersome, and the girl found herself
complaining to the driver of one of the delivery trucks.*

*"I know how y'can deal with him," the young driver said. "Meet
me after work an' I'll tell yer."*

*She met him. And one thing led to another, and before long she
found herself going out with the driver, who was called Cheech, and
seemed decent enough, although he had a bad case of acne and never
bathed.*

Of course he wanted One Thing. The girl knew by now that all men wanted One Thing. And she also knew what could happen when you gave in, so she vigorously rejected his advances.

Cheech was not used to being turned down. In spite of the acne and the body odour, girls loved him. He was a real loverboy. Cheech always made out. "I can't see you no more if'n ya don' give me no lovin'," he warned her.

"Okay," she replied.

"Okay what?" He was startled by her cool attitude.

"Don't see me."

The girl puzzled Cheech. She must be . . . what was the word he'd heard Jane Fonda use in some movie?

Frigid – yeah, frigid, that was it.

They stopped seeing each other.

One day the store manager came into the ladies' room while she was sitting on the toilet. "Get out!" she screamed.

It was after six, and the other staff had gone home for the night.

"You don't fool me," the short man said. "You want it. I've seen you looking at me with your hot eyes."

He was on her before she could pull up her pants.

For a moment she was caught off balance as he lunged for her, shoving his fat hand between her legs.

She saw that his penis was out, protruding from his trousers like a fat white slug.

With all her strength she jammed her knee up, catching him in the balls.

"Aaiieee!" he screeched, doubling over.

She ran from the store and never returned.

Two weeks later Cheech turned up at her rooming house. "Why didn't yer tell me you was leavin'?" he asked.

"Why should I?" she replied.

Grabbing her around the waist he said the words she had been waiting to hear. The words that would protect her from the world forever. "Let's get hitched."

They were married two days later in a civil ceremony. She told him she was nineteen and an orphan. They were well suited, for his only relative was an older brother whose house they moved into.

Cheech wanted sex five minutes after they walked through the front door, and she obliged, because now she was his wife she could hardly keep on saying no.

He pulled her into the small room they were to share and lifted her skirt. Then, pushing her down on the narrow bed, he went to work, grunting all the time.

"Yer not a virgin," he said, after a minute.

"I never said I was."

"Fuck *me!*" he screamed angrily. "Yer not a fuckin' virgin. Yer tricked me, bitch!"

He slapped her hard, and continued to cuss and scream.

Cheech never recovered from what he referred to as her "trickery and lies". But his anger did not stop him from thrusting himself upon her every night, and sometimes in the morning too.

His brother was a surly fellow, with a common-law wife who came and went when it suited her. She worked as an exotic dancer, and refused to do a thing around the house, so the girl found herself cleaning and washing, shopping and cooking for everyone. Including Cheech's brother's friend Bryan, who stayed over on Friday nights after their beer and poker binges. Bryan was a huge man. Six feet two inches tall, and three hundred pounds wide. He had long hair, matched by an unruly beard, and a permanent sneer.

The girl soon realized that marrying Cheech was a mistake; however, it was better than being alone. She suffered in silence, accepting her fate as inevitable. At least she had a husband, and that was something.

It was on a Friday night, shortly before Christmas, that she sensed danger in the air. Cheech came home drunk, waving a half-full bottle of scotch – a seasonal present from his employer. His brother arrived shortly after, angry because his common-law wife had phoned him at work to inform him she had met another man and was never coming back. By the time Bryan got there, both Cheech and his brother were drunk. It didn't take Bryan long to catch up.

The girl hovered in the kitchen nervously. She served them a meal of fried steak and potatoes, and then got out of their way by shutting herself in the small room she shared with Cheech.

Outside, the three of them were laughing bawdily and shouting at each other. Soon she knew that Cheech would come in and crawl all over her. At least he was quick, and when he was finished she could shut her eyes and seek solace in sleep.

Sure enough, no more than twenty minutes later, he staggered in, drunkenly mumbling under his breath.

She steeled herself to accept his advances as he lunged on top of her. No preliminaries for Cheech – he went right for the goal, chafing against her dryness.

"There's somethin' wrong with ya," he grunted disgustedly. "Yer got no juice."

Silence.

"I'm talkin' to ya," he screamed, slapping her across the face, as he had taken to doing a lot lately.

She tried to sit up, but he pushed her roughly back on the narrow bed. "Yer'll go when I say so."

He slapped her again, and once more thrust into her.

With a weary sigh she let go and relaxed. The sooner it was over the sooner he would leave her alone.

Alcohol had slowed him down, and he could not maintain an erection. With a steady stream of curses he fell off her. "It's yer fault," he muttered angrily.

His brother pounded on the door. "What's goin' on in there?" he shouted in a slurred voice. "Thought we was goin' t'a bar."

"I'm comin'," yelled Cheech irritably, standing up and zipping his fly. "You've given me a belly ache, bitch. Yer nothin' but a prick-tease."

He stormed out, and she thought it was over.

Five minutes later his brother entered the room. "Why'ja havta upset Cheech?" he whined.

"I didn't do anything," she said softly.

"He's not so bad to ya, is he?" the brother asked, sitting on the side of the narrow bed.

"No," she lied.

"He feeds ya, puts clothes on ya."

"Yes."

His big hand swooped over and enclosed her left breast.

Shrinking back against the wall she whispered, "Please don't touch me."

Whiskey breath enveloped her. "I gotta do it. I gotta see if yer normal. Cheech says ya ain't."

His fleshy mouth descended on hers, while his hands worked on dragging her legs apart.

She began to struggle as she felt the full weight of him. And then she started to scream with fury and frustration as he plunged inside her.

"Cheech's right. Yer a dumb bitch," he slurred, pinning her arms to the side with a show of macho strength.

"And you're a dumb bastard," she responded gamely, in spite of the pain he was inflicting.

"Doncha call me names, cunt." He hit her twice, across the face, quieting her futile struggle. And then he finished what he had started with an animal growl of satisfaction.

When he got off her she touched her mouth and discovered blood seeping from the corner. She explored with her tongue and felt a loose tooth. Her breasts were sore, and both eyes were swollen and blackened. It was another nightmare. There had been too many in her short life.

Shakily she attempted to sit up. Before she could, Bryan entered the room. They stared at each other warily. Bryan was drunk; if he had been sober she might have been able to talk him out of what he was about to do.

"No!" She shook her head as he approached her. "No! Please, no!"

He didn't say a single word as his huge bulk crushed her beneath him.

She must have passed out, for when she came to she was lying in the back of Cheech's panel truck, and she could hear the three of them in the front, talking.

"We'll throw her right in the middle of the city dump." She recognized Cheech's voice.

"Naw" — his brother talking — "the river's better."

"Ya stupid fuckers," snarled Bryan. "We coulda got a prostie for twenny bucks."

"You fuckin' did it," accused Cheech. "Ya fuckin' smothered her to death."

If she had known fear before, it was nothing compared to now. Her skin crawled with clammy horror as she realized that, when she lost consciousness, in their drunken state they must have thought she was dead, and that they had killed her. And now they were disposing of her body.

Shivering uncontrollably she decided not to put them out of their misery.

Twenty minutes later the truck ground to a halt. The three of them were still arguing among themselves, deciding on alibis and explanations in case anyone asked awkward questions.

Cheech finally did his own summing up. "She was just a nobody — who's gonna notice she's not around anymore?"

Grunts of agreement as they manhandled her body from the truck and flung it into a deep pit of garbage.

As she fell she knew the revenge she would take.

And six weeks later she did.

Lighting the first match was easy . . .

BOOK FOUR

Hollywood, California
November 1985

Chapter 68

"Andermon Productions," Unity said into the white telephone. "Just one moment, please."

She tapped on the glass window of the pool house, attracting Wes's attention as he lounged outside catching the winter sun — which in California is sometimes just as hot as the summer.

"Who?" he mouthed.

"Mr Samuels. Revolution Pictures."

He made the effort and ambled into the pool house office to take the call.

In three months, Wes Money had learned a lot. He had taken over Silver's career with a vengeance, and although Zeppo White was her official agent, Wes himself was her personal manager, and went over every deal with a street-sharp eye.

"Harry, baby." He had learned the lingo right away. "Have you rethought our deal?"

Harry obviously had, for they spoke for five minutes, and ended with a luncheon date.

"Put me down for a twelve-thirty at the Palm on Wednesday," he told Unity, hanging up.

Opening a large leather appointment book she scrawled in the arrangement.

He leaned over her desk. "How're y'doin'?"

"Okay," she replied primly.

She certainly looked okay. A lot better than when he'd tracked her down to that sleazy bar she was working at. Shit! Was she in lousy shape then.

One morning, a couple of months ago, he had woken up and suddenly remembered her telling him that she worked at Tito's, a bar on Hollywood Boulevard. And it was like *bingo*! He thought he might amble over, collect his thousand bucks she

337

was holding for him, and see how she was doing. Maybe he'd even get his dog back.

He hung around until Silver took off to appear in a charity fashion show, and then he was out of there. Silver had wanted him to come and watch her. "No way," he'd said. "Women in clothes bore me."

"You're such a macho man!" She had smiled affectionately, not really minding at all as long as he was waiting when she got home.

He drove the Roller to Hollywood, cruising along the seedy boulevard searching for Tito's.

He found it conveniently located between a porno movie theatre and a sex aid shop. Nice neighbourhood.

The thought of leaving the Rolls-Royce on a meter made him nervous, so he drove to the nearest parking lot, where he tipped the Mexican attendant ten bucks to keep a special watch on it. The Mexican thought he was crazy and rolled his eyes.

"You gonna do it, or shall I take my money back?" Wes asked threateningly.

"Sure, me do," sneered the attendant.

"You'd better," he warned. "If I come back and there's one single scratch on this car, I'll slice your balls an shove 'em in an enchilada."

He walked briskly to Tito's, by-passing the porno shop although he was tempted to pop in and buy Silver a gift. She would love something rude. Maybe a peek-a-boo bra for her, and a jar of Tiger Balm for him. Tiger Balm was an aphrodisiac cream that supposedly got it up and kept it there. He remembered using it once when he was sixteen and going with a twenty-year-old raver who was very demanding. Locking himself in the bathroom, he had rubbed the cream on his cock. Ten strokes later and he came all over the floor. So much for Tiger Balm!

Wes had been in seedy bars in his time, but this one was a real lulu. The barman looked like he'd just been released from Attica. The customers – all six of them – looked like his cell-mates. And a crusty old cashier, hunched over an ancient cash register, appeared to resemble Mae West's grandmother – long platinum wig and all.

"Five bucks floor show fee," she wheezed as he walked in.

"What floor show?"

"You wanna peek, ya gotta pay."

Fishing out a ten, he waited for change that was not forth-coming.

"Two drinks minimum," the old hag said, hitching at a faded scarlet dress covering withered breasts.

Over by the bar the escapee from Attica watched him suspiciously.

He slid onto a bar stool and asked for a beer. In strange locations he found it was always advisable to order something that couldn't be watered down.

A tough-faced woman with badly dyed yellow hair and black fishnet stockings peeking from a fake leather mini-skirt appeared from nowhere and sat beside him. She fished a cigarette from her purse, stuck it in her mouth, and turned to him with what she obviously thought was a provocative expression.

"Light?"

"What?"

"I wanna match fer my ciggie."

Even at his lowest point he would never have second-glanced this one. Obligingly he took out his solid gold Gucci lighter – another present from Silver – and allowed the woman to suck on her cigarette until it glowed.

"I'm looking for a girl called Unity," he said. "I understand she works here."

"Who says?"

"She told me she works here."

"When?"

"A short while ago. Does she?"

The woman shrugged. "Don' ask me."

Leaning across the bar he summoned the barman. "You got a girl called Unity here?"

"Who's askin?"

"Shit!" he said forcefully. "I feel like I'm in a friggin' James Bond movie. Does she work here or not?"

The barman pointed to a door in the back. "Second booth."

Taking a swig of beer, he eased himself off the stool and made his way through the door, which led into a dark, foul-smelling hallway. Along the wall were three closely spaced peephole windows, each one covered with heavy black-out shades. A man crouched in front of the last window along, obviously indulging in an activity most people did in private. Trying to ignore him, Wes paused in front of what he presumed to be booth two. A slot signalled the deposit of two dollars before the shade lifted. He put in the money and watched the action.

Unity appeared on the other side of the glass. He hardly recognized her, for this was a different Unity. Her pinched little face was covered with makeup, the Lennon specs were gone, and she had on a straw-coloured Tina Turner wig which made her look ridiculous.

She wore a red shiny skirt, white plastic boots, and a tight tee-shirt.

Lethargically she began to take it all off, revealing a leopard G-string and minuscule bra on a painfully skinny body.

He tried to attract her attention to let her know it was him, and that she didn't have to do this. But the glass was obviously one-way and she couldn't see him.

"Goddammit!" he muttered as she stripped off everything.

The black shade – on a two-minute timer – snapped shut.

Stalking outside, he grabbed the barman's attention. "I don't want to watch her," he said angrily. "I need to talk to her."

"Who?"

"Unity, for crissake."

"She gets off at three."

"I have to speak to her *now*."

The barman cleared phlegm from his throat and spat on the floor behind him. "It'll cost ya."

"Everything costs in this joint. Are y'sure you don't charge to take a piss?"

After a short discussion they came to a financial arrangement, and the barman went off to get her.

Unity. His uptight little neighbour. He had thought she was a waitress, not some peep-show hooker.

She came out a few minutes later, sulky looking, with a long woollen sweater covering her "ready to strip" outfit.

"Remember me?" he asked.

She stared at him, her expression a mixture of surprise and insolence. Before he could utter a word she blurted, "I spent the money. I didn't think I'd see you again. And after the way they beat up on me, I reckon I deserved it."

"You spent *my money*?" he asked, outraged. He might have given it to her, but the thought that she'd spent it without asking infuriated him.

"I had to get out, didn't I? What was I supposed to do, wait for 'em to come back?"

"Wait for *who* to come back?"

"Your drug friends. You should have warned me it was drug money."

"It wasn't."

"Don't give me that. I may look stupid, but I'm not."

"I'm tellin' you, it was *not* drug money."

She shrugged. "I don't care either way. I spent it, an' there's nothing you can do about it." She continued to stare at him, daring him to do something.

Shaking his head he said, "You're a fucking thief."

"And what are *you* – a boy scout?"

"Jesus *Christ*!"

"Can I go now? I've got to make a living, you know."

"Some living. Taking it off for a bunch of jerk-off artists."

"Maybe I should deal dope instead. Pays more, doesn't it?"

They glared at each other.

"Where's Mutt?" he demanded.

"I've got him."

"I want him."

"No way."

"I can give him a good home now."

"Bully for you. He's stayin' with me."

What a pain in the ass she was with her semi-cross eyes and stupid crazy wig. She'd stolen his money, wouldn't give him back his dog, and apparently suffered no guilt about ripping off his thousand bucks.

"What are you workin' in a toilet like this for?"

"Because it pays my rent."

"I'll give you fifty bucks for Mutt."

"Mister Generous," she sneered.

"He's half mine anyway," he stated self-righteously. For some insane reason he had a burning desire to recover the dog they had once shared.

"Sue me."

Maybe it was the wig, or the place, but Unity was like a completely different person. It occurred to him that she might be high. "What are you on?" he asked.

"Fuck *you*."

Grabbing her arm, he rolled up the sleeve of her sweater

before she could stop him. And sure enough he found what he was looking for — a thin line of recent track marks.

She snatched her arm away with a jerk of fury. "Whyn't you piss off out of here?"

"When did y'start *this* charmin' little habit?"

"None of your goddamn business."

"I guess my thousand bucks financed you."

Staring at him arrogantly, she said, "You could say it started me off. When your *friends* came in an' beat the shit out of me, forcin' me to move on, I figured why not? I had the money for once."

He felt immediately responsible. And although he didn't do anything about her that day, he went back twice to see her, finally suggesting that she give up her present lifestyle and come to work for him as a secretary.

"*You* need a secretary!" She hooted with mirth. "What for?"

"Because I married well. My wife is Silver Anderson."

"No shit? And I've been dating Don Johnson!"

She took some convincing, but he was very persuasive. There was something waif-like and appealing about Unity — and he wanted to use a little of his good luck to try and get her back on the right track. He offered her a drying out period in a drug rehab clinic, and then the job.

"We'll have to tell Silver you're my cousin. I don't want to go into long explanations."

Three weeks ago she had started work. The old Unity. Quiet and serious looking, with her John Lennon shades, makeup-less heart-shaped face, and pulled-back light brown hair.

It seemed to be working out well.

*

"It's a wrap," the first assistant announced, after the director had called "Cut" on the set of *Romance*.

Silver swept off to her dressing room, trailed by her entourage of Nora — who now worked for her exclusively — Fernando, her hairdresser; Raoul, her makeup artist; and Iggi, her personal stylist and dresser.

Being a movie star again meant great luxury. Compared to the daily grind of episodic television it was absolute ecstasy. Silver adored every moment.

She had an expensively furnished and large dressing room three times the size of the rat-hole City Television had given her for emoting three days a week on *Palm Springs*. A rat-hole she

342

would no longer have to languish in, thanks to the swift, no-nonsense negotiating clout of the admirable Zeppo White. Thank God she had listened to Wes, and returned to the all-encompassing power of Zeppo. Quinne Lattimore had been distraught – naturally. But as Wes so forcibly (she was crazy about his forcefulness) pointed out – business was business. And since she had never signed a formal contract with Quinne, she was free and clear.

Goodbye, Quinne.

Hello, Zeppo.

Wes took care of the details.

Zeppo had taken one look at her contract with City Television and thrown a fit. "Slave labour!" he tut-tutted. "Shouldn't be allowed. Whoever had you sign this should be shot!"

He knew perfectly well who allowed her to sign it. Quinne Lattimore. She felt sorry for him at first, but when Zeppo and Wes explained to her how she had been taken advantage of – money and perks-wise – she didn't feel so sorry any-more.

Wes sat her down one day and gave her a lecture. "You're a beautiful woman."

She preened.

"And a great actress and a wonderful singer."

This was getting better. She loved compliments, especially from Wes, on whom she grew more dependent each day.

"But you're not getting any younger."

Her smile turned to frost. She hated mention of her age. Forty-seven was only three years away from fifty. And fifty was only ten years away from sixty. And . . . oh God, she felt quite faint.

"What are you trying to say?" she asked icily.

Catching her vibes, he jested around before getting to the main point. "You'll *always* be the sexiest broad on the block – no doubt about *that*. But I don't want you bustin' your ass in a few years' time. I want you to be able to sit back an' say fuck 'em – I don't think I'll work this year. And to be able to do that we've got to rake in the big money now. Quinne held you back a couple of years. With Zeppo we've gotta go for it. An' we gotta go for it *now*."

She recovered her composure. He was right. It might be quite a change to sit back and do nothing – when it suited *her*. "I agree," she said.

"The thing is," he went on, "don't freak out, but Zeppo is trying to break your contract with City Television."

She was aghast. Appearing on *Palm Springs* three days a week was certainly hard work, but without it what would she do? *Romance* was not going to take forever, and she had nothing else lined up.

"I enjoy doing *Palm Springs*," she said quickly. "And if Zeppo negotiates more money . . ."

"*Palm Springs* got you back, made you a star again. Now you don't need it anymore. Zeppo can keep you as busy as you want to be. He's already talkin' about an hour special with NBC. An' he's talkin' mega-bucks. There's a recording deal in the works. Commercials, endorsements. Christ, Silver, do you realize the money we can make?"

"Are you *sure*?" she asked tentatively. She suffered from every performer's lack of confidence when it came to viewing her own future.

"Yeah, I'm sure, otherwise I wouldn't be talkin' this way. Zeppo wants to explain everything to you himself – I figured I'd run it by you first."

That conversation had taken place three months ago. And in those three months, everything Wes and Zeppo promised had happened. Right now she was in the midst of shooting *Romance*. True to his word, Zeppo had got her out of her contract with City Television. How he did it she had no idea. But the great thing was that she was to guest on *Palm Springs* four times a year – at her own convenience. And for that four weeks she was to receive the same amount of money they had been paying her for a full year.

Unbelievable!

Wes was more than right. Moving to Zeppo was the second-best thing she'd done in her entire life. The first was marrying Wes. Contrary to everyone's belief that he was going to grab all her cash and run, he had turned out to be a canny operator – who was making sure she made even more bucks. And he looked after all her interests too. Banking, investments, tax, accounting. She still paid so-called professionals to do it, but Wes watched and interfered and made sure they did it right, and didn't steal from her.

Oh, the relief of having a real man around the house. She didn't care what his background was. She trusted him, and that was enough for her.

They had their fights of course, real screaming matches. The making up was worth every delicious spiteful insult. Wes was the lover she'd been searching for all her life. A powerful animal in the sack. A real man.

Recently he'd come up with a cousin, and a mangy dog. She wasn't exactly thrilled that he'd installed them in the house. The girl was a nonentity, the dog an aggravation.

Wes insisted they both stay. "She's my only family," he said firmly. "Put her in one of the maids' rooms, they're empty anyway."

How could she argue? He was doing so much for her, and as it turned out Unity was quite useful to have around. She kept to herself and didn't bother anyone.

The dog was another story. Silver wished it would fall in the pool and drown! She hated dogs at the best of times – especially pedigree-less mongrels.

When *Romance* was completed it was all go on her television special. And then she had an album of old show tunes to cut, and a commercial for Savvy perfume.

The money was rolling in. Right now Silver was content. Except for the matter of Zachary K. Klinger, who quite blatantly refused to leave her alone. He was pursuing her relentlessly, and his unwelcome attentions were beginning to unnerve her.

So far she had managed to keep it from Wes, although it wasn't easy. She was inundated with red roses daily – fortunately they arrived at the studio, where he also sent her expensive pieces of jewellery which she always had Nora return.

Occasionally he even visited the set. After all, it was an Orpheus picture, and he owned Orpheus.

Studiously she managed never to be alone with him. But she knew Zachary. When he wanted something or someone he never gave up. And he wanted her.

Toying with the idea of telling Wes, she finally decided against it. There was nothing he could do, and pitting Wes against Zachary Klinger would be like placing a small rowboat in front of an ocean liner.

She would just have to wait it out, and hope that Zachary faded quietly back into her past where he belonged.

Chapter 69

Jade Johnson was everywhere. Or rather her face was. She stared down from two giant billboards on Sunset. She was in every magazine. Her image – larger than life – decorated all the Cloud make-up departments in every one of the better stores. Her series of television commercials – daring, amusing, depicting her as a true woman of the eighties – had created quite an impact wherever they were shown.

In a short period of time she was better known than she had been in her entire career. And for the first time she was seriously considering taking it one step further. Orpheus Studios and Howard Soloman kept on making her offers she was finding hard to refuse. The more she said no, the more they said yes. Going so far as to promise she could debut in the story of her choice. And proposing a very lucrative deal indeed.

While she wasn't an actress, Jade also wasn't a fool, and she knew that opportunities like this only came once in a lifetime. She had read a book called *Married Alive*, whose central character was a young fashion designer who falls in love with a married man. It was a comedy – reminiscent in a way of *A Touch of Class* – one of her favourite movies of all time. Saying yes – if the book's film rights were still available – seemed like a tempting prospect.

Beverly D'Amo urged her to get together with Zeppo White. "You have to be with the right agent," she insisted. "Look at what he's done for me."

Beverly was currently shooting *Romance* with Carlos Brent and Silver Anderson. After that she was due to go to work on *The Murder* in a featured role.

Jade nodded. She agreed that the right representation was important, and with that thought in mind she arranged a lunch with Zeppo at The Palm on Santa Monica.

When she walked in he leaped to his feet. "You've taken your time, kiddo," he said.

"I always take my time," she replied coolly.

He cackled. Beautiful women turned him on. Especially beautiful women with razor-sharp minds of their own.

"So . . . you wanna be a movie star," he mused.

Shaking her head she said, "No, Mr White. I want to make enough money to buy myself an island, so that when the bullshit gets a little too thick on the ground, I can just take off and do whatever I want."

He cackled again. "I like it! I like you! Tell me what the thieves are offering you, an' I'll get you double."

She nodded. "For ten percent I shall expect you to do just that."

*

All things considered, Beverly D'Amo was quite happy with the way her career was progressing. Two movies and plenty more on the horizon if she continued to please Zachary Klinger. And there was no reason why she couldn't do so. He was easy to please – kinky – but what the hell – she had met a few in her time.

Zachary's particular kink was making it with her while two ladies of the night watched attentively. Of course, first she and Zachary had to eyeball the two hookers, which could get a little tedious if you weren't into that action. But Zachary loved it, and who was she to spoil his pleasure?

Beverly had never thought the day would come when she had to screw to get ahead of the game. After two and a half years in Hollywood, getting exactly nowhere, she had decided to go for it. And there was nobody bigger than Zachary K. Klinger. He was the top man.

They had an agreement. She would put out for him. And he would put out for her. Fair enough.

The only drag was he expected her to find the professionals. Easy it was not. He required new ones each time, and they always had to bring along a clean bill of health. Not that he ever touched them. Never went near them.

Beverly was seriously thinking of having a whole bunch of phoney doctors' letters dummied up. He would never know the difference, and it would surely make her job a lot easier.

The first time she slept with him he demanded a doctor's certificate from *her*. Goddammit. She nearly told him to shove the deal. Who needed the humiliation?

When he purchased the huge house on Carolwood Drive in Bel Air, he invited her to move in with him. She liked that — it showed that in his own peculiar way he cared. Another man in his position might not be so anxious to set up house with a black woman. Zachary didn't give a damn. In a funny way she loved him for it.

She had her own bedroom, her own maid, and her own Rolls-Royce. When he entertained — which admittedly wasn't often — she played the official hostess part. What with the work and the status, it was a role she could live with.

A very different role from the one she had played while growing up.

*

Rodeo Drive was quiet when Jade slipped into Lina Lee after lunch and did some serious shopping. She spent three thousand dollars on clothes, and wondered guiltily if she was going Hollywood.

It's my money, she thought defiantly. *It's not like I'm spending some poor guy's hard-earned dollars.*

She loved clothes, and recently she had needed a new outfit every day, what with personal appearances and television talk shows. In New York she used to get a lot of stuff given to her, just so she would wear it and everyone would say, "Where did you get *that*?"

The spending spree was a celebration. She had instructed Zeppo White to represent her in her negotiations with Orpheus. If all fell into position she *would* do a movie. It would be crazy-time not to.

"Jade?"

Turning, she did not recognize the short blonde woman in a peach jumpsuit and large dark glasses. Beside the woman stood a tiny child, identically dressed.

"Poppy," the woman reminded. "Poppy Soloman. You were supposed to call me. Lunch. Remember?"

"Oh, yes. How nice to see you," she said graciously, quickly trying to recall where they had met.

"And this is Roselight Soloman," Poppy continued. "Isn't she adorable? Everyone says she looks just like me. But I can see a touch of Howard in her, can't you?"

Ah! Mrs Howard Soloman. They had met at Mortons, the night Beverly was bird-dogging Zachary Klinger.

"She's lovely," Jade said kindly. The child wasn't lovely at all. She was on the plump side – just like mommy – with a petulant, screwed-up little face. "How old is she?"

."She'll be four in two weeks." Poppy paused, then added airily, "We're taking over Disneyland."

"How . . . original."

"I think it will be different, don't you?"

"Uh . . . certainly different."

"Children so easily get bored these days," Poppy confided. "Last year it was a tent and clowns and donkeys in the garden. This year she'll expect more."

"Absolutely," Jade agreed, looking for an escape.

"Now," said Poppy firmly. "While I've got you here, I absolutely *refuse* to take no for an answer. I *insist* upon giving a lunch for you. What day can you manage? Just name it, I'm all yours."

"I'm not sure when I'm free . . ."

"Monday?"

"No."

"Tuesday?"

"No."

"How about Wednesday?"

"Wednesday, let me see . . . ah . . ."

"Wednesday it is," Poppy said firmly. "Twelve-forty-five at the Bistro Garden. No excuses. I'll invite a few close chums. Is there anyone in particular you'd like?"

'Er . . . Beverly D'Amo."

Poppy gave a bitchy laugh. "She's quite a lady, isn't she? Although I guess *lady* isn't *quite* the right word."

Jade jumped in. "What is?" she demanded.

"Me wanna pee pee," interrupted Roselight.

"Be quiet," said Poppy sharply.

"What is?" repeated Jade.

"Character," smiled Poppy, recovering fast from her almost gaffe. "A charming, original *character*. And *such* a funny comedienne. Howard *raves* about the dailies on *Romance*. He says she's like a beautiful Whoopi Goldberg."

Jade relaxed. "I have to go," she said.

"Me too," agreed Poppy. "Busy, busy, busy. There's never enough time in the day is there? I'll see you on Wednesday."

A sudden noise startled both of them.

Roselight had peed in her pants, and the result was trickling to the ground.

Jade laughed all the way home. Poppy Soloman's face was a picture postcard of undisguised horror.

★

"Where's your sister?" Norman Gooseberger asked.

"She'll be here in eight minutes exactly," Corey replied, consulting his watch. "Jade runs ten minutes late on everything. No more, no less."

"Unlike baby brother," Norman said with a smile. "Always punctual, always correct."

"Not always," replied Corey.

Their eyes met and locked and did an intimate little dance all their own.

"Do you know," said Norman, "that this is the longest time I've ever been faithful?"

"Really?" replied Corey.

"Really."

They continued to stare at each other. A long stare where plenty was said, yet no words were spoken.

For the first time in his life, Corey felt completely at ease with himself. For years he had been forced to live a lie; now finally, with Norman, he was free to be himself. Norman had no hang-ups about being gay. "I knew it when I was fourteen," he had confided to Corey. "And a year later I told my parents. They freaked at first, but after a while they got used to it."

Corey had nodded. There was no way he could tell *his* parents. How could he? All they ever talked about was Jade, and how wonderful and successful she was. It wasn't easy being the under-achiever in a family used to excellence.

Jade entered the restaurant, causing the customary stares and comments. She kissed Corey on both cheeks, and then did the same to Norman. After her initial shock, she had accepted her brother's homosexuality with good grace. After all, if she were to suddenly change tracks she certainly wouldn't expect him to judge her.

"I met with Zeppo White at lunch today," she announced. "And I've decided to let him go ahead and negotiate with Orpheus for me."

Norman clapped his hands. "Bravo!" he said. "You'll be our new client. B & B signed the Orpheus account last week."

She smiled. "Not so fast, there's a lot to be worked out."

"You *should* be with us anyway," he commented.

"I know. I spoke to the Cloud people this week, and told them I wanted B & B to take over the publicity on the campaign."

"That's great!" he exclaimed.

"Great," Corey echoed, although he wasn't sure that he wanted Jade working with Norman. She had this habit of taking over on friendships — she didn't mean to do it, somehow it just happened. He loved his sister very much, only he was tired of always being in her shadow.

Dinner passed, gossip was exchanged. Jade told her Poppy Soloman story, and had Norman in hysterics.

Norman had a few stories of his own about Whitney Valentine and Chuck Nielson. "They battle non-stop," he confided. "He is *soooo* jealous of her, and she is career crazy. They're the Hollywood couple I always dreamed of representing. They break up — regularly — every ten days. *True Life Scandal* would go out of existence without them!"

Corey tried to come up with some gossip of his own. And then he thought, why even try? Norman had all the controversial and famous clients. He was stuck with Deacon the Dog, and a sixty-two-year-old male star of a television sit-com. Exciting stuff.

"How's your love life?" Norman asked boldly.

"Extremely dull," she replied matter-of-factly. Since her break-up with Mark no one had come along to pique her interest. And unlike her friend Beverly, she never slept with guys just for the hell of it. There *had* been a time when she was twenty-two that she remembered with mixed feelings. Her wild period she called it. She hadn't counted, but a lot of guys passed through her life then. Enough for her to realize that sex and nothing else was never enough. The sex was only important if it included a relationship.

"Aren't you seeing *any*body?" Norman persisted.

"I've got a lot of friends."

"We'll have to find you a winner."

Laughingly she said, "Thanks, but I'm not looking."

Driving home that night, Norman was full of how great she was. Corey had heard it so many times — he didn't need to hear it from Norman too.

They ended up arguing over something inconsequential, and Corey slept on the couch.

*

Two days later Jade and Norman lunched alone. It was a

business lunch: Norman had a promotional plan he wished to present to her.

She went over his ideas carefully, and liked what he had in mind. "You know I can't do anything without Cloud's approval," she said. "Not until my contract with them is up."

"I think you'll find that everything I'm suggesting will more than please them. It's all publicity for the product. Let's face it, you *are* the product."

She made a face. "Thanks a lot!"

"I mean the product is *you*."

"I'm not sure I like that either."

He had the blackest, curliest hair she had ever seen, and a most appealing smile. She found herself wondering if he had always been gay.

"How's Corey getting on?" she asked briskly.

"Fine. He's happy." A meaningful pause. "*I* make him happy."

"I'm sure you do," she responded quickly. Discussing their relationship still made her feel vaguely uncomfortable.

"When are you coming by the house?" he asked.

She had been avoiding it. Somehow she wasn't quite ready to see them at home together.

"Soon."

"Promise?"

"Absolutely."

After lunch she went straight to her apartment, changed into a bikini, and lay out by the pool for an hour. There was nobody around — the building was half full, and most of the tenants only used the pool on weekends.

As she re-entered her apartment the phone was ringing. Hurrying inside, she grabbed it.

"Yes?"

"Miz Johnson?"

"Yes."

"My name is Aretha Stolley. I'm calling on behalf of *Face to Face with Python* — you know, the Jack Python show?"

"Yes?"

"We'd be honoured to have you on as a guest, and Mr Python suggested I contact you directly. He always feels it's much simpler than going through agents and managers, etcetera."

"*Does* he?"

"He sure does. And I must say I agree with him. At least this way we get a direct yes or no. Usually a yes. *Very* few no's."

Jade remembered Jack Python with a taste of anticipation. Lord Mark Rand was not only dead, he was now buried.

"Tell Mr Python," she said slowly, "to call me himself." She paused. "And tell him . . . to do it soon."

Chapter 70

Aretha hung up and squawked with mirth. She put on a low, sexy voice and did a lively imitation. "Tell Mr Python," she said huskily, "to call me himself. And tell the randy sonofabitch to do it soon!"

"*Whaaat?*" said her secretary.

Aretha laughed. "I think our Jack just got lucky – yet *again*!"

"Who with this time?"

"The usual. A beautiful, stacked, *famous* lady. Are there *any* he's missed?"

Her secretary shrugged. "Don't ask me."

Aretha sailed into the production meeting with a big smile plastered across her face. She was enjoying Jack's freedom more than he was. Every week there was a different romance going on – it sure kept life interesting. Since his break-up with old sourpuss – as Aretha had nicknamed Clarissa Browning – he was back in action with a bullet.

"I called Jade Johnson," she told him.

He rubbed his unshaven chin. "And?"

"*And*, she would like to hear from you personally."

He tried not to show any particular interest. "Why's that?"

"How should *I* know? Maybe she wants to jump on your decrepit old bones. I'm paid to *do* – not *ask*."

Casually he shuffled some papers. "Does she want to appear on the show?"

"You've got to call her and find out for yourself."

"Who are we talking about?" Aldrich, his producer, joined in.

"Jade Johnson," Aretha replied, with a wink.

"We don't need another Clarissa Browning fiasco," Aldrich warned. "Are you sure she can hold a conversation, let alone one hour of prime-time television?"

"What is this?" Jack said shortly. "I don't pick duds. She'll be just fine."

He had no idea whether she would be a good guest or not. Somehow it didn't matter. He wanted to see her again. For the last few months her image had haunted him. Everywhere he looked, there she was. Beautiful. Challenging. Direct.

And yet he hadn't called her. He couldn't explain why. Perhaps it was because he needed space between Clarissa and his next serious relationship.

When the production meeting was over he shut himself in his office and stared at the phone for a while. Tonight he was taking out Kellie Sidney, a blonde, smart, divorced film star, who produced her own movies which made mega-bucks, and yet she still looked like a fresh-faced cheerleader.

The night before he had been with a slinky, dark-haired singer, who gave "sleek" new meaning.

Tomorrow night was the French actress with inviting eyes and smoky voice.

He was certainly occupied − if that was the appropriate word.

All this occupation . . . all these different bodies . . . and yet no one seemed to satisfy him. He felt restless and hemmed in. What he really needed was someone to fly with.

He picked up the phone and went for it.

"Jade Johnson?"

"Yes."

"This is Jack Python."

She sounded politely friendly. "Well . . . hi. How are you?"

"It's been a long time."

"Quite a while."

"Las Vegas, wasn't it?"

"Right."

Silence.

Long silence.

Christ! He felt like some schmuck about to request a date.

"Hey . . . uh . . . my assistant called you about doing the show, didn't she?" he asked.

"That's right, she phoned today."

"So all I need is a simple yes or no, and we can start working out schedules."

"The thing is . . ." She paused. "The thing is, I love your show. I always watch it —"

"I'm pleased to hear *that*."

"But . . . uh . . . I don't think I'd be the kind of guest you're . . . uh . . . looking for."

He was taken aback. "Why not?"

She hesitated before plunging ahead. "I just don't know what I can talk about for an hour. I guess I'm a well-known face, but I'm sure the public really doesn't know who I am. And what's more, I shouldn't think they care."

"Very modest."

"Very truthful."

"Listen, *I* want you on the show. I think you'll be great. Can you do it for me?"

"Why? So you can watch me make a fool of myself?"

"Sure. Let's all have a good laugh at your expense," he teased.

"No, thank you."

"I refuse to take no for an answer. Will you at least think about it?"

"Hmm . . . maybe . . ."

"And what can I do to help you come to the right decision?"

She could think of a lot of things he could do. Only she wasn't about to make the first move.

"Call me next week."

The moment was right to ask her out. *Are you still involved?* he could say casually. *I'm not, and I'd like to see you.*

"Fine, I'll call you next week. It was really nice speaking to you again."

"You too."

He replaced the receiver and could have kicked himself. He was a forty-year-old adult male with a certain reputation, and he couldn't even ask her out! He was behaving like fourteen not forty. *"Shit!"* he said loudly.

Aretha put her smiling face around the door. "What's up? Is she doin' it?"

"Were you listening?"

"No way."

"She's thinking about it."

"Big frigadoon deal!"

"Aretha."

"Yes, boss?"

"Piss off."

★

She could have sworn he was going to ask her out. Jack Python, with the dangerous green eyes and killer smile. Jack Python, who every day was pictured somewhere or other with a beautiful woman attached to his arm.

How about dinner? she had expected him to say.

No, she would have replied.

Jade Johnson had never considered herself to be one of the pack. She didn't want to be added to his ever-lengthening list.

Still . . . he could at least have asked.

There was only so much work one could bury oneself in. Beverly kept on fixing her up with likely candidates, and she felt no click with any of them. "Please stop," she had told her after the last one – a skinny lizard of a man with dull conversation and several billion dollars.

"But he's rich rich," Beverly insisted. "Almost as rich as Zachary."

"Who cares?" replied Jade.

She loved Beverly, but lately all her friend seemed to think about was money. Zachary K. Klinger was not the greatest influence in the world. She couldn't warm to him, and she sensed that he was uncomfortable with women. Especially strong, independent ones.

Beverly would not hear one word against him. "You don't understand Zachary," she informed Jade crossly.

"Yes I do."

Shane Dickson, the director of her Cloud commercials, was the only man she thought about getting involved with. Since his divorce he'd become quite persistent. He wasn't perfect, but he was available.

That evening she was dining with him at Spago, so she dressed accordingly. White pants tucked into boots, and a loosely belted oversized white cashmere sweater.

When he picked her up at a quarter to eight she was ready.

★

At five to eight, Jack Python arrived at Kellie Sidney's house on Sunset Plaza Drive. She wasn't ready. Kellie always ran late.

The house was filled with dogs and children. Kellie's three-year-old son had two friends over. And the dogs were a Labrador, an Alsatian and a golden cocker spaniel. A cheerful maid cooked up a storm in the huge open-plan kitchen, and televisions blared in every room. Domesticity ruled.

Jack wondered if he'd ever fit into a scene like this. It had been difficult enough keeping an eye on Heaven during the couple of months she had spent at the beach with him. He hated to admit it, but when she returned to the Valley and George, he had been relieved.

What really pissed him off was that the entire time Heaven had been his responsibility her dear and caring mother, Silver, had not called once. The woman was unbelievable.

Kellie greeted him half dressed, with rollers in her hair. She gave him a distracted wave. "I'll be two minutes," she promised. The beaming cook poured him a tumbler of scotch, and he reflected further on Silver's coldness towards her only child. Like everyone else he had often wondered who Heaven's father was. It seemed extremely callous of Silver not to at least tell her daughter. He had no respect for her because of it.

Half an hour later Kellie appeared, wholesomely pretty in a pale blue dress and dangly earrings. Word had it that she was a tough businesswoman when she got involved in producing her own movies. You would never have guessed it from her carefree appearance.

"Where are we going?" she asked, petting the dogs, kissing the children and issuing instructions to the maid – all at the same time.

Obviously she'd forgotten that when he made the date she had requested Spago, "Because I *adore* their smoked salmon pizza," she'd said.

He jogged her memory. "Spago."

She smiled happily. "*Perfect* choice. I *adore* their smoked salmon pizza!"

*

Shane had just signed a contract to direct his first feature film. He was in a celebratory mood, ordering champagne – which always left Jade with a ferocious hangover – and talking excitedly about his future. A former New Yorker, he had a certain street-smart sexuality. He looked like Al Pacino. And like Al Pacino, he was short. It was a minor turn-off as far as she was concerned. Because she was so tall, she liked men of at least

357

equal stature. Shane was several inches shorter than she, and up until now it had put her off getting involved with him, although he kept trying.

Tonight, maybe she would change her mind. All work and no play . . . And he *was* an attractive man, although he *did* talk about himself a lot. He had just completed two years of psychoanalysis, and now thought he could cure the mental ills of the world.

She glanced idly around the noisy restaurant as he described a meeting he'd just had with his recent ex-wife – a waspy Bostonian whom he should never have married in the first place.

"You know something?" he said eagerly. "For once I didn't want to slap her."

"How civilized of you," she remarked dryly.

"No. You don't understand. For me that's a major breakthrough. We are talking *major* here."

"Are *we*?"

"Yes. I can look straight into the bitch's eyes, and *not want to go for her throat*."

"Amazing."

"Damn right."

He kept talking and she kept on glancing around the celebrity-filled restaurant. Johnny Carson over here. John Travolta over there. Elizabeth Taylor and George Hamilton making a grand entrance.

She wondered if Shane would talk about his ex-wife in bed. Or even if he would talk at all.

And then she wondered if it was true – the rumours about short men being over compensated in other areas . . .

"What are you grinning about?" he demanded. "I'm pouring my guts out to you here, and you think it's *funny*?"

"Sorry! I just remembered something Antonio did in the studio yesterday. He's *such* a character!"

"Yeah, right. So let me get back to what I was telling you . . ."

She tuned out. Sometimes he was suffocatingly boring. Attractive, but boring. Attractive, but short . . .

Jack Python entered the restaurant.

Jack Python with Kellie Sidney.

She sat up straight and watched him as he paused at the reservation desk to jest with the girl there, and was then led immediately to his window table. A table that put him directly across from her.

He didn't see her at first as he leaned over and said something intimate to Kellie, who laughed. And then, just as he was about to order drinks, he noticed her and did one of those classic double-takes.

"Hey —" He smiled and waved.

She smiled back. "Hello."

Both Kellie and Shane turned around to see who their respective dinner dates were waving to. As it happened they knew each other, and exchanged greetings of their own. And then Kellie effected introductions. "Shane Dickson, Jack Python."

And Jack said, "Kellie Sidney, Jade Johnson."

And everyone came out with banal compliments before turning back to their own conversations.

"I always wanted to meet him," Shane said. "Interesting guy. Where do you know him from?"

"I met him with Antonio," she replied vaguely.

Kellie said, "She's stunning. Where did you meet her?"

"Las Vegas, I think. One of Carlos Brent's parties. Who's the guy?"

"Shane's a director from New York."

"Movies?"

"Commercials. Although I hear he's getting offers. He directs the Cloud commercials. They're wonderful — very original, have you seen them?"

"No," he lied.

"The camera work is superb. I wouldn't mind looking like she does in my next movie."

I bet, he thought. *Only pretty as you are, my sweet — no chance.*

Dinner was interesting. Shane and Kellie, back to back, had no idea of the electricity sparking between the tables. Jade tried to concentrate on her date — an impossible task with Jack Python so close. While Jack tried to give Kellie his undivided attention, as surreptitiously he watched Ms. Johnson's every move.

She couldn't eat.

"You said you were starving," Shane remarked.

She gulped more champagne — to hell with the hangover, it was needed. "Just thirsty, I guess," she said lamely.

Jack ordered smoked salmon pizza, and was relieved to see Kellie finish every piece. She was telling studio stories. Horror tales of male executives' attitudes to female movie stars who took control of their own destinies.

"I wish you'd mentioned this on the show," he said. She had been his guest three weeks before.

"I'll come back again," she said sweetly. "When I have another movie to plug."

He glanced up and met Jade's gaze head-on. They had been conscientiously trying not to stare at each other all night. This time neither of them looked away.

She felt the burn right down to the soles of her feet, and knew that Shane Dickson had just lucked out.

Chapter 71

The frigging asshole bought a mansion and moved himself out to Beverly Hills. Howard Soloman nearly had a heart attack. It was bad enough having Zachary K. Klinger driving him loco from New York – but right on his own frigging doorstep? Jesus H. Christ. Somebody up there was not looking out for him.

"It's not so terrible," Poppy tried to console him.

"How would *you* like it?" he demanded. "I'm supposed to be running a studio, not waitin' to wipe Zachary's ass every time he goes to the john."

"Does he really interfere that much?" she asked.

"Yes," he replied sourly. Actually, it wasn't that bad. Zachary's main concerns were the two movies he considered to be *his*. *Romance* and *The Murder*. The rest of the product he left alone – allowing Howard more or less *carte blanche*.

Howard had gone development crazy. Out of pique, he was spending the studio's money at an alarming rate. Buying properties, commissioning screenplays, purchasing best-selling novels, and giving the green light to a slew of producers, writers and directors with passable ideas.

Fuck it. He didn't give a damn. There were other studios to run. Orpheus was not the be-all and end-all.

Howard Soloman had a yen to move on.

*

And on the set of *Romance*, the two stars had fallen out, causing a certain frostiness all round.

Silver Anderson said it was Carlos Brent's fault.

Carlos Brent said it was Silver Anderson's.

"The man is an egomaniac," Silver said.

"The old broad is a pain in the tonsils," Carlos said.

"His voice is gone," from Silver.

"She can't sing anymore," from Carlos.

"Box office arsenic," announced Silver.

"They'll only watch her on television," announced Carlos.

Orville Gooseberger tried to patch things up. They both told him to go play with himself.

Zachary arrived on the set most days to observe the filming. Silver complained to Orville, "He makes me uncomfortable."

Orville shrugged. This one he could do nothing about. The man owned the studio.

Silver said she had a sore throat and claimed she couldn't work. Each week the film crept more and more over budget.

Meanwhile, on location in Arizona, where *The Murder* was shooting, a new romance was blossoming. It startled everybody, including Whitney Valentine, who like everyone else stood on the sidelines and watched.

Mannon Cable and Clarissa Browning came together as if they had been waiting for this moment all their lives.

One love scene in front of the camera, and they disappeared for an entire weekend.

Whitney was shocked. For some time now she had sensed Mannon was getting ready to ask her back into his life, and in spite of his pregnant wife and her own involvement with Chuck, she had considered the possibility of saying yes. She had even gone as far as discussing it with Norman Gooseberger. He not only handled her publicity, but had become a friend, whose advice she listened to.

"Take him back if he asks you," Norman had urged. "Chuck's a destructive influence. He's no good, and he drags you down with him."

Agreeing, she waited for Mannon to make his move.

He didn't. He started his ridiculous affair with Clarissa Browning, and everyone wondered what she had that was so special.

First Jack Python.

Now Mannon Cable.

Two of the best-looking men in Hollywood.

And while Clarissa was undoubtedly a magnificent talent, she would certainly never win any prizes in the beauty stakes. Plus her charm was non-existent. Most of her co-workers couldn't stand her. She was critical, demanding and tight with every cent, never so much as buying the crew a drink if she happened to be in the hotel bar when they were all present.

On screen she was magic. It was as simple as that. Her acting was flawless, and because of her, Mannon accomplished a lot more than his usual macho strut and self-deprecating sly glances to the camera. He was giving a very fine performance.

Whitney felt betrayed. Not only had Clarissa Browning taken her role, she had taken her man too.

The bitch would pay. Whitney knew how to make people pay . . .

Chapter 72

It was Jack's idea they all join up for coffee and dessert, and Kellie was amenable. "Ask your friend," he suggested.

She turned around and nudged Shane, who was surprised and pleased. "Is it okay with you?" he checked with Jade.

"Sure," she replied, trying to keep her tone casual.

They got up and moved to Jack's table, where Kellie immediately patted the empty chair beside her. "Sit here," she said to Shane enthusiastically, "and tell me *all* about the camera operator you used on the Cloud commercials. I *love* his work."

"*He* is a *she*," he replied. "A very talented lady."

"*Really?* I'm wild about working with women. My goodness – if females can't support each other I just don't know who will. Do you?"

As Kellie chattered away, Jack turned to Jade and said very quietly, "Hello."

"Hello," she replied, immediately getting lost in his green eyes.

There was no need to say anything more, for they both knew where they were heading.

Under the table she felt the pressure of his thigh against hers. "Have you thought about whether you'll do the show or not?" he asked.

Laughing softly she said, "Give me a break, I've got other things on my mind."

Kellie leaned forward and peered across the table at her. "You must tell me, who does your makeup?" she asked eagerly.

"I usually do it myself."

"How *clever* of you. I'm hopeless with shading. Fortunately, I have this wonderful Algerian boy who always takes care of me for photo sessions — and then . . ."

Jade did not hear a word the blonde actress was saying. All she knew was that she was in the throes of a wild sexual heat, and she did not care *how* many women Jack Python was photographed with. She only knew she wanted him. And she wanted him now.

Abruptly she rose from the table. "Excuse me," she murmured. "Just going to the ladies' room."

Her legs were weak, her throat dry.

Get a hold of yourself, Johnson, she cautioned. *He's only another guy.*

Both restrooms were occupied, so she leaned against the wall by the pay phone and attempted to pull herself together. It had been a long time since she'd felt this way.

"Hello." He was beside her.

Weakly, she managed, "We've got to stop meeting like this."

He thought she was heartbreakingly beautiful, and he had an insane desire to touch her face and body; bury himself in her hair; kiss her eyes and her mouth and her breasts and everything else she possessed. She had him under a spell, and he couldn't remember when he'd felt like this before.

"What's going on with you and the guy?" he asked urgently.

Shaking her head, she murmured, "Nothing." And after a slight pause, "How about you and Kellie?"

"She means nothing to me," he replied truthfully.

Suddenly he couldn't hold back any longer. Pinning her against the wall with his hands each side of her shoulders he kissed her long and hard. A forceful, penetrating kiss, which she didn't try to block, but responded to, just as he knew she would.

After a few moments he pulled back and said, "We're getting out of here."

"We can't do that."

"We can do whatever we want to."

Ida White emerged from one of the restrooms and smiled glassily. "Good evening. Jack, dear." She was stoned as usual. Oblivious to everything.

He waited until she had wandered off before whispering to Jade, "Come with me. Don't say a word." Taking her hand, he led her through the crowded restaurant to the back entrance.

"We can't just leave them sitting there, waiting for us," she protested weakly.

"It's not our problem. I've picked up both checks, and left a message with the waiter that you got sick and I had to escort you home."

"They'll never believe it."

"Who cares?"

His Ferrari was waiting, engine running, an attentive valet ready to usher them into the car.

She got in and leaned back against the plush leather. "This is crazy behaviour," she said, tingling with anticipation.

"Crazy," he agreed.

"And exciting."

"You got it."

The car surged forward, scattering photographers and fans. He drove down the short hill, waited impatiently at a red light, and took off like a rocket all the way to his hotel.

"Why here?" she asked, as he helped her from the car.

"Because it's where I live."

"Good evening, Mr Python," said the doorman.

"No apartment? No house?" she persisted.

"This is home."

"Good evening, Mr Python," said the desk clerk as they walked past.

"No family? No roots?"

"Has anyone ever told you that you ask too many questions?"

"Frequently."

"Good evening, Mr Python," said the elevator operator.

They rushed into his suite like impatient lovers – which any minute they were to become. And as soon as the door closed they fell on each other with indecent haste – removing clothes with a no-nonsense speed bordering on the obsessive.

"Christ! You're beautiful!" he breathed.

She trailed her fingers down his chest. "And you're just as beautiful."

There was no conversation after that as he took her with a powerful urgency. It was something he had to do before he could even begin to think straight.

And it was like that for her too. They were both holding back, and their mutual release was fast and sweet – earth-shattering and very, very necessary.

Now they could relax and enjoy the sinful pleasures of discovering each other's body. Which is exactly what they did, slowly and luxuriously.

Leading her into the bedroom he laid her on the bed, and began – with exquisite restraint – to carefully explore every inch of her smooth, taut body.

She responded by touching his skin with the tips of her fingers, tactilely feather-stroking his chest, until his further pleasure became only too obvious.

"I'm glad to see you're a man of action," she murmured happily.

"For you – anything!"

"Just because you want me on your show . . ."

Tantalizingly he started to kiss her neck, moving down at a leisurely pace, relishing the piquant taste of everything about her.

She enclosed his hardness with her hands and teased his unquenchable desire, until the slow, erotic pace of things turned once again into fervent, reckless lovemaking.

And after the second time they fell asleep, wrapped in each other's arms, peaceful and voluptuously content.

Chapter 73

"Wow!" sighed Heaven. "It's like *totally* killer!"

Rocky nodded his agreement. He felt pretty confident standing in the recording studio listening to the final mix of her record. She had people swarming all over her – the producer, the sound engineer, a couple of record company executives – but he felt confident because *he* was the one who had set the whole gig up, and *he* was the one with a signed management contract in his pocket, giving him a hefty fifty-one percent of her. And it was signed by her grandfather – who happened to be her legal guardian, even though he lived in cloud-cuckoo-land. She had told the old guy it was something important to do with school – dragged in the housekeeper and a television repairman as witnesses – and he had signed away without even reading it.

Rocky had warned her – up front – that unless she got the contract signed, he wasn't doing a thing.

Well ... once he realized who she was he'd had to protect himself, hadn't he? She was the under-age, unwanted daughter of – guess who? Silver Anderson. Sweet coincidence.

When Jack Python had walked into the beach house that night, three months ago, Rocky had thought the television king was her *boyfriend*. It soon became clear he was her uncle, and a very pissed off uncle at that. He had wasted no time in throwing Rocky out. Hey – it wasn't the first time.

Rocky had driven off into the night with no thought of ever seeing the kid again.

Two days later she called him. Out of curiosity he arranged a meet at Charmer's Market, in Venice.

When she arrived he sat her down, brought her a cup of coffee, and got the full scam.

She was Silver Anderson's kid. How could he resist?

First of all he came up with the legal papers giving him fifty-one percent of any deals. And once it was safely signed, he got hold of the guy he knew at College Records.

His contact was a major buyer, who was really only interested in scoring the best dope to supply to the recording company's biggest stars.

"I've gotta girl I wancha t'hear," Rocky told him. "She sings the ass off Madonna."

The man sighed wearily. "So does my niece, my janitor's daughter, my bookie's girlfriend, an' the checkout flim at Safeway. *This* is what I need from you." He then gave Rocky a hefty order for cocaine and Quaaludes.

Rocky filled the order, and shoved Heaven's tape at him. "She's Silver Anderson's kid," he said. "Pass this on to someone who can listen. If anythin' happens there'll be a cut for you."

A week later the man came back to him. "What does she look like?"

"A sixteen-year-old prick-tease. We're talkin' juicy."

"Get me over a picture. No snaps. Something professional."

"It's done."

Rocky had to wait for her to call him. He was bad news at the beach house – Uncle Jack had put up a few rules.

When she finally phoned he asked her about photographs.

"Antonio – you know, the famous photographer – has like these incredible shots," she said. "Only I can't get hold of them."

"Leave it t'me," Rocky said. "Just give me his address."

The next day he sauntered into Antonio's studio, displaying greased-up muscles and a crooked smile.

"Hiya, beauty," he said to the receptionist, who was all L.A. style – with punked hair, orange makeup, and sixties geometric clothes.

She stared at him. The last time she'd seen anyone who looked like Rocky was on a television programme called *Hollywood Close Up* – when they did a segment on Sylvester Stallone.

"Can I help you?" she asked.

"Baby – y'can help me all ya want. I'm yours!"

He ended up swapping a full ounce of prime coke for one twelve-by-fourteen glossy print of Heaven, which he had to admit was a dynamite photo.

"Don't you *dare* ever say where you got this," the receptionist warned. "It's appearing in *Bazaar* soon, and Antonio will kill me if he finds out I did this."

Rocky touched his lips with his index finger. "Your secret — my secret. I live by the code of silence."

Without showing the picture to Heaven, he delivered it to his contact, who must have handed it directly to the right person, for the next day Rocky got the call he'd been waiting for — "Bring her in."

So he did. And after that it all happened.

Now, here they were, months later, with a very hot record all set to hit the airwaves.

Hey — he'd had a hunch his break was on the way.

Heaven was it. And he owned fifty-one per cent of her.

*

She accepted everyone's compliments with a warm glow, hardly believing that it was finally happening for her. All she needed was the record to be a hit. And it would be. She *knew* it. Even though it wasn't exactly the record *she* would have made. For a start it wasn't a song that she'd written, and the arrangement was too upbeat — she would have preferred a slower tempo. And the title of the song — *Gonna Eatcha Tonight!* — was kind of gross. The lyrics were certainly bound to cause *mucho* controversy, which wasn't such a bad thing.

The hook went:

> I'm a Maneater . . . yes I am . . .
> Maneater . . . sure I am . . .
> Maneater . . . and baby —
> I'm gonna eatcha tonight!

Real sophisticated stuff. But she had given it her all. And it sure sounded good!

Sneaking a glance at Rocky she decided he looked pleased, and so he should, for he had half of her action, which as far as she was concerned he deserved. Without Rocky, none of this would have happened.

When Uncle Jack had walked into the aftermath of that bummed-out party, he had vented his wrath on poor Rocky — who was really innocent of any blame. After kicking him out of the house he had turned on her. "I don't want you *ever* seeing that creep again. Do you understand me?"

"Why?" she had asked defiantly.

"*Why?* Are you asking me *why*?"

She had never seen him so angry.

"I'll give you a list of reasons why." He continued in a tightly controlled voice. "One — he's a lowlife. Two — you're a child and he's almost old enough to be your father. Three — he's —" He stopped, exasperated. "What am I explaining this to you for? I trusted you and you let me down. In future you'll listen to me, and *when* I say you'll do something, you'll do it. No questions."

What a summer to look forward to! She was better off with her distracted grandfather.

As it happened, all turned out okay. After a few days Jack cooled down, and things returned to normal.

Secretly she contacted Rocky, and after the hassle of traipsing over to the Valley and getting George to sign the contract Rocky produced, it was all go.

Now she actually had a record ready to come out, and it was the most exciting day of her life!

Unfortunately there was nobody she could share it with. Only Rocky, for he was the only one who knew about it.

Soon, everyone would know. College Records planned a big party to launch her upon an unsuspecting world.

"They'd kinda like it if your mother came," Rocky had told her a couple of days ago.

"NO WAY!" she'd exploded. "Like I don't want any trading on *her* name or Jack's name. I really mean it."

"Forget it," he'd said easily. And promptly told the publicity department to drop the information into any column that would run it.

Hey — the kid was a kid — she'd soon learn. Use whatever you have.

Rocky loved the idea that he might soon become a successful personal manager. Jeez! What a kick. Just like Wes Money he could move into the big time without a backward glance. And taking a ride with the same family too. What a double kick! Wes got the old broad, and he got the kid. Not that he'd made a move on her — yet. There was plenty of time for that. Plenty.

Chapter 74

"Have you noticed the way he watches me?" Silver asked Nora edgily, as they sat in her dressing room eating a light lunch.

Nora picked an olive out of her salad and put it to one side. "They should only allow those things in drinks," she grumbled.

"Listen to me when I'm speaking to you," Silver said authoritatively. "Zachary Klinger can't take his eyes off me."

"I'd be flattered if I was you."

"You are *not* me – thank God! And stop being so flippant."

Nora crunched on a lettuce leaf. "The man had an affair with you. He's never forgotten it. That's not such a crime, is it?"

"You don't *know* Zachary. When he wants something, he *always* gets it. He was like that when I was with him before, and he wasn't as powerful then as he is now."

"So?"

"He makes me nervous."

Nora swallowed a laugh. The thought of Silver Anderson nervous about anything was too ridiculous to contemplate. Silver ate people for breakfast, and spat them out half-digested. On this film she had already seen to it that three crew members were fired because she didn't like their "attitude".

"You'll get a reputation for being difficult," Nora had warned her.

"Professional," Silver had corrected. "There *is* a difference, you know."

Silver thought everyone on the film loved her. Some of them did. Some of them didn't. Right now the crew was split into three camps – Silver's, Carlos Brent's, and Orville Gooseberger's. The poor director didn't have a chance. He just shot the script and hoped for the best.

That afternoon there was a heavy love scene scheduled between Silver and Carlos.

Nora watched her pop a piece of raw garlic in her mouth and suck on it. "What *are* you doing?" she asked, as if she didn't know.

"It's *so* good for the blood," Silver replied innocently.

"Breathe it over Zachary," Nora remarked. "*That'll* get rid of him forever."

"You're not taking this seriously," Silver scolded. "What if he decides to . . . do something to Wes?"

This time Nora *did* laugh aloud. "I'd like to see any*one* do any*thing* to Mr Money that he doesn't want done. Your husband can look after himself. Of that I'm sure." She pushed the salad away and reached for a cigarette. "And talking of family, how long is it since you've seen Heaven? It's her birthday next week, you know."

"She's not a child," Silver responded sharply. "The phone works both ways. She could have congratulated me on my marriage."

"Did you invite her?"

Abruptly Silver stood up. "Are you trying to aggravate me? Is that it? Sometimes, Nora dear, you're a real pain."

Nora drew deeply on her cigarette. The mystery of Silver and her daughter continued to confound her. Whatever the circumstances of the child's birth, flesh was flesh, and Silver *had* kept Heaven with her until she was ten. "Shall I send her a present from you?" she inquired.

"Do what you like."

Nora decided to mention it to Wes. Maybe *he* could persuade Silver to change her attitude. Now that they had been married for a few months, Nora found she was changing her opinion of him. He had certainly done wonders for his wife's career. And so far all her hard-earned cash was still intact.

Wes Money — the mystery man — could turn out to be a surprise winner after all.

*

The eruption took place the moment they clung together in romantic bliss.

"Goddammit!" screamed Carlos Brent. "The fucking bitch has got a mouthful of fucking garlic!"

"Language! Language!" chided Silver, infuriating her co-star even more.

371

Orville, hovering on the set as was his habit, leaped into the fray. "Carlos. I'm sure you're mistaken."

"Mistaken, for crissake. You can smell the fucking bitch from here to Palm Springs!"

Zachary K. Klinger stepped out of the shadows. "I hardly think that's a gentlemanly way to address Miss Anderson," he said menacingly.

"Go fuck yourself," snapped Carlos. "Who gives a shit *what* you think?"

Zachary, who was only a few years older than Carlos Brent, but at least four inches taller and fifty pounds heavier, hauled off and hit him straight on the chin.

Carlos staggered and fell.

An amazed silence took over the set.

Silver broke it with a small, triumphant laugh. "Well," she said succinctly. "I guess that takes care of shooting for today. Can we all go home, please, Orville, dear?"

*

"Where are you from?" Wes asked curiously.

"Why do you want to know?" Unity replied.

He sat on a corner of her desk in wet swim-shorts. "Is it a secret?"

"Virginia," she replied shortly.

"I've never been there," he said, sizing her up and deciding that whatever her reasons she was lying. "Do you still have family living there?"

"No family," she said shortly. "They all got it in a train wreck. I came to California with a man. He left me. End of life story."

"Pretty exciting stuff."

"Yeah. Do you think they'll buy it for the movies?" she said sarcastically. "It'd be a natural for Sissy Spacek. She plays all the losers, doesn't she?"

Regarding her warily he wondered what was going to happen to her. This time he'd been around to give her a helping hand. It wasn't always going to be that way.

Outside, in the garden, Vladimir tried to see what was going on in the pool house. Ever since Madame's husband had brought that girl home, saying she was his cousin, Vladimir had harboured a deep suspicion. *He* thought they might be lovers. *He* thought they could be planning to *murder* Madame and run off with all her money.

This was America.

Anything could happen.

Chapter 75

Jack awoke with a sudden jolt, automatically groped for his watch, and realized it was only four in the morning and he was not alone. Jade was asleep beside him. She lay on her side, her arms stretched languorously above her head, the sheet tangled around her waist.

The window shade was up, and a misty dawn filtered through the windows casting a faint morning light.

Leaning back against the headboard he watched her intently as she lay motionless. God! She was so beautiful and desirable. There was something about her that really reached out to him. And it wasn't just a sexual attraction, although the sex was incredible. Instinctively he knew Jade Johnson was destined to be much more than just a great time in bed. He had known it the first time he saw her.

Stirring in her sleep, she shifted slightly.

"Hey," he said, very softly. "Are you awake?"

"Mmmm . . ." she murmured, still fast asleep.

Gently he reached out and touched her breasts, lightly caressing her nipples.

"Mmmm . . . ." she sighed again.

Caught up in the sharp burn of desire, he felt as if he hadn't been with a woman in months, and yet, only a few hours ago, they had made love twice with hardly a pause for breath.

Christ! He, who usually had such admirable control, was ready for lift-off almost immediately.

Sliding down beside her, he let his hands roam her body, as his insistent hardness pressed up against her cool, smooth skin.

She was asleep – but she felt him.

She was asleep – but she wanted him.

How little she knew of Jack Python, and yet already he was an addiction. Her eyelids fluttered – almost awake ... almost.

He teased her breasts with his tongue – slowly – surely – small strokes destined to stimulate and excite her.

What was it about this man? Arousal was immediate.

Stretching luxuriously she whispered, "Is it morning?"

"I guess if you usually have breakfast around four a.m. we can consider this morning."

"Oh, no! Why are you waking me?"

His laugh was husky contentment. "Take an educated guess, beautiful lady,"

She felt a deep flood of pleasure, and opened up to allow this intimate stranger to transport her to the edge of ecstasy.

He was filled with pure energy as they began the incredible ride.

Almost immediately she was swept away, her breathing constricted, a rush of voluptuous sensuality waiting to explode.

Usually he could wait. It was a trick, a game. Making love was an art.

And yet, with Jade, he couldn't even consider waiting. They were so in tune, and conscious of each other's every need.

He rode her with a compelling exquisite certainty. They were heading in the same direction ... Breathing the same intoxicating air ...

"Ohhh ... God! This ... is ... *sooo* ... fantastic ..."

A sudden jolting rush.

A simultaneous shudder of satisfaction.

And then a slow, dreamy drift back to sleep, once again wrapped contentedly in each other's arms. Two soulmates who had finally found each other.

*

"Good morning." Jade ventured onto the set, fully made up with her hair done, ready to shoot the second batch of Cloud commercials. She'd had two hours' sleep, but it didn't matter. Everything about her was alive and glowing.

Shane Dickson threw her a stony look. "Feeling better?" he asked sarcastically.

"I'm sorry about rushing off last night," she said apologetically. "I couldn't help it."

Shane was a picture of jealous fury. "Was he as good as his reputation?" he asked bitterly.

She ignored the question.

"I'm surprised at *you*," he said incredulously. "Miss Commitment and Caring. According to Kellie – who was completely humiliated by the entire incident – Jack Python sticks it into anything that doesn't struggle."

She refused to be baited into a conversation about Jack. Maybe she was dreaming, but as far as she was concerned, from now on he belonged to her, and she belonged to him.

Not that they'd discussed it. In fact they hadn't discussed anything at all. Just savoured the unlimited pleasures of each other's body. In the early morning she'd had to leave while he still slept. A cab took her home to change, and then a car picked her up and delivered her to the studio, where she'd sat dreamily in the makeup room thinking about him.

She smiled. A big, satisfied smile which irritated Shane even more.

"Wipe that dumb grin off your face," he said brusquely. "Today we're shooting the dream sequence."

She didn't feel at all like working. She just felt like smiling and singing and looning about.

Was it like this with the English asshole at first?

She couldn't remember. In fact she couldn't remember one damn thing about Lord Mark Rand, except that he was married, and a liar.

*

She was gone.

He groped for her cool velvet body and found that she was no longer there.

Jack got up and investigated. She was not in the bathroom. Her clothes, left trailing across the living room floor last night, were missing. The lady – as the saying goes – had vanished.

Disappointment flooded over him. And then he found her note in the kitchen, propped against the toaster, and the moment he read it he felt great.

> Good morning. Thank you for putting a smile on my face that will probably stay there until I die! If I was with you now I'd make you toast, or maybe I'd just make you . . .

Gone to work to shoot a commercial. I'll be home after seven. If you want me to, I'll cook for you.

JADE

He was doing his show later, and the guest was an interesting and controversial senator. Last night, after dinner with Kellie, he had planned to read a lengthy bio on the man. Now he couldn't even concentrate on getting dressed, let alone anything else.

Throwing on clothes, he headed for the studio, where he immediately instructed Aretha to send six dozen yellow roses to Jade Johnson.

"Is this persuasion or thanks?" Aretha asked jauntily.

"Don't be so inquisitive."

"Any message along with the flowers?"

"Just say 'And you cook too?' Have them put a question mark *and* an exclamation point."

Aretha rolled her eyes knowingly. "My, oh my! I guess that answers the question!"

"Oh, and have somebody call that French actress we had on – you know who I mean."

"Big bazoombas and a frog in her throat?"

"You got it. In fact, do me a favour and call her yourself. Lie a lot on my behalf. Tell her I can't make dinner tonight."

Aldrich hurried into the office looking harried, his usual expression on the day of a show. "Have you read all the material?" he asked anxiously.

"Honey," sighed Aretha, "the only thing *this* man read last night was the stars in his lady's eyes!"

*

"It's not going to work," Shane said shortly. "Can't you at least try?"

"I *am* trying," Jade replied patiently. He had been on her case all day.

"You're supposed to look ethereal and dreamy. Why are you grinning like a fucking Cheshire Cat?"

They both knew only too well why she was grinning, and it wasn't helping matters.

"Imagine something serious," he said sternly. "Like getting AIDS or the clap. That's what happens when you sleep with a person who fucks like he's on an assembly line."

376

The smile disappeared from her face. "That's an uncalled-for, *dumb* remark."

"Think about it," he repeated vehemently. "I'm only telling you what everybody in this town already knows."

"No. *You* think about *this*," she said furiously. "*I'm* the star of this commercial. *You're* the director. You can be replaced – *I* can't."

She hadn't planned on being quite so forthright, but he'd been asking for it all day.

After her outburst, they finally got some work done, and she was able to get out of there just after six. Instructing her driver to stop at the Irvine Ranch Market in the Beverly Center, she bought thin slices of veal, potatoes and vegetables, butter pecan ice cream, a rich chocolate cake, and two bottles of wine.

Gathering an armful of fresh flowers, she rushed home, where she was surprised by an apartment full of glorious yellow roses, placed in vases by her cleaning lady – and Jack's voice on her answering machine. Listening to his message three times, she glowed with delight.

How was it possible to be *this* crazy *this* fast?

She didn't know and she didn't care.

I'm doing the show today, said his voice on the machine. *And after that I can't think of anything I'd like more than you cooking for me.* A pause. *Yes, as a matter of fact I can. Let's forget about food. I'll see you later.*

He had a great voice. A great everything else.

She put Springsteen on the stereo, and without a trace of tiredness began to unpack the groceries.

Chapter 76

"I gotta fly to Arizona," Howard announced disgustedly.

"Why?" Poppy demanded.

"Because Whitney Valentine is trying out for cunt of the year."

Poppy pursed her lips. "You know I don't like that word, Howard."

"Sometimes there's just no substitute."

"Try and find one," she said sternly.

"Back off, Poppy. I'm not in the mood for your 'holier than thou' number."

One thing about Poppy, she knew exactly how far she could go, and when he told her to back off she did so at once.

"I've had a day that was pure murder from beginning to end," he grumbled, and proceeded to tell her about the Silver/Carlos/Zachary incident on the set.

Her eyes widened. "Zachary Klinger actually *hit* Carlos Brent?"

"Punched him right out."

"What's going to happen?"

"Guess who spent the afternoon sorting it out?"

"You, of course."

"Right on. Silver started it all. Another cunt."

"Howard!"

He held up a restraining hand. "Okay, okay, no more cunts."

"Is everyone speaking?"

"Barely. Carlos is threatening to walk – and he can do it – you know the kind of temper *he* has. The good thing is that he needs us more than we need him. What other studio is gonna give a burnt-out bum like him the lead in a twenty-million-dollar movie?"

"Oh, Howard," Poppy exclaimed, little-girl voice in full swing. "You're so clever!"

Poppy knew how to trowel on the flattery just when it was needed.

"Anyway," he continued, "we had to stop shooting for the rest of the day, and hopefully, by tomorrow, all will be calm."

"Shouldn't you be here to make sure?"

"You bet your ass I should. But we've got bigger problems on *The Murder*. If I don't get down there and get Whitney's ass back in gear, *that* production's gonna have to stop. She's only playing a cameo role, but all her stuff takes place on the location shoot in Arizona."

"And what's she doing?"

"Pretending to be sick, which is bull. She's pissed off because Mannon and Clarissa are steamin' up the screen."

"Isn't Chuck with her?"

"He was. And yesterday they had another fight and he took off. That's when the – uh – that's when she supposedly got sick and took to her bed."

"It's so unfair," Poppy wailed. "All these problems, and only *you* to solve them."

"I'll do it," he said bravely, thinking this might be the perfect opportunity to fling a fast fuck into Whitney. God knows, he'd waited long enough.

"Shall I pack you an overnight bag?" Poppy asked, the concerned wife.

"You'd better. I shouldn't be gone for more than twenty-four hours."

He was on the company plane shortly afterwards.

Poppy, left to her own devices, called Carmel to find out Orville's version of the story. Then she reported the entire event to Ida, who already knew, and couldn't have cared less anyway.

"Don't forget my lunch tomorrow for Jade Johnson," she reminded everyone. "The Bistro Garden, at twelve-thirty."

She tried to decide whether to call Melanie-Shanna or not. *No*, she thought. Very soon Melanie-Shanna could be the *ex* Mrs Mannon Cable, and there was nothing more boring than having to pretend to be friends with an ex-wife. Once the husband was no longer around, what was the point?

On the other hand, shouldn't someone *tell* Melanie-Shanna about Mannon and Clarissa? After all, it was only fair that she should know. If Howard was dropping his pants elsewhere,

379

Poppy would most *certainly* want to be alerted. *And* the poor girl was about to give birth any minute, so maybe Mannon wouldn't dump her, and she would remain Mrs Cable.

Poppy sighed. Ah, decisions, decisions. Her manicured hand reached for the phone.

*

Dirk Price, the director/writer of *The Murder*, met Howard at the airport in Arizona. He was a long-haired, twenty-eight-year-old graduate of UCLA Film School, and had made two other movies, both of them teen-oriented (naked virgins, horny boys and the trashing of public property) and both of them enormous money-makers. This was his first venture into grown-up territory, and the dailies — flown to Howard in Hollywood every day — were quite impressive. Especially Mannon's performance: he was really marvellous, surprising everyone. Clarissa, of course, was incandescent as usual. And Whitney looked sensational and acted like she'd just got out of drama school.

"I want to replace her," were the first words out of Dirk's mouth. "She's ruining my film."

"*Our* film," Howard corrected. "And we have a contract to honour."

"She's not honouring *her* part of it," Dirk said heatedly. "I had to shoot around her all day, and it's going to put us over budget."

"That's why I'm here. I'll talk to her."

"Why can't we just pay her off?" Dirk demanded. His long hair was tied back in a ponytail, and he wore one diamond stud earring.

"Because," Howard replied patiently, feeling about eighty-five years old, "we can't. It's as simple as that."

"Fuck!" snapped Dirk.

Howard patted his toupee to make sure all was in place. Dirk had a receding hairline. What good was all that hair at the back going to do him when there was nothing left up front?

They had booked him a room in the same hotel as Whitney, and he showered and changed clothes before going to visit her.

The door of her suite was opened by her stand-in, who also doubled as her secretary. "Mr Soloman," the woman said. "Thank goodness you're here. Whitney has been expecting you."

She waited, sitting cross-legged in the middle of her bed. She wore a pale pink tracksuit, pastel running shoes, and a petulant expression. Her trademark hair was tamed in two schoolgirlish braids, and her face was devoid of makeup, although with her healthy tan that didn't matter.

He felt a message from Father Christmas, and hoped that it wasn't obvious in the light grey pants he had slipped on with a casual sweater.

"Howard!" she wailed. "They're trying to crucify me!"

"Who?" he asked patiently, sitting on the edge of the bed.

"All of them!" Her aquamarine eyes filled with true tears.

Ah . . . if she could only act *on* the screen like she could *off* it.

"Tell me everything, baby," he soothed.

Lower lip quivering, she came out with a litany of complaints. The director didn't want her; Clarissa was a bitch; the crew weren't friendly; Mannon was a bastard; everyone was ganging up against her.

"After all, Howard," she finished off indignantly, "I accepted a cameo role in this movie, when I *should* have been playing the lead."

"I know," he agreed sympathetically. "And you won't regret it. This role will open up all the doors you ever wanted. You're obliterating Clarissa in the dailies. It's *your* film."

She brightened considerably. "Really?"

"Would I lie?"

"You know I trust you."

Trust me with this, he wanted to say, as his hard-on chafed uncomfortably in place.

"Listen, baby," he said. "Don't be your own worst enemy. Get your fanny back on the set tomorrow – *pronto*! You're makin' Clarissa a very happy woman by not showing up for work. She figures *this* way she'll be able to squeeze you out." He paused, getting ready to nail a point. "And if you don't . . . jeez, Whit, the lawyers are gonna move into action, an' there'll be nothing I can do. I'd hate to see you ruin your career with one dumb move."

She stared at him thoughtfully, mouth downturned and expression intent.

And then – like the sun appearing from behind a cloud – she smiled. Whitney Valentine had the most dazzling smile in the world. A lot of teeth and very patriotic.

"You're damn right, Howard. And I love you for being so honest." Crawling across the bed she kissed him.

The kiss was aimed at his cheek, only he managed to move

quickly enough for it to land on his mouth. Grabbing her in a bear hug, he gave her the famous Howard Soloman smackerooney. In high school his kisses were the stuff legends were made of.

She gave a little struggle — not too hard — and then he had her! She was responding. And there it was, a long, passionate, real soul kiss.

Pushing him away at last she sighed, "Oh, Howard, we shouldn't be doing this, you're married."

"In name only," he said, faster than the speed of sound. "Since we had Roselight, Poppy can't have sex. The doctors say it's psychological. We're working on it. Meanwhile I'm still a man, Whitney. And a lonely one."

"Surely not lonely? You have so many opportunities . . ." She trailed off.

"I've thought about this moment for years," he said excitedly. "You, me . . . Nobody else around . . ."

She didn't believe his story about Poppy for a minute; however, an affair with Howard would certainly secure her position on the set, *and* infuriate Mannon — who might not care about her anymore, but would no doubt be affected if she and another of his ex-best friends got together.

"Later," she promised in a low whisper. "After dinner. Just you . . . and me . . ."

Chapter 77

"Get that *horrible* dog away from me," Silver screamed. "For God's sake, Wes, it's filthy!"

"He's not," he argued, ruffling Mutt's fur.

"And I suppose you're going to tell me it doesn't have fleas either?"

"Naw. Except this one!" He plucked an imaginary insect from Mutt's shaggy coat and waved it at her.

She shrieked hysterically, while he doubled up laughing. "Only joking," he confessed.

Glaring at him she hissed, "You stupid bastard. I don't know *how* I ended up marrying someone with the mentality of a ten-year-old."

"Easy. You married me for my money."

"Oh, so *that's* what it was."

"And my charm."

"Why didn't *I* think of that?"

"And my big dick."

"I've seen bigger," she sniffed.

"Yeah?"

"Absolutely."

"Well, cop a look at *this*, lady."

Soon they were playing games on her king-size bed, while Mutt raced excitedly up and down the carpet, barking.

"Get . . . rid . . . of . . . it," she warned insistently.

"Now?"

"*Right* now."

"Are you sure you want me to stop?"

"*Right now, Wes*. I am *not* joking."

With a grunt of resignation he rolled off the bed, grabbed the dog by the scruff of its neck, and gently shoved it out of the room.

"I *never* want to see that animal in here again," she said, watching him intently as he walked back towards the bed. She never tired of checking out his body. He was so masculine. His strength impressed her, and his complete lack of ego when it came to his looks. An actor would kill to get near a mirror first. Wes couldn't care less. He had a natural animal sexuality, and she loved it, and he knew it, which made them both very happy.

So he was younger than her. She really didn't give a damn. It was the ridiculous newspapers and gossip columns who made it into some sort of big deal. She was hardly snatching him from the cradle. Carlos Brent was sixty something, and his current girlfriend, Dee Dee Dionne, was in her early thirties. There was at least thirty years between them and nobody said a word.

Wes climbed into bed and clicked the television on with the remote control.

Silver took it from him and switched it off. "We were in the middle of something," she reminded.

He looked surprised. "We were?"

"Yes."

"Jeez .. I got me a mother of a headache . . ."

She threw a magazine at him. "Don't start with me."

Grinning, he said, "I thought that's exactly what you wanted."

★

Downstairs, Vladimir prepared dinner, while Unity, out in the pool house office, fielded phone calls. They were coming in fast and strong: Orville Gooseberger to speak to Wes; Zachary Klinger for Silver; three calls from Zeppo White for Wes; Poppy Soloman for Silver; Nora for either Wes or Silver.

However urgent any of them said it was, Unity had strict instructions never to disturb the happy couple while they were upstairs in the bedroom. Dutifully she took messages, and promised everyone their calls would be returned in due course.

At six o'clock she decided she was finished for the day, and turned on the answering machine. This job was no big deal. Sure, she was grateful to Wes for helping at a time when she needed it — but the loneliness of living in the huge mansion with nobody to talk to was beginning to get to her. Queen Silver and ever-faithful Wes. Who needed it?

She wandered into the kitchen, where Vladimir ignored her as usual. He had hardly spoken more than three full sentences to her since her arrival.

"What are you making?" she asked.

"Chinese chicken salad," he replied resentfully. He hated having Unity around all the time, certain that she spied on him, making it difficult for him to smuggle in his transient lovers. Even in his own apartment above the garage he had no privacy. She had knocked on his door the other day for some inane reason. "It's my time off," he had shouted through the closed door. "Vill you *never* please disturb me here again."

The Italian waiter he was servicing at that particular moment became paranoid that it was his wife searching for him, and was unable to get it up. Vladimir was livid.

"Can I taste it?" Unity asked. "It looks delicious."

"There's not enough," Vladimir replied waspishly. "The cold spaghetti in the fridge is for you."

Mutt came bouncing into the kitchen, wagging his stubby tail.

She bent to fuss the little dog.

"No animals in the kitchen vhile I'm preparing food," snapped Vladimir.

"I wish you could be halfway polite," she snapped back, surprising both of them. Up until now she had acted like a timid mouse and not complained about anything.

He recovered at once. "Vat vill you do? Report me to your . . . *cousin*?" he sneered.

Her face reddened. "I'm not a spy," she retorted hotly.

He was glad to hear *that*. But he made no comment, continuing to cut and slice and chop.

"Listen to me," she said sharply. "The truth is I hardly know my cousin. He's just helping me out because I was in trouble."

Finally she had Vladimir's interest. "Vat kind of trouble?" he asked curiously. "Vere you pregnant?"

"No." She shook her head. "Nothing like that. It was . . . drugs."

Vladimir perked up even more. Laying his work knife aside, he put a sympathetic arm around her shoulders. "Vhy don't you tell me all about it?"

★

Wes left Silver to bathe and dress, and loped downstairs. He couldn't smell anything cooking, which was a disappointment. Vladimir, in spite of his numerous faults, was at least a knockout cook – the one reason Wes hadn't dismissed him the moment he moved in.

Flinging open the door to the kitchen he was startled to find Unity and the gay Russian sitting at a table engaged in intimate conversation. He was startled. Up until now the two of them had managed to stay out of each other's way, which suited him just fine. He didn't want Unity revealing anything – especially about his past.

"What's going on? Where's dinner?" he asked.

Vladimir was on his feet in a second. "Is Madame ready to eat?" he inquired solicitously.

"Yeah, she's ready," Wes replied. "What is it?"

"Chinese chicken salad," Vladimir replied, scurrying back to his chopping board.

"Chinese chicken *what*?"

"Salad."

"You mean it isn't hot?"

"No."

"Shit!"

"Madame requested it personally. She mentioned that in her opinion you could lose a pound or two." Vladimir knew he had scored a point and enjoyed Wes's discomfort.

"Did she?" Wes stalked from the kitchen, followed by Unity, who relayed his messages to him. "Put them on my desk in the study," he said shortly. "I'll return the calls after dinner."

"Mr White said it was urgent. So did Mr Gooseberger."

"Okay, okay."

Settling himself in the study he placed a call to Orville. The producer had never telephoned him before, and he was curious to know what it was about.

"Did Silver tell you what she did today?" shouted Orville.

"No," Wes replied.

"You mean you don't know?"

"Spit it out, Orville. I never liked *Twenty Questions*."

"We had to close the set down this afternoon. Silver had a chunk of garlic hidden in her mouth when she kissed Carlos. He went berserk and insulted her, and Zachary came to her defence. Carlos then insulted *him*, and Zachary knocked Carlos out."

Wes did not believe what he was hearing. All this had taken place and she hadn't mentioned a word.

"Go on," he said flatly.

"Well," Orville continued, "between Zeppo, me and Howard Soloman, I think we got everyone calmed down. However, tomorrow is another day, and I don't trust your wife. For some reason she's got a knife at Carlos's throat. I think she'd like him to walk off the picture. The gossip on the set is she thinks he's too old for the part, and wants a younger co-star."

"Yeah?"

"I don't have to explain to *you* what it would mean to this production if Carlos Brent walks. You're a businessman, you understand these things."

"I sure do."

"So .. Howard, Zeppo and I thought it might be a good idea for you to accompany her to the set tomorrow and whenever you can, to keep an eye on things. If you'll excuse my French – when you've got a difficult woman on your hands, the one who controls her is the one who's *fucking* her. In my experience it always works."

Wes laughed without humour. "Yeah. I get your point. I'll try an' be there."

Orville thanked him effusively and hung up – whereupon Wes had an almost identical conversation with Zeppo White, who was slightly cruder than the old producer, but made exactly the same point.

By the time he was finished with the two of them, he was furious. Why hadn't she told him? What was he? The houseboy? The lackey to screw in the afternoon when she had nothing better to do? Didn't she have any respect for him?

Striding angrily into the hall, he picked up the keys of the Rolls and yelled, "Vladimir!"

The flaxen-haired Russian appeared at the door of the kitchen.

"Tell *Madame* that I *will not* be home for the Chinese chicken salad. And tell her that I won't be back until later – *much* later. If at all."

With that he stalked out of the house.

Chapter 78

" 'Ellooo, Jacques." The French actress with the inviting eyes and smoky voice was in the Green Room when he put his head around the door a few minutes before showtime. Tantalizingly she undulated across the room, kissing him on both cheeks with Gallic style, drenching him in a powerful musk scent. She was dressed all in scarlet.

Senator Peter Richmond, his guest for the evening, jumped up and followed her over. "Jack." His handshake was hearty. "Good to see you again. I'm looking forward to crossing swords with you tonight. Only be gentle – it's my first time – with you, that is," he added with a twinkle.

Searching desperately for Aretha, Jack tried to figure out what was going on. Signals were crossed somewhere along the line. Aretha was supposed to have cancelled his date with Danielle

Vadeeme, and unless she was here to be with the very married Senator Richmond he was in trouble.

He gave them both the benefit of a friendly smile. "It's my pleasure to have you here, Senator."

"I flew in specially." The Senator winked. "And Miss Vadeeme here has invited me to join you both for dinner. I keep on telling her the last thing you want is me along, but she absolutely insists. At least I'll have something to look forward to while I endure a full hour's torture!"

"With time out for commercials," Jack said, automatic charm on full pilot, thinking how he would strangle Aretha when he found her, although murder was probably too gentle a punishment.

Meanwhile, what was he supposed to do about Jade? He could hardly ask her along. And yet all he wanted was to be with her.

"Five minutes, Mr Python," yelled Genie, the assistant floor manager.

Senator Richmond's researcher hurried to his side.

Danielle leaned close to Jack. "Later, *chéri*," she whispered seductively. "We get reeed of Meester Senator, an then we make the — how you say — beeeauteefool looove."

He had no desire to make anything again, unless it was with Jade. Christ! How did he ever get caught in this trap?

"Where's Aretha?" he asked Genie, as he followed her to the studio ready to confront his expectant audience.

"In the booth, I guess," she replied.

"Goddammit!"

"Something wrong?"

"Get a message to Aretha and tell her to call Jade Johnson. Have her say I can't make it, I'm going to be held up at the studio, and I'll contact her later. I want that taken care of at once."

"Yes *sir*!"

*

Jade changed into jeans and a sweater. Then she changed the sweater three times. Then she changed the jeans for tracksuit pants, hated the way they bagged, and changed back into jeans.

First, she had scrubbed off her studio makeup, applying a much more subtle look, and had washed her hair, leaving it to dry naturally — framing her face with a wild tumble of shaggy curls.

High on pure energy, she went to work in the kitchen, marinating the veal in lemon, slicing potatoes, chopping parsley, stringing *mange-tout*.

Next she soaked strawberries in Grand Marnier, and whipped sour cream with brown sugar.

Not bothering to set the table, she laid place-mats on the coffee table in front of the television, just in case he felt like watching *Hill Street Blues*. And if he didn't, she put Sade on the stereo.

After opening a bottle of cold white wine, she switched on the television, just in time for the beginning of his show. *Face to Face with Python*.

Happily she settled down to watch.

*

The Senator was affable and slippery, a true politician who answered all questions with bland good nature, at the same time getting in every point he wished to make.

Jack found him an interesting study. How could one man talk such a crock, and *still* manage to come across as disarmingly nice? Senator Richmond succeeded. And for once Jack let him get away with it – his mind elsewhere.

"That was one prize of a sluggish hour!" a frustrated Aldrich complained after the event. "You gave him the chair. For Christ's sake, Jack, it was the Peter Richmond show."

"Where's Aretha?" Jack asked tightly, ignoring the criticism. "I said –"

"I *heard* what you said. I'm not in the mood to discuss it."

He found Aretha in the office. When she saw him coming she gestured helplessly. "I know, I know. I'm sorry. What can I tell you?"

"You can tell me what the fuck happened."

"I *did* telephone Danielle earlier. She wasn't in, so I spoke to some foreign person who seemed to understand the message I left."

"Which was?"

"That you had to cancel dinner. I even spelled your name, just to make sure."

Shaking his head he paced around the office. "Now not only do I have to take *her* to dinner, I'm stuck with the goddamn Senator too. You're incompetent, you know that?" He snatched a cigarette from her desk. "What did Jade say?"

"Uh . . . Jade," she said blankly.

"Don't tell me you screwed that up, too?"

Aretha looked vague. "Was I supposed to do something?"

"Jesus Christ!" Now he was really angry. "Haven't you phoned her yet?"

Frowning, she said, "Stop screaming at me please."

Taking a deep breath he said patiently, "I told Genie to pass you a message in the control booth to call Jade and tell her I can't make it tonight. Did you do that?"

"Oh yeah, yeah."

"How did she sound?"

"Calm."

He gave a resigned sigh. "Book me a table for three at Chasen's."

"You got it."

As soon as he walked out of the room she grabbed her phone book. Genie had passed on no such message, and Aretha knew that as soon as Jack heard the news he would fire the girl. Genie was new and enthusiastic, and Aretha didn't want to see that happen.

Covering up for her, she made the call. It was nearly nine-thirty.

*

Putting down the phone, Jade couldn't help feeling a wave of disappointment. Why hadn't he called himself? Why had he waited until nearly nine-thirty to have someone phone and cancel for him?

"Jack has to have dinner with the Senator," his assistant had explained.

If that was so, why hadn't he asked her to accompany them?

Maybe she was expecting too much. After all, she knew her own feelings, but to Jack Python perhaps she *was* just another one-night stand.

Anger flushed her face. He had a reputation, Shane had warned her – why hadn't she listened? The roses were probably standard practice. And she had acted like a gullible idiot.

Well, there was no way she was going to sit around and cry. Corey had called yesterday and invited her to a private party for Petrii, the New York dress designer.

Antonio had also left a message on her machine insisting she be there. And that's exactly what she intended to do.

*

It didn't take a genius to figure out that the very married Senator had eyes for the provocative French actress. With a little creative match-making, Jack decided he could be out of Chasen's in an hour, and if Jade still wanted to see him . . .

He thought about her as Danielle droned on in her monotonous smoky voice, and the Senator's eyes feasted hungrily on her cleavage. There was something wonderfully different about Jade. Beautiful and exciting as she was, those attributes were not the main attraction. She was a free spirit. He'd sensed it the first time he saw her, and now that they'd embarked on a relationship he wanted to get to know her properly. In fact, he couldn't wait . . .

Glancing impatiently at his watch, he decided he could slide off and phone her without being missed. "Excuse me," he said politely.

As if they'd notice.

*

The doorman summoned a cab, and she was on her way, having quickly changed into a short black leather dress worn with masses of silver jewellery.

"Chasen's," she told the Iranian driver, who took off as if he was being pursued by half the L.A.P.D.

In the cab she lit a cigarette, had one drag, then stubbed it out. Opening up her purse she took out her compact and carefully checked her makeup. She noted — with a buzz of annoyance — that she had that look about her. The glow of really great love-making. Ah . . . if only someone could bottle it, they'd make the fortune of all time.

God *damn* Jack Python. Why had he walked into her life?

The cab driver began to talk, while executing his death-defying dash along Wilshire. "Where you from, lady?"

"New York," she muttered, not wishing to engage one second of his concentration.

"I thought so. You look New York. I got two brothers live there. One — he marry this beautiful girl. The other, he . . ."

She stopped listening, wishing that she'd taken her car instead of subjecting herself to the driver's family history.

*

There was no answer in Jade's apartment. Her machine wasn't on, so he couldn't even leave a message.

She's probably gone out, he thought. After all, he couldn't expect her to just sit around waiting for his call. Now, if he could only get rid of the Senator and Danielle at a reasonable hour, he might drop by her apartment and wait for her.

The thought cheered him. He wasn't prepared to be patient.

As soon as he returned to the table, Senator Richmond jumped up. "I have an early appointment tomorrow morning," he said, by way of explanation.

"You do?"

"Seven-thirty."

Danielle extended her hand. "*Au revoir*, Senator."

"Goodnight, Miss . . . uh . . . Vadeeme. It was a real pleasure."

"*My* pleeeasurrre, Senator."

Jack looked from one to the other. What was going on here? He had thought they were all set.

The Senator made a fast exit, leaving him stuck with Danielle.

Snaking her hand along the back of his neck she moved closer. "He want me to sleep with heem," she whispered huskily. "I promise to veesit hees hotel later." With a mysterious smile she added, "What I do, Jacques?"

Without a doubt she expected him to tell her no way. And normally he would have done so, but now things were different, and all he desired was to get rid of her.

"Hey . . . Danielle," he said sensibly. "A promise is a promise."

Disbelief crossed her face. Danielle Vadeeme was used to men getting down on their knees. "You sonofabeetch!" she exclaimed in surprise.

"I may be a sonofabitch, but I'm a truthful one," he said, lightening his words with a killer smile.

Staring at him knowingly she said, "What happen, Jacques? You fall for someone?"

Nodding, he was almost embarrassed to admit such a weakness.

With a Gallic shrug she said, "Then why you weeth me, *chéri*?"

"Circumstances."

"Ah, Jacques. You *sooo Américain*." And she patted him on the hand matter-of-factly. "We go. I veesit the Senator. And you . . ." Another shrug.

Miss Vadeeme was a very understanding lady.

*

Naturally the cab driver did not have change for the fifty Jade offered him. It just wasn't her night.

"I'll get it broken," she said irritably, walking into Chasen's and stopping at the front desk for change.

The driver followed, obviously thinking she was going to vanish out the back. He was still babbling on about thieves and robbers and the dangers of carrying more than twenty dollars in change.

She broke the fifty and gave him his money, whereupon he left with a grunt.

Turning to go in, she was stopped by a hand on her arm. "Jade?" said an unfamiliar voice.

She turned and looked into the eyes of a complete stranger.

Seeing she didn't recognize him, he introduced himself. "Hi, I'm Penn Sullivan. We met with Beverly D'Amo a few months ago at Mortons. I was with Frances Cavendish – the casting agent. It was a business dinner."

Looking faintly amused she said, "It was?" Then she remembered him. Beverly had said he was an actor. "I hope it did you some good," she added, also remembering the terse exchange between him and the elderly casting woman in the parking lot.

Brushing his hand through a wiry mass of hair he said, "I'm working. It beats waiting tables – which I did for *three* years in this town."

He couldn't be more than early-twenties, and he was undeniably attractive.

"I'm going to the Petrii party. Are you having dinner here?" he asked.

"I'm here for the Petrii party too," she said.

"Alone?" he asked, definitely coming on.

*

Jack helped Danielle from the table. As Howard would put it - the old French broad had come up trumps. Maybe as a favour he would introduce her to Howard, get him to put her in one of his films. In France she was a huge star, but in America she had yet to break through in a meaningful way. After all, she was behaving like a lady, and he admired her style.

Putting a friendly arm around her shoulders, he began to walk her towards the entrance.

*

Just as Jade was about to repel Penn Sullivan's very obvious come-on, Jack and Danielle strolled into the vestibule of the restaurant. They seemed entranced with each other. His arm was around the French actress's bare shoulders, and she was gazing up at him lovingly. As they appeared, she murmured "*Merci, chéri*," and stood on tip-toe to kiss him on the cheek.

Jade was momentarily stunned. What a bastard! She could hardly believe her own eyes!

Hardly taking a beat, she recovered her composure and turned to Penn. "Let's go party," she said boldly, attaching herself to his arm.

"Great!" he replied, happily surprised.

At which point Jack spotted her. "Hey –" he began. "What are *you* doing here? I was just –"

She smiled, but her eyes were cold steel. "Jack Python," she said, keeping her tone light. "How *nice* to see you. Have you met my good friend Penn Sullivan?"

He had no desire to meet the handsome, young actor. And what the fuck was she doing with him anyway?

Christ! It didn't take Jade Johnson long to get over a broken date – and he had thought she was different.

Chapter 79

It was an extraordinarily balmy night. Howard could feel the sweat forming under his hairpiece before he even left the hotel. He was trying out a new glue and it worked really well, only perspiration wrecked it, and he couldn't afford any mishaps on this night of nights.

After visiting Whitney, he had taken a trip to the location, where Mannon and Clarissa were sequestered in her motor home. It took ten minutes of knocking loudly on the door before it was opened.

Wonderful! Howard thought. Especially during the times they might be needed on the set immediately.

"We call them twenty minutes early," Dirk had confided. "That way we get them there on time."

Mannon emerged eventually, rumpled and smiling. "Howard! This is a surprise. What are you doing here?"

"Trying to see that we get a film made," Howard said grimly. "Remember? That's why we're *all* here."

Grinning, Mannon said, "Am I giving a performance or *what*?"

"Yup," Howard agreed. "The dailies are something."

"Something? Is that all you have to say? Clarissa thinks if we keep up this energy, and the studio does its job when it comes to nomination time – well, she reckons we're *both* on for the ride."

"Nobody would like that better than me. I'd also like to see Whitney happy."

The sound of her name wiped the smile from Mannon's face. "I hate to be the one to say this – but that lady is strictly amateur night. She shouldn't be in this film. We need a real actress in the role."

From 'love of his life' she had gone to 'that lady'. Clarissa must have some heavy influence.

"The thing is," Howard said patiently, "she is in the film. We have a contract. And it would be nice if she got a little support."

"Fire her," Mannon said callously. "I don't care."

Howard – who never gave much thought to anyone's morals, including his own – was shocked. "This is *Whitney* we're talkin' about."

"I know."

"Well, goddammit, two months ago you would've kissed my ass to get her back. Now you want her thrown off the picture?"

"Listen, Howard," Mannon lowered his voice to a confidential whisper. "Clarissa knows what she's talking about, and she says Whitney is dragging the movie down. Dirk agrees. And the crew, everyone."

"So you'd like me to fire her?" Howard asked tightly.

"Right."

"Fuck you. Your contract gives you plenty of power, but you and Clarissa are not runnin' the friggin' studio – an' until you are, *I* decide who gets the axe. And *I* still have some loyalty to old friends."

Clarissa appeared at the door beside Mannon. "Howard," she greeted him curtly.

"Clarissa," he replied, just as curt.

"We only want what's good for the film."

He would never understand her success. What was it that took place between her and a camera?

"I know that," he said. "And I want *you* to know *this*. Whitney stays. I'm flying in a special acting coach for her. She'll improve. She'll be okay."

"If you say so," Clarissa said stiffly.

It occurred to Howard that neither one of them was about to invite him inside. Actors! Actresses! Stars! Phoney, insecure assholes who woke up one morning and got lucky. What made them think they were all so special?

"You're both doing a sensational job," he said, with insincere friendliness. "Keep it up, an' try to go easy on the kid."

"Hardly a kid," murmured Clarissa bitchily.

"Yeah . . . well . . ." He stared at his good friend Mannon, and went for the jugular. "Poppy's seen Melanie a few times. She says she looks healthy enough for someone who's about to drop a baby any second. Do you want me to relay a message?"

Mannon provided a quick flash of guilt. "No," he said. "I speak to her all the time."

Howard did not approve of the way Mannon was treating his pregnant wife. Shrugging, he said, "Gotta go kick ass. See ya."

What he actually had to do was arrange for an acting coach to be flown in at once. And then break the news to Whitney.

She took it better than he expected, glad of the support.

The only acting coach the studio had been able to arrange at such short notice was Joy Byron, an eccentric old Englishwoman who presided over Joy Byron's Method Acting School in Hollywood. Her main claim to fame was that she had discovered Buddy Hudson – currently *the* hot new star. Joy was thrilled to be asked, and arrived on the next plane.

Now Howard had to take them both to dinner, plus Whitney's secretary – who apparently accompanied her everywhere on location. *And* her publicist, Norman Gooseberger, who had also flown in that day.

Howard wasn't worried about dinner. Getting through that would be a breeze. It was *after* he kept on thinking about. Finally, he and Whitney would be alone together. She, so beautiful and vibrant. He, so . . . what?

He was short.

Nearly bald.

He had a paunch.

And more pubic hair than she had probably ever seen in her entire life.

He snorted too much cocaine before leaving the hotel, and gulped a couple of Valium. What a combination! The coke to bring him up, and the Valium to calm him down.

Biting his nails, he allowed a limo to deliver him to his fate.

*

Howard's snide comments about "loyalty" and "old friends" really pissed Mannon off. Whitney was an actress. She had a job to do, and if she couldn't deliver, then she *should* be out. Clarissa had explained that to him. In fact, Clarissa had explained a lot of things to him – especially about acting, and that's why he was giving such a great performance.

For over fifteen years he had played movie star. Now, with Clarissa's help, maybe he'd get a little critical acceptance as a damn good actor. And why should he feel guilty about trying to bump Whitney from the film when she deserved it? Screw Howard and his smartass remarks.

The trouble with Howard was they had known each other too long, and instead of Howard treating him with the deference a star of his stature deserved, he talked to him as if they were equals.

"You don't have to be nice to him," Clarissa pointed out. "He's nothing more than a coked-out buffoon. Zachary Klinger's messenger."

"You think he's on something?"

"Don't be naive. The whole town knows."

Mannon digested this information in silence. Back in the sixties, when he had shared an appartment with Howard and Jack, they had all experimented with various drugs. Jack and he got into smoking grass for a while. Howard was the straight one. He tried everything once, and never came back for seconds. "Addles the brain," he had said. Now *this* little revelation.

"Cocaine?" Mannon asked.

"Exactly."

"Jesus!"

He wondered if Jack knew, or even cared. Lately the three of them saw less and less of each other. Really they had nothing in common anymore.

He hated knowing Clarissa had been with Jack. For almost a year, too. It took all his control to stop himself from asking what his good friend was like in bed, and if he was better.

Clarissa would never say. She was secretive about past loves. He had to curb a strong desire to kill all of them. Clarissa was an unusual woman. He had never been with anyone remotely like her.

If someone had said to him before the start of the movie that he was going to fall in love with Clarissa Browning, he would have told them they were stark, raving crazy.

It had all happened so fast. He had knocked on the door of her hotel suite the first night they arrived on location, just to say hello and be friendly. Four hours later he was still there, discussing script changes, characterizations, and the film in general.

"We fall in love in this movie," she had said. "We make love."

"We sure do!" he had joked in his usual light-hearted way.

"When we interact on screen it has to be real," Clarissa continued seriously. "We have to generate *excitement* and *passion* and *longing*."

"Just try me, baby!"

"Do you know what I believe in, Mannon?" she had asked him gravely.

"What?"

"That we should work our roles through *before* we get in front of the camera."

"Really?"

She'd stared at him intensely. "Let's make love."

He had no idea this was a line she used with all her co-stars, and he fell for it immediately, immensely flattered such a serious actress would want to go to bed with him.

Lying back, he had enjoyed every moment of her fiery passion. After that they were an inseparable team.

The newspapers got wind of it — blind column items appeared daily. He knew he had to tell Melanie-Shanna, but as usual he kept on putting it off. She was expecting their baby any day, and he was only too aware what an uncaring louse he would look if he walked out on her now. His timing was off. "Wait six months," his lawyers had told him.

Clarissa never mentioned his wife. She behaved as if he didn't have one. He managed to phone Melanie-Shanna every few days. She sounded fine, and in spite of his passionate affair with Clarissa he was looking forward to becoming a father for the first time.

Mannon Cable wanted it all. And he saw no good reason why he couldn't have it.

*

The dinner was a bore. Howard never had been good at playing Entourage. For that's what the people around Whitney were. Norman, an adoring fan; her secretary, a willing slave; Joy Byron, a wacky, off-centre flatterer. Every one of them spent the entire evening buttering Whitney up, while Howard fidgeted uncomfortably.

"Let's get *outta* here," he muttered over coffee. "Say goodbye to the go-fers, an' let's split."

Whitney yawned. "I'm *sooo* tired," she announced.

"You need plenty of sleep when you're working," Joy Byron said crisply. "Peace, calm, work, and rest."

"Yes, Whitney," Norman joined in quickly. "We're being selfish, keeping you up. Why don't I take you back to your hotel?"

"*I'll* take her," said the secretary possessively.

"Perhaps you would like to go through a scene or two before sleeping?" Joy suggested.

Howard managed to kick Whitney under the table. A kick that said, "Get rid of them," as sure as if he had spoken the words.

"Um, I have some business to discuss with Mr Soloman. So why don't you all take my car to the hotel, and I'll be back later."

Within five minutes they were alone in the restaurant.

"Thanks," Howard said.

She looked at him serenely. "You're welcome."

His eyes dropped to her breasts, their magnificent outline clearly visible beneath the pale pink angora sweater she wore.

"I've been waiting for this night for years," he said, his voice thick with desire.

"Are we being fair to Poppy?"

Clutching her hand he came up with "Think of it as an act of mercy." Frantically waving for the check he said, "Let's get out of here."

Hand in hand they walked outside to his waiting limo. He was as excited as he'd ever been, and on the way to the hotel he thought about how it would be.

Good. That's how it would be.

Sensational.

Fucking sensational.

399

Sensational fucking!

With a practised move he pressed the button, raising the dark glass separating them from the driver. And then he grabbed her, his hands reaching for her fabulous breasts beneath the soft angora.

"Howard! Not here!"

Silencing her objections with his lips, he plunged his hand beneath her bra, and popped a tit.

Oh, Jesus! He thought he was going to come in his pants. This was better than high school!

Bending his head, he sucked on the rosy nipple bursting from the rim of white lace.

"Not in the *car*," she protested.

Her struggles were in vain as he sprawled all over her.

"HOWARD! WE'RE HERE!"

The limo pulled up outside the hotel. Quickly he leaped off her, as she hurriedly pulled her sweater down.

There was a nuclear explosion waiting to go off in his pants. He hoped he could make it upstairs.

The driver opened the door and they climbed out.

"My suite or yours?" he asked, bursting with expectation as they entered the hotel.

Before she could reply, Chuck Nielson came bounding eagerly out from behind a potted palm. He carried flowers in one hand, and a huge stuffed toy panda in the other.

"Baby!" he yelled. "I'm sorry. I love you. I'm a bum. What can I tell you?"

Howard's hard-on deflated like a pricked balloon.

Chapter 80

Drawing into the parking lot behind the Bistro Garden, Jade wondered what she was doing. Surely she could have thought of *some* excuse to extract herself from Poppy Soloman's lunch?

She *had* tried, phoning Poppy at ten in the morning. "I don't think —" she'd started to say.

"I hope you're not even considering telling me you can't make lunch," Poppy interrupted. "You *are* the guest of honour. And I *have* gone to a great deal of trouble." A pause. "Of course, if you're dying . . ."

"No, I'm fine," she'd said, coward that she was. "I'll be there."

"*Won*derful. Your friend Beverly is coming. Melanie-Shanna Cable, Ida White, and Carmel Gooseberger. We'll have a good time."

"Great."

It wasn't enough that Jack Python had turned out to be just another cheating liar. Now she had to get stuck at some ladies-only lunch she was dreading. Well, at least Beverly would be there.

The day was a Californian blisterer. A freak November blazing sky, and the temperature way up in the eighties.

Last night she had ended up drinking too much and staying out far too late with a group that included Corey, Antonio, and Penn Sullivan. A strange combination but they all seemed to get along surprisingly well. Norman Gooseberger had flown off to Arizona to visit Whitney. "I don't see why I should sit around while he's out of town," Corey had said defiantly.

"No," she'd shrugged. "Nobody should sit around waiting for anybody."

And then she had proceeded to get good and drunk.

Corey brought her home at three in the morning. He guided her to bed, and camped out on the couch. In the morning they shared coffee and a companionship that had been missing far too long.

"Are you happy?" she had asked him.

"Getting there," he'd replied. "How about you?"

The phone had saved her from answering. A business call about her upcoming trip to New York for a special Cloud promotion party. She was glad to be rescued. There seemed no need to burden Corey with her problems.

*

It was easy to get rid of Danielle. Jack just dropped her off at Senator Richmond's hotel, bade her goodbye, and she was history.

Considering that Jade was out on the town without a

moment's pause, gazing into the eyes of her next conquest, he should have kept Danielle, taken her to *his* hotel, and vented some of his frustration and disappointment.

He was more than disappointed. He could have sworn that he and Jade Johnson were on for a beautiful, long, crazy ride.

Wrong.

Another one hits the dust.

She couldn't even wait *one* day. What an operator!

And yet . . . he remembered her note – all about how it was impossible to wipe the smile off her face, and did he want her to cook for him.

Sweet.

Phoney.

Shit!

He went to bed and slept badly. In the morning he was woken by Heaven on the phone. She sounded suspiciously cheerful, and suspiciously guilty.

"What's up?" he asked. "Do you need money?" He saw to it that she received a healthy allowance, only most months she seemed to run out of funds.

"Nope."

That was a surprise. "Don't tell me you've heard from your mother?"

"Get serious, Uncle Jack."

"You can drop the uncle. Aren't you going to be seventeen next week? I think plain Jack'll do just fine." He groped for his watch and realized it was only seven-forty-five. Too early for idle conversation.

"I'm seventeen the day after tomorrow," she corrected.

Damn Aretha. He'd told her to remind him – now it looked like he'd forgotten. "I know that," he said quickly. "Just testing to make sure *you* remembered."

"Very funny." A short silence. "I'm dropping out of school."

Struggling to sit up, he said, "You're doing *what*?"

"Don't freak out. It's okay – really. I've got something exciting to do – it's not like a job exactly –"

"Can we discuss this over lunch?"

"Why?"

Why. The kid asked him why. He was in no mood to play the father figure, but it seemed unavoidable.

"Meet me at Hamburger Hamlet on Sunset at twelve o'clock. Be there," he said sternly.

"I don't see why I have to . . ."

"I said be there." He hung up abruptly.

*

Poppy Soloman adored her ladies' lunches. They gave her an ideal opportunity to star in her own productions.

She dressed up accordingly, and wore important pieces from her ever-growing collection of fine jewellery. Sometimes she had her hair and makeup done by a professional. It was nice to look one's best, especially when most women were super-critical — usually behind her back.

Howard had phoned early in the morning. Poor Howard. He could hardly survive without her. "I've got a stomachache," he'd complained. "I feel lousy."

"Get on a plane and come home," she'd said sensibly.

"I will, as soon as Whitney gets her ass back on the set."

"Hurry, pusskins, Poppy misses you."

She knew he loved it when she babied him. There was no doubt about it, she could take care of him better than his other three wives put together.

Sighing, she consulted her watch. It was nearly twelve-thirty, and her guests would soon be arriving. She always liked to be there first so she could decide on the seating and position herself in a key spot.

The garden restaurant was already abuzz with activity. She waved to several acquaintances, and blew kisses to a favoured few. Poppy Soloman was a force in so-called Hollywood society. As the wife of a studio head she expected and received deferential treatment wherever she went.

How different from her first months in Hollywood, when she worked as a lowly secretary . . . How very different . . .

"Don't even tell me I'm the first! Jeez! And you look so lonely sittin' there all by yourself. Hi — I'm Beverly D'Amo. What a pleasure to *finally* get to have lunch with you."

Poppy looked up at the extremely tall, exotic black woman. Beverly certainly was striking.

"Sit *here*," she said, indicating the chair next to her. "I'm delighted you could come today."

Beverly rolled her eyes and winked wickedly. "Girl, I *come* whenever the opportunity presents itself! Doesn't everyone?"

Poppy was saved from answering by the appearance of Jade

403

Johnson, clad all in white and looking spectacular. "I'm not late, am I?" she asked breathlessly.

"Not at all," replied Poppy, patting the chair the other side of her and saying, "Please sit here."

"Hiya, J. J.," Beverly greeted Jade. "Who's the guy? Seems to me you're sending out those special signals."

"Huh?"

"You heard."

"I don't know *what* you're talking about."

"Babee, it's *me*. C'mon, tell."

"Champagne, everyone?" interrupted Poppy.

"Why not?" replied Beverly. She grinned at the waiter. "Make mine a Mimosa. Fresh orange juice, the best bubbly, an' a little shaved ice."

Poppy could see that if she wasn't careful, Beverly would take over her entire lunch. Quickly she asserted herself, making her position clear up front. "Beverly," she said sweetly, "Howard speaks *so* well of you. He's *very* impressed with your performance in *Romance*. Even though it's only a small role he says you have great potential, and he hopes to use you again soon." Actresses had to be put in their place. Firmly.

Beverly's grin widened. She, too, could play power games. "No shit? The little guy said that about me? Hey – I'm *really* flattered. I guess that must be why old Zach's promised me the lead in my next flickeroony."

Before anyone could say anything else the odd couple arrived – Ida and Carmel. Poppy busied herself with introductions, placing Carmel next to Jade, and Ida beside Beverly. There was one chair left for Melanie-Shanna, who was late.

"Didn't I see you at Spago with Jack Python?" Ida said, peering myopically across the table at Jade, her striking white hair shimmering in the sunlight.

"Uh . . . yes, I guess so."

"Ah *ha!*" yelled Beverly triumphantly. "Jack Python, huh?"

"A rutting dog," boomed Carmel. "He's had more women in this town than Silver's had men."

"Silver?" echoed Beverly. "As in Anderson?"

"They're brother and sister, you know," said Poppy. "It's not a well-publicized fact."

"I never knew that," said Beverly. "They don't look anything alike."

"Of course, she'd much older than he is," Carmel confided

knowledgeably. "Silver and I go *way* back."

"She had Orville once, didn't she?" remarked Ida.

"No, she didn't," replied Carmel crossly. "I wish you'd stop suggesting that Orville has had every woman in this town."

"Probably one of the few he missed," chortled Ida, surprisingly lively for once.

Carmel glared at her.

"It sounds like brother and sister have covered the waterfront," observed Beverly. "And *I* wouldn't mind covering *him* any day of the week. How was he, Jade? All tight pants, teeth an' talk? Or is there gold in them there hills?"

Shrugging vaguely Jade said, "I've no idea. We were just . . . uh . . . talking business."

Beverly raised a quizzical eyebrow. "Business?"

Sometimes Beverly got completely on her nerves. "Yes, business," she said shortly. "He wants me to appear on his show."

Noting her guest of honour's discomfort, Poppy switched subjects. "And what is everyone's opinion of the new *Mr* Silver Anderson?" she asked.

"A sly one," Ida said without hesitation.

"Who is he? Where does he come from?" Poppy mused. "That's what *I* wonder."

"Orville says he's quite sharp," interrupted Carmel.

"Must be," Ida said. "He got her to marry him, didn't he?"

"Has she ever had anything *lifted*?" Poppy asked curiously. "She looks so wonderful – for her age."

"There are more plastic surgeons in Los Angeles than anywhere else in the world," Beverly announced authoritatively. "My gyno told me. Amazing what they'll come out with when they're eyeballin' one's snatch!"

"I wonder where Melanie is," fussed Poppy. She had called her the day before, dropped a big hint about Mannon and Clarissa, then invited her for lunch. "I hate people who think they can walk in half an hour late. It's so rude."

"Does she know about hubby dearest?" inquired Carmel, lighting a long thin cigarillo.

"I really have no idea," replied Poppy innocently. "Isn't the wife always supposed to be the last to find out?"

Jade felt lost in a sea of idle gossip. She abhorred the casual way they were picking everyone over. Jack Python probably *was* a rutting dog, but she didn't want to hear about it from this group.

"Like I think you gotta let me do this," Heaven said earnestly. "And if it doesn't work out, I"l go back to school, college, the whole bit. Uncle Jack, you gotta understand – if I *don't* do it, I could like totally miss out on the greatest opportunity of my life."

"You should have told me at the beginning," he said sharply. "Before you signed contracts, and made a record, and committed yourself."

"You would've stopped me," she countered.

He had to admit she was right. "So what you're telling me is that you want to drop out of school for a year, and pursue a singing career. Is that correct?"

"That's it."

"And what if this record of yours flops?"

Pouting, she said, "Thanks!"

"Hey – don't get carried away, young lady, it could happen."

Picking at her hamburger, she said, "Not to me, I've had enough bummed-out scenes in my life."

Staring at his pretty, forlorn niece, he wondered what was in store for her. She had come to him with a whole scenario, and he knew if he stepped in and said no, she would hate him forever. Why hadn't his father asked him about it? How could George just go ahead and sign contracts without knowing a thing about the business? Goddammit. If he'd spent more time with her she might have come to him *before* the event.

"I don't know," he said unsurely.

"Yes you do," she wheedled.

"What about Silver?"

"What *about* her?"

"I guess if you're going to drop out of school, someone should tell her."

"Why? Do you like honestly believe she cares?"

Once again he had to admit she was right.

Pushing her plate away, she went on, "It's settled then? You agree?"

"Would it make any difference if I didn't?"

With a guilty laugh she said, "I guess not."

"Show business is a tough number to conquer."

"Easy sucks. I'm into struggling."

"When do I get to hear your record?"

"The record company's having a party for me. Sort of like to introduce me to disc jockeys and the newspaper people. I want you to come. Only, Uncle Jack, promise not to get mad at me?

The thing is, I just don't want to advertise the fact we're related. Okay?"

He began to laugh. "Ashamed of me?"

Giggling, she said, "You got it in one!"

"Once again I suggest you drop the uncle — it does kind of give things away."

"Thanks, Unc — I mean — Jack."

"You're welcome." He called for the check. "When is this party anyway?"

"On my birthday."

"Give me a time and a place. I'll be there."

*

As soon as the waiter suggested coffee, Jade was out of there. She had heard enough about face-lifts, and who was sleeping with whom, and designers, and servant problems, and character assassinations.

Beverly left with her, and they both burst into hysterical laughter as they hit the parking lot and handed over their respective tickets.

"*Shee-it!*" exclaimed Beverly. "Heavy duty."

"*Bor-ing*," Jade said. "I never intend to get trapped at one of those lunches again."

"Right on. Poppy Soloman is somethin' else," agreed Beverly.

"You can say that again."

The parking valet drove up in a maroon, impeccably polished Rolls-Royce — licence plate KLINGER I.

"I see the beat goes on," Jade remarked dryly.

"Sure does. Why don't you come back to our simple little mansion and we can *really* spill our guts? Leave your car here — I'll get one of the slaves to pick it up later."

Jade hesitated. She felt like confiding in someone, but on the very few occasions she had been in Zachary Klinger's company he made her uncomfortable.

Reading her mind, Beverly said, "It's all clear on the Bel Air front. Big Daddy's at the studio — I think he's hoping to get another pop at Carlos Brent!"

"Is it true he actually hit him?"

"Whacked old Carlos out, an' proud of it."

"Why would he do that?"

Beverly tipped the valet and got in the car. "I think he's got a secret crush on Silver Anderson. How hysterical can things get?"

And at the studio, Zachary Klinger stood silently in the background and watched.

He had more than a secret crush on Silver. He had an all-consuming passion. And very soon he would win her back.

One way or the other she would be his again, and nobody was going to stand in his way.

Chapter 81

"You're a first-class cooze," Carlos Brent muttered.

"And you're a broken-down old swinger," Silver replied coolly.

"Pulling that stunt with the garlic yesterday. What kind of crap was that?"

"I had this mad urge to see Zachary Klinger knock you down."

"Yeah, you would." Grabbing her in an affectionate hug he added, "You're not such a bad old broad. I guess I'll have to put up with you."

"Are we ready to shoot?" the director called nervously, wary of his stars coming to blows after yesterday's débâcle.

"Whenever you are," Silver replied sweetly, extracting herself from Carlos's embrace, and strolling in front of the camera.

Following her, Carlos walked with the jaunty swagger of great fame.

Silver had to admit that he was still an extremely attractive man, in spite of the hair transplant and extra pounds which filled out his once gaunt frame. And he was an American legend. Which is more than she could say for Wes Money – who wasn't even American, let alone a legend.

She was furious with Wes. How *dare* he walk out on her last night. How *dare* he do such a thing.

And – even worse – he had not returned home. When she left for the studio in the morning, the bastard was still missing.

She had not married Wes Money for him to walk out on her. Oh, no. Absolutely not.

And she had no intention of letting him get away with such behaviour.

Vladimir had been quite triumphant about the whole episode. When she drifted downstairs last night with a faint smile and a languorous air, Vladimir was waiting to greet her. "Mr Money vill not be dining vith you tonight," he said smugly.

"And why is that?"

"Mr Money vent out for the night, madame. He instructed me to tell you he vill not be back until later."

"Where's he gone?"

Vladimir professed ignorance.

She tried to find out from Unity if *she* knew the reason for Wes's sudden departure. Unity didn't know, and what's more she didn't seem to care.

Silver felt uncomfortable with the girl: there was something about her she didn't like – a cold, unspoken insolence. "Did Wes speak to anyone since coming downstairs?" she had asked.

Unity shrugged. "I think he returned a couple of calls."

"To whom?" Uneasily it occurred to her that maybe there was another woman in his life. After all, he was hardly keeping it zipped in his pants when she found him. He was probably embroiled in affairs with cheap women all over the place.

"Orville Gooseberger left an urgent message to return his call, and so did Zeppo White," Unity said flatly.

The picture became clear. Orville and Zeppo telling tales. And Wes becoming miffed because *she* hadn't told him.

With a sigh of annoyance she had tackled a solitary dinner, and waited for the return of her husband.

As far as she was concerned, she hadn't been keeping any secrets. Why *should* she feel obliged to report everything to him?

Deep down she knew that she hadn't told him because he would have said she behaved childishly. Screw him. Silver Anderson didn't have to answer to *anyone*. She hated criticism, and wasn't about to hear it from her own husband.

When he failed to come home, her anger grew. Just who exactly did Mr Money think he was dealing with?

On the way to the studio that morning she had decided to teach him a lesson. One he wasn't likely to forget in a hurry.

The first thing she did was send a note of apology to Carlos, and then she sat back and waited for his reaction.

It was predictable: she knew Carlos of old.

After their mild exchange of insults on the set, he invited her to his dressing room for lunch.

She hadn't had Carlos in twenty years. Why wait any longer?

*

After storming from the house, Wes headed straight for the nearest bar, where he downed a couple of fast scotches and took stock of the situation.

As he began to calm down he realized what Silver had done – or rather not done – was no big deal. She merely needed a little reminder that *he* was the boss of the household, and as such deserved some respect. By not telling him about the furor on the set she could have made him look like a prize jerk to Orville and Zeppo. Fortunately, he was a quick thinker, and had saved the situation by pretending he knew all about it when he spoke to the two of them on the phone.

It was about time Silver realized she couldn't treat him as her latest resident stud and nothing else. If he stayed out late the lesson should be well learned. After all, it wasn't like he was risking anything – they were married now, and there was nothing she could do about it.

He didn't like the bar he had chosen. It was dimly lit and stuffy, filled with an assortment of secretaries trying to score, and men in three-piece suits. Deciding more familiar haunts would suit him better, he drove down to Venice, to a bar/ restaurant he used to hang out at. The place was not Chasen's, nor even Spago. It was rough and noisy, with a loud juke box, and an assortment of hookers and drug dealers hanging round the bar.

This was your life, Wes Money, he said to himself – and he knew immediately how difficult it would be ever to go back.

*

One thing about Carlos, age had not slowed his sexual prowess. Once a cocksman, always. And Silver enjoyed the visit from an old friend.

A revenge fuck. Fast and furious. Ha! She would make sure Wes found out about it.

"You're one hell of a sexy old broad," Carlos said with a chuckle, as he pulled up his pants. "Why'd we ever break up?"

"A matter of ego," she said crisply, adjusting her clothing.

410

"Yours. It threatened to engulf both of us." Rising, she went straight to the mirror and inspected her makeup to make sure nothing was disturbed. "And kindly don't call *me* old. You're at least twenty years ahead of me. If *I'm* old, what does that make you?"

"Men don't get older, only better," he said boastfully.

"Stuff it, Carlos dear."

"I thought I just did!"

Feeling strangely unsatisfied, and a tiny bit guilty, she decided that maybe she wouldn't tell Wes after all.

Then she remembered he'd been out all night.

The hell with *him*.

*

He saw a few friends, only they didn't seem so friendly. Brief exchanges stilted conversation.

"What's the matter with everyone?" he asked his ex-local hooker.

Looking battered and worn, like an old used car, she mumbled, "Ya ain't one of us anymore, Wes." She ran a hand through yellow hair with black roots. "Ya rich now, an' famous."

"*I'm* not famous," he said. "My wife is."

Staring at him curiously she asked, "What's she like?"

"Great," he replied, and found that he meant it. Silver could be surprisingly great when she dropped the "big star" act.

The sad–looking hooker wagged a finger at him. "Ya got a break. A real lucky break."

"I know," he replied truthfully.

She scurried off, even though he wanted to buy her a drink. "Gotta get back t'work," she explained.

By the time she left he was deeply depressed, and he decided Silver had been punished enough. He was going home to Bel Air, where he belonged.

Outside, in the back parking lot, two men walked slowly towards him.

He smelled trouble before it happened, went to defend himself, and was felled by a heavy blunt instrument.

Oh, Christ, not again, he thought, just before drifting uneasily into the land of nod.

Chapter 82

Bazaar hit the stands in the morning, and Heaven hit an un-suspecting public the next day with what was destined to become the hottest single of the year.

Her combination seventeenth birthday and *Gonna Eatcha Tonight!* promotion party turned out to be a blast, covered by *Entertainment Tonight* and a host of other media, as there was nothing else going on that night. It took place at Tramp, the private club. Giant blow-ups of her Antonio pictures covered the walls, while white and gold balloons inscribed *Heaven* and *Gonna Eatcha Tonight!* decorated the ceilings.

Heaven glimmered and glittered her way through the party – an irresistible mixture of innocence and seduction in a white lace body stocking worn with a black leather micro-skirt, lace-up gold boots, festoons of diamanté jewellery, and a trailing gold trenchcoat.

Lindi, the publicity girl from College Records, had taken her on a shopping spree down Melrose, and the result was slightly bizarre, very individual and stylishly effective. "We're calling it the Heaven look," Lindi told a group of hungry journalists – always on the alert for a new trend. "This kid'll make Madonna look like a non-starter. Just wait until you hear her."

Speaking to the press was a completely new experience. She knew her mother had complained about it all her life, but Heaven couldn't see what was so bad, talking about herself non-stop. Pushing her hands through her multi-coloured hair, she answered questions on clothes, style, fashion, school and background.

"I spent my childhood in Europe with my parents," she half lied. "And now I live with my grandfather in the Valley."

"There's a rumour going around that you're Silver

Anderson's daughter," said a fat woman in a peasant blouse, with jangles of beads around her plump neck.

Heaven glared at her. "Really?" she said. "I guess I'll be Cyndi Lauper's *sister* next!"

Everyone laughed, and Lindi spirited her away to get ready for the debut of her record.

"You know," Lindi said sympathetically, "we're never going to be able to keep it under wraps."

"What?"

"That you *are* Silver Anderson's daughter. I know you want it kept a secret, but that's not easy when your manager is going around telling everyone."

She was aghast. "Rocky?"

"'Fraid so."

"I could *kill* him."

Lindi shrugged philosophically. "It *will* get out eventually, one way or another. So we may as well scoop it now, then at least it's behind us."

"Why?" she asked stubbornly.

"Because if the media thinks you're trying to hide something, they'll *really* go all out. We don't have to announce it – it's just best you don't deny it. Okay?"

She nodded resignedly. Deep down she had known it was an impossible secret to keep.

The debut of her record was planned for eight o'clock, and she was supposed to mime to it. Shaking with nerves she changed into a slinky leopard catsuit, and then slipped on a long black leather coat worn open. The Heaven look.

Several of the College Records executives crowded round her, wishing her good luck. Rocky appeared at her side, mumbling *his* encouragement.

This was it. This was the opportunity she had been waiting for.

She heard the opening beat of the record, and tensed up.

Lindi gave her a little push, propelling her in front of the disc jockey stand, where a spotlight hit her in the eyes.

Oh, no! She wanted to throw up! Everyone was staring at her expectantly. Waiting, watching, expecting great things!

And then, as the music enveloped her, she began to move her lips, stiffly at first, intimidated by the crowd and the lights. This wasn't like performing at some high school dance with Eddie in attendance. This was it. This was the big time.

Get loose, she told herself. *Lighten up*.

Miraculously something clicked, and she was suddenly gloriously, *wonderfully* into the music.

> I met a guy who's big and strong –
> his muscles make me quiver
> I look at him – he looks at me –
> Oh, wow, he makes me shiver.
> There's one thing I will do to him –
> because I know he wants it
> I get real near – with message clear
> I whisper low – all systems go
> I'm a Maneater . . . yes I am . . .
> Maneater . . . sure I am . . .
> Maneater . . . and baby –
> I'm gonna eatcha tonight!

By the time she finished her adrenalin was really pumping and she felt sensational. The crowd of guests gave her a rapturous reception. And Uncle Jack told her how proud he was of her.

"You were *fantastic*," Lindi whispered, grabbing her arm as soon as Jack left. "Come with me, the photographers want a shot of you and Penn Sullivan."

Heaven tried to hide her excitement. Penn Sullivan! The actor! He was *gorgeous*!

Things were *certainly* looking up.

Somewhere in New York . . .
Sometime in the seventies . . .

The girl arrived in New York on a freezing Saturday afternoon. Clad in a thin cotton dress and a cheap nylon jacket, with one small suitcase clutched in her hand, she stood in the Port Authority bus terminal and wondered where to go.

New York had seemed like such an exciting idea when she first hatched her plan to travel to the big city. Now, as she ventured out onto West Forty-second Street, she wasn't so sure.

The street was filthy, full of garbage and dirt. A crazed bag lady hurried by — pushing a shopping cart full of brown paper bags and newspapers. A skinny black man in a pink jacket with matching eyes hey-babied *her. Two punks eyed her suitcase, contemplating grab and run. They'd be very disappointed if they did, for their entire haul would consist of two old sweaters, some worn underwear, a pair of jeans, scuffed sneakers, and two packets of Oreo cookies.*

Those were all her worldly possessions. And in the pocket of her nylon jacket she had eighty-four dollars in assorted bills.

That was it.

A police car screamed by, just as a sharp-nosed white man in a sheepskin coat approached her. "Hiya, sweetie."

Ignoring him, she began to walk quickly along the street.

Companionably he fell into step beside her. "You look like ya need a friend," he said.

"I'm okay," she replied, shivering as a blast of icy wind penetrated her light clothing.

"Where ya from?"

"California," she lied.

"Yeah? I was there once. Got me a tan and a blonde cutie."

She stopped and turned towards him. "What do you want?" she demanded bluntly.

"Jest bein' friendly," he replied, taken aback.

"What do you want?" she repeated.

"Sex," he said hopefully. "I'll give ya ten bucks, an' tell ya where t'get connected."

"Connected?"

"Y'know, I'll meetcha the right people. Ya need a job, doncha? An' someplace ter park yer butt."

Sighing wearily she said, "Get lost."

He pulled up the collar of his warm sheepskin coat. "Ya turnin' me down?"

"That's right."

"Well, fuck you," he spat. "See how far you'll get without my help."

"Go away."

He walked off, muttering to himself.

Waiting until he was out of sight, she leaned against the wall and clumsily opened her suitcase. Removing both her sweaters, she took off the nylon jacket and struggled into them, feeling warmer at once. Then she put her jacket back on, asked directions to Herald Square, and set off, walking briskly until she reached Macy's, the famous department store she had read about. It was supposedly one of the biggest stores in the world — occupying a full square block of space.

Inside, the activity was frantic, shoppers mingled with tourists, everyone rushing back and forth anxious to spend their money.

Approaching a bored-looking redhead stationed behind one of the cosmetics counters, she asked, "Can you help me? Who do I see to get a job here?"

The redhead stared. "You're going job hunting with a suitcase?" she questioned. "No chance."

"No chance of what?"

"No chance of them hiring you."

"Why?"

"For a start, you look like you just got off the bus."

"I did."

The woman laughed derisively. "Holy cow! I suppose you're broke, with nowhere to live, and probably knocked up."

"Two out of three. Any suggestions?"

"I hope it's the right two. Get a room at the Y overnight, and then catch the next bus home."

The girl did neither. She had made up her mind that in New York things were going to be different, and one way or another she was going to rise from her crummy beginnings and make a success of her life. No job and no place to stay were minor setbacks. She was a survivor.

416

Hadn't she proved it? Failing to land a job at Macy's, she was able to get a room at the YWCA, where she deposited her suitcase, and then took a walk to Times Square. She looked around, finally noticing a DISHWASHER NEEDED sign in the window of Red's Deli, a huge, noisy restaurant.

One thing she knew — she was never going to succumb to the easy money she could make selling her body. Even dishwashing was better than that.

Washing dishes non-stop on a seven-hour shift was back-breaking work. The girl threw herself into it, in spite of the hostility of the other three dishwashers — all male. Even at such a low level of employment, men resented a female's intrusion. They made sure she got the dirtiest work of all. The huge frying pans covered in hard grease. The garbage pails to clean out. She was even allotted the cockroach run — cleaning out the lower cupboards once a day, and getting rid of the mice and rat droppings before the health inspector appeared. Working hard, she kept to herself, discouraging the friendliness of several of the waiters and short-order cooks. The girl knew that relationships could get her into trouble.

She never felt guilty about what she had done in the past — for all her victims deserved it. But she didn't want to keep on having to punish people . . . and running . . . running . . .

There was one waiter called Eli. He was black, gay, and unfailingly cheerful. He talked to her whether she wanted him to or not.

"Woody Allen's sitting at table four," he confided. "And yesterday Liza Minnelli was in — she just loves our apple strudel. It's not fair that you don't get to see anybody. Why don't you ask for a job as a waitress? Stella's quitting, there'll be a vacancy. How about grabbing it?"

"Does it pay more?"

"Yes. Yes. Yes!"

She took his advice and asked for the job. And she got it.

"Good," Eli said, "now you can come and live with me. I am in desperate need of someone to split my rent."

His kindness made her suspicious. Nobody had ever been kind to her unless they wanted something in return. Warily she moved into his cramped Greenwich Village apartment, paying half the rent, and waiting patiently to see what he was after.

"I'm an actor," Eli confided. "And a dancer, and a singer. What are your ambitions?"

Just to survive, she nearly said. Only Eli wouldn't understand. Nobody would. The tragedy of her life was her secret, and she would never reveal it to anyone.

BOOK FIVE

Hollywood, California
December 1985

Chapter 83

A shout of annoyance from the general direction of Silver's bathroom indicated she was not ready to leave the house. Wes cast an eye at the clock. They were running late for the wrap party of *Romance*. Nothing new about *that*. Silver ran late for everything. She and Elizabeth Taylor held the record for tardy arrivals.

Yawning, he sat on the edge of the bed and clicked on the television. He'd been ready to go for forty-five minutes.

Another scream. "Damn!" Silver yelled, emerging from the bathroom. "I look like a hag!"

She was clad in a beige suede gaucho outfit which didn't suit her. The shoulders were too wide, the skirt too long, and the waist too cinched. It was an outfit suitable for a twenty-two-year-old six-foot model.

"What do you think?" she demanded belligerently, knowing full well it wasn't right.

"Great," he said mildly.

"Liar!" she shouted, and marched into her dressing room, slamming the door.

Slipping off his shoes, he put his legs up on the bed. He could bet on at least another half-hour before she was ready. It didn't bother him. He felt perfectly safe and secure lying on the bed waiting for her. The trip back to his past six weeks ago had straightened out any desire he might have had to go wandering. Getting beaten up in a seedy parking lot and dragged off to meet with some fat drug pimp was not exactly his idea of a wonderful time.

He recalled the evening with distaste. The *whole* fucking evening, for they hadn't released him until the next day.

He was sure somebody had squealed on him when he went

visiting his old haunts. And he had a hunch it was his pathetic hooker friend. Not that he blamed her – anything for a buck – although it would be interesting to find out what the going price for fingering him was.

It was fortunate he possessed a concrete skull. The mother-fuckers had hit him with something heavy, dragged him into the back of a car, and taken him to visit the black dude with the shit-eating grin and big white sunglasses.

This time the meet was in a deserted warehouse. When he regained consciousness, he found he was slumped on a dusty concrete floor, his hands and feet bound with wire.

For a moment real fear had taken over. Mr Silver Anderson was going to end his days alone and unloved – just as he had begun them.

His heart jumped about like an out-of-control tennis ball, and he almost relieved himself in his pants.

STAY CALM a voice screamed in his head. THEY CAN'T DO ANYTHING TO YOU – YOU'RE A SOMEBODY NOW.

"What you think, man?" The black man prodded him with his foot. "You think we be dumb-ass fuckers? You think we gonna wait forever for our money?"

He'd groaned, and quickly tried to collect his wits.

"You owe us, white boy, an' we ready to collect."

"I owe you fuck all," he managed. "You set me up."

"We want our money," the man said. "We be fair. You pay us the twenny-two thou an' we forget about drugs you steal."

Struggling to free himself he said, "I don't fucking believe this!"

"You think fast 'bout payin' money you owe."

A swift kick caught him in the lower abdomen, landing dangerously close to his balls, making him gag with pain.

"Think carefully. I be back tomorra."

They left him, trussed like a chicken, all night long. In the morning a henchman returned to set him free. "Ya bring the money t' the same parkin' lot Tuesday nite, eight o'clock."

By the time he got the circulation going in his wrists and ankles, made his way back to the car, and drove to the house, Silver had departed for the studio. When she arrived home later that night to find him stretched out on the couch with an ice-pack on his forehead, she was furious.

"Hangover? Serves you right," she had snapped coldly.

"I got mugged," he objected.

Sarcasm flowed. "What a *shame*."

"How about some sympathy?"

"Whistle for it."

She had swept upstairs and ignored him for several days.

Obviously, everything was okay on the set, for both Orville and Zeppo phoned to thank him. "I don't know what you said to her," Orville chuckled. "Or *did* to her. But she and Carlos are behaving like best friends."

Concealing his surprise, he had accepted the congratulations as if they were his due. "I told you everything would be all right," he said magnanimously. "Any time you want her pulled back into line, just call on me."

Orville and Zeppo loved him. It took a while before Silver did again. She liked getting her own way – without exception. He had challenged her, and she did not enjoy the experience.

Slowly he charmed his way back into her good graces. Sex. Silver needed it, wanted it, hated to be without it. But they had both learned a lesson from their brief estrangement.

Meanwhile, he had no intention of paying back the twenty-two thousand dollars. Fuck 'em. They had planted the money on him, and as far as he was concerned it barely compensated for the screwed up Laurel Canyon caper. Besides, it was his "fuck you" money. He had it stashed in a safe-deposit box at the First Interstate Bank – minus the rent he had paid Reba – and he did not plan to go anywhere near it. There was nothing they could do. He was back in Bel Air, safe and protected by the new security system he had persuaded Silver to install. For insurance he took the gun – another souvenir of Laurel Canyon – out of hiding, and carried it for protection. No way was he getting caught again. Wes Money was back in the big time.

At last Silver appeared, clad in a gold jacket worn over a short black dress. "*Do* come on," she sighed impatiently. "Aren't you ready?"

Ha! *She* was berating *him*. He had been ready for over an hour. Lately her mood had been lousy. He knew the reason. And the reason had a name. Heaven. Silver's well-kept secret daughter was an emerging rock star, and it was driving her crazy.

*

Sound stage six at Orpheus Studios was set up for a party. There were balloons, round tables with pink cloths, a small combo playing music from the film, an open bar, and a buffet table covered with food. The party was crowded, but not with stars. A wrap party was a thank you from the producers to the cast and crew, and usually they were allowed to bring their respective mates.

The stars generally put in an appearance. Always late. Certainly brief.

Neither Silver nor Carlos had shown. However, Howard Soloman was there, a bejewelled Poppy in close attendance. She distributed largesse and sweetness. Poppy considered it excellent public relations to be nice to the "little people". "After all," she told Howard earnestly, "I was once one myself."

Yeah, he remembered only too well the days when Poppy was his secretary. It hadn't taken her long to change roles.

Since getting back from Arizona, and his aborted affair with Whitney, Howard had been on a downhill slide. He was doing more coke than ever, spending the studio's money rashly, and indulging in even more scams where the gains went straight into his own pocket.

Paranoia reigned supreme – he thought that everyone was talking about him. And for the first time in his life he was off sex.

Once that happened, Poppy noticed. "Howie, baby, is anything wrong?"

"Work pressure."

"Poor sweetie. We need a vacation. Shall I book a suite at the Kahala in Hawaii?"

"I'll let you know."

Going away was not the answer. He didn't want to be stuck in confined quarters with Poppy, where she could find out about his habit. He had finally admitted to himself that it *was* a habit. Not an unbreakable one. He could stop any time he wanted.

The problem was – he didn't want to.

*

Carlos Brent made his entrance first – walking with the same swagger as in his youth. He travelled with two bodyguards, a secretary, a personal publicist, and his long-suffering girlfriend, Dee Dee Dionne.

His attendants hovered around him like anxious butterflies.

Shortly after, Silver arrived, with Wes and Nora. "I hate these things," she muttered to Nora. "All this smiling makes my face muscles ache." She waved to the lighting cameraman – always an actress's best friend – and graciously stopped by his table to meet his wife.

Now that the film was finished shooting she was feeling slight tingles of apprehension. Had she done the right thing leaving *Palm Springs*? A television soap gave her constant exposure to a more than fickle public. Would that same public go to see her in *Romance*? Would they watch her upcoming television special? Would they still *love* and *adore* her?

She wasn't ready for rejection. Silver *needed* adulation, just as Howard needed his cocaine.

And Zeppo White was not Quinne Lattimore. Quinne used to be available for her calls day and night. She could summon him to attend to minor problems any time she wanted. Zeppo was another matter. As a star agent he refused to jump, and that annoyed her.

"I'm not sure Zeppo is the right agent for me," she'd complained to Wes.

Looking at her quizzically he'd said, "Zeppo is the tops. From now on it's only the best for you."

She was harbouring guilty feelings about cheating on Wes with Carlos. What if he ever found out?

Of course, he never would. How could he? And if he did, she would merely deny it. Nora was the only one who knew. Well, Nora was privy to all her secrets – why should this one be any different?

"Can I beg a favour from you?" the lighting cameraman's wife asked.

Silver smiled generously. The woman probably wanted an autographed photo – everyone did.

"Certainly."

"It's not for me."

Of course not. It never is.

"It's for our grand-daughter."

Grand-daughter! Her fans were getting younger every day!

Still smiling, she noticed Wes talking to Carlos and wondered what they were discussing.

Hey – did you know I fucked your wife the other day?

Really? I hope you enjoyed it.

Yeah, why not? She's a good old broad.

"Little Marybethe will be thrilled to pieces if I can promise her an autographed picture of your daughter, Heaven. And if she can sign it – to Marybethe – M-A-R-Y-B-E-T-H-E."

Silver's smile was fixed on her face like a concrete mask, while shivers of annoyance mixed with jealousy mixed with disbelief ran up and down her spine.

Goddammit! What the hell had she ever done to deserve *this*?

Chapter 84

Getting away was the best tonic Jade could think of. Only it seemed that every time she made a trip, she was running from a bad relationship. Los Angeles to escape from Mark. Now back to New York to forget Jack Python. Although she could hardly call *him* a relationship. More like a night of passion with a professional stud. Making conquests was obviously his hobby.

How *could* she have been so gullible? It wasn't as though she hadn't been around.

In New York she tried to put the entire incident behind her, and threw herself into seeing old friends. There were lunches at the Russian Tea Room, Mortimer's, and Le Cirque. Evenings at the Hard Rock Café, Twenty-One, and Elaine's – depending on her mood. And crazy shopping trips to the three great B's – Bendel's, Bergdorf's, and Bloomingdale's.

Walking the streets she breathed the freezing city air and had a wonderful time doing it. Then she visited her parents in Connecticut for a long, blissful, promotion-free weekend.

When she'd signed the Cloud deal, she had not fully realized the extent to which they expected her to sell their product. After complaining to her modelling agent, she was shown a copy of her contract, and there it was in black and white – *Ms. Johnson will undertake eight weeks of personal appearances during a twelve-month period.*

Ms. Johnson had signed.

Ms. Johnson had to do.

She was certainly incredibly well compensated. The Cloud deal had set her up for life. Now she could venture into movies on her terms, or not at all.

Zeppo White called to inform her that Howard Soloman had

purchased the film rights to *Married Alive*, and that a top screen-writer was tailoring the script to accommodate her.

"I got you the sweetest deal in the world," he crowed. "Everything you asked for an' more. I'm couriering the contract to you overnight. Get it back to me right away, kiddo."

"How's L.A.?" she asked, shivering in the borrowed apartment of a friend.

"Hot. Christmas is coming. I'm havin' my turkey out by the pool. How about you?"

"I'll spend Christmas with my family and be back right after the holidays."

"Looking forward to it. Ida wants to throw a party for you."

She was all partied out. The Cloud Gala, held at the top of the World Trade building, had been a lavish affair attended by a mix of New York's movers and shakers, plus press, and the most avid stylesetters.

Men had hit on her from all directions. A plump politician with an indecipherable accent. A Broadway star who liked to score. A former consort of Silver Anderson's. And a tall, thin dress designer who swung both ways.

She'd declined every offer, having decided – quite firmly – that men were out, career was in.

Christmas was only a few days away, and when it was over she planned to return to Los Angeles and shoot the final batch of Cloud commercials and photographs. Actually she was looking forward to it. After nine months of living on the Coast she'd gotten used to the L.A. pace, the beautiful weather, and friendly people. She even missed her apartment, and thought she might buy a couple of cats when she returned. If the movie deal panned out she entertained the thought of renting a house – maybe at the beach.

Christmas shopping in New York was frantic. The stores were packed. Choosing presents was fun – paying for them a nightmare. And Jade found that everywhere she went she was recognized. Losing her freedom was quite a blow.

Finally, all shopped out, she was ready for a family Christmas. Corey was flying in from the Coast, and when the holidays were over they planned to travel back to L.A. together.

The day before she was all set to leave for Connecticut, Mark Rand re-entered her life with a vengeance.

He was divorced, and ready for commitment.

*

"We need decisions, Jack," Aretha said, in her best persuasive voice. "Otherwise we are going to be producing shows with just li'l ole you sitting all on your lonesome in front of the camera."

"I told you," Jack said stubbornly. "I want Jade Johnson on the show."

"And I told *you*," Aretha replied patiently, "she is in New York, and will not be back until after Christmas."

"I'd like to have a definite commitment from her people that she'll do the programme the week she returns."

Sighing, Aretha fluffed out her hair. "I'll do my best. Ever since Norman Gooseberger took off from Briskinn & Bower, it's a bitch getting them to return a call – let alone anything else. They're all a bunch of deadheads over there. Our show is hotter than Carson, an' those assholes can't even put their finger in the dial."

"Get her," Jack said sternly.

"I'm *workin'* on it. Meanwhile, the Carlos Brent booking looks like a definite. And we're still working on Zachary Klinger."

"Sounds good."

As he walked from the office, Aretha made a face behind his back. He'd been a real pain in the ass for weeks now. Usually he was such a sweetheart, but when he had something on his mind – watch out! Somehow foxy Jade Johnson had gotten under his skin. Aretha couldn't figure how or why, she just knew he was hot to confront her. If Jack wished to destroy someone, he did it in front of a camera, and *Ms.* Johnson was his next proposed victim.

She placed another call to Briskinn & Bower, this time asking for Bernie Briskinn. Aretha had found that if you couldn't get what you wanted from the employees – go to the boss. It always worked.

*

Jack hit the freeway in his Ferrari, already late for a meeting with Heaven and his business manager. Suddenly his little schoolgirl niece was an earner – heading for big bucks, and he wanted to make sure her money was well protected and invested correctly.

What a shock he'd had the day of her launch party. Expecting some minor hype which would fizzle out to nothing, he'd walked into a major event.

428

Heaven was all set for stardom, and when he heard her record he flipped. She had a sensational voice. Without a doubt he knew she possessed that very special quality which would propel her right to the top. She was going to be a star. Just like her mother.

At first he was assailed by so many different emotions. She was too young to get caught up in the crap. And then he felt an almost parental pride that she was good, a winner, for Jack was a winner himself, and he knew what it was like to have to struggle for achievement.

How was Silver going to feel? It would be interesting to observe her public reaction if the kid actually *did* make it.

After Heaven had lip-sync'ed her song, he made his way over, pushing through the crowds of congratulators.

"Hey – I'm one proud uncle," he whispered, aware she didn't want anyone making the family connection.

"Really?" She glowed with triumph and delight.

"Call me tomorrow. I know you're busy now, so I'm taking off."

She nodded excitedly, amber eyes gleaming.

Lindi moved in. "I'm getting questions about why Jack Python is here," she said, smiling at him. "Hi, I'm Lindi Foxworthe. In charge of P.R."

"And I'm making a fast exit," he said, kissing Heaven on the cheek, and slipping her a small gift-wrapped package. "Happy birthday, sweet seventeen."

He hadn't seen her since, although they spoke on the phone often. As soon as her record took off he had suggested this meeting with his business manager.

"I *have* a manager," she'd said, which was news to him.

"Who?"

"Remember Rocky?"

Sure – he wasn't likely to forget Rocky. And how'd she ever got caught up with *that* creep, when he'd issued specific instructions she wasn't ever to see him again?

Goddammit! He wasn't her father. He was her uncle. She would be eighteen in a year, and how could he prevent her from doing what she wanted? At least when she reached eighteen he could stop worrying.

"Bring all the contracts George signed on your behalf and meet me at my business manager's office in Century City, Thursday at two-thirty," he instructed.

She was there, and so was Rocky – a walking nightmare in a white suit, black shirt, white tie, and two-toned shoes.

"Hiya, man," Rocky greeted him, friendly as an over-boisterous puppy.

Jack ignored him, checked out the contracts with his business manager, and was shocked to discover that Rocky owned fifty-one percent of her blossoming career.

"Why didn't you show these to me *before* you got George to sign them?" he steamed.

"Because," she shrugged, "you're always so busy. Anyway," she added saucily, "you might've not let me do it."

Indicating Rocky he said, "This Stallone clone owns fifty-one per cent of you. Does that seem right?"

"Hey, man," objected Rocky, adjusting his cuffs, "I *got* her the gig with College. Without me she'd be just another little girl tryin' to make it."

"Back off," warned Jack. "These contracts are going right over to my lawyer's office."

"They're legal," Rocky scowled. He didn't appreciate being treated like a nothing.

"We'll see."

"Stop!" announced Heaven. "I'm perfectly happy with Rocky getting his cut. Lay off him, or I'm going home."

Could it be his imagination, or was there the faint shadow of Silver emerging? Was this budding young rock star going to turn out to be just like mommy?

The least he could do was see that the money she earned was well looked after. Then she was on her own, if that's the way she wanted it.

*

Heaven skipped out of the meeting, a disgruntled Rocky trailing her. "Your uncle treats me like a real shitheel," he complained. "I bin good t'ya. Haven't I?"

"Yep."

"So what's his problem?"

"I guess he just wants to see that I'm okay. He's my only family, y'know."

"No shit? You gotta grandfather, *and* a mother. S'more than I've ever had."

"You must have had a *mother*."

"Naw. I got dumped on the steps of a church when I was born. Nice, huh?"

Staring at him earnestly, she said, "I didn't know that, Rocky. It's like really awful."

"What can I tell ya – I survived," he mumbled.

They walked towards her car, a bright red Chrysler convertible – Uncle Jack's birthday present. The gift-wrapped package he'd handed her at the launch party had contained the keys. How thrilled and surprised she'd been. What a hot car!

"Mebbe I should get *me* a business manager," Rocky mused. "Handle all *my* loot."

Sliding behind the wheel she said, "Why don't you?"

"HEAVEN! HEAVEN!" Two teenage girls ran over to the car. "Oooh, you're so pretty! Can we touch you? Can you write your name on our hands? Oooh!!"

"Get *outta* here," Rocky growled, jumping into the passenger seat.

Not quite sure whether he meant the girls or her, she started the car and zoomed off. Being recognized was such a blast! She loved it more each time.

As they drove along, Rocky threw her a sidelong glance. Sweet, sweet baby flesh. And he hadn't laid a finger on her, although the prospect was tempting.

He knew he was in on a pass – one false move and maybe her uncle *would* start checking with his big-shot lawyers. Everything was legal . . . but if Jack wanted him out of the picture . . .

Hey – he had no urge to go back to dealing drugs. It was a dangerous occupation and he'd had about enough. This kid was going all the way. And he was going all the way with her. Meanwhile, she was still living with her grandfather. He had to get her out of there, set her up in her own place. And to make things *really* tight – how about if he *married* her? Then Uncle Jack could go take a hike.

The thought appealed.

"Listen, babe," he said lightly. "Ya wanna go t'a party tonight?"

Rocky had never asked her out socially; it was always business. "I don't know . . ." she replied guardedly. "Whose party?"

"Friend of mine at the beach. You've bin cooped up writin' that theme song for *The Murder* all week. It'll be a trip t'get outta the house."

"I guess . . ." she said hesitantly, wishing it was Penn Sullivan asking her out. Meeting him at her record launch party had been a real thrill. Unfortunately it was true – since her success it was all work work work, and no time for play. Eddie had telephoned on a couple of occasions, and she hadn't even had time to return his calls. Getting the plum assignment to write the theme song for *The Murder* was probably more exciting than *Gonna Eatcha Tonight!* climbing the charts faster than anyone expected. It was currently at number four with a bullet on the *Billboard* chart – which meant it was still rising.

"You're gonna be number one!" everyone at College Records assured her. And then they had asked her if she would like to write and perform the theme song for *The Murder*.

Would she? wow!

Originally Orpheus had wanted Cyndi Lauper or Madonna. An executive at College Records had taken a meeting with Howard Soloman and convinced him that Heaven was the hottest and youngest meteor on the horizon.

The Murder was still filming, behind schedule, in Puerta Vallarta. Heaven had been shown a rough cut of the dailies, and even she knew the finished product was going to be a smash. Clarissa Browning was staggering; Whitney Valentine looked breathtaking; and Mannon Cable gave a wonderful performance. It wasn't a youth picture, but she loved every scintillating minute –for it combined all the elements of exciting moviegoing.

"You like?" Howard Soloman asked, having snuck into the screening room while she was watching.

"Brilliant!" she enthused.

"Write us something tricky," he requested with a wink.

"I will, Mr Soloman, I will!"

And she had. As far as she was concerned it was the best song she'd ever written.

Grandfather George was in his workroom when she returned home, which meant that he wouldn't emerge for the rest of the night.

She had dropped Rocky off at his Hollywood apartment. "Pick me up at ten," he'd said.

"Ten!" she'd exclaimed. "What time does this party start?"

"Babe – no party worth goin' to starts before eleven."

"If I can get out."

"If ya can get out!" He'd laughed derisively. "We gotta start thinking 'bout movin' you to a place of your own."

The seed was planted. He had to pull Heaven away from any sign of family. She was going to be a rock star. What kind of a rock star lived in the *Valley* with her *grandfather*?

Yeah, Rocky decided. Tonight was the night his sweet little piece of baby flesh was going to grow up all the way.

Chapter 85

Puerta Vallarta was hot in more ways than one. If the days were steamy while the cast and crew toiled away shooting the final scenes of *The Murder*, then the nights were even more so.

Everyone was on edge. They all knew the film was special. They all wanted to be finished with it before Christmas, and get home to their families.

Between Arizona and Puerta Vallarta there was only a three-day break. Clarissa had said to Mannon, "What shall we do?"

"Honey," he'd replied apologetically, "I've got to go see Melanie-Shanna and my baby. There's no way I can't."

On the day Poppy Soloman had thrown a lunch for Jade Johnson, Melanie-Shanna had given birth. Somehow, bearing Mannon Cable's son had seemed a more pressing engagement. Mannon had wanted to fly to L.A. as soon as he heard, but Clarissa stopped him.

"For the first time in your career you are giving a fine performance," she had told him. "If you break your concentration now it will spoil everything. Trust me."

He trusted her. Clarissa was like no other woman he'd been with in his life. Her intensity had him caught in a web he really didn't want to escape from. With Clarissa Browning he was not a macho superstar with startlingly blue eyes and a way with the ladies. He was a *real* man, with honest feelings. And he was a damn good actor.

Strutting, sexy, good-humoured Mannon Cable had taken a walk. Clarissa taught him to centre his feelings and care about himself more.

"You're much too nice to people," she'd said. "They walk all over you, and treat you like a fool."

He hadn't realized that. So he withdrew a little, became more aloof, stopped being so unassuming and good-natured.

"And you eat like a wild animal," she informed him. "No more red meat, sugar, salt, alcohol."

"Hey —" he'd objected.

"Trust me," she'd said patiently. It was her favourite expression.

He'd trusted her, and he knew it was working, because he'd never felt so physically healthy in his life.

There was no way she could stop him from visiting his son. Wasn't he entitled to be excited about becoming a father for the first time? Even if he *did* plan on divorcing Melanie-Shanna, as soon as his lawyer gave him the go-ahead. So, in spite of Clarissa's objections, he flew to Los Angeles. She wasn't pleased.

"What'll *you* do?" he'd asked her, before leaving.

"Don't worry about me. Please," she'd said icily.

"I don't want you to be angry."

"I'm not."

He knew she was, but he figured he could straighten everything out once he got to Puerta Vallarta.

Clarissa had formed an alliance with Norman Gooseberger. He had arrived in Arizona to take care of Whitney Valentine, but once Clarissa ascertained he was very good at what he did, she decided she wanted him for herself. Placing a direct call to Howard Soloman, she demanded Norman's exclusive services for the remainder of the picture.

Howard was bemused. "You refuse to do publicity," he pointed out. "Why would you want Norman?"

She did not reply that she had a whim to take him away from Whitney. She just said one word — "Because."

Howard understood *Because* when it was spoken by a star. "He's yours," he said resignedly, wondering how Whitney would take the news.

Howard phoned Norman personally to give him the good news. "I've cleared it with Bernie," he said. "Just do whatever she wants, and stay close."

Norman was thrilled. Clarissa Browning was his idol. He regarded her as one of the finest actresses of her generation — she ranked alongside Meryl Streep and Vanessa Redgrave as far as he was concerned.

Corey was not so thrilled. Norman had left for the weekend,

and now could be away for weeks. "You mean you're not coming back?" he asked anxiously.

"Don't sweat it," Norman replied. "I'll fix it so you get a few days in Puerta Vallarta. Meantime, pack me a suitcase and get it out on the next plane."

Clarissa and Norman spent the three-day break between locations redefining Norman's sexual urges.

"You're not *really* gay," she teased him, the night Mannon and the crew took off. They were in her suite, lying on the bed fully dressed, downing lethal concoctions of grapefruit juice, vodka and gin.

He nodded affirmatively. Not many people discussed his sexual preferences.

"Come *on*," Clarissa said lazily. "How do you *know*?"

His voice sounded surprisingly dry. "It's always been that way."

"Always?"

Another nod.

"You mean you've never had a woman?" She trailed delicate fingers across his cheek.

Shaking his head he remembered his mother's loud voice when she discovered *Penthouse* magazine hidden under his pillow. He was thirteen at the time. "Filth!" Carmel had boomed. "Pornography! You want to grow up just like your father, humping every open-legged starlet you see?"

No. He didn't want to be like Orville. He'd heard the fights in the huge mansion the three of them inhabited with four Filipino servants. He'd seen the anger and hurt they inflicted on each other. So one day, when an older boy at Beverly Hills High made a suggestion to him, it seemed like a safe alternative. If he wasn't to be just like Orville, he had to strike out in the other direction. And the other direction turned out to be extremely pleasurable.

Dropping out of school at seventeen, he went to New York, and enjoyed himself in the fast lane of the gay culture for several years. His parents, although horrified when they first found out he was what Orville called "a faggot" and Carmel termed "queer", were only too delighted that he chose to do his growing up out of sight. They gave him financial support, and the feeling they'd be happier if he stayed away.

When he decided to take a job and start shaping his life, Orville arranged a position for him in the San Francisco offices of Briskinn & Bower. He turned out to be excellent at what he did. P.R. was his vocation.

After meeting Corey, he felt the time had come to go home, and without delay he bought a house in the Hollywood Hills with some trust money he'd inherited. Setting up housekeeping with Corey was a real challenge. Norman was a grasshopper – he liked the thrill of many different sexual partners. So far he had managed – only just – to remain faithful to Corey.

"You don't know what you're missing," Clarissa said softly, allowing her fingers to creep down to the buttons of his shirt.

Laughing uneasily he tried to figure out what she wanted. Clarissa Browning was a star, an Oscar-winning actress. She had Mannon Cable – what could she possibly want from him?

"You're very handsome, Norman," she said, lightly touching his exposed nipples. "It seems to me such a waste . . ."

"What is?" His voice cracked. He knew exactly what she meant. In spite of himself he felt a hardness in his pants. *My God! She's actually turning me on!* he thought.

"You know what," she replied huskily. "Don't you ever wonder about a woman's body? Oh, I know you can look at pictures if you so desire. But pictures can't tell you about touch and taste and smell, can they?"

As she spoke she continued to massage his nipples, and by the time she began to unbutton her blouse he knew he was ready to do whatever she asked. The excitement of the unknown was pounding through his body. Norman Gooseberger was twenty-six years old, and he had never had sex with a woman.

"Take off your clothes," she commanded.

With trembling hands he started to do just that.

Clarissa opened her blouse as she watched him. She wore no bra, and her breasts were small, with sharply extended nipples. As he stripped off, her eyes never left him. Distractedly she touched herself.

Now he was naked, and she was still dressed. His hard-on dominated the room.

"Very nice," she murmured. "I want you to straddle me and touch it to my breasts."

He could hardly breathe as he obeyed her request.

"Easy," she said, taking his erection in her hands and rubbing it back and forth, the tip playing against her erect nipples. "Just take it slow and easy."

How could he? All he wanted to do was come, and there was no way he could control it any longer.

"Clarissa – I'm going to –" Before he could get the word out, it happened. A throbbing, pulsating explosion.

And as his semen pumped all over her, she smiled – a secret smile. "We'll make a man of you yet, won't we, Norman?"

*

The first thing Mannon did when he arrived back in Los Angeles from the Arizona location was to instruct his driver to stop at a hamburger joint and get him two double burgers with everything on. This health kick Clarissa had him on was all very well, but he needed a break. Fuck it, he was doing his best – she couldn't expect miracles.

Munching the burgers in the limo on the way to his house, he felt one hundred percent better.

Arriving home, he marched inside, the conquering hero returning from the wars of location to see his son.

There was no one to greet him. "Where is everyone?" he hollered.

The Mexican housekeeper appeared. "Meesus Cable, she out."

"And the baby?"

"He out."

Wonderful. He'd rushed home specially, and everyone was out. What a welcome!

Not only were they out, but they did not return for another two hours. By this time he was furious.

"Where have you been?" he demanded, as Melanie-Shanna entered the house. Behind her stood a uniformed nurse carrying his three-week-old son, Jason. Not waiting for an answer, he rushed over to the nurse and inspected her small charge. "Jesus!" he exclaimed. "He looks just like me!"

Later that night, after he'd spent plenty of time staring at his son and heir, and consumed a hearty roast beef dinner and a couple of scotches, he took a second look at Melanie-Shanna. He had to admit it – she was gorgeous. Of course, Clarissa had taught him that gorgeous wasn't everything, and he missed her already, but Melanie-Shanna *was* still his wife, and maybe – until he broke the divorce news – he would be wise to pay her a little attention.

They had just got into bed when he reached for her. "How're you doing, pretty?"

Edging away from his touch she replied, "Fine, thank you."

"You fine – me fine – baby fine. It's good to be home."

"For how long?"

He detected hostility in her voice. Was it possible she'd heard about Clarissa and him? *Deny it. Deny it* and then *Deny it.*

"Only three days, but the rest of the location'll pass faster than you can buy yourself a present at Cartier."

"I want a divorce, Mannon."

What? What did she say? Was he losing his hearing? *I want a diamond necklace* he could understand. *I want an emerald ring* was easy. But *I want a divorce*? Come *on.* That was *his* line. And he wasn't ready to say it. Not yet, anyway.

"Huh?"

"I said" – her voice was clear and calm – "I want a divorce."

"Are you goddamn *crazy*?"

"No. I'm perfectly sane."

"Why?"

"You know why."

"Have you heard things about me and Clarissa?"

No reply.

"*Have* you?"

No reply.

"You've been listening to that cunt Poppy Soloman, haven't you? Well, I'm here to tell you it's lies – *all* goddamn lies."

"I've seen a lawyer."

"You've *what*?"

"He insisted I shouldn't allow you back in the house, but I said you're entitled to spend at least one night with your son."

Fury overcame him. "WHO IS THIS FUCKING SONOFABITCH? I'LL KILL THE MOTHERFUCKER!"

"I want you out, Mannon. I'm divorcing you, and nothing you say will stop me."

He had ranted and screamed, raved and roared. And eventually he'd had to leave for Puerta Vallarta. But not before meeting with *his* lawyer, who told him it was the best thing that could possibly happen. "*She's* throwing *you* out. Can't you see how much better that looks?"

No. He couldn't see it at all. He was very angry.

Clarissa welcomed him back with a wintry smile and a new constant companion – Norman Gooseberger, who followed her everywhere like an obedient and adoring dog.

"If he wasn't a fag I'd say he had the hots for you," Mannon remarked one day.

"Maybe he's *not* gay," she replied mysteriously.

"Ha ha! What a joker."

And so the filming continued, and Mannon tried to forget about Melanie-Shanna and her unfair behaviour.

Clarissa helped him slip back into his role. He was soon as spellbound by her as ever.

Chapter 86

Christmas shopping was an ordeal Silver was glad she didn't have to put up with more than once a year. Under sufferance, Wes agreed to go with her, if only to park the Rolls as they went from Neiman Marcus to Saks, and then across the street to Rodeo Drive. It was a California Christmas, the fancy street decorations and the bright sunshine forming an incongruous alliance.

"At least Rodeo is civilized," Silver remarked, throwing off benevolent waves of good cheer to all who recognized her. She was in rather a good mood, thanks to the way she had handled the Zachary Klinger situation.

Zeppo had called her. "We'll have a lunch, kiddo. Just you an' me."

"As long as you promise not to jump on me, Zeppo dear."

Cackling with amusement he'd said, "Don't think I can't."

"I wouldn't *dream* of thinking *any* such thing. I know you are perfectly capable — you scoundrel, you!"

Zeppo White thrived on flattery, and Silver knew how to pile it on.

Something told her she should make a special effort, so Fernando was summoned to do her hair, and Raoul for her makeup. She chose to wear a devastatingly glamorous Yves Saint Laurent suit.

Arriving at The Beverly Hills Hotel, for lunch in the Polo Lounge, she looked every inch the star.

"Greetings, Miss Anderson," said the maitre d'. "How lovely to see you again."

"Thank you, Pasquale," she said imperiously, and swept to booth one, where Zeppo waited.

Standing up, he said, "Gorgeous, kiddo. Ravishing."

"How kind of you."

"Kind — bullshit. You're the last of the great stars, and don't you ever forget it."

"I'll try not to," she said modestly.

"What a gal!"

During the meal — lightly grilled sole for her, a rare steak for him — they discussed her future career. Zeppo had plenty to talk about, but not one *firm* offer for her to do another movie. Oh yes, there were guest spots on *Palm Springs*, the NBC special, and talk of a record album, but where were the starring film roles he had promised?

"People gotta see what happens with *Romance*," he explained. "When that goes through the ceiling — we name our price."

"You're sure of that?"

"Do dogs crap in Central Park?"

"*So* eloquent."

"So what? As long as you get the game plan." He shifted uncomfortably.

She had a feeling he wanted to say something but wasn't quite sure how to go about it. Unusual for Zeppo.

And then Zachary Klinger walked in, and she knew why she'd taken such care with her appearance. A confrontation was inevitable. Zeppo, the unscrupulous little turd, had arranged it.

"Silver," Zachary greeted her formally.

"Zachary," she replied with cool aplomb.

"Do you mind if I join you?"

Before she could say — *Yes, I do mind very much*, Zeppo was on his feet. With feigned amazement he peered at his oversize watch. "It's two o'clock. Jesus, kiddo, I'm running late. I'm leaving you in excellent hands — the best. This man is a king!"

"Goodbye, Zeppo." She didn't care to listen to his ass-kissing speech. Enough was enough.

Zeppo raced off, and Zachary sat down. There was a long silence. Finally he said, "Tell me, Silver, what is it going to cost me to get you back?"

She glanced edgily around the restaurant. "Too much for even *you* to afford."

"I own Orpheus, you know."

"I'm well aware of that."

"I could make you the most famous woman in the world."

A hint of sarcasm entered her voice. "I'm not doing *too* badly as it is, thank you very much."

"If I don't wish to put *Romance* out, I don't have to. What will *that* do for your career? Everyone will think the film is so bad it can't be released."

Narrowing her eyes she said, "Just try it."

Taking a Dunhill cigar holder from his pocket, he extracted a fat Cuban cigar and lit up, blowing a steady stream of smoke in her direction. "Maybe you'll force me to."

She refused to be intimidated by this man. He had used her. Why did he have to come back after all these years and expect her to fall into his arms?

"Maybe," she said coolly.

He began to laugh. "I always admired your spirit, it always excited me."

"Let this excite you," she said evenly. "I am married. *And* I am in love with my husband. So kindly leave me alone with your disgusting threats and blackmail."

"You're married to a bum," he stated.

"My choice, and I like it." Swiftly she rose.

Putting a restraining hand on her arm he said, "I can spend millions to promote *Romance*, or I can let it languish on a shelf. One night of your company might persuade me to spend the money. Think about it."

"Good*bye*, Zachary."

"I'll be waiting for your call."

Well, she hadn't called him, she had contacted Carlos Brent instead. In his own peculiar way, Carlos had as much power as Zachary Klinger. It was rumoured he was connected – politically and otherwise.

"Carlos, dear," she'd said, glad they were friends again. "What would you do if you found out Orpheus might not release *Romance* because of some *whim* of Zachary Klinger's?"

He'd laughed. "Don't even think about it. *Romance* will be the hit of the year, *I'll* make sure of that."

She wasn't worrying. And she was pleased with the way she'd dealt with Zachary.

They walked into Giorgio, Silver and Wes. He sat at the private bar in the middle of the store while she tried on everything in sight.

"I thought we were *Christmas* shopping for *other* people," he said pointedly.

"Ah, yes," she replied, choosing a beaded handbag for Nora, plus an assortment of Giorgio scent. Then she decided she had to have the most delicious gold beaded Fabrice gown she had ever seen. It was six thousand dollars. "Come and see it, darling," she called to him. "I'll wear it on New Year's Eve."

Strolling over, he said, "What do I care? It's your money. Enjoy it."

He went back to the bar, and was just settling into a nice cold beer, when a familiar voice exclaimed, "Wesley!" And Reba Winogratsky, his former landlady, was all over him with unwelcome wet kisses and a hug or two.

Extracting himself – she was like an over-made-up spider – he gave her a lukewarm greeting.

"Wesley! Wesley! Wesley!" she sighed, with a knowing shake of her head and an affectionate wink. "Look what happened to my Wesley."

Her Wesley?

"How's it going, Reba?" he asked, with more enthusiasm than he felt.

"All the better for seein' you." She spotted Silver emerging from a dressing room and gave an orgasmic yelp. "Introduce me, Wesley. Oh my God! Do I look all right?"

Reba, in a creased beige linen suit – the skirt too short – with bare scorched legs and feet encased in stiletto heels, did not look all right. She looked like a cheap tramp, in spite of the extra-large diamond ring he spotted winking and blinking on her finger.

Noticing his focus of attention, she waved her hand in front of him. "I'm back with my old man – a reconcili-present."

"Nice," he said.

"Intro*duce* me," she hissed again.

Silver strolled over, ignored Reba, and took Wes possessively by the arm. "We can move on, darling. I'm all through here."

"Er . . . this is Reba," he said awkwardly. "She wants to meet you."

Silver gave her the distant but charming smile reserved for

442

fans. "Hello," she said — and then promptly ignored her again.

Reba sprang into action. "I *looove* you in *Palm Springs*," she gushed. "And I'm so thrilled you and Wesley have gotten married."

"Thank you," Silver replied coolly.

"Wesley an' I are old friends," Reba continued, tripping over her words as she peered at Silver closely to see if she'd had a face-lift. "You *could* say that we shared a house."

Silver voice was pure acid. "How *cosy*."

"Reba was my landlady," Wes explained hurriedly, lest she get the wrong impression.

"And more!" Reba said with a saucy wink. "I was separated from my beloved at the time. And of course, Wesley hadn't met you. And —"

Silver's eyes glittered dangerously as she interrupted Reba in full swing. "*Do* excuse us, we're running late." With a stony expression she swept towards the entrance of the store.

Wes shrugged as he went to follow her. "Bye-bye, Reba."

"What's the matter?" she asked spitefully, blocking his way. "Aren't I good enough to talk to movie stars?"

"Sure you are," he replied easily, trying to dodge past her. "Only we've got a lot of ground to cover today."

A thin smile spread across her face, cracking her carelessly applied makeup. "Pay the money you owe, Wesley. The big boys are impatient. I wouldn't screw with them if I was you. It's gettin' dangerous."

Chapter 87

The New Year's Eve invitations were sent out three days before Christmas, arriving in most homes on Christmas Eve.

Beautifully embossed, and printed on white cards with festive red lettering, they read:

Zachary K. Klinger
requests
the pleasure of your company
for a
New Year's Eve cruise
on
December 31
1985

Within hours it was known to be the hottest event of the year, and if you hadn't received an invitation – forget it! Leave town. Crawl under a stone. Kill yourself!

Only fifty invitations were sent out. Zachary had decided that only fifty couples would get lucky. One hundred choice people to see the New Year in with him.

Since Zachary Klinger was one of the richest men in the world, plus he owned a Hollywood movie studio, nobody could afford to turn his invitation down. Zachary had decided that at the party he would announce plans for Orpheus to film a remake of the classic *All About Eve*. The coveted Bette Davis role was a part Silver would kill for. He should have known blackmail wouldn't work, but she was an actress after all, and if the bait was right, maybe he could win her back that way. It was worth a try. And a magnificent party was a small price to pay to gain her attention.

Beverly D'Amo had a great time checking out the guest list with Zachary's fleet of efficient secretaries. She made sure Jade and Corey were included, and then, with a wicked grin, double-checked to ascertain whether Jack Python's name was on the list. It was. Frankly, she saw no harm in getting the two of them together again. After the things Jade had told her she figured they must really be something as a duo. Not that Jade had revealed any gory details – sexual descriptions were not her style. However, by listening to what she *hadn't* said, Beverly knew instinctively they should give each other another chance. There was nothing she would like better than to see her friend settled with the right guy.

"Why are you having this party?" she asked Zachary.

"The start of the New Year should be celebrated in a proper way. I'll make this celebration memorable," he replied.

"I bet you will," she murmured, already aware of some of his plans to make it an event to be remembered. Belly-dancers.

444

break-dancers, a Brazilian trio, disco music, fireworks. And all on a spectacular cruise between Long Beach – where the party guests would join the yacht, courtesy of a fleet of limos – to Laguna and back.

Beverly found that living with Zachary – in spite of his age – was an adventure. And the only part of the adventure she couldn't stomach was his predilection for having sex while hookers watched. God – how she hated it! At first she had thought of it as one of life's more bizarre experiences, shutting her eyes, gritting her teeth, and going with the flow. Now the whole sordid scene disgusted her.

She had moved in with Zachary to advance her career – no use in kidding herself on *that* score. Unfortunately she had fallen in love with him.

Not with his money.

Not with his power.

Beverly D'Amo loved Zachary K. Klinger – the man.

God help her.

Chapter 88

There was only one more day and night left before the cast and crew of *The Murder* left Puerta Vallarta and winged their way back to Los Angeles just in time for Christmas.

As a location it had not been an easy one. The oppressive heat made everything a constant effort. And when it wasn't hot and muggy, it rained – putting the film even more behind schedule. Plus most of the cast and crew suffered at one time or other with what one wag had christened 'the Mexican Hot Trot'.

Clarissa was one of the fortunate few. She ate only fresh vegetables, fish and fruit, flown in daily from L.A. and because of this had not succumbed to the dreaded runs.

Mannon was okay while he stuck to her regime, but a couple

of days before leaving he cheated with an enchilada and a few tequilas with the crew, and lived to regret it.

"It's your own fault," Clarissa said bluntly.

Sometimes he thought she didn't have a sympathetic bone in her body.

He made it through the day's filming, and then lay groaning on his bed all night.

Clarissa did not visit him.

Clarissa was conspicuous by her absence.

"You know, you're a real cold-hearted bitch," he complained to her the next day.

"I am not a nurse," she replied. "If you hadn't filled yourself with junk food, you wouldn't be sick."

True. But still . . . she *could* show a little sympathy.

They had decided that when they returned to Los Angeles, he would move in with her. He hoped he was making the correct decision. Melanie-Shanna fussed the hell out of him if he had so much as a cold. And Whitney always had, too. But then how could he expect Clarissa to behave like other women? Indeed, he wouldn't want her to. She was different, a true artist, and her blazing talent was her main attraction.

He felt a little better the next day, but by the evening his stomach was churning again, and he didn't care to risk being anywhere except close to his bathroom.

Clarissa visited him later. Her fine hair was twisted in a knot and threaded with gardenias. She wore a white off-the-shoulder dress instead of her usual uniform of baggy slacks and a shirt.

"You're all dressed up," he remarked.

"It's the last night. I'm going dancing."

"Who with?"

"Norman."

He should have guessed. Norman Gooseberger. Her faithful slave.

"Have fun."

"I'll try."

"See you in the morning."

Restlessly he lay in bed thinking. Tomorrow was the start of his new life. *The Murder* was the start of his new career.

And yet he couldn't help worrying about the son he was leaving behind.

Jason.

The boy looked just like him.

Was he making the right move?

Yes. Clarissa was his woman now. She combined class and talent. She would bring him up to a new level.

When he awoke several hours later, he was bathed in sweat and had an awesome erection. Best of all, his stomach felt calm. In fact, he was in good shape. The pills the makeup girl had given him had obviously worked. "Take these," she'd said. "You'll wake up singing."

Getting out of bed he showered, waited for his erection to subside, and when it didn't, decided to pay Clarissa a visit, sure she would enjoy it.

Fortunately, they were on the same floor in the hotel, just a few doors apart. Naked under a white towelling bathrobe, he padded barefooted down the corridor, humming softly to himself. Fitting the spare key to her room in the door, he entered quietly.

She was asleep – the room was in darkness. Faintly he could hear the steady rhythm of her breathing.

Slipping off his robe he slid into bed beside her.

She had her back towards him, and he nestled up against it, willing his hard-on to wake her. Or if she didn't want to wake, he would be quite happy to accommodate her while she slept. Cupping her ass with his hands, he prepared to slip in through the back entrance.

Several things happened at once.

Mannon encountered balls.

Norman Gooseberger let out a yell.

And from the other side of the bed Clarissa mumbled a sleepy "What's going on?"

"Jesus Christ!" shouted Mannon, with a rush of realization, leaping from the bed.

Norman sat up equally startled, just in time for Mannon's fist to connect with his jaw.

There was a sickening splintering sound.

Howling with fury, Mannon dragged Norman from the bed, hitting him again and again.

Desperately putting up his hands to defend himself, Norman began to scream with pain. His jaw was hanging as if unhinged, and he knew it was broken.

"You fucking phoney faggot!" Mannon roared. "You cock-sucking ass-licking little *prick*!"

He continued to beat up on Norman, who slumped un-conscious under the vicious rain of blows.

Clarissa went wild, first trying to grab Mannon's arms and then kicking him on the legs. She couldn't stop him. He was out of control with anger.

Spinning around, he whacked her across the face. "You cheating *bitch*! How dare you cheat on me."

"Fuck you!" she began to scream. "Who do you think you are? Leave him alone, you *monster*. LEAVE HIM ALONE! YOU'RE KILLING HIM, FOR GOD'S SAKE!"

Chapter 89

Christmas morning.

Jack Python took a trip over to the Valley for lunch with Heaven and his father. George appeared to be even more vague and preoccupied than ever. The old man attended lunch, prepared by the housekeeper, then rushed off to his workroom, muttering about a new braking device he was working on.

Heaven waited until George was safely out of the way, and made an announcement. "I'm movin' out," she said. "Rocky found me a great apartment — like with security an' all that stuff."

If she was looking for a fight from Jack, she wasn't going to get it. He didn't blame her.

They exchanged presents, then she went off to see Rocky, and Jack drove over to Kellie Sidney's house, where there were children and dogs and family and food.

Being on his own, Christmas was not Jack's favourite time. Last Christmas he had spent with Clarissa in New York, and hated every minute. He had heard the rumours about her affair with Mannon. What a strange combination! It was difficult to imagine those two together.

Briefly he thought about Jade Johnson, and wished that it had worked out.

It hadn't.

No good thinking of her.

★

Rocky greeted Heaven, ushered her into his high-rise Hollywood apartment (cheaply furnished and functional) — and then ushered her into his bed.

She was lonely, but not that lonely.

★

Howard Soloman flew back from fixing things in Puerta Vallarta a nervous wreck. How come, when anything bad happened, the first person they called on was him? What was he? The original fixer?

The director of *The Murder*, Dirk Price, had telephoned him in the middle of the night in a total panic. "Mannon's beaten up Clarissa and almost *killed* someone," he screamed hysterically down the phone wires.

"Calm down," Howard responded, already climbing from his comfortable bed. "No police. No hospitals. Use the unit doctor, an' keep everything under wraps until I get there. I'm on my way to the airport now."

"How can I do that?" whined Dirk.

Howard toughened up. "If you ever want to work again, you'll find a way," he warned, and then as an afterthought added, "Who did Mannon nearly kill?"

"Norman Gooseberger."

"Holy shit!"

It had taken clout, but he had fixed it. Norman Gooseberger was in a private nursing home in Mexico City with twenty-four-hour guards to keep out any snoopers. He had suffered a broken jaw, a broken nose, kidney damage, and various cuts and lacerations. His condition was stable.

Clarissa was back in her rented house on Benedict Canyon. She was bruised and shaken, with a black eye Marvin Hagler would have been proud of inflicting.

Mannon had insisted on returning to Melanie-Shanna.

Keeping it out of the newspapers was a nightmare. Finally, Howard huddled with the unit publicist, and they released a short statement.

ON LOCATION IN PUERTA VALLARTA, MEXICO, STARS OF *THE MURDER*, CLARISSA BROWNING AND MANNON CABLE WERE

449

INVOLVED IN A CAR ACCIDENT. BOTH SUFFERED MINOR BRUISES.
NORMAN GOOSEBERGER, PUBLICIST TO MS. BROWNING, WAS
ALSO HURT.

End of statement.

It took an hour before the rumours swept Hollywood like a tidal wave.

The most difficult part was telling Norman's parents. Howard called them from Puerta Vallarta and gave them the same story as the press release.

"What's the truth?" Orville asked bluntly.

"Not an attractive scenario," Howard replied. "We'll talk when I return. Meanwhile, Norman's fine. All taken care of."

"Should we fly in?"

"Not necessary."

So they didn't.

When Howard returned from Mexico, Poppy grilled him as if she was the F.B.I.

He didn't crack – Poppy had a mouth like the Grand Canyon.

*

Mark Rand accompanied Jade to Connecticut for the Christmas festivities. He was a new Mark Rand – attentive, concerned, caring. He was also divorced.

"I did it for you, sweetheart," he told her in his fine English accent. "Life was very dull without you. You *do* know we belong together, always. And now we can get married."

She was confused. Mark was the man she had lived with and loved for six long years. Theirs had never been a perfect relationship, but she couldn't deny they had experienced a lot of very good times indeed. And when Mark wanted to be, he was the most charming man in the world. He charmed her mother *and* her father.

"Isn't it about time you two got married?" her father asked. "You've waited long enough."

"Just think," her mother whispered excitedly. "When you marry, you'll have a *real* title, you'll be Lady Jade!"

Fortunately, her parents were old-fashioned enough to put them in separate bedrooms. Jade was relieved because, much to Mark's chagrin, she was not ready to leap back into bed with him as though their ten-month break had never happened.

"I want us to get married at once," he informed her.

Was it what *she* wanted?

Hell, she'd wanted it for six years – why not now?

Jack Python. His name kept on intruding into her thoughts.

Damn Jack Python. He was one night of great sex.

That was it.

Period.

In yesterday's newspapers there was a picture of him with Kellie Sidney at a film premiere.

How nice.

She hoped the two of them would be very unhappy.

"We'll get married in California," she promised Mark. "On New Year's Day."

"You'll never regret it, sweetheart," he replied with heartfelt sincerity. "I'll make up for all the time we've wasted."

Since arriving from California, Corey had seemed fidgety and nervous.

"What's up, bro?" she asked.

"It's Norman," he said. "Everything was going so well between us, until he went off to work on *The Murder*."

"There's nothing wrong with that, is there? It's his job, and you know he's the best at what he does."

"I know," Corey confessed miserably. "And at first he phoned me every day. But since he became Clarissa Browning's personal P.R., I haven't heard from him in weeks. He was supposed to be back in L.A. by now. I keep on calling the house, and there's no reply."

"Try his parents," she suggested. "It's Christmas Day – I bet he's over at their place."

"Will you do it for me?" he begged.

Sighing, she said, "Give me the number."

Orville answered the phone, and wanted to know exactly who she was and why she was calling.

"My name is Jade Johnson," she said. "I'm a friend of Norman's, and a client. Can I speak to him?"

"Norman's not here," Orville said, lowering his voice. "He had a car accident in Mexico, he won't be back for a while."

"I'm sorry to hear that. It's nothing serious, is it? Is he all right?"

"Perfectly all right. He's . . . er . . . recuperating. Somewhere, I'm not sure where."

"I'd like to send flowers."

"They'll have to wait until he gets back. I have no address for him."

When she put down the phone, Corey was frantic to know what had happened. She relayed Orville's conversation.

He nodded, dully accepting the fact that Norman had no doubt found someone else.

Jade felt so sorry for her brother. She wished there was something she could do, only somehow words didn't seem enough. "Are you okay?" she asked full of concern.

He attempted a wry smile – didn't quite make it and gestured helplessly. "I changed my life for Norman," he said.

"No." She shook her head. "You didn't change *just* for Norman. You changed because it was what you *wanted* to do."

He realized the truth in what she was saying and nodded again. "You're right. Living a lie was killing me."

"And now you're free."

"I guess I am."

She squeezed his hand. "You know what Beverly always says – miss one taxi – there's a dozen more around the block."

"I'm not looking."

"You will."

He couldn't help smiling. "Love ya, sis."

"You too, baby brother."

*

Melanie-Shanna baked the turkey herself. And she fixed sweet potatoes, broccoli, corn bread, fresh peas, and a thick country gravy to go with it.

"Sen . . . *sational*!" Mannon praised, holding his plate out for seconds.

Piling more food on his plate, she wondered at the sudden difference in her errant husband. He had arrived back from Puerta Vallarta a changed man. The first words out of his mouth were "I don't want a divorce. I love you. I love the baby. That movie made me crazy. WE ARE NOT GETTING DIVORCED. I want to sell this goddamn mansion and buy a place in Mandeville Canyon – near the beach. We'll have room to keep horses and dogs. And I want us to have six more children. What d'you say?"

At first she had refused even to entertain the idea. But Mannon could be devilishly persuasive – not to mention charming, and eventually she succumbed. After all, she loved the man.

"That place was a nightmare," he told her. "Next time I go on location you're coming with me. You and the baby. No more lonely nights."

He'd hugged her so tight she thought she might break in two.

"What happened, Mannon?" she asked very quietly.

"Nothing," he said. A pause. "Nothing I want to talk about . . . not yet anyway."

*

Nora was at Silver's Christmas lunch, along with Fernando, his friend Boyce, her makeup artist Raoul, and her ex-agent Quinne Lattimore – who had recently separated from his wife of twenty-eight years.

"I can't *bear* to think of anyone alone at Christmas," Silver confided to Wes.

"Yeah," he agreed, thinking of all the Christmases he had spent alone and broke, usually ending up in bed with a woman as lonely as he.

Happiness was Silver speaking to him again. After bumping into Reba at Giorgio, she had flipped out – throwing a total jealous fit.

Who was that woman?
Have you slept with her?
My God, Wes. Where is your taste?
Or should I call you Wesley?
Wesley, indeed!
Was she hot in bed?
She looks like a prostitute.
An old prostitute.
A cheap hooker.
How could you?
When?
Recently?
Since we've been together?
I hate you!

A jealous Silver was a new Silver. Despite her acid tongue, he was glad she cared. So glad, in fact, that with a gesture of defiance he marched into the First Interstate Bank, requested his safe-deposit box, and took out the money he had stashed there. Screw the perpetrators of the Laurel Canyon scam. He was not returning one red cent. He had earned every dime.

And screw Reba Winogratsky too. What did she know anyway?

With the money in his pocket he strolled calmly into Tiffany's, the jewellery store, and announced his requirements. "I want a necklace for around nineteen thou," he said casually. "Tax included. Show me what you got."

The result was a ruby heart, embedded in pavé diamonds, on a diamond-studded gold chain. He hadn't given it to her yet. The moment had to be just right.

"Delicious turkey," Fernando said, dabbing his lips with a napkin.

"Delicious," echoed Boyce, his quiff of silver hair bobbing agreement.

"Did you cook it, Silver darling?" teased Raoul.

"*Naturellement, mon chéri!* Don't you all know how handy I am toiling over a hot stove?"

Everyone laughed.

In the kitchen Vladimir and Unity faced each other across the table and solemnly raised their shot glasses of the finest Russian vodka in a toast.

"To freedom," Vladimir said, downing the colourless liquid in one fast gulp.

"To money," Unity said.

They smiled at each other like conspirators. Which they were. *True Life Scandal* was paying them one hundred and twenty-five thousand dollars for the *real* story of Silver Anderson, Wes Money and Heaven. It was to be serialized over three weeks, and the first instalment was due to hit the stands on the Monday after New Year's.

By that time, Unity and Vladimir would be long gone.

Somewhere in New York . . .
Sometime in the seventies . . .

The girl found that living with Eli was the beginning of her life. He was the most unfailingly cheerful and good-natured person she had ever met, and after a while she couldn't help responding to his kindness.

"Where are you from?"

"I don't want to talk about it."

"What do you wanna do?"

"Being a waitress is fine."

"No, it's not."

"Why?"

"Because we are all put onto this earth to do something amazing with our lives. Make a goal, an' go for it!"

She didn't have any goals. Just living was enough.

Eli wouldn't allow her to drift. He insisted she accompany him to his singing classes and dancing lessons. One day he took her to his drama group, and she watched enthralled as he acted out a role in Macbeth.

"It's Shakespeare," he told her.

"What's Shakespeare?"

"Are you kiddin' me, girl?"

On her birthday he bombarded her with books on great playwrights, and text of their best work. "You gotta be more than just a pretty face," he told her.

She was captivated by the realistic scenes of great pathos and drama.

Occasionally Eli brought a friend home. She hated it when this happened, and if it was early enough she would go out and walk the streets rather than listen to the unwelcome sounds of their lovemaking.

One day he brought a friend home to stay. "This is Luke," he said, and she shivered with certain knowledge of bad things to come.

Luke was a burly, British blond with bulging muscles and a permanent sneer. He never dressed in anything but crotch-hugging Levis and torn tee-shirts.

"Luke thinks he's Marlon Brando," Eli joked.

"Don't fockin' laugh at me — yer spade fairy," Luke spat.

Eli winced and took it.

Luke didn't work. He sat on the roof all day, concentrating on his suntan and guzzling beer.

The girl did not understand what Eli saw in him. She knew it was only sexual, and hoped the attraction would soon pass.

At night she heard them together and buried her head beneath the covers, desperately trying to shut out the disturbing sounds.

Luke soon became violent. After several weeks he began to take Eli's money, and go out on drinking binges.

He tried to steal money from her one day, but she turned on him with such ferocity that he never went near her again.

She slept with a knife under her pillow, and was ever watchful.

"Get rid of the fockin' bitch," she heard him tell Eli.

"She stays," Eli replied, standing up to him for once.

"She goes or I go."

"So be it," replied Eli bravely.

To her enormous relief, Luke departed.

"I don't know what happens to me," Eli confessed. "When it comes to the Lukes of this world I just can't control myself."

They talked late into the night, and for the first time, falteringly, she began to confide in Eli, as he was confiding in her. They shared a closeness that was very special.

Sometime in the early morning, Luke returned. The girl was roused by stifled noises. Luke was not alone, he had two friends with him. They were taking turns holding Eli down and using him.

She felt the fear leap into her throat as she remembered that time — not so long ago — when she had been abused in the same way. Leaping from her bed, she brandished her knife in the air, shouting, "Stop it! Go away! Get out! STOP IT!"

They took their time before leaving, finishing what they'd set out to do.

The ambulance arrived too late.

Eli bled to death from internal injuries on the way to Emergency.

Several weeks later the girl tracked Luke down to a seedy walk-up he was sharing with a male prostitute in a condemned building. She waited until the prostitute was out plying his trade, and then she torched the building.

Lighting the first match was easy . . .

BOOK SIX

**Hollywood, California
New Year's Eve
December 31
1985**

Chapter 90

"Our limousine awaits," Mark said, with a twist of irony. "I do love you Americans – you do things with such panache. The driver tells me there are forty-nine identical white limos with fully stocked bars and a supply of the best caviar, to transport Zachary Klinger's illustrious guests to his waiting yacht. You'd think he might want to double up, save a bob or two. I wouldn't have minded more of the incredible Zeppo White, and that strange zombie-like lady he's married to."

Jade stifled a laugh. "Don't be so rude."

'You must admit, they do make strange bedfellows."

"Well . . ."

Taking her hand he said, "Speaking as a premier photographer of wild and beautiful creatures, you, my dear, are the most beautiful of all."

"Thank you."

"Surpassing even a pregnant leopard I recently had the privilege of observing."

"You're such a flatterer."

"Part of my English charm."

"And *sooo* modest."

"One tries one's best."

She had to admit that being with Mark again was pleasurable. He made her laugh with his dry sense of humour. And she was almost convinced that marrying him was the right thing to do.

It better be. They had taken out the licence, had the requisite blood tests, and tomorrow was the big day.

Beverly had freaked out when she'd told her. "*Whaaat?* You an' the English asshole? This girl does *not* believe it."

"Now that I'm marrying him, Bev, let's drop the asshole bit, huh? I don't think it's really appropriate, do you?"

"Whatever you say. I'm easy."

When Beverly realized that Jade was seriously getting married, she offered the use of Zachary's mansion for the ceremony, sure he wouldn't mind.

"No guests," Jade warned. "We just want to do it quietly, and then take off for a couple of days in Carmel before I have to shoot the final batch of commercials."

"Try this for fit. The two of you. Corey. Me. A sunlit garden – if the goddamn weather doesn't change – and a nice friendly preacher. Zachary's flying off to New York right after the party. How does the scenario grab you?"

"Perfect!"

"It's arranged."

Mark had liked the idea when she told him. "I can't wait, my darling," he'd said.

She knew why. She still hadn't slept with him, and he couldn't stand that she was making him wait.

"Aren't I worth waiting for?" she'd teased him.

"Jade. This is ridiculous. We lived together for six years. Why are you doing this?"

"Because it's romantic. Besides, it's such a short time, and it'll make our wedding night really special."

For Zachary's New Year's Eve cruise she had chosen to wear a black cashmere Ralph Lauren sweater, sleeveless, with one shoulder completely bare; white silk pants; a bronze buckled belt; and a whirl of delicately thin bronze bracelets around her upper arm. Hoop earrings, and slave bangles on each wrist, completed her look. On her engagement finger was the antique sapphire and diamond ring Mark had presented her with on Christmas day.

"Let's go," she said, with a dazzling smile. "I promised Corey we'd pick him up on the way."

Mark was ready.

*

Poppy was in gold. From the ornament in her hair to the shoes on her feet, everything was gold, including her nails.

Howard took one look and decided she should be frozen in time, reduced in size, and placed on somebody's mantel – next to an Oscar.

He did not feel well. After snorting cocaine all day, gulping a few Quaaludes, and a Valium or two, he felt like shit.

Once, cocaine was the answer to everything. A couple of toots and he was King Kong. More, and he was ready to take over the world.

Now the rush didn't last. It brought him up, and sank him back down almost immediately. And his nose was killing him. Every time he snorted, the pain was like a thousand tiny needles jabbing the sensitive membrane in his nostrils.

Of course, he knew there were other methods of doing it. If he wasn't so queasy about needles, he could inject himself with the magic potion.

He'd tried it once and nearly passed out. Besides, injecting drugs? Wasn't that getting a little desperate? He was no junkie.

"Honeybunch, have you set the tape machine?" Poppy asked. "I don't want to miss Zachary on the Python show."

"If I know old Zach," Howard said, with a manic twitch, "he'll have a screening room on the boat, and we'll all have to sit and watch. Talk about a captive audience! That's probably why he's having the party on his yacht in the first place. Nobody can escape."

Poppy adjusted a huge gold earring. "*I* think it's a *wonderful* way to spend New Year's Eve. I'm bored with normal parties."

"As long as you don't get seasick."

"Oooh. It's not going to be *rough*, is it?"

"Just kidding."

On their way out to the car, Roselight's nanny came running after them. "Mr Soloman," she called, "there's a call for you from Mexico City. The operator says it's urgent."

*

"I can't imagine like *why* they invited *me*," Heaven said, excitedly gobbling caviar as the white stretch limousine transported her and Rocky to Long Beach, and Zachary K. Klinger's exclusive party.

"'Cos you're a star," Rocky said confidently. "An' don' forget who did it for ya."

"Maybe Uncle Jack suggested they ask me," she mused.

"Naw. Why'd he do that?"

"It's New Year's Eve. He always tries to see me then."

"Yeah?"

"Yes."

"Forget about ya Uncle Jack," Rocky said, flicking on the built-in television. "You're a big girl now – ya got *me*."

*

"I must have been unhinged to even *think* about letting you get away from me," Mannon said, his arm around Melanie-Shanna as they entered the limousine.

"I was sure it was what you wanted," she replied softly. "You were so cold towards me. I could never do or say the right thing. And when I got pregnant it was like you couldn't care less."

"I guess the idea of becoming a father made me nervous."

"It wasn't exactly easy for *me*. Especially with your attitude . . ." She hesitated. "And Whitney . . ."

He hadn't thought of Whitney in months. One thing Clarissa had cured him of was his obsession with his ex-wife. And now he was cured of Clarissa too. Christ! When he remembered that night in Puerta Vallarta he was so ashamed. Beating that boy, half killing him. The memory was a nightmare. Thank God for Howard, who kept the whole deal out of the press, and spirited him out of there.

The fucking pills the stupid makeup girl had given him had made him crazy. Not to mention Clarissa. Thinking of her now, he shuddered. The woman was a fling, an interlude, and an unfaithful liar.

He couldn't care less if he never set eyes on her again.

*

They'd taped *Face to Face with Python* early, ready for viewing later that evening, and it was a smash. Zachary K. Klinger was the kind of guest Jack wished he had on every week – forceful, opinionated, jagged, and sharp as a stiletto.

"What a show!" Aldrich congratulated him. "Dynamite! Especially when you got him talking about his personal life, and his sorrow at never having kids. Jesus, Jack – it's compulsive viewing."

Jack agreed. He knew it was a sensational show, and he also knew it presented an in-depth portrait of a man who had everything – and yet yearned for what he thought he was missing. Great insightful television. It wasn't often he could say that.

Zachary had been pleased too. Considering he never consented to do interviews, it was a real coup for the Python Show to get him.

"I'll see you at my party," Zachary said as he departed, accompanied by several assistants. "I understand you're bringing Senator Richmond with you. I'm delighted. I haven't seen him for a while. I had no idea he was out here."

Jack didn't say – *He's visiting Danielle*. He merely nodded, and wondered how he had become the beard for Peter Richmond.

They were all going to the party together: Jack with Kellie Sidney, the Senator with Danielle Vadeeme.

Peter Richmond had phoned him and asked, "Are you attending Zachary Klinger's party?"

When he'd said yes, the Senator had inveigled an invitation for himself and the French actress. "Danielle wants to go," he'd explained. "If we come with you it will appear *you're* with her."

"I'm taking Kellie," Jack had explained.

"With your reputation," Peter guffawed, "everyone will naturally assume you're with the two of them. I have to be careful. I *am* a married man, you know."

On the cheat.

Weren't most of them?

Sometimes Jack found it useful to store favours, so he'd agreed.

Kellie kept him waiting as usual. He was used to it now, as the dogs crawled all over him, and her three-year-old son greeted him with a sticky hug. Kellie walked the tight-rope between movie-star, mom, and producer with careless style.

"Ooops!" she exclaimed, rushing into the living room clad in a sexy long dress. "Odd earrings!"

"And shoes," he pointed out.

"No?"

"Take a look."

Glancing down at her feet, she clapped a hand over her mouth. "What a putz!"

"But a lovable one."

She grinned at him. "Thanks!"

It had taken effort on his part, getting connected with Kellie again. After the Spago incident, when he had slipped away with Jade Johnson, she had not been inclined to see him again. It had taken roses and persuasion, for out of all the women he'd dated since Clarissa (excluding Jade, of course – *she* was something else) Kellie was the nicest. And he admired her strong sense of family.

"I can't wait to meet the Senator," Kellie said. "I hear he's quite a boy in Washington."

"So I believe."

"Politicians are *very* highly sexed."

"How do you know?"

She giggled. "I never said I was a virgin when we met!"

*

Up in Benedict Canyon, Clarissa let the driver wait as she finished getting ready. She wore a navy blue pants suit and a white sweater. Nothing fancy for Clarissa Browning. She didn't need the phoney glitter of Hollywood.

Leaning close to her mirror, she traced the outline of a faint black eye – a souvenir of Mannon Cable. The violent bastard.

Earlier, she had called the private nursing home in Mexico to ask after Norman. They refused to give out information on the phone, even though she had a private number to contact.

She brooded about Puerta Vallarta and what had taken place there. Mannon Cable should have been properly punished for behaving like a maniac, but no – Howard Soloman had arrived with his warnings and threats. "If you let out one word of this," he had told her, "your career will be over, finished. Just like that."

Hollywood folk.

They had their own laws.

Hollywood folk.

Sometimes she loathed the whole pack of them.

*

Beverly D'Amo was rushing from the house on her way to Long Beach to meet Zachary when the messenger arrived, carrying a brown manila envelope marked:

EXTREMELY URGENT

PRIVATE PAPERS

Attention of: ZACHARY K. KLINGER

Hand-delivered envelopes arrived for Zachary every day – often marked URGENT. But extremely urgent?

She decided she'd better bring it with her. Not that he would want to be bothered in the middle of his party – only with Zachary, one never knew. And if she *didn't* take it he'd probably ask if it had arrived, and then berate her for *not* bringing it.

Couldn't win.

She tossed it on the back seat of the limo and promptly forgot it for the moment.

*

"Happy New Year, Vladimir. And you too, Unity, dear," Silver said graciously, thinking to herself what an absolutely bizarre couple they made – her gay Russian houseman, and Wes's little cousin. They seemed to have formed some peculiar kind of liaison "Are you going out?"

"Yes, madame," Vladimir replied courteously. *We are going out and never coming back*. With sixty-five thousand dollars apiece, finding somewhere to go should present no problem.

"Perhaps you'd like your picture taken with me," Silver said with a winning smile. "Wes – get your camera."

She knew she had never looked better. Wes Money was like a rejuvenating tonic. Her skin was smooth and clear with the flush of regular sex, her body trimmer than ever. And the six-thousand-dollar Fabrice dress she had invested in was spectacular. Not to mention Wes's surprise gift – a stunning diamond and ruby heart necklace. She'd been quite taken aback when he presented her with it on Christmas night. "Tell me," she'd whispered later, "did *I* pay for it?"

"No, you didn't," he'd replied, insulted.

"Well, where did you get the money?" she'd asked, perplexed.

"My life's savings," he'd replied jauntily. "Consider it well spent. Now I really *am* busted out."

How touched she was by his generous gesture. "I've been thinking, we should put you on the payroll," she'd said. "After all, you've been handling all my affairs. Does ten percent of my earnings seem fair? We can have my lawyer draw up contracts."

He'd laughed. "While we're together what's yours is mine. Right? Let's leave it that way."

Time and time again he had proved that he wasn't after her money. Thank God she'd chosen him, and not that dreadful, power-hungry, social-climbing Dennis Denby.

Wes picked up his new Nikon camera – a Christmas gift from Silver, along with a metallic silver Ferrari ("Every time you look at it, darling, you'll think of me!"), a Sony video camera, and a virtual closetful of new clothes.

"Come here, Vladimir," she called. "And Unity, dear, would you like to be in the picture too?"

Vladimir threw Unity a commanding glare. This photograph would be worth another few thousand! What luck!

Silver stood between Vladimir and a reluctant Unity, her arms around each of them, a perfect smile in perfect place. Pictures with the staff were part of the game. Oh, how they loved it!

Vladimir would be able to show the snap to all of his friends and boast endlessly of his famous employer.

"Perhaps Madame vould like a photograph of herself and Mr Ves together?" Vladimir suggested respectfully.

"What a good idea," she said, beaming. "Oh, and Vladimir, you may sleep in tomorrow. No sense in you getting up at six as usual. Shall we say nine o'clock?"

"Thank you, madame." Selfish woman. She wouldn't leave *her* bed until at least noon. Besides, New Year's Day was supposed to be a holiday.

Why should he care? He would be long gone. Hawaii was his first planned stop. Hawaii, with a tall and tanned ex-stripper, who sang like Sinatra, and gave great toe massage.

Snap.

"Another one," Silver said.

Snap.

"Just one more." She snuggled closer to Wes.

Snap.

"That's enough," said Wes. "We can't be late, they'll sail without us."

Silver raised an amused eyebrow. "You *are* joking?"

"Mr Ves," Vladimir said humbly. "Just one vith you and your cousin."

Wes didn't need a picture with Unity – she'd turned out to be a miserable cow, not at all grateful for his help. Serious thought was going into how to get rid of her – without the whole story being revealed.

It seemed simpler to pose and get out of there. Vladimir took the picture, and Wes took the camera from him. "Shall we bring it with us?" he asked Silver.

Laughing delicately, she said, "Darling, this is the most important and exclusive party of the year. If *you* want to look like a Japanese tourist, bring it by all means."

And on that line she exited. Ever the star. And ready to party.

Chapter 91

Everyone was aboard. Music played, champagne flowed, and the white yacht – christened *Klinger II* – set sail from Long Beach on time. Zachary's main yacht – *Klinger I* – stayed permanently on the Mediterranean coast. But *Klinger II* was no slouch in the luxury stakes. A large sleek vessel, it accommodated Zachary's party with ease. The hundred guests mingled happily, giving off a certain air of triumph. They were the lucky ones, the chosen few. This would be a party to remember.

The heated main deck was festooned with fairy lights, flashing and winking in the dark night sky. Small, intimate tables surrounded a dance floor, while a trio of musicians played appealing Brazilian sounds.

"Kiddo!" Zeppo stood up and waved to Jade, beckoning her over to his table. "Join Ida and me."

"Shall we?" she whispered to Mark.

"Certainly," he replied. "The man is a riot!"

"Okay with you?" she checked with Corey.

"I think I'll just wander around," he said.

"Are you sure?"

"I'll feel more comfortable doing that."

Leaving his sister and her bridegroom-to-be, he made his way into a magnificent dining room, where white-coated waiters were putting the finishing touches to a sumptuous buffet of lobster, cold salmon, oysters and numerous salads.

Corey was in a deep depression. Norman leaving Los Angeles was bad enough. But not to even call, to just drop him without a word over Christmas and New Year's, was unforgivable. He had left his wife and child for Norman, completely changed his way of living, and now his whole world had crumbled.

"Looks good enough to eat, doesn't it?"

467

"Huh?" Corey glanced over at the speaker, a skinny blond waiter with bright sharp eyes and a thin mouth.

"I guess, if we're lucky, we'll get the leftovers."

"Yes," Corey agreed vaguely.

"Are you in the biz?"

Slowly Corey realized the waiter was coming on to him. Jesus! he thought. Don't tell me it's beginning to show. One glance and they *know*.

"I'm married," he said quickly.

"No law against *that*," the waiter replied with an encouraging wink. "*I* don't care if you don't."

Retribution. A suitable punishment for Norman. They had sworn to each other that they wouldn't play around. AIDS was the Russian Roulette of the eighties, and only a fool would risk promiscuity.

*

The butterflies were churning as Heaven accepted compliments from all and sundry.

You're an original!

Love your record!

My daughter worships you!

My son wants to know if you have a poster out?

She was being fêted by every old fogey in town!

And none of them was mentioning her mother!

A blast.

A mega-blast.

"I'm famous," she informed Rocky.

"Told ya I'd do it for ya," he boasted.

Swirling her fake leopardskin coat around her, she revealed a cut-out lace body suit underneath, and a lot of bare midriff. "They like what I do!" she squealed.

"Hey – hey – hey – why shouldn't they?"

Bobbing her head confidently, she said, "You're right. Why shouldn't they? I'm almost a star, and I *loooove* it!"

Rocky grinned. He loved it too. Only he couldn't let a party like this go to waste. There were big spenders aboard. Studio heads and movie stars. He was almost bailing out of dealing drugs. Almost . . . not quite. There were some opportunities he just couldn't let slip by.

"I gotta go t' the john," he said quickly. "Don't go away."

Where did he think she was going? She was having the time of her life. She'd already greeted Uncle Jack, successfully avoided her mother, and now she was enjoying all this newfound attention.

"Hello, again."

She turned, ready to accept another compliment, and found herself facing Penn Sullivan.

Oh God! She felt sick, nervous and hesitant all at the same time. Penn Sullivan! He was totally gorgeous!

"Uh . . . hi," she mumbled, sounding like a stupid idiot.

"Having fun?"

"Are you?" she managed.

"Well, now that I've seen Heaven . . ."

Was it her imagination or was he coming on to her?

"Do you know something?" he asked.

"What?" she gulped.

"We're the youngest people on board. Somehow, I think we got railroaded into the wrong party."

She couldn't care less *what* they'd got railroaded into. Penn Sullivan was utterly amazing!

*

"When are you visiting Washington? I'd like very much to be your official guide," Senator Peter Richmond said to Kellie Sidney. He was a Kennedy clone, with a John Lindsay profile, and – one of these days – a fair shot at the main chance.

"I wasn't planning a trip in the near future," she said brightly.

"You're missing a lot of fun," he replied, double entendre at full mast.

"I'm sure I am." She looked at Jack to save her, but he was allowing her no mercy, forcing her to handle the randy Senator all on her own.

Whitney Valentine, undulating past, rescued her. The Senator took one lecherous look at the quivering Ms. Valentine – sheathed in body-hugging silk jersey with nipples on show – and was on his feet in a flash.

Jack almost laughed aloud. Washington meets Hollywood. What a *perfect* combination. Real power and real glamour. He remembered the Kennedy scandals and Marilyn Monroe. The entire country had shivered on the edge of ecstasy for months.

Unfortunately, Danielle Vadeeme had failed to materialize. Earlier, when Jack and Kellie had arrived to pick them up, the Senator was alone. "Food poisoning," he'd explained. "Danielle insisted I mustn't let you down."

469

Now he was hot to boogie. With whoever cooperated.

"Hasn't the man ever seen a woman before?" Kellie whispered, as they both watched him go to work on Whitney, who seemed to take him quite seriously.

*

Zachary held court in his library. The large yacht featured several entertaining areas, and the guests could wander around as they pleased.

Poppy Soloman sat as close to Zachary as possible. She was worried about Howard. He had been behaving very strangely lately. In the car on the way to the party he was like a zombie, and he wouldn't even tell her what the urgent phone call from Mexico was all about.

"What's the matter?" she'd asked.

"Migraine."

After that he'd refused to speak, in spite of valiant efforts on her part.

"I've been meaning to ask you something," she said to Zachary in her breathy, little-girl voice. "You do know that Howard lives, eats, and breathes Orpheus? The studio is his life."

"I've always appreciated loyalty," Zachary replied, puffing on his cigar. "I pay well for it."

"I'm sure you do. And you can't get anyone more loyal than my Howie."

Zachary couldn't be bothered with people who didn't get right to the point. "What are you getting at?" he asked brusquely.

"He needs a vacation, he really does," she sighed.

"I'm not stopping him," Zachary pointed out.

"I know," she said, very seriously, realizing that if Howard caught her having this conversation he would be furious. "But he refuses to take one. And unless you force him, he'll just keep going until he drops."

Zachary nodded. He was quite impressed by her concern. Poppy had never struck him as a caring wife until now.

"I'll see he takes a vacation," he promised. "I'll order him to. Will that suit you?"

"Thank you," she said gratefully, already planning Paris, Rome, maybe even London — the shops were great in London.

*

Meanwhile, Clarissa had cornered Howard on one of the upper decks.

"I phoned the nursing home earlier," she said sharply. "They refused to give me any information about Norman. You know perfectly well they're supposed to tell me how he is. Have you changed the instructions and forgotten to leave my name?"

"Uh . . . things are a little different."

"Different? What are you *talking* about?"

He looked around to see if they were being overheard. "It's not a matter for discussion tonight."

"*What* isn't?" Aggravation filled her voice.

"Tomorrow, Clarissa. I'll come by your house in the morning."

"I don't need you in my house, Howard. I want to know what's going on, and I want to know *now*."

Howard muttered something she didn't hear. "What?" she snapped, making him repeat it.

"He's dead," he mumbled.

Mesmerized, she watched a muscle twitch wildly by his right eye, while a cold, clammy feeling swept over her, a mixture of fear and hate. "Dead?" she echoed dully.

Taking a deep gulp of night air, and wiping the sweat from his brow, he said, "'Fraid so."

Chapter 92

He knew she was aboard — Beverly had told him. Only Jack Python had her number now, and he wasn't about to fall a second time.

Casually he strolled around the yacht looking for her. He had told Kellie he was going to the men's room, and she seemed quite happy chatting to an amenably stoned Chuck Nielson.

When he spotted her, he thought — Ha! So she's beautiful. So what? And like a magnet he was drawn towards the table where she sat with the Whites and a sandy-haired man.

"Hello, Zeppo. Ida, how are you?"

Zeppo jumped to his feet. "Jack, my boy. The report on tonight's show is fabulous."

Zeppo always knew everything — sometimes before it happened.

"Thanks. Zachary's putting it on later, are you going to watch?" He could smell her scent; it reminded him of no one else.

"Wouldn't miss it, kiddo," enthused Zeppo. "Do you know Jade Johnson?"

"Yes, he does," interrupted Ida knowingly.

"We've met," Jack replied, staring straight at her.

"And her fiancé, Lord Mark Rand."

Her *what*?

"Congratulations," he said, almost too quickly. "I didn't know you were engaged. When's the wedding?"

"Tomorrow," she said calmly. "How are you?"

"Fine, great, I couldn't be better."

Her eyes were wide and flecked with little pieces of gold coin. He knew what her hair felt like, soft and silky. And he could remember in an instant how incredible it was to be in bed with her.

She was engaged, *goddammit*. She was about to marry someone else.

"'I saw the show you did with Lord Snowdon," Mark said. "A very interesting piece of journalism. You asked all the right questions." Turning to Jade he added, "Didn't we see it together, darling?"

Together? The show with Snowdon was three years ago. This must be the English jerk she'd mentioned. The English jerk she'd said was out of her life.

"I don't remember," she murmured vaguely.

The Brazilian trio were playing *The Girl from Ipanema*.

> Tall and tan and young and lovely
> The girl from Ipanema goes walking
> And when she passes each one she passes goes
> Ahhh . . .

"Do you mind if I steal a dance with Jade?" Jack asked abruptly.

"It's up to the lady herself," Mark replied with a hearty chuckle. "She always makes her own decisions."

"Shall we?" He held her gaze with his deadly green eyes.

Oh God! Why did she feel like this whenever she saw him? *I swear I'm regressing*, she thought. *I'm sixteen, and standing next to the football hero at my first prom.*

She wasn't about to let the professional stud think he'd got to her. "Sure," she replied casually, wondering why her voice sounded like an idiot's squeak.

They moved to the dance floor, held each other at arm's length for a beat or two, and then – as if by mutual consent – he pulled her closer to him, and she felt her flesh burn where his hand rested on her bare shoulder.

"Hello," he whispered, as if nothing had happened.

*

"*Adore* your dress," Silver said to Dee Dee Dionne.

"Adore *yours*," Dee Dee replied. "Fabrice?"

"But of course."

"Shit! I hate it when broads gab on about clothes," Carlos said loudly. Zachary and he had forgotten about their fight, and were now talking again, hence his appearance at the party.

"It's just our way," soothed Dee Dee.

"Broads are good for fuckin', suckin' an' shoppin'. Give 'em anything else t'do, an' they're lost souls." Carlos roared with laughter at his own humour, expecting Wes to do the same.

Wes didn't. He wasn't entourage material, and Silver loved him for it.

Carlos was three-quarters of the way through a bottle of Jack Daniels, and feeling no pain. "Wassamatter?" he slurred. "Not funny?"

"No," Silver said curtly, remembering why their affair – so many years ago – had broken up. When Carlos got into heavy drinking he became a pig. "Vulgar and *very* unamusing."

Ignoring her, he nudged Wes. "Ever had a black chick suck your dick?"

Dee Dee's mouth tightened with disapproval and embarrassment.

"Black chicks are the best," Carlos continued. "*The . . . very . . . best.*"

"Come on, darling, let's go get some food," Silver said quickly.

"'Course, our little Silvy here doesn't want to hear that," Carlos sniggered. "'Cos our little Silvy thinks *she's* the best cocksucker in town. She th –"

Wes hauled back and punched him right in the mouth.

Carlos slid to the ground like a pole-axed bear.

It was over in seconds.

Summoning a couple of waiters, Wes said, "Carry Mr Brent downstairs an' put him to bed, he's not feelin' well."

The waiters exchanged glances, then proceeded to pick up the fallen superstar and cart him off, a concerned Dee Dee in attendance.

"You shouldn't have done that," Silver said, her eyes bright with admiration.

"Why not? He insulted you."

"Darling, he was drunk."

"Yup. An' that's the only way to deal with 'em. When I was working bar I used to do it all the time. He won't even remember when he wakes up."

"Someone will tell him. And Carlos Brent is not a nice man to have as an enemy."

"You think I care? Listen, Silver, I may be a peasant, but where I come from – if someone insults a lady, they're askin' for it. 'Specially if that lady just happens to be my wife."

Inexplicably she felt like crying. Nobody had ever defended her before – except Zachary, and he didn't count.

*

The news was brought to Zachary by a minion.

"Put him in my stateroom," he said generously.

"Yes, Mr Klinger."

"What happened?" Beverly asked.

"A little fracas. Carlos seems to have a penchant for inviting a right hook."

"That man is one rude sonofabitch."

"We're fortunate he left his bodyguards on shore. A brawl was hardly my plan for this evening."

"Maybe he'll sue you," Beverly said flippantly.

"He didn't sue when *I* hit him. Why should he do so now?"

"It's your boat."

"Perhaps I'll go see him."

Beverly stopped him with a hand on his arm. "What *is* it with Silver Anderson? She's not exactly Brooke Shields, and yet every time there's a fight, she's involved."

Zachary paused to think of the right answer. "She's a true star," he said at last. "She excites loyalty."

*

"Has anyone ever told you that you are —"

"Whatever you're going to say — don't. Okay?"

"Why?"

"Because I can't stand bullshit. You've drowned me in it once, and I don't need a repeat performance. Shall we sit down?"

"No." He had her in a tight hold, and he couldn't help noticing that she didn't attempt to break it. "Are you seriously getting married?"

"Yes, I seriously am."

"Why?"

"I don't really imagine it's any of your business, do you?"

"As a matter of fact I think you owe me an explanation."

Now she did struggle, but only slightly. "*I owe you* an explanation?" she asked incredulously.

"We had a great time, didn't we?"

"Oh, sure. One *helluva* night. Only that wasn't enough for loverboy Python, huh? It was on to the next victim, with hardly a pause for a coffee break."

"What are you talking about?"

"Forget it."

"I don't want to forget it."

"Well, *I* do."

"You hardly waited around, did you?"

"What?"

"You heard."

"Will you quit holding me so tightly. I want to sit down."

"No you don't."

"Yes I do."

"No — you *don't*."

"You're a bastard."

"You know something? I think I'm going to forgive you."

Her voice was icy. Her body uncomfortably warm. "For what?"

"For standing me up."

"Standing *you* up. You stood *me* up, with that French jam tart."

"If you mean Danielle, she was with the Senator."

Caustic sarcasm. "Sure."

"And who was the guy *you* were walking into Chasen's with? Some half-baked actor, huh? I credited you with better taste."

"I guess you would have been happier if I'd sat at home thinking about what a wonderful time we had together, and

475

hoping that one of these days you'd call me again. You know – when you had nothing better to do." She paused, her voice alive with indignation. "I actually *cooked a meal for you*. Your slave phoned me at nine-thirty. If you couldn't see me, why didn't *you* call me earlier? Or are you too big a star to pick up the phone yourself?"

"Aretha phoned you before the show at eight o'clock and told you I was tied up at the studio, and that I'd contact you later. You couldn't even wait, could you? Out on the town without missing a beat."

"Don't tell *me* what time she called and what the message was. It was after nine-thirty. And there was *no mention* of you contacting me later."

"Hey, lady – when you're angry I think I love you even more."

"Can I break in?" Mark smiled smoothly as he pried them apart, but there were daggers of anger in his eyes.

Jack half considered saying – *No – you can't*. And grabbing her back. But it was already too late. She was in Mark's arms. He was whirling her around the dance floor as the fairy lights twinkled, and the yacht headed on its way to Laguna and the New Year.

*

Carlos Brent sprawled snoring in the middle of Zachary's bed in the master stateroom. Dee Dee Dionne sat in a nearby chair, her ebony features calm and composed, like a beautiful carved statue.

As Zachary walked into the room he wondered why she put up with the ageing superstar. She was a talented singer, with a certain amount of stardom of her own – she didn't need Carlos Brent.

"How is he?" Zachary asked.

"Sleeping it off," she replied. "He won't even remember. He was very drunk."

"Has he ever considered A.A.?"

"Carlos? Never." Faint amusement lit her face. "He enjoys drinking. It never upsets *him*, only other people."

"How do you manage?"

She smiled wanly. "Oh . . . I manage. When you love someone you always do."

Zachary felt like an intruder in his own room. With a blustering cough he walked into his bathroom. Propped against the mirror was an envelope addressed to him marked EXTREMELY URGENT.

Nice of whoever had delivered it to hand it straight over. Staff. They were never good enough.

Without hesitation he ripped it open. He was in need of a pause before rejoining his party, which seemed to be going extremely well, in spite of the fact that Silver was successfully avoiding him.

At first all he saw was a magazine, one of those cheap supermarket rags which everyone claimed never to read, yet knew the contents off by heart. Attached to it was the white card of one of his personal assistants in New York, with a handwritten note:

> *A contact got an advance copy of this over to me today, and I'm couriering it straight to you rather than discussing it on the phone. It hits the stands on Monday. Please advise if you wish to take action.*

The magazine was called *True Life Scandal*. And the headline proclaimed in huge black print:

FATHER OF SILVER ANDERSON'S SECRET LOVE CHILD REVEALED!!
BILLIONAIRE ZACHARY K. KLINGER IS HEAVEN'S DADDY!!

And underneath, in smaller type:

VLADIMIR KIRKOFF AND UNITY SMITH REVEAL THE SENSATIONAL TRUE-LIFE DRAMA OF SILVER ANDERSON'S LIFE! READ ALL ABOUT THE FORMER BARTENDER AND DRUG DEALER SHE MARRIED! HOW SHE HATES HER DAUGHTER — SEVENTEEN-YEAR-OLD ROCK STAR SENSATION HEAVEN! AND DESPISES HER FORMER LOVER — HOLLYWOOD TYCOON AND BILLIONAIRE ZACHARY K. KLINGER!

READ THE SECRETS!

READ THEM HERE!

Revealed by the two people who know her BETTER THAN ANYONE ELSE!

Full story on PAGE TEN.

Zachary blinked rapidly a few times. Then he took off his steel-rimmed glasses and stared blankly in the mirror above his black onyx sink.

If this garbage was true he had a daughter. A seventeen-year-old daughter. And for seventeen years Silver had kept them apart.

Damn the woman.

Damn the bitch.

She'd got away with everything all her life. Forget the announcement he'd planned as the party's climax. If this was true, he would personally see to it that she paid, and paid in full.

Chapter 93

"I wouldn't have expected it of you," Mark said, an annoying, supercilious curl to his lip, as they sat down.

"Huh?" In her mind she was still dancing with Jack, caught up in his arms, listening to his voice.

"You and the leg-over merchant."

"I beg your pardon?"

"Leg-over merchant, my dear, is a quaint old English expression meaning a man who likes to put it about."

"Put *what* about?" she asked, irritated by his superior attitude.

"For Christ's sake, Jade. A *stud*. You do know what that is, don't you?"

"Fuck you, Rand, what are you trying to say?"

He went very red in the face, a sure sign that he was angry. "Oh, tough talk. The liberated woman. Bravo, darling. Was he enough for you in bed? Is that why I haven't had the pleasure?"

Was she *really* marrying him in the morning? Had she *honestly* made that decision?

The Whites returned to the table after a quick whirl around the dance floor.

"Invigorating!" exclaimed Zeppo.

"Boring!" muttered Ida.

Jade arose. "Excuse me," she said politely. "I'm going to find Corey."

Leaving an angry Mark sitting with the Whites, she took off.

*

"You're not eating, Howie," Poppy complained. "The lobster is delicious."

"If I've told you once I've told you fifteen times – I *am not* hungry, so stop shoving food at me. Just back off."

"Grouchy, grouchy! Maybe the belly-dancers will cheer you up. I hear there's *three* of them. Hand picked by Zachary, and *gorgeous!*"

The sick ache in his stomach would not quit. If he was smart he would have cancelled out on this whole deal, flown off to Mexico, and found out what the fuck had happened.

Norman had been getting along fine, they'd told him that yesterday – the asshole doctors he'd hired.

Correction. They weren't assholes. They were the best.

He'd paid plenty to keep the situation under wraps. He'd lied to all and sundry, and in a matter of weeks Norman Gooseberger was supposed to stroll back into town fit and well, with a brand new position as head of publicity at Orpheus.

Dammit! What went wrong?

The kid was dead. Massive internal haemorrhaging, he'd been told.

Technically Mannon had killed him. Oh, Jesus!

Carmel and Orville were somewhere at the party. Who was going to tell them? And what would happen when they found out? Were they going to just sit back and take it in the good old Hollywood tradition of keeping silent to protect the guilty?

Clarissa was wrecked. Maybe he should have waited to reveal the news to her, but he'd had to share it with someone, and she was sworn to secrecy.

"Mannon has to be punished," she'd said, white with grief.

"No," he'd replied. "The knowledge alone is gonna be with him forever. That's punishment enough."

"I don't understand. Justice must be done."

"You're sounding like a movie. It's too fucking late for justice. I've told you before – the scandal and publicity will ruin *both* your careers, and kill *The Murder* stone cold. You want that? For what?"

"Yes. I want that."

"Get serious, Clarissa. Bigger stars than you have been dragged down by a lot less. Imagine yourself in court, telling *your* side of the story. Jeez! They'd crucify you. In France the blame would be *all* yours. Don't forget, if Mannon hadn't caught you in the sack with another guy none of this would have happened. You were involved in a hot and heavy affair with Mannon. Everyone knew about it. One word of the truth and it's over for you. I'll *personally* see to that, along with Zachary Klinger and most of the other people aboard this yacht tonight. You'll end up doing art movies in Siberia. Is that what you want?"

"It's all so sick."

"And I guess you in bed with a confirmed fag is normal?"

She'd pulled her jacket close around her and shivered in the breeze, while all around them the party went on, unaware of their personal drama.

He'd reached over to touch her, a small gesture of sympathy to show he wasn't completely heartless.

She drew away as if he had communicable herpes.

"You'll get over it, Clarissa. Hey – *we all* liked Norman. I'll fly in tomorrow and take care of everything. He's going to suffer a burst appendix. I hope to Christ he's still got one."

"You'll be an accessory to murder," she'd said slowly.

"No, I'll be helping everyone out – *including* you."

He'd left her alone on the deck – a solitary figure. She'd be all right. Clarissa wasn't some dozy-headed starlet – she had guts. She'd survive.

"Hello, Howard and Poppy." Whitney wafted into sight wearing a dress that would give any healthy male a hard-on for life.

"So *lovely* to see you," enthused Poppy.

"Have you met Senator Richmond?" Whitney asked, taking his hand and pulling him forward.

"*The* Senator Peter Richmond?" Poppy said triumphantly. She was never at a loss for a name – especially an important one. "No, we've never met, but I'm *delighted*. Are you visiting? Is your wife with you? We'd *love* to give a dinner for you. Something small and intimate, say fifty or sixty people?"

*

The belly-dancers appeared with dessert: nubile young women clad in full Eastern garb – their smooth, round stomachs on display as they undulated from area to area, pulsating and fluctuating their agile hips.

Chuck Nielson tried to grab one as she slid by, her eyes bright with promise above the veiled part of her face.

"C'mere, baby," he crowed, pulling at the flimsy chiffon twirling between her legs.

"Get lost, pox face," she muttered out of the corner of her mouth, skilfully moving on.

Only Beverly and Zachary knew the true identity of his exotic belly-dancers. They were all hookers, trained especially for tonight's performance. It amused Zachary to entertain his guests with the unexpected.

After the belly-dancers came the break-dancers – six talented black youths.

"They're *sooo* jazzed," Heaven exclaimed excitedly.

"Yeah," agreed Rocky, although he couldn't see what all the fuss was about. He preferred the belly-dancers himself. Now they were something else!

*

Below decks, in the powder room, Melanie-Shanna found herself washing her hands next to Whitney Valentine. They hadn't seen each other since the famous fight between Mannon and Chuck upstairs at the Bistro.

Whitney hitched the top of her clinging dress a touch higher. "Hello, Melanie. How are you?"

"Oh – hi, Whitney, I didn't see you."

Nobody could miss Whitney Valentine in all her glory. She had a body capable of reducing grown men to tears.

"Congrats on the baby," Whitney said. "I'm sure it's made Mannon very happy, he always wanted kids."

"Thank you."

Whitney glossed her lips and fluffed out her hair. "I'm so glad you two stayed together. Believe me, Clarissa Browning is a grade A cunt. She would have made him nothing but miserable."

Melanie-Shanna, busily applying lipstick, nodded her agreement. "It's all worked out," she said quietly. "We're over Puerta Vallarta and his affair with her. He's happy being back with me and the baby. He says Clarissa was just a bad nightmare."

"Good," Whitney said firmly. "Let's be friends, huh?"

Melanie-Shanna could hardly see that happening, but at least he finally felt secure with his ex-wife. Whitney didn't want Mannon, and he didn't want her anymore. "How's Chuck?" he asked. "Are you two still together?"

"On and off." Whitney shrugged. "Tonight more off than on. He's such an asshole when he drugs out — like right now." She leaned confidentially towards her new friend. "I have met *the* most attractive and interesting older man. His name is Peter Richmond. *Senator* Peter Richmond. And I think he likes me."

"Isn't he married?" Melanie-Shanna asked, putting away her lipstick and closing her purse.

"In name only. When you're in politics getting divorced is a definite no-no. Anyway — he says —"

They left the powder room chatting amicably.

Clarissa waited a beat of ten before emerging from a locked toilet.

*

"So you're not talkin'?" Wes asked.

"I never *said* we weren't speaking," Silver replied, an argumentative edge to her voice.

"She's sitting right over there, an' you haven't said one word to each other. What's the deal? You don't talk to your brother and father. And now I find out you don't even talk to your kid."

"I think she should come over to *me*, don't you?"

"I think you're full of crap."

Silver put on her haughtiest tone. "And what exactly do you mean by *that* remark?"

"Just what it sounds like. She's your *daughter*, for crissake — not some deadly rival. Loosen up an' at least say hello."

"Keep your nose *out* of it, if you please. It's not your business."

"You're being unreasonable. An' if *you* don't wanna say hello, *I* will."

Glaring at him angrily, she said, "Don't you dare!"

"Why shouldn't I? I'm her stepfather. I'm goin' right over an' introducing myself."

Silver was unaware of the conversation he'd had with Nora concerning her relationship with Heaven.

"Why doesn't she want to have anythin' to do with the kid?" he'd asked.

Nora had shaken her head. "Some kind of guilt about the girl's father."

"Who was that?"

"Nobody knows."

"Come *on*. You know."

"No, I don't."

"Yes you do."

"I *don't*."

"Swear on your life."

"If you could forge some sort of relationship between the two of them it would be nice. See what you can do, Wes. You're the only one I've ever seen her listen to."

Silver picked up her champagne and drained the glass. "If you go over to her, I will not speak to you for the rest of the night."

"That'll make a whole bunch of us you're not talkin' to."

"I mean it, Wes."

"We'll see."

"I said I *mean* it."

He stood up. "I'll be back in a minute."

★

Jade couldn't find Corey. She wandered from area to area, bumping into Poppy along the way, an unfriendly Howard, and finally getting stuck with Chuck Nielson, who introduced himself and then wouldn't leave her alone.

"You're somethin'," he kept on mumbling. "An' I'm just a bum."

He offered her a joint.

She turned him down.

He offered her cocaine.

She turned him down.

He offered her his body.

She laughed.

"Don' *laugh* at me," he said, roughly grabbing her.

"Leave the lady alone." Jack was there, dangerous green eyes and killer smile.

Chuck backed off without a word.

"Do you know what we are?" Jack asked, his voice caressing her.

She shook her head.

"We're unfinished business. And there is no way I am letting you marry that jerk tomorrow. No way at all."

Chapter 94

Clarissa left the powder room, her pale face impassive. She ignored the activity around her – giggling women dressed to the hilt, two belly-dancers hurrying to their makeshift dressing room, waiters rushing back and forth.

She headed down the corridor, away from the noise of the party, entering the part of the large yacht where the staterooms were located.

She was approaching Zachary Klinger's private suite when a uniformed security guard stopped her.

"Can I help you, Ms. Browning?"

"You startled me!"

"I'm sorry."

"I suppose you're just doing your job."

He grinned happily – after a night of solitary boredom he was finally meeting a star. "Sure am!"

"I bet you're an actor," she said.

"How'd you know that?"

"We all had to moonlight at one time or another."

"You too?"

She smiled. "Me too. What have you done?"

"A few television shows. It doesn't pay the rent. I've been doubling with this job for three years."

"You'll get a break."

"D'you think so?"

"It happens."

"From your lips . . ."

"Can you do me a favour?"

By this time he was ready to do anything she asked. "Nam it."

"One of my future projects takes place on a yacht."

"No, really?"

"It's true."

"Is there a role for me?" he asked boldly.

"You never know . . ."

He'd heard stories about Clarissa Browning being aloof and difficult to work with. This woman standing before him was so nice and natural. Friendly too, not at all a big movie-star phoney.

"There's just a little information I need," she said lightly. "Perhaps you can give me a quick tour. Nobody will miss you, will they?"

"I'm not supposed to leave my post."

"It doesn't matter."

"But, for you –"

She smiled. "Thank you."

Chapter 95

"Mr Klinger wants to meet you."

"He does?" Heaven's eyes were wide saucers of surprise. "Why?" She was still recovering from her exciting encounter with Penn Sullivan, who Rocky had frozen out with a baleful glare. "Catch you later," Penn had said as he left, giving her hope for the future.

Beverly grinned. "I guess he gets off on your music. C'mon, girl, he's waiting."

"Me too?" asked Rocky hopefully.

"Nope. But hang around, big boy – if Central Casting ever sees you, you've got a job for life!"

As she spirited Heaven off, Wes appeared. "What are *you* doin' here?" he demanded of Rocky.

"Hey – hey – hey. The big time only suitable for *Mister* Anderson? I found the kid, y'know. I like – discovered her."

Wes couldn't conceal his amazement. *"You?"*

"Yeah, *me*. Ya think I'm not good enough or somethin'? I'm makin' it too." Rocky smoothed down the lapels of his rented white tuxedo, his muscles bulging. "An' while we're talkin', the word is out you're cat food if you don' pay back the money ya owe."

"I don't owe *one fuckin' dollar*," Wes said angrily. "I was set up – you know that better than anyone. A fine friend *you* turned out to be."

"I told ya t'be careful," Rocky said sulkily.

"I was. An' that's why I'm here today. An' they ain't gettin' back *one thin dime* of the bucks they planted on me. Fuck 'em. Let's see what they can do about it."

"Blow you away," Rocky muttered.

"Just let 'em try. I'm ready."

*

"I can get into Los Angeles once a month," Senator Richmond said, devouring Whitney's delectable flesh with ravenous eyes. "No problem."

"Why would you want to?" she asked demurely, her breasts rising and falling, nearly escaping from the confines of her sprayed-on dress.

"Because I've met you," he said with deep sincerity. "And you're special."

Lowering her eyes she murmured, "What a lovely compliment."

"Why don't we go downstairs to one of the staterooms where we can talk properly?" he suggested. "There's so many people here, so many interruptions. I'd really like to get to know you better."

"Well . . . I don't want to miss the fireworks display. I understand it's going to be spectacular. I've always loved fireworks, haven't you?"

"My passion," he said, glancing at his watch. "They're not due to go off until midnight. We have an hour."

*

There was something about being on a boat, confined for hours on end, that Mannon didn't like. It gave him a trapped feeling, which indeed he was. Everywhere he went there were the same familiar faces with the same predictable questions.

What film are you doing next?

Who's producing?

Who's directing?

Who's your co-star?

Quite frankly, he'd had the movie business for the time being. He needed to take a long vacation with Melanie-Shanna and the baby. He needed to go someplace where they didn't even know what a movie *was*.

In the distance he saw Howard approaching. Manic Howard Soloman, whose outrageous coke habit was the talk of the town.

"Can we have a word together privately?" Howard requested.

"What do you suggest we do – jump off the deck and swim alongside?" Mannon said sarcastically.

Howard didn't crack a smile. "It's a serious matter."

"I'll be back in a moment, sweetheart," Mannon said to Melanie-Shanna.

Howard walked with him to a quiet spot along the main deck. "Bad news," he said soberly. "I'm gonna give it to you straight. Norman Gooseberger died tonight."

"What?"

"Complications. An internal haemorrhage. I don't know . . ."

"Jesus Christ! Does this mean *I'm* responsible?"

"Technically – yes. In the real world – no. I'm taking care of it. Paying off the right people. It'll be fixed."

"And I'll be forever in your debt. Is that what you're trying to say?"

Howard shrugged philosophically. "Hey – that's what friends are for."

Angrily Mannon stared down at the dark, cold water rushing by. "I let you talk me into a cover-up," he said bitterly. "You promised me everything was going to be all right."

"Listen, sport, I'm not God. *I* didn't kill the poor bastard – *you* did. You wanna come out in the open now? Is that it? You wanna play Truth and Consequences an' let the media rip you to shreds? Be my guest."

Mannon leaned over the side and began to sob.

Embarrassed, Howard turned away.

*

"Nice to meet you, Heaven."

"You too, Mr Klinger."

He peered at her intently, searching for a clue. She was pretty in spite of her outlandish makeup, hair and clothes. But he couldn't spot any striking resemblance.

"I understand your record is doing extremely well."

"Zoomin' up there. Like it's number two with a bullet. Which means by next week it could be —" she paused to draw a huge expectant breath. "Number one!"

"I hope so."

"Yeah! What a blast!"

"Heaven."

"Yes, Mr Klinger."

"I have some information that I think you should know."

"Yes, sir?" She waited expectantly, quite awed to be in the presence of such an important and powerful man.

"Er . . . there seems to be a possibility — only a possibility, mind you — that I might be your father."

Chapter 96

The breeze was cool on her face. She knew what she was doing, and she had no regrets. They all deserved it. Every one of them.

IT'S TOO LATE FOR JUSTICE.

Really, Howard. Is that what you think?

BELIEVE ME, CLARISSA BROWNING IS A GRADE A CUNT.

Thank you, Whitney. It takes one to know one.

YOU'LL END UP DOING ART MOVIES IN SIBERIA.

Better than ever having to do anything for you again, Howard.

HE SAYS CLARISSA WAS A BAD NIGHTMARE.

Did Mannon say that? Poor Mannon, he doesn't know what a nightmare is. Yet.

ONE WORD OF THE TRUTH AND IT'S OVER FOR YOU.

And you, Howard. And all your Hollywood friends.

SHE WOULD HAVE MADE HIM NOTHING BUT MISERABLE.

You should know, Whitney. You tried for long enough. Now you'll never make anyone miserable again.

I'LL PERSONALLY SEE TO IT, ALONG WITH ZACHARY KLINGER AND MOST OF THE OTHER PEOPLE ABOARD THIS YACHT TONIGHT.

Will you, Howard. Will you?

Lighting the first match was easy . . .

EPILOGUE

February 1986
Seven weeks later

There were two major events taking place in Hollywood on a cool weekend in February 1986.

The first was a funeral.

The second, a wedding.

Some people felt obliged to attend both. Although, of course, they changed outfits for each occasion.

*

Compared to what took place on *Klinger II*, the night of December 31, 1985, the impact of *True Life Scandal* hitting the stands a few days later was considerably diminished. Who cared about Silver Anderson's indiscretions, when an entire yacht – filled with Hollywood celebrities – had been blown sky high the night of Zachary Klinger's exclusive New Year's Eve party.

No movie could beat *this* story. A desperate struggle for survival in the cold night sea, while explosions rocked the luxurious yacht, raging fires spread from one end of the boat to the other – and an insane fireworks display gone wrong shot rockets and stars, blazing wheels and jumping crackers, into the dark sky.

This was the most headline-making drama possible, with the most expensive cast ever assembled. Every ingredient was there. And the world couldn't get enough.

The horrific accident was quite obviously sabotage. Investigators sifting through the debris of the gutted vessel found traces of rags soaked in gasoline near each of the firework displays, and elsewhere on the boat.

The tragedy was not caused by one fire, but by a series of them, set by a person or persons unknown to cause the maximum amount of damage. Obviously, by sparking the fireworks – resulting in explosions and chaos – mass mayhem and panic took place. Fortunately, the lifeboats had been successfully launched, otherwise the tragedy could have been infinitely more serious.

Now, seven weeks later, things were finally quietening down. And today, after the wedding and the funeral, maybe the focus would shift from Hollywood and people could resume their normal lives.

The funeral was due to take place at eleven o'clock, the wedding at three in the afternoon. There was plenty of time to attend both.

*

Poppy Soloman, draped in black Saint Laurent, glanced anxiously at Howard standing next to her at the Forest Lawn cemetery. He looked all right, a touch pale. It was taking some getting used to – seeing him without his hairpiece – but at least he was well again.

Howard had suffered a heart attack the night of the accident. Huddled in the lifeboat, he had suddenly clutched his chest and started to groan. By the time they were picked up by rescue teams, he was unconscious. She had thought he was dead.

The last few weeks had not been easy. He had been rushed straight to the hospital, and Poppy found herself alone – unprepared and frightened.

His doctors had been embarrassingly frank with her, talking about his cocaine problem as if she knew all about it.

She'd had no idea he took drugs. Oh, the shame!

When Howard recovered, he told her he was stepping down as head of Orpheus.

Poppy saw her whole world crumbling. "Why?" she wailed.

He'd looked at her for a long time, and finally said, "If it doesn't suit you, Poppy, we can separate. I don't need the pressures any more."

She'd thought about what he'd said, and then she'd thought about life without him. True, she loved being the wife of a studio head, but that wasn't the only reason she was with Howard. She loved her husband. It was as simple as that.

*

Nearby, Melanie-Shanna and Mannon held hands. It had been a terrible few weeks. Mannon had insisted on standing up and

494

taking full responsibility for Norman Gooseberger's death, only nobody wished to prosecute him. "An unfortunate accident," said the Mexican police. "There is no case." And that was that.

He had behaved like a hero the night of the yacht disaster. Along with Jack Python and Senator Richmond he had helped to launch the lifeboats, and after seeing that Melanie-Shanna was safely aboard, bodily thrown frightened, screaming women into them. After that he had dived repeatedly into the sea to rescue survivors with horrible burns who had flung themselves into the water. Carmel Gooseberger was one of the people he saved. Somehow that made him feel better.

There had been five fatalities. Four bodies discovered within days.

Funerals for Chuck Nielson, a security guard, and two waiters had taken place almost immediately. The Chuck Nielson funeral had been a lavish affair, with many touching speeches from producers and directors who had refused to employ him for the last year and a half of his life. The only genuine gesture was from Whitney Valentine, who laid a single red rose on his coffin and wept discreetly.

And now the fifth victim was being buried – Hollywood-style. The body had washed up on shore, and been found by a beachcomber only a few days ago.

*

Senator Peter Richmond attended the latest funeral as a mark of respect. Never underestimate the glamour connection between politics and Hollywood. The public loved it.

Besides, the funeral gave him an excuse to visit Whitney Valentine. She stood nearby, her blonde hair shrouded by a black lace veil, her brilliant eyes shielded by opaque dark glasses. Next to her stood Kellie Sidney, and then Zeppo White. Ida had been the unfortunate recipient of an exploding firework in her face. She was lucky not to have lost the sight in her left eye. Currently she was undergoing extensive plastic surgery.

Orville and Carmel were also present, with heads bowed. The tragic death of their only son had quieted them both down. They lived, shrouded in their own guilt.

*

Jack Python stood at the back, his handsome face impassive, well aware of the gangs of waiting photographers, the ghoulish crowds, and the television cameras.

Hollywood was burying one of its own. A true luminary. And the world was watching.

Clarissa Browning was certainly getting a star's send-off.

*

Meanwhile, at Zachary Klinger's Holmby Hills mansion, preparations for a wedding were underway. Caterers' trucks stood in the driveway, last-minute flowers were being delivered, security guards patrolled the grounds, and a nervous future bride stared at her reflection in a full-length mirror. "I don't know why I let you talk me into this," she said, in a verging-on-the-edge-of-panic voice.

"Because you'll love it!" Beverly replied confidently. "And as Zachary says – this town needs a beautiful wedding. A new beginning. And, girl – there ain't *no*body more beautiful than you!"

"I wanted a small, quiet ceremony," Jade said, adjusting the zig-zag skirt of her exquisite white silk wedding gown. "You and Mark tricked me into this."

"Honey, you were in the hospital – *somebody* had to make the arrangements. And when Corey called your parents and invited them, it just seemed right to make it an *occasion*. Mark loves the idea – I'm tellin' you, girl, he'll go Hollywood in no time at all! I hear that Zeppo's bachelor rip for him last night was something else."

"Good."

"You're a disappointment to me, Jade, y'know that?"

"Why?"

"*We* should have done somethin' last night. Gone to Chippendale's and watched the guys take it all off. Or had our *own* party."

"Sorry. Next time I get married I'll try not to disappoint you."

They both giggled.

"Hey, did anything happen with you and Jack Python?" Beverly asked curiously. "I always had a feeling you two might get together again."

"Whatever gave you that impression?"

Beverly smiled. "Vibes."

"A fine conversation when I'm just about to marry Mark."

"You two were dancing at the party, the night of the disaster."

"I don't remember."

"Yeah, well . . . I guess I gotta go check everything out. Do you need anything? A stiff drink? A stiff prick? Anything! A bride's last request will always be met."

"Springsteen."

"Bruce?"

"Is there another one?"

"Hey — I've heard of last requests, but this guy might be just a *little* hard to get hold of. Now — if you'd only given me time . . ."

"His music, schmuck! Do you have any records or tapes?"

"Oh. His music. Easy!" Beverly dived into a stack of albums piled next to an elaborate stereo system and produced a special re-mix twelve-inch version of *Cover Me*. Pulling out the record, she handed Jade the album. "Horny, huh?"

There was a picture of Springsteen sitting on the door of a white convertible, legs apart, wearing jeans, scuffed boots, a wide leather belt, striped sleeveless tee-shirt, and a bandanna round his head.

"It's his music that turns me on," Jade said.

"Yeah? You'd say goodbye on a rainy night, huh? *Sure* you would. Eyeball those muscles an' tell me that." With a ribald laugh, she left the bride alone.

Springsteen's voice came across loud and clear, flooding the room.

Jade closed her eyes. She was lucky to be alive, she knew that — enough people had told her. Apparently, when the yacht started to blow apart, she must have been hit by falling debris and knocked unconscious. Someone had helped her into a lifeboat, and eventually she was taken to hospital, where she lay in a coma for a week. Waking up one morning she felt fine, and remembered absolutely nothing about the entire experience. Her last recollection was getting ready to go to the party. "I remember you saying something about forty-nine identical white limousines, and that's it — complete blank-out, until I woke up in the hospital," she told Mark.

"You're fortunate, my darling — it wasn't a pleasant time."

He'd sprained an ankle, but other than that was unscathed.

They were both lucky. And Corey too, although he'd suffered few minor burns helping to get people into the lifeboats, including a young waiter who'd had a leg blown off below the knee.

Naturally, she and Mark had postponed their wedding. And the next thing she knew she had allowed herself to be talked into this circus. Pretty stupid for someone who liked things private. But too late to do anything about it now.

*

"You okay?"

"Of course."

"Y'look friggin' fantastic for an old broad."

"Darling, I know he's your hero, but *do* try to stop sounding like Carlos Brent on a bad day."

Wes laughed. "Just jokin'!"

"Oh, goody. I do so *adore* your sense of humour."

Bantering back and forth was just their way. Since the *True Life Scandal* revelations, Silver and Wes had become closer than ever. He had blown his stack about her recent dressing room affair with Carlos, and she had not been thrilled about his supposed drug-dealing activities – he'd denied everything. But all in all, they weathered the bad times, relieved to be alive after the night of horror on Zachary's yacht from which they'd both escaped without injury, thanks to Wes's quick thinking. He had hustled Silver into a lifeboat, and at her insistence gone back and found Heaven, bringing her to safety too.

Suddenly, with chaos all around, a reunion had taken place. Mother and daughter were together again. Temporarily.

After the appearance of *True Life Scandal* on the news-stands, Silver had been forced to admit reluctantly that Zachary Klinger was indeed Heaven's father. And with both Wes and Nora urging her on, she had met with Heaven privately, and falteringly tried to explain why she'd kept it a secret. Of course, she hadn't told her the real truth – she'd just said that he was a married man at the time, and she'd done what she thought was best.

To Silver's annoyance, Heaven and Zachary forged an immediate and wonderful relationship. Heaven moved into the Klinger mansion – and to make matters even more aggravating, her record went to number one.

Wes couldn't understand her pique. "She's your own *daughter* You should be goddamn proud. I thought everything was okay between you now."

Silver wasn't proud she was jealous. She just couldn't help it

Now they'd promised Zeppo White to go with him to Jade

Johnson's wedding, and there was no getting out of seeing Zachary and Heaven together — a sight Silver dreaded.

*

Corey visited Jade just as Springsteen faded.

"Dad's on his way up," he said. "How are you feeling?"

"Like I'm entering prison with no hope of a reprieve!"

"I told mom to stay downstairs — she'll only make you cry."

"How do *you* feel?" Since Norman's death he had become even more quiet and withdrawn.

"I'm quitting the publicity business," he said. "It's not for me. I think I'll be better away from the atmosphere."

She took his hand, "I think you're right, and remember, Corey, whatever you do, I'm always here for you."

A knock on the door announced their father. Oh God! Father of the bride. She was really doing this.

She felt hot and cold, dizzy and sick.

She was getting *married*!

HELP!

*

As Wes drew out of their driveway, with Silver sitting beside him in the Rolls-Royce, a black sedan appeared from nowhere and cut in front of him, forcing him to brake abruptly.

"Sonofabitch!" he yelled angrily, leaning on the horn.

"Don't get excited," soothed Silver, taking out a compact and checking her appearance yet again.

The sedan came to a stop, blocking the narrow street up in the hills of Bel Air.

Without thinking, Wes got out of the car and started to walk towards the other vehicle, swearing.

The gunshots took him completely by surprise.

*

"And do you, Jade Johnson, take this man, Mark Rand, to be your lawful wedded husband?"

Yes, I do.

No, I don't.

She stared at the preacher in the magnificent grounds of Zachary Klinger's opulent estate. He was a Californian preacher. Blond streaked hair, blue eyes, and a suntan.

A helicopter hovered overhead, causing an unpleasant breeze.

"... forty-nine identical white limos with fully stocked bars and a supply of the best caviar, to transport Zachary Klinger's illustrious guests to his waiting yacht ..."

SHE COULD REMEMBER!

Picking up Corey, the ride to Long Beach, boarding the yacht, and joining the Whites.

SHE COULD REMEMBER!

The preacher cleared his throat, a gentle reminder that they were waiting for her reply.

She turned to Mark. He nodded encouragingly.

Tall and tan and young and lovely
The girl from Ipanema goes walking

Jack Python.

Jack Python with the deadly green eyes and the killer smile. Was he really going to let her go through with this?

Impatiently the preacher cleared his throat again and decided to repeat himself. "Do you, Jade Johnson, take this man, Mark Rand, to be your lawful wedded husband?"

"Are you seriously getting married?"

If you don't stop me I am.

"You know something? When you're angry I think I love you even more."

Well then, where are you when I need you?

The noise of the helicopter was getting louder.

"Answer," hissed Mark, becoming red in the face.

She remembered him saying — *"Was he enough for you in bed? Is that why I haven't had the pleasure?"*

Yes. Right, Mark. On both counts.

Instinctively she looked up, just in time to see the helicopter swoop down and lower a rope ladder.

Thank God! Rescue was at hand.

Without a second thought she gathered up the flimsy skirt of her white silk dress, kicked off her shoes, and made a dash for the ladder, freedom, and most of all — Jack Python.

"Holy *shit!*" yelled Beverly, with a hoot of crazed laughter, as Jade scrambled up the precarious rope stairway. "One thing about Johnson — she always *was* a wild one!"

And the helicopter rose like a bird, and whirled off into the future.

NINE MONTHS LATER

Zeppo White gave up agenting, and became the new head of Orpheus Studios.

His wife, Ida, recovered from her burns, and as the result of extensive plastic surgery looked twenty years younger.

Zeppo continued to chase nubile females who lusted after an acting career.

Ida gave up drugs, and took to very young men instead.

Zeppo made her a producer. She never produced anything, but gave endless auditions.

They remained locked in marriage.

*

Whitney Valentine posed nude for a prestigious men's magazine, and was paid a record amount of money. A million bucks for revealing paradise. Her movie career took off like a rocket, and she became the highest-paid bad actress in the world.

Senator Peter Richmond flew in from Washington once a month to visit her, and after a few months swore faithfully he would leave his wife and marry her.

He never did.

*

Vladimir Kirkoff stayed in Hawaii, living off his revelations of life with a star. He liked the climate. He liked the people. And most of all he liked the huge, bronzed surfers with their wicked grins and penchant for thrills.

Vladimir never forgot Silver. He kept her picture in a silver frame with a single orchid beside it. If Madame ever called, he would be there.

*

Unity Smith was picked up by the police in Amarillo, Texas, working in a peep-show bar. She had spent her money from *True Life Scandal* on drugs and a hustler with lean hips and a way with the ladies. He dumped her when the money ran out.

She was recognized from her picture in the cheap tabloid.

Unity Smith's real name was Unity Serranno, and she was wanted in the state of New York for the cold-blooded murder of a young couple during the course of an armed robbery in 1983.

Her husband and partner in crime helped finger her. He was doing time for the same murders, and when he saw her photograph in *True Life Scandal* he whined to the police – "This is her – how come she's runnin' around free while I'm locked up? *She's* the one pulled the damn trigger."

Unity Serranno was taken back to the state of New York and sentenced to life imprisonment.

*

Mannon Cable bought a home in Carmel. A large, rambling, comfortable ranch house, perched high on a bluff, overlooking the ocean.

He was acclaimed for his fine work in *The Murder*, and the quality of the material sent to him improved considerably.

"I'm taking a year off to enjoy my family," he told his agent, Sadie La Salle.

"Work comes first," she admonished. "I've got a script for you that Redford would kill for."

"Bye-bye, Sadie. See you in a year."

Melanie-Shanna became pregnant again. She glowed with health and happiness. Every day Mannon woke up and thanked God for his son, Jason, and his wonderful wife, whom he finally appreciated.

For the first time in his life Mannon Cable let go. And it made him a very secure and contented man indeed.

*

Carlos Brent married Dee Dee Dionne in a lavish ceremony in Las Vegas. It was his fifth wedding, and he bought the bride a magnificent diamond necklace as a betrothal present.

His daughter, Susanna, was incensed. "You see that bitch," she told anyone who would listen. "That bitch is walking around with *my* inheritance hanging round *her* neck!"

*

Orville Gooseberger retired from the movie business and moved to Palm Springs with his wife.

Palm Springs was too quiet for Carmel. They divorced after thirty years of marriage, and he remarried – a twenty-one-year-old mud wrestler.

Carmel moved to Houston, Texas, and found herself an oilman. She, too, remarried. Unfortunately her new husband expired six weeks after the wedding, leaving her most of Houston.

Orville divorced his mud wrestler, got back together with Carmel, and they returned to Hollywood where they both belonged.

*

Howard Soloman went into "indie prod" – independent production – and gave up cocaine with the help of a fine organization called Cocaine Anonymous.

He genuinely loved the movie business, and had no intention of ever getting out. But the pressures of running a studio were not something he missed. Now he was his own boss, the pace of his life was a little less frantic: there was time to take the occasional trip, no need to go out every night, and if he wanted to spend a day at home just lazing around the pool – he did so.

Poppy adjusted. She was very adaptable when she had to be.

And, of course, she still gave great parties.

*

Corey Johnson gave up his P.R. job at Briskinn & Bower and moved back to San Francisco. It took him a long time to get over Norman, but eventually he met a successful writer called Ted, who invited him to move in. He did so, and six months later Ted died of AIDS. For a while Corey was numb with grief – he had nursed Ted through the last helpless months, and Ted had left him his house and a reasonable monthly allowance. The doctors told him he had not contracted the disease.

After much thought, he decided to use Ted's house as a hospice. He opened it up as a haven for AIDS victims who had nowhere else to go, and helped them through the final difficult days, allowing them to die in dignity and peace, with someone nearby who cared.

*

Wes Money almost died. He took two bullets, one dangerously close to the heart.

Silver Anderson, who without any thought for her own safety had left the car and rushed to his assistance, was also shot.

As the black sedan raced off, leaving them both on the ground wounded, she had managed to memorize the licence plate as the car sped away. And then she crawled to the Rolls and phoned for help.

More Hollywood dramas! The press was ecstatic! Silver Anderson alone could keep their circulation rising!

They were rushed to the hospital. Wes was operated on immediately for the removal of two bullets, and Silver was treated for minor lacerations – a bullet had merely grazed her shoulder. "You can go home tomorrow, Miss Anderson," she was told.

Silver never stepped from the hospital until Wes was out of intensive care and off the danger list. When he drifted back into the real world, she was there beside him, her hair a mess, no makeup, dressed in a crumpled tracksuit. "How dare you!" were the first words out of her mouth. "If you think you're leaving *me*, Mr Money – you can think again! I *need* you, barman. And don't you ever forget it!"

She postponed her NBC special to nurse him back to health, personally cooking him greasy chicken soup and burnt scrambled eggs.

"Silver," he begged her weakly. "If you ever want me to recover, you'd better quit with the cooking!"

Thanks to Silver's diligence, the black sedan was traced to a known drug kingpin, Sol Winogratsky. Within hours he was picked up and charged with attempted murder.

*

Nora Carvell decided she was getting too old for all the excitement and that it was time to retire. She gave up smoking and went to live with her sister in Florida.

Before leaving Hollywood she was delighted to be present at a reconciliation lunch between Silver and her daughter, Heaven. The two of them finally seemed to be getting along.

*

Reba Winogratsky took over her husband's business while he was doing time for an attempted murder rap he should never have gotten involved with in the first place. It was all the fault of that stupid magazine *True Life Scandal*. Printing that she'd had an affair with Wes Money. Really!

Like a fool she had left the magazine on the floor in the can, and Sol had read it on one of his marathon craps.

"Is this the same motherfucker who ran off with my money?" he screamed.

How many Wes Moneys married to Silver Anderson did he think there were?

"Yes, Sol."

"An' you *fucked* him?"

"Yes, Sol. We were separated at the time. You were *schtupping* the female bodybuilder with the big biceps. Remember?"

Sol had a hot temper. It was his undoing.

*

Heaven adored living with her father, even though it was unbelievable to realize she was Zachary Klinger's daughter. He was such an important man, so rich and powerful. At first she was in complete awe of him, but gradually – with the help of Beverly – the two of them began to get to know each other.

And things with her mother were looking up. Since the shooting incident, while not exactly close, they were in regular contact, and it pleased Heaven a lot. At last she felt she was part of a real family.

And her record went to number one. What a blast! But best of all, she and Pen Sullivan had become an item – as they say in Hollywood.

At twenty-three, Penn was old enough to look after her, and young enough to understand.

They really enjoyed being with each other.

When Zachary K. Klinger suffered a mild stroke, his daughter and Beverly were by his side, a close-knit family unit.

It was the relationship Heaven had yearned for all her life.

*

Rocky was cast adrift right after the great yacht disaster. Zachary K. Klinger bought his part of Heaven's contract for a princely sum, and banished him from her life.

Heaven didn't care – she hardly seemed to notice.

Rocky bought a Porsche, a closetful of new clothes, and a penthouse in Marina Del Rey.

He met an Amazon woman with Nordic bones and a voice

like the crunch of gravel on a wet day.

"Gonna make ya a rock star, babe," he promised her.

He was still trying.

*

Lord Mark Rand stayed in Hollywood and directed a film for Zeppo White and Orpheus. Zeppo was under the misguided impression that anyone with a title could do no wrong.

Mark's directorial debut was the flop of the year. Fortunately for him he was still invited to lots of parties. After all, he was a Lord, and Hollywood was crammed with social-fucks.

*

Jack Python assisted at the birth of his first child with all the aplomb of a seasoned veteran. He held the baby immediately after the doctor, placing it lovingly on Jade's stomach. "It's a boy," he said for the sixth time since his son had entered the world.

"A boy," she murmured happily. "Looks just like daddy, I hope."

"Take a peek."

She raised her head. "Gorgeous! All that hair!"

"I think we should get married," he said seriously.

"Why?"

"Because."

"Because what?"

"Because I love you, *goddammit!*" he said, exasperated.

"Let's stay single," she suggested.

"Why?"

"Because."

"Because what?"

She smiled. "Because I love you, *goddammit!*"